Praise for the *Henrietta and Inspector H*

A Girl Like You

"Michelle Cox masterfully recreates 1930s Chicago, bringing to life its diverse neighborhoods and eclectic residents, as well as its seedy side. Henrietta and Inspector Howard are the best pair of sleuths I've come across in ages—Cox makes us care not just about the case, but about her characters. A fantastic start to what is sure to be a long-running series."

—Tasha Alexander, *New York Times* best-selling author of *The Adventuress*

"Fans of spunky, historical heroines will love Henrietta Von Harmon."

—*Booklist* starred review

"Flavored with 1930s slang and fashion, this first volume in what one hopes will be a long series is absorbing. Henrietta and Clive are a sexy, endearing, and downright fun pair of sleuths. Readers will not see the final twist coming."

—*Library Journal* starred review

A Ring of Truth

"An engaging and effective romp rich with historical details."

—*Kirkus Reviews*

"There's a lot to love about the bloodhound couple at the center of this cozy mystery."

—*Foreword Reviews*

"Set in the 1930s, this romantic mystery combines the teetering elegance of *Downton Abbey* and the staid traditions of *Pride and Prejudice* with a bit of spunk and determination that suggest Jacqueline Winspear's Maisie Dobbs."

—*Booklist*

"The second book of this mystery series is laced with fiery romance so delicious every reader will struggle to put it down. If you devoured *Pride and Prejudice*, this love story will get your heart beating just as fast."

—*Redbook*, "20 Books By Women You Must Read This Spring"

"Henrietta and Inspector Howard make a charming odd couple in *A Ring of Truth*, mixing mystery and romance in a fizzy 1930s cocktail."

—Hallie Ephron, *New York Times* best-selling author of *Night Night, Sleep Tight*

A Promise Given

"Cox's eye for historical detail remains sharp. . . . A pleasant, escapist diversion."

—*Kirkus Reviews*

"Series fans will cheer the beginning of Clive and Henrietta's private investigation business in an entry with welcome echoes of *Pride and Prejudice*."

—*Publishers Weekly*

"Enjoyable, escapist read with some truths to savor."

—*Historical Novel Society*

"Fans of Henrietta and Inspector Howard will delight in Michelle Cox's latest novel. Romantic and atmospheric, *A Promise Given* offers an intriguing glimpse in 1930's Chicago, by weaving in authentic period details and exploring the social tensions of the day. The unlikely pairing of the Howards—two characters from very different worlds—provides a tender love story."

—Susanna Calkins, award-winning author of the Lucy Campion Historical Mysteries

A Veil
Removed

A Veil Removed

A HENRIETTA AND INSPECTOR HOWARD NOVEL

BOOK 4

MICHELLE COX

SHE WRITES PRESS

Published 2019
Printed in the United States of America
ISBN: 978-1-63152-503-2 pbk
ISBN: 978-1-63152-504-9 ebk
Library of Congress Control Number: 2018964807

For information, address:
She Writes Press
1569 Solano Ave #546
Berkeley, CA 94707

She Writes Press is a division of SparkPoint Studio, LLC.

To Amy Wheeler

Those innocent days of exploring first the halls of Mundelein College, then Chicago, and then the world beyond with you are some of the happiest of my life. Thank you for those, and for being my friend, always.

And posthumously to:

Sr. Joan Frances Crowley, BVM, 1919-2009

Thank you for your own part in broadening my understanding of the world beyond by pointing me in the direction of the past and for showing me that ultimately, love wins. Your zest for life was contagious.

Chapter 1

Elsie lay on the bed engulfed in darkness. The misery she felt threatened to overwhelm her. Harrison was gone. She supposed she should feel grateful—even happy—that things had turned out as they had, but she just couldn't. Instead she felt ashamed and wretched. She turned over on her side, toward the window, not that it mattered. The thick velvet curtains covering the windows of her Palmer Square bedroom, drawn as they were now, let in little light. It must be nearly morning, though, Elsie surmised, and she felt sure that she hadn't slept at all.

What would she tell Henrietta? she groaned inwardly. She and Clive were due to arrive home late that afternoon. They had docked in New York the day before and were taking the train to Chicago today; at least, that was what she had been told. Elsie knew she probably wouldn't see Henrietta for several days, as her sister would undoubtedly be caught up in the arrangements for Mr. Howard's funeral, which had been postponed, she had heard, until Clive and Henrietta could get back from their arrested honeymoon. Poor Clive, she thought. She knew what it was like to lose a father. And how terrible for both of them to have had to abandon their lovely trip! Elsie winced at the thought that her own deviousness, her own sinful behavior, would surely add to their current woes.

1

At first, she had been hopeful that perhaps her letter, in which she had revealed that she was eloping with Lieutenant Harrison Barnes-Smith, might not have reached Henrietta before she and Clive had had to rush home at the news of Alcott's death. She had eventually realized, though, with a sickening sort of dread, that even if her letter *had* arrived too late for Henrietta to have read it, both she *and* Clive (how mortifying!) would surely hear the news from Julia at some point, anyway. Elsie had begged Julia to swear that she wouldn't tell Ma what had—or had almost—happened, to which Julia had thankfully agreed, but not without warning Elsie that she could not, in truth, promise anything more.

Elsie had been surprised that fateful afternoon, as she was hurriedly packing for her evening escape with Harrison, which she had assumed was to be her wedding night, when Karl had knocked and said that she had a visitor. Elsie was horrified to think that it might be Harrison, that he had arrived early (she still had so much to do!), but Karl had informed her that no, it was not the lieutenant, but rather, a young lady, a Mrs. Julia Cunningham.

Julia?

Elsie panicked. What would Julia be calling on her for? Perhaps it had something terrible to do with Henrietta or Clive, and Julia had been sent to tell her! She hurried past Karl, who was still standing dozily in the hallway just outside her bedroom door. Elsie entered the parlor and embraced Julia quickly, her face betraying her anxiety, and subsequently breathed a heavy sigh of relief when Julia responded in the negative to her distressed inquiries regarding Clive and Henrietta's well-being.

Once assured that they were truly not in any danger, Elsie tried to collect herself and proceed with the visit as propriety might demand, awkwardly offering Julia a chair and perhaps some tea? Julia had declined any refreshment but had accepted Elsie's invitation to sit down. As she did so, Elsie's mind uneasily began to guess at what other reason Julia might have to condescend to visit her—and unannounced at that. Worriedly, she supposed that it couldn't be anything good.

Julia, as it happened, did not leave Elsie guessing for long. She entreated Elsie to recall the conversation she had had with her and Henrietta in the bride's room at Sacred Heart on Henrietta's wedding day, as the three of them had held hands and declared their love for one another, just before Henrietta had walked down the aisle.

"That makes us like sisters, does it not?" Julia asked, sitting beside her on the settee. Elsie very enthusiastically agreed, to which Julia then proceeded to ask, quite delicately, if there was anything Elsie might like to tell her—anything at all.

Elsie, growing nervous now, demurred, but Julia pressed. She had received a letter from Henrietta just the other day, she said, in which Henrietta had expressed concern about a certain lieutenant . . .

Elsie blushed profusely at the mention of Harrison but did not answer.

Julia went on to say that she felt it her duty to inform Elsie that, as charming as Lieutenant Barnes-Smith might appear, she was very sorry to tell her that he possessed quite a bad reputation. Lowering her voice, then, she asked if Elsie had not heard the story of poor Alice Stewart?

Elsie bravely met Julia's eyes at the mention of the unfortunate Alice Stewart, saying that she had indeed heard of her and that she had, as a matter of fact, asked Harri—the lieutenant—about her and that he had told her that it was a common misunderstanding, that he was not to blame in that very disagreeable situation. He had told her everything, Elsie said, not without a little bit of triumph in her voice.

Julia reached out and took her hand. "Did he?" she asked quietly. "Did he mention how he secretly engaged himself to her and got her with child?" She said this last bit barely above a whisper.

Elsie's throat tightened.

"But when Alice's father refused to settle any money on her as long she took up with the likes of him," Julia went on, "the 'honorable' lieutenant released himself—and her—from any betrothal promises."

Elsie could not help letting out a little murmur at this point, as she had, quite unconsciously, been holding her breath.

"Alice was sent to live with relatives for the duration of her confinement," Julia continued, "and the lieutenant walked free—denying everything."

"Didn't . . . didn't her family do something? Force him to marry her, perhaps?" Elsie asked, a slight crack in her voice.

"No, they wanted to be well rid of him, calculating that the mild scandal would be worth it. Alice had to give the child up, of course, and then her mother took her to Europe for the season to escape all of the bad rumors. I'm afraid her reputation is in tatters now, though. Her only hope is to marry a foreigner," she sighed.

"You're . . . you're sure?" Elsie asked, shocked that Harrison had not only lied, or had left out a very large portion of the story, at any rate, but that he also had *a child* somewhere out there. Hastily, she wiped away a tear from the corner of her eye.

"Very sure, dearest," Julia said quietly.

Elsie burst into tears, then, her body racked with sobs as she gave in to her despair. She knew it was unladylike in the extreme, but she couldn't help it, nor did she really care. Julia didn't seem to mind the breach in etiquette, either, and quickly moved closer to her and put her arms around her. Elsie confessed the whole sordid tale, then, how she had very nearly succumbed to the same devious plan as had been tried on the unwitting Alice Stewart, but had left out the very important detail of how he had already seduced her, how she had given her virginity to this wretch. In truth, however, she had not given him anything—he had *taken* her virginity, their dalliance that night having been closer to something forced more than anything else. But poor Elsie could not, even now, admit that to herself, much less utter the words to one such as Julia; she was ashamed enough already. Elsie thought that she might tell Henrietta when she returned, but then again, maybe not.

Julia listened calmly to all of Elsie's sad story, and when it was done, she entreated Elsie to come and stay with her for a few days.

Elsie declined at first, but when Julia pointed out that she was in no fit state to face Harrison when he appeared—apparently, in just a few hours—Elsie reluctantly acquiesced and left a note for him, which Julia made sure to discreetly read first, with Karl. Mrs. Von Harmon would not know or care if Elsie went to stay with the Cunninghams: she believed her to be going to stay with her Aunt Agatha and Uncle John, anyway, as was her usual arrangement on Wednesdays, and which had been the proposed cover for her escape with Harrison.

Julia herself had helped Elsie pack a small portmanteau and had taken her back to Glencoe with her. Once she had settled Elsie in one of the guest rooms to sleep off the exhaustion from the emotion of the afternoon, which had included some additional rather violent sobs, Julia had quickly telephoned her father to employ his help in the matter.

Upon receiving Julia's worried call, Alcott had been very sorry and, indeed, quite incensed to hear of poor Elsie's woes and had promptly attempted to put a call in to the reprobate's uncle, Major Barnes-Smith, who had not only been Clive's commanding officer in the war but who had also been Clive's best man at his wedding, which is how Alcott had come to know him better.

After several precious hours of trying to reach the major at his home, Alcott attempted to instead telephone him at Fort Sheridan and was promptly put through to one Colonel Perkins, who crisply informed him that Major Barnes-Smith had been summoned to Washington, DC, several weeks ago now to report for duty, but that was really all he could divulge. It didn't take too long for Alcott to add up what had probably been going on in the major's empty house while he was away, and he felt a fresh burst of anger toward Harrison Barnes-Smith for more than likely using the major's home as a den to lure the innocent Elsie. Why, she was little more than a child!

Alcott then explained to Colonel Perkins that he very desperately needed to speak to the major regarding a matter that was somewhat delicate in nature. Could the colonel possibly get a message through, asking the major to telephone him at Highbury as soon as possible? Colonel Perkins grudgingly took down Alcott's information before he rang off and said he would do what he could, but no guarantees.

Alcott sat back in his chair in his study then and poured himself a brandy as he considered what to do next. He supposed he should ascertain whether Elsie had been interfered with—but he would leave that to Julia. Dwelling on such a subject for any length of time made him decidedly uneasy. He contemplated confronting the lieutenant himself and possibly trying to detain him, but what good would that do? he mused. No, he would leave it up to the major; after all, Harrison was *his* nephew. Alcott predicted that once the major was finished with him, the lieutenant would very soon find himself stationed somewhere remote, held by a very short rope. He would tell Clive, of course, when he came home. He contemplated writing to him, but why bother him with such a thing on his honeymoon? No, he would handle it on his own.

He should probably tell Exley, though, he sighed, as he took a longish drink of his brandy. That was sure to go badly, but Alcott knew that if it were he in Exley's position, he would want to know, if only to perhaps keep a closer eye on what Elsie got herself into. John and Agatha had told him and Antonia that the girl was coming to stay with them regularly, with the intent of exposing her to society, as per Exley's instruction, but obviously the lieutenant had wriggled his way through that particular line of defense. Alcott wondered whatever had happened to that neighborhood boy Elsie had turned up with at the engagement party. They had seemed well suited—not that his opinion ever counted in such matters. Knowing the Exleys as he did, however, Alcott presumed that the boy had probably been long since chased away by now.

No, he sighed, he supposed he would have to drive over and see Oldrich in the morning. Not that he had time, really; not with this other business pressing so hard as of late. Alcott stood up, unsettled, and gazed at the papers lying on his desk, his eyes unfocused. At the bottom, he knew all too well, carefully tucked under the blotter, was yet another letter from Susan, this one more pressing, more demanding. Alcott moved from behind the desk and began to pace.

What was he to do? It had gotten worse since Clive's wedding, oddly, and was almost out of hand now. He cursed himself for not having confided the whole miserable business to Clive earlier. Enough was enough, as it were. If he allowed it to go on any longer, he risked putting Highbury itself in jeopardy—but more than that, he didn't want Clive to inherit the problems he himself had forged. After all, Clive would have enough to worry about when he took the helm.

Alcott walked to the fireplace and braced himself against the mantel, his arms outstretched as he stared into the flames. He should never have gotten himself involved with these—what would he call them?—ruffians! He had always refused to call them by their more common name—the Mob—though as time had gone on that was what he felt sure they were a part of.

Shortly after his marriage to Antonia, her father, the powerful Theodore Hewitt, had unveiled his plan that Alcott and Antonia should move to the Midwest and capitalize on the emerging automobile industry in Chicago and Detroit. Both had been loath to do so, but Mr. Hewitt had assured them that he would have a mansion built for them to rival any in New York, and Alcott, it was known, had always had a penchant for luxury racing cars. Not that that would be the thrust of his business, Mr. Hewitt had explained to him over countless glasses of cognac and cigars, but he could always dabble on the side, he had wryly suggested. Alcott had at first tried to protest this proposal, saying that he had read Greek at Cambridge and had no idea regarding business affairs, even in the slightest. Hewitt had told him not to worry, that he would surround him with business aficionados and that he need act only as a figurehead of sorts. Make sure everyone was on the up-and-up, as it were, someone to make sure Hewitt wasn't being cheated at the end of the day.

Alcott, eager to prove himself in his new country—and remembering the third of Antonia's fortune that had been wired to the coffers of the crumbling Linley Estate back in Derbyshire as part of their marriage contract—knew where his duty lay. If he were to be the sacrificial lamb for Linley, then, by George, he would throw himself into it wholeheartedly. Admittedly, marrying the beautiful socialite, Antonia Hewitt, although a relative stranger to him, had not taken much persuasion, but he had balked slightly, in the beginning, when the arrangements were being negotiated and drawn up, at Hewitt's decree that the young couple live on American soil. Knowing it was a fight he couldn't win, Alcott had manfully given up life in his ancestral home and had taken the hand of his bride and led her to the palatial Highbury, built for them, as promised, by Theodore Hewitt as a wedding gift.

Antonia, for her part, Alcott later learned, had likewise been reluctant to leave her home amid the New York social scene, especially considering the decided advantage becoming the wife of an English aristocrat would have given her in all future social situations. She had been convinced in the end, however, by her mother, who craftily explained that this way, Antonia instead had the opportunity before her to be the reigning queen in Chicago. And so, separately won over by the powers that be, Alcott and Antonia had dutifully agreed to depart and establish themselves just north of the city in Winnetka, Illinois.

It hadn't taken long for the Mob, or the Outfit, to catch wind of a new business opportunity, and they eventually got around to introducing themselves—in decidedly cheap suits, Alcott noticed right away—but perhaps that was to be expected in this part of the world? With rather crude language and in no uncertain terms, they explained to Alcott that all Chicago businesses, especially ones importing luxury items, needed protection and that their "firm" just happened to offer such services. "Protection from whom?" Alcott had asked, but was never given a solid answer. The conversation had then strayed into distasteful, even frightening, topics of warehouses robbed, deliveries held up, cargo lost at sea, and even, in some unfortunate cases, terrible attacks on family members.

Alcott, a true innocent at the time, quickly deduced that Chicago was indeed a more dangerous place than he had first realized. He contemplated asking Mr. Hewitt about said protection services, but as if they could read his mind, these Outfit chaps had instructed him that this was a private, quiet arrangement. No need to tell anyone— simply pay the monthly "fee," as it were, and nothing bad would happen. Somewhat against his better judgment, Alcott had then fatefully entered into this "contract" with them, careful to make the payments from his own money and not from the company's account.

After six months or so of getting his feet wet and gaining experience in the business world, however, Alcott attempted to extricate himself from said arrangement. He explained, somewhat nervously to these thugs, that while he was grateful for said services, they would no longer be needed, he didn't imagine, and that he therefore wished to end their relationship. He had expected perhaps some refutation, but certainly not physical violence, which, indeed, was what had transpired. Two men had attacked him in an alleyway as he was coming out of the Burgess Club in the city and had told him he might want to reconsider pulling out of the arrangement and that the next time he made trouble, an unfortunate accident such as this one might instead befall his beautiful new wife.

Shaken to the core, Alcott had told Antonia that he had been held up, nothing more, when he showed up back at Highbury with a split lip and perhaps a cracked rib. She had fussed and fumed and said this was what came of living in what one could call a frontier town! Never before had she witnessed such lawlessness and violence, she had exclaimed and positively pined for the days when she had been able to lunch at the Waldorf or spend the summer at Newport.

In truth, Alcott was privately inclined to agree. Never had *he* experienced this kind of violence either, even as a first-year at Eton, and he was, in truth, quite frightened. Dutifully, then, he had gone on paying the "fee," which he now recognized as outright extortion, but which he could not see any way out of it. He had told no one, of course, under threat of more violence, except Bennett at the firm, though even to him he had not elaborated the whole story, but had merely hinted, until recently, that is. Bennett, however, had a way of perceiving things, and Alcott was pretty sure he had guessed what was really going on before he had openly shared it with him.

The arrangement had gone on this way for years, Alcott paying the "protection tax," as it came to be called, and no more incidences of violence had occurred. He was communicated with through untraceable letters and was informed, usually yearly, when the "tax" was increasing. It had been particularly difficult to pay during the Depression years, when Alcott had already dipped into his private salary to help keep the company afloat.

Consequently, there had been less money to spend over the years on Highbury itself, which needed constant repairs and cost a small fortune just to run, not to mention the money needed to entertain and thereby maintain a certain standing in the upper echelons of the glittering society in which they dwelled. As a result, he had been forced to let things slip. He knew Clive noticed each time he visited from the city and was utterly ashamed at his poor steward-ship, but what could he do? As it was, he was worried that he might have to begin dipping into the accounts of Linley Standard before too long. He had come into the marriage relatively cash poor, and he had already spent everything he had and everything he had sub-sequently earned. Luckily, the company itself was doing well—the board had invested wisely in steel and the railroads, besides being heavily involved in manufacturing automobile parts and importing luxury cars. Somehow, he had managed to get by.

But just recently, the arrangement had taken a different turn. Alcott had begun receiving odd letters from one Lawrence Susan, informing him that a new outfit was taking over his "contract" and that they had consequently decided to double the amount of his pay-ments. Outraged, Alcott, who had always been content to communi-cate with these ruffians via letters to a post office box, as instructed, especially after his violent experience with two of this firm's members all those years ago, demanded an actual meeting with this Lawrence

Susan. He had had enough! He was no longer afraid, tired of hiding the truth, and conscious of the fact that if Clive really were to take over Linley Standard soon, he was going to have to find a way to end this once and for all. He dreaded Clive's ever discovering his dishonor of having allowed himself to be extorted from all these years, made worse by the fact that Clive was, or had been, an inspector with the Chicago police!

Surprisingly, this Susan had agreed to a face-to-face meeting. Alcott had made his way to the predetermined rendezvous place in the city, a filthy bar called Duffy's on Canal, where Alcott was ushered into a back room to find Susan waiting. Much to his bewilderment, Susan had not been what he was expecting at all. He was small and slight, with thinning hair and crooked, yellowing teeth, and he gave off a stale, acrid odor as of smoky garbage or rotting flesh, tempting Alcott to put his hand over his nose, which he managed, just in time, to resist doing. From the man's thin, almost nonexistent lips dangled a cigarette.

For a brief moment, Alcott contemplated whether he, even in his advanced years, might be able to defeat this Mob boss in a physical altercation, however distasteful that would prove to be, but quickly saw the futility in such a move, though his anger and his fear ran high. For one thing, Susan was surrounded by two large, beefy goons, who added a bizarre element of contrast to the thin, greasy man seated between them. For another, he knew that killing, or even injuring, this spider would not necessarily extricate himself from this web. No, he would need to be craftier.

The creature before him laughed when Alcott demanded that the arrangement come to an end.

"Oh, I don't think so," Susan said soberly. "The arrangement ain't over just yet. You've gotten off cheap all these years, I'd say. Moretti was soft on you. So now yer gonna start payin' what you should have been payin' all along. Double, I think. And a one-time fee—call it back taxes, if you want. Ten grand oughta do it," he said with as much of a smirk as his thin lips would allow. The goons shuffled and grinned.

"That's preposterous!" Alcott blustered. "Look here, I'm finished with all of this now. My arrangement was with this Moretti fellow, not you. I should have ended this long ago."

"But you didn't, did you?" the creature said coolly, his black eyes boring into Alcott. "And you ain't gonna now either," he said, ash spilling from his cigarette onto his jacket. "Know why? 'Cause of those two little grandsons of yers. Randy and Howie is their names, ain't they? Or should I call them by their proper names—Randolph and Howard?" He grinned when he saw the unmistakable look of horror cross Alcott's already flushed face. "And they're enrolled at Sacred Heart Academy, ain't they? Ridin' lessons on Tuesdays. Fencin' on Thursdays. Always a walk in the park on Saturday afternoon with Nanny. Am I close?" He laughed.

Alcott felt his heart constrict.

"It'd be a shame if one of them was to have an accident, wouldn't it? So easy to be thrown from a startled horse, or even led astray while Nanny dozes. Boys will be boys, you see. And there's plenty of dangerous criminals out there. You should be *thankin'* us for the protection services we offer, that's what I'm thinkin'. *Grateful* is what you should be," he wheezed.

Alcott forced himself not to recoil. Sweat had broken out on his forehead now and was dripping down the back of his neck, but he did not make a move to wipe it. His mind raced, searching for something—anything—to bargain with. He knew he shouldn't show fear, but he was thoroughly out of his depth. He should never have come. It was turning out worse than he had imagined.

"Look here" he said, trying his best to sound firm, "I've had enough of your bloody attempts to frighten me. I'll not be threatened any further, I'll have you know. I've made up my mind, and I'm going to the police," he said, with much less force than he had hoped for.

The creature merely tilted his head ever so slightly, causing one of the goons to break rank from behind him and quickly stride over to where Alcott was standing. With incredible alacrity and force, the goon grabbed hold of Alcott's shoulder, and with one fluid movement, sank his other fist into Alcott's gut, causing him to groan and double over. Barely able to breathe, Alcott would have collapsed, but the goon gripped his jacket and held him up, only to punch him again before he finally let him slump to the floor on his knees.

"Now then," Susan said calmly, "I hope that got yer attention. And as for the police, funny you should bring that up, considerin' your son's a high-and-mighty detective inspector. Must not be too good a one to not even know how deep his own father is involved with the, shall we say, less-than-desirables, such as myself. Tsk, tsk. It does look bad, don't it?"

Susan stood up, then, absently trying to brush the ash from his waistcoat. "But maybe he's just distracted, shall we say? That little wife of his is a ripe cherry, if ever there was one. Be a shame if some-thin' happened to her, wouldn't it? Almost had her, I did. Twice," he snarled. "But she slipped through my fingers. She won't be so lucky next time."

He walked to where Alcott was still on his knees on the filthy floor and spit on him. "You bring us the cash, and you don't say anything to anybody. Understand?"

Alcott gave an almost imperceptible nod, and Susan and the goons left him then to further contemplate his options.

Alcott stirred himself from the fireplace and the memories of that terrible night, which he tended to recount over and over in his mind, and looked up at the mantel clock. It was getting late. He supposed he should telephone Julia and let her know what had come of his attempts to locate the major. It was good that Julia had had the foresight to remove the girl to her own home in Glencoe. Barnes-Smith must surely have been surprised when he turned up at the Von Harmons' only to find that his prey had escaped him. As he thought about it, Alcott rather uncharacteristically felt the desire to release some of his own pent-up anger on the unsuspecting lieutenant in the form of a severe scolding—or perhaps more—but that was madness, obviously. But he sincerely hoped that the major would contrive of some way of punishing the wretch, or at least some way of getting rid of him.

But that, of course, was the least of his worries. Ever since that night several weeks ago at the bar on Canal, he had been struggling for a way out of the web in which he was still entangled. He had raised the "back taxes" that Susan was demanding by reluctantly selling one of the paintings from the upstairs gallery. He had selected one of Isaac Levitan's lesser known works, knowing that Antonia was not overly enthralled with this artist, anyway, calling him amateurish and Impressionistic, which was absurd of course, as Alcott considered him one of the last of the golden age of the Russians. But now was not the time to quibble over art. He had Billings replace it with a similar work stored away in the attic, but he knew it was only a matter of time before Antonia would discover it. Well, he would deal with her later. The cash, the whole ten thousand, was stored in the wall safe here in his study, ready for his rendezvous with Susan or his goons or whomever it was he was to meet in the end. He had been instructed via the usual unmarked letter—letters which, of late, had strangely begun to appear on his desk rather than in the post box, making him uneasily suspect that at least one person on the staff was in cahoots with this outfit—that the hand-off would be in one week's time at the train station in Winnetka. Obviously, they knew his movements, knew that Fritz drove him every day to the station to catch the 9:04 into the city. It gave him the chills to think that he was so closely observed. Well, that would be the end of it, he hoped, as he formulated a plan—perhaps a reckless one, but it was all he could think of.

Wearily he picked up the telephone and asked the operator to put him through to the Cunningham residence, Glencoe. He sighed, waiting for the connection to be made. He hoped that Julia had been able to offer the girl some means of comfort; Julia was good at that sort of thing, after all. Exley, however, would be furious when he heard what had gone on.

—

Elsie forced herself out of bed. She knew that preparing all of them for Mr. Howard's funeral would fall on her. Not for anything in the world would she burden Henrietta with having to make sure they were all properly attired; she would have enough to worry about. Ma had not said much regarding Mr. Howard's death, just that it was a shame and that no one ever knew the time or place. More than once, Elsie had lamented aloud the fact that poor Henrietta's lovely honeymoon was being cut short, but Ma had merely snorted that "something was better than nothing." Elsie knew that Ma was right of course, especially considering Ma's woeful experience—but Elsie couldn't shake her sorrow over Henrietta's failed trip. Maybe it had something to do with her own failed attempt to fly away, crude and melodramatic though it may have been in comparison, like so much bad poetry in the face of a sonnet.

She winced at the memory of how she had so stupidly fallen for Harrison's manner of seduction, which consisted of, among other things, reading her poetry that he had originally tried to pass off as his own. Had her virginity really been exchanged for this? But there had been more to it than the poetry and the whiskey, she told herself defensively. There was a part of her that had liked—no loved!—being with Harrison, and a small part of her still mourned the loss of him. She knew this to be wickedly wrong of her, but she couldn't help it. Despite his apparent deviousness, she couldn't help but miss him just a little and the attention he had given her. As Ma had said, wasn't something better than nothing? And, if truth be told, she couldn't help but to still feel sorry for him, even in the midst of this debacle in which she herself had been the victim. She grieved not only for herself, but also for him. For how misunderstood he was. And what of Harrison's child, somewhere out in the world? Did the two of them even know of the other's existence? Thus, on more than one occasion, Elsie found herself crying not only for herself, but also for this lost child, and for Harrison, too. Harrison was bad, certainly, but it wasn't really his fault, was it? He was practically no more than a lost child himself.

But it would never do to say this to anyone, even to Julia. No one seemed to understand her. Elsie had stayed with the Cunninghams for almost a week until she began to feel underfoot, especially where Julia's boorish husband, Randolph, was concerned, and declared quite suddenly one day that she felt much better—truly!—and that it was time for her to go home. In truth, as the week had gone on, she had felt Randolph's withering glances acutely and longed to escape back into the confines of the tomb-like Palmer Square house, which held its own set of problems, Ma being the first and foremost of course, but which was safe, at least, in its lack of visitors and society in general.

Julia had been averse to let her go, entreating her to stay even a few days longer, so much so that Elsie began to wonder if there was something more to her entreaties than mere concern for her own pitiful situation. No, she told Julia, she must be getting back, lest Ma begin to suspect something. Julia had finally acquiesced, knowing as she did that the lieutenant was no longer a threat, as her father had informed her that the major, infuriated when he had eventually learned of the situation, had had Harrison mysteriously transferred to Oregon where various army troops were assisting the CCC in building ranger stations deep in the Oregon forests.

Julia had been kind enough to tell Elsie that no real harm had come to Harrison as a result of his treachery, that his punishment had consisted only of being transferred somewhere far away. Elsie was grateful of course for the news, but she was surprised by the whole range of emotions she felt at his exile, anger oddly surfacing at times to mix with the sadness and the pity. But she had thanked Julia just the same for all she had done, though Julia had been the primary agent, one could say, of the breakup of the lovers in the first place.

Elsie had spent at least some portion of every day since then crying, though she managed to do it in secret. Ma remarked several times, however, complaining that Elsie seemed an awful mope these days, and what had gotten into her? And then had come the terrible news of Mr. Howard's death, after which Elsie's tears could flow openly, masquerading as sorrow for her sister's father-in-law. Not that she wasn't sad of course; Mr. Howard had seemed kind and had treated her respectfully at both the engagement party and the wedding itself. But she had not really known him well, and so most of her tears, in truth, fell for herself and her lost love.

As the days wore on, monotonously marching toward the funeral and Henrietta's return, her tears had finally ebbed until she was left with merely a barren sort of dullness. Where she had once felt so much so tortuously, now she seemed to feel nothing at all, and instead went through the days in the same dreary way.

Elsie dressed slowly and went downstairs for breakfast. Ma was nowhere in sight of course, and the boys were already off to school. Thankfully, Eddie and Herbie had black suits they could wear, and God knew Ma had more than enough black dresses to choose from, but Doris and Donny and Jimmy would have to be fitted with something new. As Odelia bustled in with some coffee for her, Elsie tried to muster up the energy to make a plan. She supposed she should go up to the nursery after breakfast and ask Nanny to accompany her downtown with the twins to shop. She would have to take Jimmy tomorrow, or maybe she should wait for him to get home from school and take him and the twins together? She should have kept him home from school! Oh, why couldn't she think? This wasn't that terribly complicated, and yet she found it difficult to concentrate on anything as of late. Absently, she poured herself some coffee from the silver carafe in front of her and rested her forehead on her fist.

What was she to do? Is this what her life was to be now? Stanley was gone; Harrison was gone. Her grandfather, she knew, wished her to make some sort of stupendous match with the son, or the fountainhead himself, of some eminently wealthy or powerful family, and that Aunt Agatha and Uncle John had been specially discharged to oversee this mission, she also knew. As Elsie poured some cream in her coffee, her stomach clenched as she wondered how much of the Harrison escapade her grandfather was aware of. She prayed that

Mr. Howard had not confided in him before his death. She would be mortified, and no doubt he would be furious. But, she thought then, a realization slowly coming over her as she added some sugar to her cup, that perhaps him finding out that she was "damaged goods," as Harrison had called her, might not be so bad after all. Perhaps everyone might leave her alone then to her own devices. Elsie had no idea what those might be, at the moment, but at least she would be free from her new relatives' machinations and scheming attempts to marry her off.

Elsie sighed. To be fair, Aunt Agatha and Uncle John had been very kind to her, and she actually enjoyed their company and the lovely concerts and plays they had taken her to see in the city. And, in truth, the young—or not so young—men of their set whom they made sure to introduce her to weren't *terrible*, per se, though she always felt strange and awkward around them. She hadn't the slightest thing in common with *any* young man of their acquaintance it seemed, and yet no one seemed to recognize or acknowledge this, at least not out loud. She had once tried to voice her reservations to Aunt Agatha, explaining that she didn't know what to say to any of them, that she found conversation difficult at times even with the easiest of companions. Aunt Agatha had tut-tutted her, saying whatever did conversation have to do with it? That all that was required of *her* was to smile demurely and appear in lovely gowns. *And*, Aunt Agatha had been pleased to say, Elsie was progressing nicely in the learning of bridge, which would be an asset as well.

But did Elsie really want a man who merely sought a rich, well-dressed wife who could play bridge? What about love? She knew that if she raised this question, in all seriousness, she would be given some sort of pat answer, such as "Well, of course love is important, darling, but it doesn't always happen right at the beginning!" But what, wondered Elsie, if it never came?

But worse than all of these doubts was the guilt, the shame that she now carried around, like a heavy bundle on her back. She could not escape her feelings of self-deprecation regarding her lost purity.

All these rich men, looking for a chaste, obedient wife to display in their mansions . . . but she was no longer that, was she? And so she felt doubly inadequate, an imposter on two counts. First, she was not of their class (not really, despite what everyone said about her being an Exley and a Von Harmon), and secondly, she had shamefully and irrevocably tainted herself. She felt so very different now and was amazed that no one else seemed to notice what was so plain to her. She had been praying ever since that fateful night with Harrison that her sin wouldn't become clearly obvious to the greater world, in the form of, say, being with child. Each day that passed in which her flow did not come had added to her misery, so that when it did finally begin—a week late!—she had flown to St. Sylvester's and said a rosary in thanksgiving.

She roused herself, again, from her dreary thoughts, and pushed back the plate of toast that Odelia had set before her. She couldn't eat, and even that made her sad. What an ungrateful girl she was! There had been a time, not so very long ago, when they would have fought over an extra piece of toast—and with real butter on it, to boot! She sighed and looked around the exquisitely appointed room of the house her grandfather had purchased for them. How dare she dwell on her own miseries when she should instead be grateful. But she didn't feel grateful, and that made her wretched, too.

She stood up resolutely, determined to extract the twins from the nursery and do something useful, simultaneously resolving to stop reading Jane Austen, or at least romance novels, and certainly poetry, anyway, for the foreseeable future, maybe forever. That chapter of her life was decidedly over. She would simply have to allow fate to take its course. But she shouldn't use the word "fate," she reprimanded herself; she should say *God*.

She had worked up her courage just yesterday to go to church and confess her sins to Fr. Finnegan, who was severe in his reaction to them. She hadn't really felt forgiven, though he had of course absolved her. She had dutifully and prayerfully—and she hoped sincerely—said her penance, but in her heart, she felt it wasn't enough.

Well, she would allow God to inflict whatever punishment He saw fit upon her. And if that meant marrying whomever the Exleys put before her, then she supposed she would and she would try to be happy in the process. After all—a lovely home, pretty clothes, a family—isn't that what she had always dreamed about as she sat sewing in Mr. Dubala's dusty shop?

But that was not all she had dreamed of in those days, she knew. Love had been the intertwining thread, but that seemed impossible now. She would just have to school herself to believe that love was a fantasy, an illusion; that was obvious, wasn't it? A stray thought of Henrietta came to her mind, then, like an errant sprite, but she pushed it away. Henrietta's situation was different, of course. *She* had found true love, but that was rare. And if it *were* such a rare, precious thing, it made sense that it had come to her beautiful sister and not to the likes of her—plain and, well, dirty.

Chapter 2

As welcoming as the sight of Highbury had been, there was a decided pall of gloom about the place now as the Rolls approached. Clive and Henrietta had arrived at Union Station well past six o'clock and were met by Fritz, who arranged for their luggage to be safely deposited in the car while he saw that his new master and wife were well placed within, but not before giving Clive a sorrowful handshake and offering the sincere condolences of not only himself but of the staff as a whole.

Clive had said little on the drive up to Winnetka, but Henrietta had clutched his hand tightly—not because she was nervous about returning to Highbury, as she had been wont to be before their marriage, but because she was worried about him. He had positively brooded on the ship back across the ocean, speaking hardly at all and merely staring, for hours it seemed, at the vast expanse of the ocean before him, which did not change from day to day except for the patterning of the clouds and the differing amounts of light that shone through. It was as if something dark had risen up from his past—perhaps memories of the war?—and she could not seem to reach him.

Antonia must have been waiting somewhere near the main hallway because she stepped out onto the stone steps as soon as they drove up, clutching her cardigan tightly around herself as the November wind whipped at her skirt. To Henrietta's eye, she seemed smaller and more fragile than she remembered, but perhaps it was just the darkness, or maybe it was the massiveness of Highbury looming behind that dwarfed her. At any rate, Henrietta's heart went out to Antonia, and tears flooded her eyes when she saw Clive hurry up the stairs and embrace her. With no guests in the immediate vicinity, their mutual tears could flow freely and without embarrassment. When Clive released her, Henrietta, who had followed more slowly up the thick stone stairs, embraced Antonia, too, mumbling, "Antonia, I'm so very sorry." Antonia did not say anything, but held onto her tightly.

After several moments, Antonia released her, saying, "Come in, then, you must be exhausted." She turned and went in, Clive and Henrietta soberly following. Henrietta was surprised that not only did Clive take her hand as they entered, but that it was slightly trembling.

"Welcome home, sir, madam," Billings said in his familiar nasally voice from where he stood at attention by the door. Most of the servants were also present in the foyer, offering their greetings and welcoming them back as they bustled about, gathering their coats and carrying luggage. There was an air of muted excitement among them that the newlyweds had returned home safely from their long travels, but it was edged with more than a hint of somberness. Edna was on hand of course, eager to take up her role as lady's maid for Henrietta. She would begin unpacking immediately, she informed her mistress, and asked in a low voice if there was anything in particular that she needed. Henrietta took Edna's hand and said no and gave it a grateful squeeze.

In a muted voice, Antonia directed Billings to bring tea through to the drawing room, and the three of them made their way there in silence. As they sat down across from each other, Henrietta looked around and was struck by how much this felt like home now.

Antonia asked disjointed questions about their voyage and

about the state of Montague and Margaret, Clive's uncle and aunt with whom they had stayed at Castle Linley, but once the tea had been dutifully delivered, she immediately veered into the subject of Alcott's terrible death, wanting to tell the whole story from beginning to end. She began stoically enough, but more than once she required her handkerchief, her voice uncharacteristically catching from time to time.

Henrietta was distressed by Antonia's rare show of emotion, but she did not know how to respond. She knew that if she were to attempt to comfort her *own* mother, she would be rebuffed, and so with that in mind, she remained silent and instead quietly sipped her tea, looking now and again at Clive for clues. For his part, he did not appear overly affected by his mother's tears and instead seemed deeply engrossed in listening to Antonia's tale, taking in all of the details as if he had never heard the story before, though Antonia, Henrietta knew, had already told Clive all of this on a transatlantic call to him at Linley Castle. Silently he sat through the retelling, his lips pursed and his hands firmly gripping the tea cup he held.

It really had been a most unfortunate accident, Antonia repeated yet again, that Alcott had apparently slipped on the new snow and had fallen in front of the oncoming train. Hadn't she advised him to wear his new galoshes? Hadn't she warned him that his old ones were nearly worn through?

"At least he didn't suffer," she cried quietly, putting her handkerchief up to her eyes again. "It was over so quickly."

"Yes, a blessing," Henrietta added sadly.

"And no one saw him fall?" Clive asked, pulling his eyes from the tea he'd been swirling in his cup and looking up at his mother intently.

"Saw him fall? What an extraordinary question, Clive! How would I know? I . . . I suppose there might have been other people on the platform who saw it happen. How horrible for them," Antonia sniffed.

"*Were* there other people on the platform?"

"Really, Clive. How would I know that?"

"Did anyone think to ask?"

Antonia stared at him for a few moments. "No, they did not. What are you getting at, darling? Are you thinking someone could have saved him, perhaps?" She looked at him expectantly.

"Has it not occurred to anyone else that Father's death seems, well, unusual? I mean . . . he slipped on the snow and fell in front of a train? That seems extraordinary, to use your word."

"Are you suggesting that his death was not an accident?" she asked slowly, appearing increasingly horrified as this idea sunk in.

Clive shifted uncomfortably. "Well, perhaps . . . it just seems odd, don't you think?"

Antonia stared at him, bewildered. "Are you suggesting . . . your father would never do such a thing! How dare you even think such a thing, Clive!" she exclaimed.

"No, of course I don't mean *that*, Mother," Clive said hurriedly. "I just mean that, well, that maybe he was pushed—"

"Pushed?" she asked in a high voice. "But who . . . who would want to harm your father? He was a pillar of society. The kindest, most gentle . . . oh, Clive!" She began sobbing in earnest now, her hands covering her face. "What am I to do?"

Clive immediately stood up and went to her, sitting beside her and putting his arms around her. "Shh . . . Mother. Forgive me. This is not the time for this. I'm sorry. It will be all right." He looked across at Henrietta, his own eyes full of tears as well.

Henrietta noiselessly set her cup down and rose from her place on the sofa. She walked across to where the two sat huddled and stroked Clive's shoulder. Then she bent down and kissed the crown of his head and retreated. "I'll give you some time to be alone together. Please don't hurry."

Clive blearily smiled his thanks, but Antonia kept her face buried.

Henrietta valiantly tried to stay awake, waiting for Clive to come upstairs. For a long time, she sat in one of the red, plush armchairs by the fire, trying to read Dorothy Sayer's latest, *Gaudy Night*, which she had hurriedly picked up at a book stand on their way through New

York. She was sitting in Clive's old suite of rooms, which Antonia had had redone before the wedding, making this upper wing of the house like a little apartment for them. They had not spent any time here, however, having spent their wedding night in the old cottage down by the lake, Clive's nuptial surprise for her. And while Antonia had graciously asked her opinion on various items of décor, Henrietta, at the time, had not really grasped that these rooms were to be wholly theirs and had let Antonia do as she wished. Now that they were back, however, with the excitement of the wedding and the honeymoon over, Henrietta was able to take stock of the suite and found it to be rather charming. As she wandered through, she noted that there were one or two things she might have done differently, but all in all, she was grateful and was of the opinion that Antonia had done quite a good job. But what did any of this matter at a time like this? she sighed, her mind turning to what lay before them.

She had always known that when they returned to Highbury, they would have to take up a new list of duties, that their new life would have certain challenges, but she could never have foreseen that it would start off with such monumental ones. She pitied Clive not only for losing his father, but also for having to start immediately at the firm, a position he had struggled to accept in the first place and which he had only recently agreed to. He had thought he would have years before having to take over. And, of course, he would have the burden of the grieving Antonia.

Well, thought Henrietta, perhaps she could help with that. She had been surprised upon their arrival that no other guests were in the house and thought to ask Edna about it when the girl had quietly knocked, eager to begin her duties by helping Henrietta to undress.

Accordingly, while she hung up Henrietta's dove-gray Piguet traveling suit, Edna explained that John and Agatha Exley had indeed been there almost every day and had in fact just left right before they had driven up. "Likely you might have even seen them on the road, had you a mind to be lookin' for them," she said from where she moved now to stand behind the seated Henrietta to unhook her jewelry for her. Edna went on to explain that Mrs. Howard's relations from New York were due in tomorrow for the funeral and that the house would then be heaving with people. It would be like the wedding all over again, only this time for a sorrowful occasion, she had sadly observed.

"But what about Julia?" Henrietta asked of Edna's reflection in the mirror of her dressing table. "I'd have thought that she at least would be here."

As much as Henrietta's mind was obviously preoccupied with Alcott's death and the subsequent problems resulting from it, a large part of her was also desperate to speak with Elsie, and she had hoped that Julia might be at Highbury to greet them so that she might have asked her more.

Julia had wired them in New York after they had docked to say that all was well with Elsie and that the crisis had been averted. They had hurried to the Savoy then, where they had planned to wait the several hours until their train to Chicago was scheduled to depart, the Savoy being so much more comfortable, and private, a place to wait than even the first-class lounge at the train station could afford. From there, Clive had been able to place a call to Julia, who had then thankfully been able to relate the little she knew—that she had managed to intercept Elsie before she could carry out her fateful decision to elope with Harrison and that Alcott, through his string of connections, had alerted the major, who in turn had the lieutenant transferred to a remote locale. Henrietta was dying to ask more, but she knew that a long-distance telephone call in a box just off the lobby of the Savoy was not the place for it and that it would have to wait. Instead, she had thanked Julia profusely and taken the opportunity to likewise express her deep sorrow for the loss of Alcott. Julia had gone silent on the line, then, for so many moments in a row that Henrietta was inclined to think they had been disconnected. "Julia?" she had asked. "Are you there?" Julia had come back on then and had replied with what Henrietta could tell was forced cheerfulness, that they would talk when they returned and implored her to give her love to Clive.

"She's been here every day too, miss . . . I mean, madam," Edna murmured with a blush. "She wanted Mr. Clive . . . I mean, Mr. Howard . . . sorry, madam . . . to have some time alone with Mrs. Howard . . . with his mother, that is . . ." she fumbled, laying out Henrietta's robe. "Oh!" she said then, turning back toward her. "I nearly forgot! Mrs. Cunningham wanted me to give you this." She drew a note out of her dress pocket—no longer required to wear an apron now as a lady's maid—and handed it to Henrietta. It smelled distinctly of lavender. Henrietta opened and quickly skimmed it, and seeing that it contained nothing disastrous, she folded it and put it on the side of her dressing table to be read more thoroughly later.

"Thank you, Edna. I think that will be all."

Before her marriage to Clive, when she had been just a guest at Highbury, Henrietta had often surreptitiously enjoyed helping Edna with her household chores behind the backs of the watchful, disapproving Billings and Mrs. Caldwell, the housekeeper, and had indeed fancied the two of them as friends, despite Edna's protests, stating the obvious difference in their class. Henrietta, however, a working girl herself before Clive had met and fallen in love with her, had been loath to elevate herself above Edna, or *any* of the servants, much to Mrs. Howard's despair and repeated scolding. Like errant school children, she and Clive had likewise refused to take a valet and a lady's maid on their honeymoon, further adding to Mrs. Howard's annoyance.

As it turned out, they had been assigned, as a matter of course, personal servants from among the staff at Castle Linley, the Howards' ancestral home, for the duration of their stay there. So it was at Castle Linley that Henrietta had really grown accustomed to servants (and demure ones, at that!), whether she liked it or not, and had dutifully played the part of the lady, if nothing else to avoid embarrassment, if not for herself than for her new husband, whom she was determined not to shame if she could possibly help it.

That experience, plus the resultant weight of Alcott's death and Clive's subsequent retreat into himself, forced Henrietta to give up any previous childish notions about being on familiar terms with the servants. She had no time for such silly antics now. Thus she found herself acting accordingly, but not unkindly, toward Edna, who seemed also to sense the change in Henrietta and was trying to feel her way through to whatever their new relationship would be. Henrietta felt a sort of kinship with Edna, however, more than the other servants, not only because she had once tried to befriend her, but because she had sorely misjudged Edna's romantic attachment to Virgil Higgins, one of the estate's gardeners, during the whole sordid Jack Fletcher affair. Henrietta was therefore happy that Edna had been assigned to her as a lady's maid, but she saw this as horribly out of date and had other ideas of how she might use Edna's services, but those would have to wait.

When Edna finally left her for the evening, assured that Henrietta had positively everything she needed, Henrietta sat in one of the armchairs to read Julia's note more thoroughly:

Dearest, Henrietta,

I know you will of course be frantically worried about dear Elsie. Rest assured that she is safe. Thanks to Father alerting the major, I am quite convinced that the lieutenant will not be interfering with Elsie again. It was perhaps Father's last beneficent act before his accident, and I am touched that it was in your sister's service. That will always be a comfort to me. We can discuss the details of the sordid affair, if you wish it, at a later date, but I will leave that for your contemplation and initiation.

There is one small point of consideration, however, that I feel obliged to relate, though it is only my humble opinion and nothing else, so you may do with it what you will. While I feel quite assured that Elsie is safe from any physical harm or secret trysts by the hand of Lieutenant Barnes-Smith, she may be, dare I say, still in danger of the heart.

It became apparent to me during her short respite with

us, that while we see the lieutenant for the wretch that he is, Elsie, though she tries to hide it, is still quite attached to him and indeed fancies herself still in love. Knowing Elsie the way that I'm sure you do, this is probably not any great surprise. Therefore, bearing that in mind, it has occurred to me that poor Elsie would be greatly aided by some sort of occupation to settle her addled spirits beyond merely being the current plaything of John and Agatha Exley. Might she not be encouraged to study, for example? To take up classes at some nearby women's college? There is a new one, Mundelein College, just by Loyola, near the lake in Roger's Park. I am told that it is run by the Sisters of the Blessed Virgin Mary, so I am sure it is respectable. I have no idea if this would appeal to Elsie, or if your grandfather would even allow it, but surely you can put your lovely charms to use, should you think it an appropriate proposal. But I will leave this with you for your deliberation.

I only meant this to be a hurried note, so I will close now. I am quite downcast, of course, regarding Father, but mostly, if I am honest, as to how it relates to poor Mother and of course to Clive, whose every fiber, I daresay, rebels against the thought of taking up Father's position at the firm. Truly I am sorry for him, but I am confident he will find a way, as he always does, especially with so lovely and devoted a helpmate by his side. How Mother will cope, I cannot say.

Know that I am well. Give my love to Clive, and I eagerly look forward to seeing you very soon, despite the very sad circumstances in which we find ourselves.

Your loving sister,
Julia

Henrietta set the note aside, touched that Julia had called herself her sister and missing her all the more. She took up the note again and reread it. *Elsie go to college?* It was an interesting idea, one that had never occurred to her, she thought guiltily, but one which seemed to grow on her as she sat and mulled it over, the premise of *Gaudy Night* not far from her mind. Why not? she mused. It was a wonderful idea, actually. Why hadn't she thought of it before? She supposed it was because she had been so busy with Clive and Highbury and wedding plans and a myriad of other things, to notice what had been going on in Elsie's life, blaming herself for the hundredth time.

She assumed that her grandfather, the domineering Oldrich Exley, still intended to execute his plan to send the boys away to Phillips Exeter after Christmas, despite Alcott's death. After all, what would Mr. Howard's death matter to her grandfather's schemes? And if the boys were gone, why should poor Elsie be left to mope around the Palmer Square house? No wonder she had become entangled with Barnes-Smith! Ma would fume, Henrietta expected, but what difference would that make? Ma was determined, it seemed, to be perpetually miserable; so be it, Henrietta thought bitterly. As far as she knew, Ma still did not know of the plan regarding the boys, only Clive (and therefore she) and Alcott having been privy to it. Henrietta wondered when her grandfather intended to unveil it to the family as a whole.

The more Henrietta dwelt on this new possibility for Elsie, the more excited she became. It was a bright spot on an otherwise bleak landscape. She assumed Grandfather would be against the idea, as no doubt he would see no point in educating women, especially when he had other plans for Elsie. He had made it quite clear that Elsie was to make a brilliant match with some eminently suitable young man from the North Shore or possibly New York as a means of elevating the Exleys even higher up the social ladder. But what no one dared to voice aloud in this whole scheme of her grandfather's was whether or not Elsie was really capable of snagging a rich husband from the North Shore.

Henrietta loved her sister dearly, but Elsie, with her big-boned frame and dull, brown hair was only mildly attractive at best. A new hairstyle and fashionable clothes had gone a long way in enhancing her attractiveness, but Elsie had a way of carrying herself that belied her self-consciousness even still. She seemed never at her ease unless curled up in an armchair somewhere reading. Henrietta had seen her share of unattractive women win handsome, rich men, but usually it was because they had a certain flair to them, as if they knew they had certain physical deficiencies but managed to make it appear as though they didn't, laughing and flirting and cooing with the best of them. Henrietta had herself learned that a display of confidence was everything, whether as a poor taxi dancer or a society woman of the North Shore, and it was a skill in which poor Elsie was decidedly lacking. However, Henrietta was beginning to see that Oldrich Exley was a very ambitious man and usually got his way in most things.

Well, Henrietta thought, she would see about all of that. She wasn't afraid of her grandfather, she liked to think, and, anyway, as *Mrs. Howard* now, she had her own supply of wealth, if it came to that. If nothing else, she determined, she would pay for Elsie's tuition herself if her grandfather refused!

Henrietta yawned and glanced at the rococo clock on the writing desk, squinting in the dim light to make out the time. Was it really past midnight? She stood up and decided to take up her vigil in bed. She untied her silk dressing gown, and placed it on the end of the bed, and slipped beneath the heavy blankets. Valiantly, she tried to remain awake, but she slipped into a doze every so often, her many thoughts begging for priority in her mind.

After about an hour of fitful rest, she felt Clive slip into the bed beside her. She hadn't heard him come in.

"How is she?" she whispered to him.

"You're awake?" he whispered back, sounding grateful and surprised.

"Of course, I am. I'm worried about you."

She reached out her hand and ran her fingers through the hair on his temple. Though the room was lit only by the light of the fire, she saw his eyes close at her touch and heard him take in a deep breath. They lay facing each other. Under the covers, Clive put his hand on the swell of her hip. "Henrietta . . ." he said hoarsely.

He had not touched her once since he had received the telegram regarding Alcott's death. Night after night she had lain beside him in their luxury state room on the Queen Mary, but he had not reached for her, and she did not know if she should approach him. Until they had received that fateful telegram at Castle Linley, they had made love every single day of their honeymoon, sometimes more than once in fact, except for the one night they had quarreled. How silly all of that seemed now.

Henrietta could sense his deep need and obvious struggle. Why did he hold himself from her? His hand on her hip here in the dark was the closest he had gotten to her. Her heart beginning to beat a little faster, she resolved to try to make it easy for him. Tentatively, she rubbed the back of her fingers along his cheek, the stubble on it thick after the long day. She leaned forward and kissed his lips, allowing her fingertips to drop hesitantly to his chest. He did not respond to her kiss, but neither did he pull away, so she inched herself closer to him and kissed him again, this time deeply. She felt him tense as he lay there stiffly on his side, allowing her to caress his lips, but still he remained rigid. She put one hand on his back, hesitating there for several moments before allowing it to drop lower until it brushed against his buttocks, causing a swift intake of breath on his part.

Encouraged, Henrietta kissed him on the base of the neck, her tongue exploring, and continued to distribute her kisses, moving to his chest and inching her way down until she heard him groan, the first sign of life she had detected in these many weeks. To her delight, his resurrection continued with him reaching for her breasts, softly stroking them through the cotton of her nightgown, as he gazed into her eyes. He leaned toward her now and kissed her lips. He was tender at first, reluctant, just barely brushing his lips against hers, until his passion seemed to ignite, and he returned her kisses fully. A corresponding flush of excitement coursed through her.

Suddenly, however, he stopped and pulled himself abruptly away.

"No, this is wrong," he panted. "We shouldn't be doing this. My father's funeral is tomorrow!" he said, almost angrily, rolling over onto the pillows and throwing his arm across his forehead.

Henrietta, her own breath coming rapidly, raised up on her elbow to look at him. "Clive, it isn't wrong. I'm your wife. Let me comfort you," she said, tentatively running her fingers along his cheek again. "How long do you plan to remain celibate? Surely this is not what your father would have wanted."

He remained unmoving, however, and after looking at him for several moments, she bent forward and kissed his shoulder nearest her. "Make love to me," she whispered in his ear. "Please." She had never been this daring. "I need you," she said, placing her hands on his chest and allowing her fingertips to wander. Slowly, she let her hand roam lower until she felt him tremble and a deep groan escape.

Swiftly, he rolled over and lay on top of her, the weight of him so welcome. He began kissing her again, tenderly at first but then more fiercely, as if he were beginning to lose control. Roughly, he tugged her nightgown up and fitted himself between her legs as she quickly opened up to him. He had never been this way with her, and though it startled her, she was aroused just the same. She gasped as she felt him enter her. He began to thrust, kissing her neck, her ear, and finally moving back to her lips. She wrapped her arms around him, clenching his back and feeling his muscles ripple. He paused only once to deftly pull her nightgown over her head, releasing her full breasts, which he bent to kiss. She groaned, her breath coming in short bursts.

"Henrietta," he said huskily after only a few moments. "I . . . I can't wait . . ."

"No," she panted. "Don't stop . . ."

With one last kiss of her breasts, his rhythmic thrusts increased, overwhelming her with pleasure until she felt him shudder violently, filling her completely. Henrietta, her hands still on his scarred back, covered now in a thin sheen of sweat, felt herself climax then, too, an explosion of light erupting in her mind as she cried out from under him, her body taut and pulsing.

When her own shuddering finally stopped, gently and gradually, like a wave slowly rolling back, he softly kissed her lips and her neck and finally her shoulder until he rolled off and collapsed beside her, breathing deeply.

Henrietta lay cradled in his shoulder, basking in her love for him.

"Did I hurt you?" he asked, not looking at her.

"You could never hurt me, Clive."

He turned to her, then, and began to rub his fingers along her shoulder and down her arm. She looked up at him and saw the deep ache in his eyes. On their honeymoon it had been she who had often cried after their lovemaking, but tonight, she saw, it was him.

"I love you," he whispered.

"I love you too, Inspector," she answered, nestling closer to him, grateful that he had at last come back to her. She had missed him.

Chapter 3

The funeral mass for the honorable Alcott Linley Fitzwilliam Howard was held on November 18, 1935 at Sacred Heart Church in Winnetka, followed by a small reception to be given at Highbury. He had been baptized in the Anglican church of course, but he had taken Antonia's faith before their marriage; hence he was buried with the full rites of the Catholic Church.

Elsie was amazed at how many people had come to pay their last respects. The Von Harmons had barely found a pew all the way in the back, having arrived several minutes after the mass had begun, which caused Elsie further despair than what she already felt. It had been Ma's fault, of course, that they were late. She had had another one of her nervous spells and had tried to declare that she wasn't well enough to go. Elsie had quickly fetched her pills and administered one and said that of course she had to go, there was no time to change her mind now—the cars were already out there, for heaven's sake! Ironically, the scolding she gave Ma could have easily applied to herself as well, as she had been sorely tempted to claim to be ill, too. But someone, she knew, had to rise to the occasion of organizing them all, and she knew it certainly wouldn't be Ma. She would just have to try to fill Henrietta's shoes as best she could.

Eventually Elsie had managed to corral all of them into the

Packard, which Karl commandeered, and the additional car that her grandfather had arranged and sent over in order to fit them all respectably. Elsie dreaded going into public, imagining that the whole of Palmer Square and the North Shore knew of her shameful sins. It was all she could do to walk into the packed church and be escorted—late!—by one of the ushers to one of the few empty pews in the back. Luckily the situation called for a bowed head, as Elsie doubted she would have had the strength to hold it up anyway.

After arranging Donny and Doris on either side of her and unbuttoning their matching black Rothschild coats, she picked up her hymnal. After a few minutes of skimming along, not really focusing on the words before her on the page, Elsie could not help but raise her eyes and eagerly search the crowd for Henrietta. Eventually, she spotted her. If she leaned to the right, she could just barely make her out through the crowd. She was in the first pew, of course, standing erect, next to Clive. She thought she caught a glimpse of Julia and Randolph, as well, but did not see Mrs. Howard until she went up for communion. She was there, kneeling stiffly next to Clive, her face resolute and ashen.

The Exleys were there, of course, including Grandfather, and though she could have been mistaken, she thought for sure that he looked at her with more than his usual severity. Did he somehow know? she wondered, the turmoil in her stomach increasing. No, she told herself; she was letting her fears run away with her, and she tried harder to focus on her prayers. But she no longer knew what to pray for, at least regarding herself, so she instead prayed for Clive and Henrietta, and Julia, and Mrs. Howard, of course. Then she prayed for her own little family assembled around her, especially Ma, that she might be happy someday. She even offered up a little prayer for Stanley and, truth be told, Harrison, wherever he was, and wiped away a tear.

Elsie was indeed so lost in her own thoughts for much of the service, that she was surprised when the concluding rite began. Fr. Michaels draped the white cloth over the casket, saying the church's final words of farewell and blessing. The pall bearers, which included

Clive, of course, and Randolph, assembled themselves at attention beside the casket and, at the signal, heaved it up upon their shoulders. The organ began to swell out under the strains of the recessional hymn "Love Divine, All Love Excelling," and the procession down the aisle began. It was Alcott's last journey. Fr. Michaels walked before him, accompanied by altar boys gingerly swinging thuribles of incense. Behind the casket walked the family, led by Antonia Howard, who was leaning heavily on Julia and sobbing quietly behind a stylish, short, black veil that covered her face. Elsie, herself caught up in the sadness of it all, tried valiantly to sing the hymn, but broke down finally as she tried to sing the last verse:

Finish then thy new creation;
Pure and spotless let us be.
Let us see thy great salvation
Perfectly restored in thee,
Changed from glory into glory,
Till in heaven we take our place,
Till we cast our crowns before thee,
Lost in wonder, love, and praise!

In her despair, however, her head bent as she cried, Elsie suddenly felt a gentle pressure on her arm and almost exclaimed aloud as her sorrow momentarily turned to joy. Henrietta had broken out of the rank of the procession to quickly embrace her and deposit a kiss on her cheek before she slipped back in line, but not before patting Doris and Donny on the head and winking at Jimmy.

Elsie smiled through her tears as she attempted to quiet the now agitated twins, hopping and squirming at the sight of their beloved sister and asking in loud whispers when they could see her. "Later," Elsie whispered back as she helped them button their coats. "We're going to go see Henrietta in her big house," she told them, and though she knew it was probably wrong to feel happy at a funeral, she had to admit that she did—just a little.

On the short journey from the cemetery to Highbury, however, Elsie tried to prepare herself for the fact that she would probably see very little of Henrietta that day. She was sure Henrietta would be much too busy to talk at any length, but it would be a comfort, she told herself, just to see her.

The twins were fighting in the car. They were getting more and more rambunctious, and it had been difficult at the gravesite to keep them quiet. Fortunately, Nanny Kuntz, who was accompanying them for the day, had brought some biscuits with her and had sparingly passed them out between them, but not without a large helping of scolding. Ma was in the other car with the boys, which Elsie was grateful for, as she did not have the strength to quarrel with her further. Another nervous spell had come upon Ma at the cemetery, causing her in the end to seek refuge in the Packard for the duration of the service, leaving Elsie and Nanny to corral the kids at the back of the crowd. Donny and Jimmy had more than once attempted to run off among the gravestones, and Elsie had had to send Herbie out to collect them. She shivered as she watched him go, a desperately pale specter weaving his way between the graves, growing as tall and thin as Pa had been, despite having only just turned twelve.

Elsie was afraid that Ma would refuse to get out of the car, now that they had finally reached Highbury, so she breathed a sigh of relief when she saw Ma emerge from the Packard ahead of them and walk up the stone steps, gripping Eddie's arm tightly as she did.

They were shown into the small ballroom, where Clive and Henrietta had had their engagement party, Elsie remembered correctly. Large tables had been set up and loaded with trays of beautifully displayed food. As she held the twins back from dashing across the room toward the food, Elsie looked around and noted how different it seemed from the night of the party. Then, it had seemed golden and glittering and ethereal almost; now it just seemed somber and dull. Still beautiful, to be sure, but muted somehow. She remembered, sadly, that it was here that she had first met Harrison, and her stomach clenched at the memory . . .

"Elsie!" she heard someone cry and turned to see Henrietta rushing toward her. Elsie could not help but smile as she embraced her
lovely sister, dressed somberly in a simple black dress with a black
lace collar with her rich, auburn hair classically pinned up. She
seemed older to Elsie than when she had last seen her at the wedding,
though it was just a short time ago, really.

Donny and Doris wriggled free of Nanny and ran to hug Henrietta
awkwardly about the legs, followed closely by Jimmy. Eddie and
Herbie, for their part, held back, eagerly watching the scene unfold,
until Henrietta held out her arms to them as well, and they sheepishly embraced her. "Look how big you've all gotten!" she exclaimed
brightly.

"Did you get us anything, Hen?" Jimmy asked excitedly.

"Jimmy! For shame," Elsie hissed. "That's not the first thing you
say!"

"Why not?" Jimmy asked genuinely.

"Of course, I brought you all something. Later," she whispered. "I
hope you've all been good for Ma," she said, finally looking over at
her mother, whom she had successfully avoided acknowledging until
now and who was seated, what looked to be uncomfortably, on a
chair Eddie had found for her. "Let me go for a minute, so I can hug
Ma," she told her siblings, and they instantly released her.

Ma stood up unsteadily, and in a rare moment of affection,
embraced Henrietta, albeit briefly.

"Hello, Ma," Henrietta said. "How are you?" Though Henrietta's
tone was even, Elsie could tell by the look on her face that she was
troubled by Ma's appearance. Elsie looked over at Ma now too and
tried to see her through Henrietta's eyes. It was true that Ma was
looking weaker and more fragile these days.

"Hello, Henrietta," Ma said coolly. "I'm sorry about Mr. Howard.
He was a kind man, more than most."

Henrietta was about to respond when Clive suddenly joined them.
"I see you've found each other," he said with a sad smile.

"Oh, Clive," Elsie said spontaneously, moving toward him. "I'm so very sorry. Sorry for everything . . ." she mumbled, not knowing what else to say, and standing awkwardly in front of him, feeling big and ugly.

Surprisingly, Clive's response was to reach out and hold her in an uncharacteristically tight embrace. "We've all had a hard go of it lately, haven't we?" he said to her quietly. He released her and gave her a sad smile, which Elsie recognized as the sort that only comes from deep grief. "You must come and stay with us for a time and cheer us up. Right, my dear?" he said, looking over at Henrietta.

"Yes, of course you should, Elsie!" Henrietta exclaimed. "We've so much to talk about, don't we?" she asked gently.

Elsie looked from one to the other, small tears emerging in the corners of her eyes. They were both so good. Elsie wanted to say something more, but before she could think of anything, Ma hobbled up behind her, holding her hand out to Clive and obliging Elsie to stand aside.

"I'm sorry, Clive," she said sincerely. "Your father was a good man."

"Thank you, Mrs. Von Harmon," Clive said tightly, clasping her hand with both of his. "Thank you for coming. This must be very trying for you."

Ma ignored this comment and sighed. "Well, what a thing to come home to," she offered instead.

"Yes, very hard," Clive said quietly. "All good things must come to an end, however, as they say."

"Yes, that's true enough."

There were a few moments of awkward silence during which Elsie again wished she could think of something to say.

"And how about all of you?" Clive asked, looking around at the assembled group. "How have you been?"

No one answered, however, and Elsie felt herself squirm in the silence. She knew that the children were still not completely sure about Clive—they had seen so little of him, and he was still like a stranger to them.

"As good as can be expected," Ma finally answered for them in a gruff sort of tone. "Keeping busy."

No one said anything else for several more moments until Clive finally spoke. "Well, if you'll excuse me, I'm sure you have much to catch up on," he said, giving Ma a deferential nod and Henrietta a quick, forced smile.

Elsie watched him slip away and approach another group now, possibly the Hewitts from New York, if she remembered correctly from the wedding. She truly felt sorry for him and wished she had been able to think of something clever, or at least comforting, to say to him. She could only imagine what was going through his mind today, and she fervently hoped her ridiculous situation did not add to his burden. But she couldn't help but wonder what he must think of her.

With a sigh, she turned her attention back to Henrietta, who was asking Eddie and Herbie about school now. Elsie had initially thought she would never tell Henrietta or anyone what had really happened between her and Harrison, but now that Henrietta was indeed before her, so genuinely happy to see her and seemingly not upset or condemning or annoyed, Elsie longed to get her alone so that she might confess all, to pour her heart out finally to someone and, she had to admit, to not only be absolved, but also be comforted. While Julia had certainly done her best, it was not the same as having Henrietta to talk to, and she suddenly felt like one of the twins, wanting to clamor for her attention. Elsie tried valiantly, however, to control her desires, knowing that today was not the day for a conversation of the heart. She couldn't possibly allow herself to be that selfish! And yet, she found her eyes traversing the room for perhaps any quiet corner in which they might have a chat, when they unexpectedly came to rest on the figure of their grandfather, making his way toward them with decided intent.

Henrietta must have noticed too, for Elsie saw her draw herself up at the old man's approach, though Elsie also observed that Henrietta's eyes remained locked on Eddie, listening to him intently, even as Grandfather arrived beside her. Elsie marveled at her confidence and her grace.

"Good day, Martha," Mr. Exely said curtly as he came upon them, nodding at Ma, who had gone back to her chair once Clive had left them, and remained there, gripping the arms of it as if preparing herself to withstand a storm. She did not return his greeting. "Good day, grandchildren," he continued, ignoring Ma's slight and looking at each one curiously. "Henrietta," he said, finally turning toward her, "I'm very sorry for your loss. Alcott Howard was a surprisingly good man of business, despite a few inconsistencies."

"Thank you, Grandfather," Henrietta said rigidly.

"Clive will take over now, though, I'm sure," he said with a bit of a glint in his eye. "He'll make a fine chairman. And in the meantime, you'll be busy learning all you can from Antonia Howard, I have no doubt."

Henrietta chose not to answer this but merely gave a small nod of acquiescence.

"I trust your voyage was satisfactory. How did you find Castle Linley?" he asked.

"How kind of you to ask, Grandfather," Henrietta responded, a false smile about her lips. "The ship was very satisfactory, thank you. Castle Linley was quite charming and Lord and Lady Linley were of course very gracious," she rattled off.

How on earth did she manage it? Elsie wondered. Such grace and presence of mind.

"It was quite an education, actually," Henrietta added.

"No doubt it was," Mr. Exley said, smiling falsely. "That's what I like to hear, however. Always watching and learning. You should take a page from your sister's book," he said, turning his critical gaze upon Elsie. "That's how you get ahead in this world," he rasped with a little shake of his cane.

"Grandfather, that's not what I meant."

Mr Exley did not respond to this but merely curled his lips. "Speaking of education," he said churlishly, as he turned to look at Ma, "there is a subject I wish to discuss with you, Martha, if you might be so kind as to name a day that would be convenient for me to stop."

"You're welcome to say what you have to say right now, Father," Ma said without emotion, her first words to him since he had joined them.

Mr. Exley bit back a scowl. "It is a subject that will take some time to relate, Martha, and is, shall I say, of a rather delicate nature. I would speak with you in private regarding this matter, in your drawing room, preferably. I merely approached you at this moment to offer my condolences to Henrietta, here, and to ascertain a date most convenient to us both."

"If you think for one moment that I will welcome you into my home, then you are sadly mistaken, sir."

"Might I remind you who pays for that home?" he snapped.

"That is of your own decision. Not mine," she answered coolly. "Say what it is you have to say, or not," she said, drawing herself up in the chair as much as her rounded back would allow.

"Very well. I trust you will not make a scene," he warned.

Ma did not say anything, but merely stared at him with pure hatred, though Elsie thought she detected a slight quiver about her eyes. She, too, was holding her breath at what her grandfather might say and, in truth, felt in danger of fainting, so weak of mind was she of late that she did not know how much more she could take.

"Very well," he began. "I've arranged for the boys—all of them, except Donald, of course, to be sent to Phillips Exeter for the spring term. They leave the fifth of January."

"No!" Elsie exclaimed and looked desperately at Henrietta, who for one quick second put her forefinger to her lips to indicate that Elsie should remain silent.

"What devilry is this?" Ma exclaimed. "You can't take my children! You said that if we moved to Palmer Square they could stay at St. Sylvester's! That's what you said!" Ma cried, her voice rising. Elsie cringed as she saw several people look at them.

"Be quiet, woman! I warned you not to make a scene!" Mr. Exley hissed.

"Don't tell me what to do! You lost that right long ago!" she said loudly.

"Let's just say, circumstances have changed," he said icily, looking at poor Elsie now in what could only be termed disgust.

Elsie's face blanched and her stomach dropped, as if she had been struck. *He must know!* Oh, God, what was she to do?

"I've allowed certain things to evolve much too freely. It's become clear that I must take them more in hand."

"What do you mean by that? Speak plainly!" Ma snapped.

"Just that there have been certain indiscretions that have come to light—"

"Indiscretions?"

"Grandfather, please," Elsie begged, unwanted tears filling the corners of her eyes. "Send me away, but not them!"

"What's Phillips Ex-ter, Hen?" Jimmy asked innocently, tugging at Henrietta's dress and looking up at her.

"It's the finest boarding school there is," Mr. Exely answered for her. "It's in New Hampshire. All Exley men go to Phillips."

"New Hampshire?" Herbie choked out, as if all his breath had left him.

"You mean I'll have to go away and live?" Jimmy cried and looked on the verge of dissolving into a fit of panicked tears.

"Grandfather," Henrietta said evenly. "I thought Jimmy was to remain behind for a year."

"You knew?" Ma asked, incredulous and outraged.

Elsie looked at her as well, horrified. Had Henrietta betrayed them? How could she? she thought, feeling slightly dizzy. She tried to catch Henrietta's eye, but Henrietta continued to stare at Grandfather.

"I've thought better of it," Mr. Exley continued. "I've spoken to this Fr. Finnegan at St. Sylvester's, and apparently James is not as behind as I first imagined. He's quite able to attend Phillips."

"But he's so young," Henrietta put in.

"Gerard attended at six."

Jimmy began to wail at this point. "But I don't want to go away and leave Hen and Elsie and Nanny and Ma!" he cried aloud, causing many people to look at them now, including Mrs. Howard.

Henrietta looked desperately around the room for Clive, but he was nowhere to be seen.

"Shhh!" said Nanny, bustling over from some remote corner, where she had apparently been seeking a few moments of quiet respite. "Come along, now! What's all this fussin'?" she said as she tried to lead him from the room. "Sorry, madam," she said in Ma's general direction.

"I don't want to go away!" Jimmy wailed, but he allowed himself in the end to be dragged from the room.

"See what you've done!" Ma snarled at her father.

"What more proof do I need that this child—that all of these children," he said pointedly, again looking at Elsie, "are in need of more discipline? It's quite shamefully evident."

"Grandfather, I—" Elsie tried to say.

"As for you, Miss," Mr. Exely said disdainfully, "from this moment on, you will go and live with John and Agatha, where a more careful watch can be kept upon you."

"No, Grandfather, I—"

"I rather think we should continue this conversation later, wouldn't you agree, Grandfather?" Henrietta put in hastily.

"What has she done?" Ma interrupted, suspicious. "Why are you singling her out? She hasn't done anything! Or is this really yet another punishment for me?" Ma said, her voice rising again. "You're still trying to get even after all these years, aren't you, Father? But why? You got what you wanted in life. Can't you just leave me in peace! Is it too much to ask?" Here she unexpectedly broke down in tears, which, though it *was* a funeral, drew attention, as the appropriate time for a public display of emotion had most probably been back in the church and not here at the reception, where, indeed a few men in the corner—Alcott's business associates, presumably—were already happily indulging in a variety of toasts to Alcott, which were accompanied by, if not hilarity, then at least a measure of thoughtful good cheer.

"Eddie, take Ma to the car," Henrietta instructed. "Karl can take her and Nanny and the little ones back. You and Herbie and Elsie can ride back in the other car."

"They won't all fit!"

"Nanny can ride in the front with Karl, I dare say," Henrietta quipped.

"Oh, all right. Come on, Ma," Eddie said with a deep sigh and helped to lift her out of the chair. Ma oddly did not say anything at this point but allowed Eddie to pull her up and then stood there unsteadily.

"Perhaps I should go, too, Hen," Elsie suggested quietly, "to see to her."

"No, you stay," Henrietta said firmly.

She turned to her mother, then, and embraced her. "Don't worry, Ma. It'll be alright," she said, and Elsie was surprised that Ma allowed herself to be held at all.

"I'll come in a few days' time, maybe tomorrow," Henrietta promised, but her words seemed to have no effect on Ma. She merely stared back at her blankly with sad, dull eyes. Henrietta gave a nod to Eddie and Herbie, who escorted her across the small ballroom, one on either side. Elsie watched them go, wringing her hands, over and over.

Mr. Exley turned his back on the retreating Von Harmons, and giving a dismissive nod now to Henrietta and Elsie, prepared to leave them as well.

"A word, Grandfather," Henrietta said, her voice sounding surprisingly calm.

"Yes?" he said flatly, turning back toward her. "What is it?"

"I have an idea regarding Elsie that might be welcome," she said looking briefly toward Elsie and then back to her grandfather.

Elsie couldn't imagine what Henrietta was about to say. . .

"Your intrigues are quite a lost cause at this point, my dear, whatever you may think, so do not waste any more time for either of us with the effort of elaborating," Mr. Exley said snidely.

"Is this how you would speak to a lady, Grandfather? You seemed only too willing to address me as such just a moment ago," she said, her eyes flashing.

Mr. Exely studied her, his black eyes heavy with irritation. "Very well," he finally said, slowly. "What is it?"

"Perhaps Elsie should go to college," Henrietta said steadily, chancing a glance over at Elsie, whose eyes, upon hearing this, grew very large. "I've done a bit of inquiring," she went on, "and there's a very good one in the city, Mundelein College, run by an order of nuns, as I understand it. Elsie would be quite safe there and would be taught correct deportment and grace, among other things of course. Romantic attachments would be out of the question with a student body of only girls—women, I should say—and nuns for teachers. It would almost be like being in a convent. She could still attend family functions with Uncle John and Aunt Agatha, if you wish."

Elsie could hardly believe what she was hearing and felt her face grow increasingly warm as she observed her grandfather's furrowed brow. He looked as if he were about to speak, but Henrietta beat him to it.

"Consider, Grandfather," she continued. "Don't you think that Elsie would be much more attractive, should I say *eligible*, with a bit of domestic education and finesse, not to mention a bit of distance from recent troubles?" she said quietly and then paused for a few terrible seconds, as if waiting for her words to sink in before adding, "It really does make perfect sense. Wouldn't you agree, Grandfather?" she asked pleasantly.

"No I wouldn't. It's preposterous!" Mr. Exely said angrily. "She has proven she is muddled in the head by thinking she could elope with that reprobate, Barnes-Smith. Why throw good money away on an education?"

At these words Elsie wanted to sink into the ground and actually considered fleeing from the room.

"Might I remind you, Grandfather," Henrietta snapped, "that as Mrs. Clive Howard, I have my own money at my disposal and will fund

Elsie's education myself, if need be. My consulting you was merely a matter of courtesy. It's time Elsie decided her own future for herself."

Elsie was studiously observing the floor during much of Henrietta's impassioned speech, but she looked up when she heard a small cough and saw that Clive had somehow silently joined them. He was standing with his hand on the small of Henrietta's back in such an encouraging way that Elsie thought she might cry. *Oh, to be loved that way!*

"Ah, Clive. I was just coming to find you. My condolences, of course," Mr. Exely said, holding his hand out to him and thereby instantly dismissing the current conversation.

"Mr. Exley," Clive responded stiffly, politely shaking the older man's outstretched hand. "Thank you so very much for coming to my father's funeral," he continued in his deep, resonant voice. "It was very kind of you."

Clive glanced at Henrietta now, and Elsie could have sworn she saw him wink.

"Perhaps we should discuss these matters at a later date," he said to Mr. Exely. "Might I offer you a brandy?" he asked as he took him by the arm and simultaneously looked back at Henrietta, giving her a tilt of his head toward the door, indicating, Elsie guessed, that this was their chance to escape.

It was only ten o'clock when Clive and Henrietta found themselves alone in their private sitting room, but it felt much later. They were both drained from the wearying sorrow of the day. Clive had remained stalwart throughout, refusing to publicly give in to tears, though Henrietta knew he had teetered on the brink when the casket was lowered into the grave. She herself felt as though she had cried Clive's share for him.

Antonia had already parted from them for the night, choosing instead to sit privately with her sister, Lavinia, one of the Hewitts who had arrived earlier in the day from New York. Clive and Henrietta had toyed with the idea of walking out onto the terrace, which had become their special place over the summer during their engagement, but the November night was wet and cold. Henrietta had told Clive that she would wrap up if he wished to go out, but he had declined, saying that they should get used to their new rooms anyway.

Antonia had taken one of the rooms in their wing, a gabled space between two bedrooms that had rarely been used, and had it converted to a private sitting room of sorts for the two of them. It had a fireplace with a low, leather sofa in front of it, complete with embroidered goose-down pillows and an Oriental rug on the floor beneath it. Along one wall ran a set of bookcases, which were somewhat sparse at the moment but which were content to wait to be filled as time went on. Beside them, a large window was cut into the gabled roofline, creating a lovely window seat. Nearby stood a cherrywood drinks cart, fully stocked of course, though they could just as easily ring for Billings, and in the corner was a brand-new wireless radio. The whole room had almost a Bohemian feel to it, and Henrietta, more than once since their return, mentally commended Antonia— this was not Mrs. Howard's taste at all, but one she must have guessed that Henrietta and Clive would enjoy.

Henrietta poured two cognacs from one of the bottles on the cart and handed one to Clive, who was slumped on the sofa in front of the fire, his jacket removed and his legs stretched out in front of him. For a few moments, neither of them said anything.

Finally, Clive spoke. "I just can't believe he's gone."

"I know."

Clive exhaled deeply.

"What are you going to do?" Henrietta asked, studying his face as he watched the flames. "Did you speak to Bennett?"

"Yes. He said to take my time and all of that. That as managing director for the interim, he'll see to things for as long as I need." He was silent for a few moments and then spoke again. "I suppose I shouldn't wait too long, though. Can't run forever." He looked at her now and gave her a tired smile. "I'll go in later in the week. Mother's asked if tomorrow I might begin going through Father's study. Making sure things are in order, I think is what she said."

"Hasn't she looked through any of it?" Henrietta asked, taking a sip of her drink.

"Apparently not. She thought it better for me to do all of that."

"I see. Not a very entertaining day, then."

"No, indeed."

"Do you think it would be all right for me to go into the city to see Ma and Elsie? They're obviously upset by what Grandfather said to them about the boys. Or am I supposed to stay here for the Hewitts' benefit?"

"Ah, yes," he said, turning toward her. "I'd forgotten all about the squabble. Forgive me for not asking before now." His eyes looked sad. "No, I don't think it matters," he said, finally answering her question. "No, you should by all means go to them." He took a drink. "It was wonderful to see you speak to old Exley that way, I must admit. He's obviously decided to act quickly based on what's happened with poor Elsie."

"Yes . . . I wonder how he found out what happened? I thought only Julia and your father knew."

"Father must have had a word with him before . . . before he died. That would be just like him. To try to do the right thing." Clive took another drink of his cognac and then was silent for a few minutes. "But what's all this about Elsie going to college?" he said, in what seemed an attempt to rouse himself from his own thoughts. "Is there such a place in the city—a women's college run by nuns? Or did you just invent that for Exley's irritation? Because if you did, it certainly succeeded," he said, another small smile appearing.

"As a matter of fact," she said slyly, "I heard about it from Julia, if you must know."

He rolled his eyes. "Why am I not surprised? What did Elsie say? I gather you enlightened her when the two of you slipped away. Thanks to me expertly diverting Exley, I might add. Apparently, there was quite a scene before I turned up . . . according to Mother, anyway."

"Yes, I'm sorry about all of the ruckus my family created. Again."

"I'm beyond caring about any of that, darling," he sighed. "But I am grateful that Mother came scurrying to find me, or I would have missed your brilliant speech."

She smiled up at him.

"Go on. You were about to tell me what Elsie had to say about planning her own future, which you've conveniently just planned for her," he added, his eyes lighting up.

"Beast!" she said, hitting him with one of the embroidered pillows, this one depicting a Bo Peep type of character, surrounded by sheep. "I'm not planning her future, merely giving her some suggestions. In truth," she said more seriously now, "I feel awful, Clive. I feel I've let her down quite terribly."

"What did she say?" Clive said, rubbing a finger down her arm along the black silk of her dress.

"Oh, you know Elsie. She tried to demure, saying she couldn't leave Ma and all that. Frankly, she was more upset at the moment about the boys going away. I could barely get a word in edgewise about her own future."

"Did she speak about the other business?" he asked quietly.

"Some, but we didn't have time for her to tell me the whole story," she answered. "She whispered bits of it to me as we were waiting for the car to be pulled up."

"Do you think he forced her?"

"To run away with him? Or to . . . ?"

Clive just looked at her.

"We didn't get to that," Henrietta sighed. "It seemed not the time to discuss it."

"Quite," Clive agreed. "But is she all right do you think? She's had a terrible blow, poor thing."

Henrietta felt she might suddenly cry at the tenderness and compassion he was exhibiting for a girl he really hardly knew. "I'm not sure. She seems awfully depressed—nervous and fidgety. I think Julia is right. Elsie needs some sort of occupation, or I'm afraid she'll go down the same path as Ma. They have similar dispositions in a lot of ways," she said, looking at the fire. "Something to do besides go about with Agatha Exley, to 'be their plaything' is I think how Julia put it."

"Indeed." Clive paused before continuing. "Not to be awkward, darling, but if memory serves, Elsie hasn't even finished high school, is this not so?"

"Well, obviously there are some hurdles to get around," she said with a twitch of annoyance, "but in theory, doesn't it make sense?"

"Hurdles?" Clive said, laughing. "Is that what you call them?" Clive reached out and brushed a lock of hair back behind her ear. "Well, it makes perfect sense to me, my love, but I'm not so sure old Exley will go for it."

"Well, really, Clive. What does that matter? I . . . I guess we've never discussed it . . . but *do* I have any money? I feel awful asking, but . . . I suppose I should know."

"Oh, darling. Of course, you have your own money. I've been distracted by all of this and remiss in telling you the arrangements. I plan to be thoroughly modern . . . that is, if you have no objections. I've been meaning to open an account just for you, separate from the household account of course. I should have told you before now and spared you having to ask."

"Thank you, Clive," she said, looking up into his eyes. "I don't know what I would possibly want," she went on in a lighter tone as she looked around the room, giving a halfhearted gesture, "but it would be nice to be able to buy things for others sometimes."

"Like a college education?" Clive smiled teasingly.

"I'm sorry about that," she blushed. "I was bluffing, of course. Obviously, I spoke out of turn."

"Of course you didn't, darling. You were wonderful. Sometimes it's hard to believe you're the same woman I fell in love with. You've changed so remarkably."

"Is that good or bad?"

He brushed her cheek with his finger and let it rest under her chin. "It's very good," he said softly. "When I proposed to you that crazy night, I didn't think I could love you more, but I was so obviously wrong. I wasn't prepared for how much more I could grow to love you. How much I need you," he said, his voice becoming thick again, as he dropped his hand and let his finger caress the hollow of her throat.

Slowly she leaned forward to kiss him softly.

"Why don't we go to bed?" she asked, her lips still close to his.

"I'd like nothing better," he said, standing up and holding his hand out to her. "I'm utterly spent."

"Come along, you poor thing," Henrietta said, standing up now too, and pulling him gently toward their bedroom. He followed her for only a few steps, however, before he stopped, and she felt a slight tremble in his hand as he pulled it from hers. She turned to look at him and saw that he stood with his head bowed, one hand pinching the brow of his nose, trying to fight back his tears.

"Oh, Clive, dearest," Henrietta said, retreating toward him and embracing him tenderly. "It's all right, sweetheart. You've been terribly strong. You don't have to be with me, you know."

He nodded and wrapped his arms around her. "I know, darling. Thank you. I just wish I could have told him how I felt about him. I wish I could have done a few things differently."

"Yes," she said softly. "But surely, he knows it now, if he didn't already feel it. He's with God in heaven, and he knows how much you loved him."

Clive gripped her tighter, and she thought she heard a small sob escape from him. He drew in a deep breath and pulled back a little. "I wish I knew what happened," he said, his voice changing abruptly. "It just doesn't make sense."

Henrietta bit her lip. He was back to this again. On more than one occasion on the trip home and now back at Highbury, he had expressed his doubts over the nature of his father's death. It was a subject he could not seem to let go of, and Henrietta was beginning to worry a bit. He seemed determined to make a mystery when there was none. *But why?* Perhaps it was a way for him to better cope with the suddenness of his father's death, the way he had turned to detective work after the war? Trying to puzzle out life by solving smaller puzzles? Or was it a way of delaying having to take up his duty as chairman of the board at Linley Standard? But tonight, she knew, was not the night to reason it out.

"Clive, darling," she said gently, "it was just an accident. A terrible one, to be sure, but an accident just the same."

"But I've spoken to Fritz. There were two men on the platform with him."

"I'm sure there were a lot of people on the platform," she said gingerly.

"But Fritz thought he saw them speaking to him."

Henrietta bit her lip again. "Perhaps they were. Does that make them murderers?" she asked, looking at him earnestly. "If Fritz was observing him, wouldn't he have also witnessed the crime?" she pointed out.

"Fritz says he drove away before the train came into the station, so, no, he wouldn't have. I know it sounds preposterous, Henrietta, but I can't explain it. Just a feeling that something isn't as it seems."

"Hmmm. Well, come along, darling. It's late. Things will look better in the morning; I promise."

He let out deep sigh, then, and allowed himself to be led to their room.

Chapter 4

"You promised I wouldn't have to do anything today!" Elsie whispered frantically to Henrietta as they sat side by side on two chrome chairs in front of a beautiful ebony desk in the registrar's office of Mundelein College in Chicago.

The new office, painted a lovely shade of aqua, was situated in the Skyscraper building, a wonderfully modern art deco structure that towered over its lowlier neighbors at an astonishing fourteen floors. The new women's college, erected on the very edge of where Lake Michigan collided with its rocky shore, consisted of only the Skyscraper and two ancient stone "mansions" that had occupied the property before the church had bought it and consequently began its construction on the new tower, giving the campus an odd and perhaps symbolic flavor of the old and the new. The mansions, now christened Philomena and Piper Halls, were apparently the only survivors of a long string of mansions that had once peppered the shore of the lake before developers had moved in and pulled them down. At least, that was what Sr. Bernard Magdalena had explained to Elsie and Henrietta during their tour of the grounds.

Carved out of this little corner of Rogers Park, just where Sheridan Road took an extreme bend, Mundelein College was the curious new little sister of its lurking neighbor and big brother, Loyola University.

And like siblings whose rooms are just across the hall from one another, Mundelein and Loyola were likewise separated merely by a sidewalk. The men of Loyola, particularly the fraternity men, who were ever in search of respectable dates for their formals, were on the whole pleased to share their lakefront acreage with this new creation and watched with curious interest when it was formally opened by Cardinal Mundelein himself and then steadily populated with the daughters of the Chicago's wealthy and the North Shore beyond.

"Well, doesn't it make sense to get it over with, Elsie?"

Sr. Bernard, the acting registrar for the day, had just absented her post behind the gleaming desk to look for the missing aptitude and placement test, which was vexingly, she had grumbled, not in the spot it normally occupied.

"But I haven't studied!" Elsie hissed, wringing her hands.

"You heard Sister Bernard," Henrietta said, looking around the room. "It's not something you study for necessarily." She looked at Elsie closely now. "The more important question is whether this is something you want. Would you want to come study here?"

Would she want to come study here? Elsie was so full of nervous anticipation that she could barely answer the question. Of course she would want to study here! Who wouldn't? It would be like a dream come true for her—a dream she had barely even been aware of.

"Yes, of course I do," Elsie whispered, on the verge of crying once again. "I just . . . this is all happening so fast. I need time to think. And what if . . . what if I do badly?" Elsie whined nervously.

"You won't do badly. And do you really need time to think? You can think about it later. After all, you can always wait to enroll next fall—a whole year from now—and go and live with Uncle John and Aunt Agatha in the interim. Is that what you want?"

She paused here as if waiting for an answer, but before Elsie could speak, Henrietta went on. "At least this way you'll know where you stand; you'll have a choice and maybe some alternatives."

Henrietta was right, of course, Elsie realized. And she didn't need time to think. She had done too much of that already, and it always left her feeling miserable and depressed. She should take the opportunity now. That was one of her supreme failings, she knew, that she hesitated too much. She would try to be more impetuous, more like Henrietta! But hadn't that been her line of reasoning the night she had succumbed to Harrison? she reminded herself uneasily. Still, she resolved, pushing that thought away, she would take the test and see what happened.

In truth, ever since Mr. Howard's funeral when Henrietta had marvelously stood up to Grandfather and proposed that she should go to college, Elsie had thought of little else. She had dismissed it at first as ridiculous, but then Henrietta had come to visit, distributing the gifts she had brought back from England and telling them all about what she had seen and done. Eagerly, Elsie had sat in the background, watching the boys unpack boxes of English sweets and biscuits, and wondering if Henrietta would again bring up the prospect of her returning to school. So silent was Henrietta on the subject, however, that Elsie began to think, as she sat there trying to work on her embroidery, if Henrietta had really been serious. Or had it just been something she had said to purposefully anger him without any real meaning behind it? But didn't she know how cruel that was? To tease her in that way just to annoy Grandfather?

Not being able to stand it any longer, Elsie stood up, then, feeling like she needed some air. She stepped gingerly over the brown paper wrappings littering the floor and wandered into the kitchen. She was surprised, therefore, when Henrietta appeared not moments later, slipping her arm through hers and suggesting that the two of them take a walk outdoors, to which Elsie eagerly acquiesced, though the sky looked as if it might snow at any moment.

Wrapping up tightly against the cold, they made their way across the street to Palmer Square Park, which had become so familiar to Elsie these last few months, having spent many an afternoon there slowly walking with Harrison or, alternately, running after Doris and Donny. To Henrietta, however, it was a new experience, and more than once she exclaimed that she wished she could have seen it all in bloom. The sisters fell into a silence as they walked arm in arm among the barren trees and bushes before Henrietta finally spoke again, asking Elsie if she might tell her more about what had happened with the lieutenant.

Elsie was silent at first, not knowing what to say, really, but at Henrietta's gentle prodding, she began, haltingly, to tell the tale, and before she knew it, she felt the dam break, and she rushed on, pouring out her heart to her sister. With a very warm face, she confessed to her how Harrison had, well, made love to her, she whispered, her voice catching as she said it, how he had insisted she marry him, telling her that Grandfather might "accidentally" find out and then she would be seen as "damaged goods" and that no one else would want her. How he insisted that they should elope in the hopes that Grandfather would do something for them once they were married . . .

Elsie heard Henrietta let out a long, slow breath, which crystalized in the cold air, and likewise saw her furrowed brow, both of which made Elsie's stomach clench at the thought of how much Henrietta must despise her now! Saying her tale of woe aloud made it sound so . . . so wretched and pathetic and vulgar. How could she have been so stupid?

Bracing herself for what she was sure would be Henrietta's admonishment, Elsie was surprised when she did not respond in any of the number of the ways Elsie thought she might, and instead utterly stunned her by asking the most painful, the most insightful question of all, which was whether she might still be a little in love with Harrison. Somehow her sister had singled out that this was the crux of the matter, not that she had lost her virginity, not that Grandfather knew of her treachery or her betrayal, but that, despite it all, she still thought of Harrison in the night and missed him.

Elsie paused, wondering if she should tell the truth. She toyed with lying but found she could not. "Is it too awfully terrible if I say perhaps just a little?" Elsie asked quietly, looking up anxiously into Henrietta's face.

"But why, Els?" Henrietta asked softly. "He treated you very badly."

Elsie shrugged. She didn't know why. Hadn't she asked herself that a hundred times? She stood looking out at the cars rumbling slowly by on Humboldt Boulevard and hoped that if she didn't answer, Henrietta would just carry on with the next question, but she didn't. She remained silent, apparently waiting for her to answer. Elsie pulled at her gloves, trying to come up with something to say. She sighed. There was nothing for it but to try to explain something she wasn't completely sure of herself.

"He . . . I suppose I feel sorry for him in a way. He . . . he's had a hard life, actually, Hen. I . . . he's so very handsome, and I guess I felt . . . well, special." Her voice cracked, and she was forced to loudly swallow, adding to her humiliation. "And sometimes he was funny . . ." she said wistfully, her voice dying away then as she realized how feeble this sounded.

She expected Henrietta to scold her, but all her sister did was put her arm around her as they walked. "Oh, Els. I'm so sorry. This is all my fault."

"Your fault? How could it be *your* fault?" Elsie asked, stopping their walk and turning to face her. "Not everything is your fault, you know, Henrietta. I . . . I'm the one who—who let him . . ." she said in a low tone. Unexpected tears began to well up. "I'm not as strong as you, Henrietta. I tried to be," she cried, "but I failed! Of course this is all my own fault."

"*Your* fault? He forced you!" Henrietta sputtered.

"No, I . . . I shouldn't have gone there that night. I shouldn't have let him . . . I'm a terribly wicked girl," she moaned, burying her face in her hands.

Henrietta had gripped her by the shoulders and gave her a little shake. "No, you're not! You're the best girl I know, Elsie. The kindest, sweetest, best girl," she urged. "Listen, perhaps it's no one's fault. I only meant that I feel as though I've neglected you. That you were too much left alone. I assumed that Stanley was . . . " At the mention of Stanley, Elsie looked up, her face wet with tears, and Henrietta broke off.

"I'm sorry," she said, gently letting go of Elsie. "I . . . how did you leave it with Stanley?"

Elsie dug her handkerchief out of her pocket and wiped her eyes. "I told him I was engaged to Harrison, and we went our separate ways. He said he was close to proposing to Rose. So, I'm sure he's happy now. To be rid of me. I don't think he ever really wanted my affections, did he, Hen?" she said, looking up at her furtively.

"That was my fault, too," Henrietta said softly. "I've wronged you so very much, Elsie. How can you forgive me?"

Elsie looked into Henrietta's contrite, pitying eyes and felt overcome with love. She could never blame Henrietta for anything, really, as she very nearly worshipped her. She was everything Elsie was not.

"Oh, Hen, it pains me for you to say that. Please don't. There is nothing to forgive."

Henrietta managed a small smile, but Elsie saw that she was still troubled. She knew she should probably leave it at that, but a part of her was curious. Besides, she couldn't imagine feeling any worse than she already did, so why not discover the whole truth? "So . . . it's true, then," she ventured tentatively. "He didn't really like me, did he? It was you he was after."

Henrietta sighed. "I thought I could convince him that you were better suited to him. I tried to persuade him to transfer his affections to you—someone so much more deserving . . ."

"Did you force him to ask me out?" Elsie asked quietly.

"Well, something like that," she said hesitantly.

"It was the day at the carnival, wasn't it? When the two of you stood off talking."

"Yes."

Somehow she had always known. She expected to feel worse upon hearing the truth, but she, oddly, did not. She supposed that she had already cried all the tears she had inside for Stanley. "Have you heard from him?" she asked.

"Stanley? No, I haven't."

"I thought maybe he would turn up at the funeral, but I guess there was really no reason for him to come. After all, he really didn't know the Howards—"

"Elsie," Henrietta said abruptly, "forget about Stanley. And Harrison, for that matter. You are wonderfully exceptional, in your own way. I wish I could convince you of that. I wish you could see yourself as I do. Someone so infinitely good and lovely and clever—"

"Henrietta," Elsie interrupted her, "I'm none of those things. We both know that," she said, irritated. "Don't tease."

"Yes, you are, goose!" she said, pulling on Elsie's hair as if they were children again. She leaned her head against her sister, and Elsie could feel the warmth radiating from her. It felt good in the cold air. "Don't settle," Henrietta whispered, serious now. "Don't settle for someone who doesn't deserve you. Go to college and learn something."

Elsie took in a sharp breath. Here was the subject that she had been waiting for!

"Be true to you and no one else," Henrietta said, standing up straight.

"But I don't know how . . . how to be true to myself."

"Then you'll learn."

"I don't know, Hen . . . I haven't even finished high school," she said tentatively, though her heart had begun to beat a little faster.

"You'll catch up. I can't imagine you're really that far behind with all the books you read."

Elsie smiled. It was true that she spent most of her long, lonely days reading.

"I don't know if I could go away, Hen. I'm not as brave as you."

"'Course you are! You just don't realize it. Anyone who has to put up with Ma day in and day out is brave beyond measure." She attempted a small laugh, but Elsie didn't join in.

"But that's another thing, Hen. What about Ma? And Doris and Donny? I can't leave them!"

"Don't worry about them! You're only going to be across town. Anyway, I'll worry about them for you."

Elsie didn't say anything, but she very much doubted Henrietta would have the time for this in light of her own situation.

"But what about Grandfather and Aunt Agatha and Uncle John? I'm sure they wouldn't approve, and aren't I supposed to be living with them now and marrying someone of their choice?"

"It's hardly the medieval age, Elsie, with Grandfather as our lord and master, dispensing of us chattel as he pleases."

Elsie could not help but laugh. "Tell Aunt Agatha that."

"Play their game, Elsie," Henrietta said seriously. "You can still attend their galas or go to the ballet, or what have you, to keep them happy. But you need a place to start over, a place of your own. And it's not as if Grandfather can really disapprove; Julia tells me the school is quite respectable, full of young ladies of the highest echelons of society. So you'll be in good company."

Elsie groaned. "Just what I always wanted. More young ladies of the highest echelons," she added grimly, but allowed herself, for a brief second, to feel hope. Just as quickly, however, a different, darker thought suddenly occurred to her. "I heard what you said to Grandfather, Hen," she said slowly, turning it over in her mind. "About it being nuns and all girls so that there would be no chance of 'romantic attachments' I think is what you said. Is that the real reason you want me to go away? So that I won't get into any more trouble? Isn't that proof that you think I'm wicked?"

"Elsie! Of course that's not what I meant!" Henrietta exclaimed.

"Are you sure?" Elsie said, looking directly into her eyes.

"Of course I'm sure. I just said that to thwart Grandfather. I can't think of anyone more virtuous . . . yes, virtuous!" she said when Elsie gave her a disbelieving look. "No more talk like that," Henrietta said, planting a warm kiss on her cold cheek. "Let's at least go and look at this school, this Mundelein. Say that you will. Please."

"Oh, all right," Elsie had said through her tears. "But just to have a look."

Sr. Bernard had accordingly spent the morning escorting them around the campus, Henrietta having lost no time in securing an appointment, just days after the sisters' huddled conversation in Palmer Square. Sr. Vincent, to whom she had spoken on the telephone, had intimated that it was not the most ideal time, as the fall trimester was just finishing and everyone was preoccupied with final exams, but she thought they might make time for a quick tour.

It had fallen to Sr. Bernard, however, to show them around, as in the interim, Sr. Vincent had broken her toe and was even now laid up in the convent, which was housed on the top seven floors of the Skyscraper. Sr. Bernard, despite being the college's president, seemed not to mind the intrusion on her time for so lowly a task, however, and gladly took them on a tour, even introducing Elsie to some of the young women, all of them hurrying to and fro, seeming to have some delightful purpose and place to be—and, of course, to be so much better than her in every possible way. Elsie also astutely noticed that the girls were quite deferential to Sr. Bernard and seemed to genuinely like her and sought her attention. A pleasant affability, almost friendship, seemed to exist between them, which was significantly different than what Elsie had experienced in her years with the more austere sisters at St. Sylvester's, and it piqued her curiosity immensely.

Sr. Bernard proudly led them through the brilliant art deco Skyscraper, which marvelously contained the whole of the college within the lower seven floors, with all of its magnificent stonework and gleaming tile and chrome accents. Besides the usual classrooms and lecture halls, there were laboratories, a dining hall, a library, a swimming pool, a chapel, a gymnasium, and even a tiny hidden greenhouse tucked away on the seventh floor. From there, they trudged across the circular courtyard to quickly view Philomena and Piper Halls, both of which served as dormitories now for the girls. Each of them also contained a small private library, which Elsie would have dearly loved to meander through, but Sr. Bernard, not wanting to disturb the girls revising for their final exams, had swiftly led them back out, explaining that all classes were primarily taught by the Sisters of the Blessed Virgin Mary, though at times, certain Loyola professors were invited to give guest lectures. In fact, there was a lively sense of comradery between the two schools with plenty of opportunity for mixing—chaperoned, of course. There were also many extra-curricular activities—tennis and golf, as well as a school newspaper, various clubs—the Student Activities Council being a very popular one—and even a few sororities, though, Sr. Bernard pointed out, the school as a whole was like one big sorority, it being so small.

Elsie excitedly considered everything they saw and tried to take it all in. Every step they had taken around the tiny campus had been in a small way torturous for her in that with each lecture hall and cozy study nook revealed, she felt her desire steadily increase to be part of this world, yet, at the same time, she found it difficult to really imagine herself here. Still, the possibility of it excited her, left her almost breathless, actually, more than any ball or diamond tiara she had ever seen in the company of the Exleys had ever done. She felt an instant connection here, deep in her soul, that this was where she belonged. And yet, how could that really be? She was completely uneducated, for all practical purposes. Self-taught, at best. And watching the other girls strolling across campus, so confident and seemingly care-free, left her feeling horribly inadequate.

But now that she knew that such a world existed, it was worse than being completely ignorant of it, as she had been but a few hours ago.

"Well, what do you think of our school, Elsie?" Sr. Bernard had asked her on the way back to the Skyscraper, their tour over. Roused from her churning thoughts, Elsie was so overcome that all she could manage was a silly, "It's lovely, Sister."

Sr. Bernard, after hearing about Elsie's limited formal education, had suggested that, as the school operated on trimesters, Elsie should take the upcoming winter and spring terms to brush up on her studies and then take the entrance exam in the summer to hopefully be enrolled next fall. Elsie's heart sank upon hearing this, feeling that that was an eternity away—almost a whole year!—but she brightened when Henrietta explained that they were hoping Elsie might be enrolled in the upcoming winter term, if possible. Sr. Bernard then commented that it was very unusual for a girl to join midyear and that such haste often suggested other troubles (here she looked carefully at Elsie), and she sincerely hoped such troubles would not follow any girl to the school, she added quietly.

"No, it's nothing like that," Henrietta said, with convincing innocence. "It's just that Elsie is eager to begin, having decided that this is the path for her."

"I see," Sr. Bernard said, though she looked a trifle unconvinced.

"If there's any inconvenience, any added work for the staff, I would be happy to compensate for that," Henrietta said smoothly.

Elsie was not sure what amazed her more, the fact that this discussion was actually happening at all or that Henrietta could be so brazenly suggestive, so able to carry herself with such confidence. Clearly, she had learned much already in her new life.

"That won't be necessary," Sr. Bernard said with a patronizing smile.

"Perhaps Elsie could take just one or two classes this next term," Henrietta suggested. "It would be a sort of trial run, to see if she's really ready."

"But we wouldn't even know where to place her," Sr. Bernard said gently. "We have no idea what she is capable of."

"She's very bright. Aren't you, Elsie?"

Elsie merely looked down at the floor until Henrietta gave her arm a little nudge and she looked up and muttered, "Well, I suppose. A little, anyway."

"Yes, I'm sure you are," Sr. Bernard responded kindly, "but—"

"Mighten she take the entrance exam today, then?" Henrietta offered, clearly ignoring Elsie's somewhat frantic fidgeting. "Just to see where she stands?"

"I don't think that would be very fair to Elsie, do you?" she asked and then paused for a moment of consideration. "Tell you what. Why don't I administer a different test today? A sort of general aptitude test, one that's not so frightening," she said, offering Elsie a smile. "And then we'll have a better idea. We'll also need your records transferred from St. Sylvester's."

"Yes, of course," Henrietta replied. "That can easily be arranged."

"This is quite irregular," Sr. Bernard added. "I can't imagine what Sr. Vincent will say," she mused. "And yet, that might be reason enough to do it," she laughed.

Elsie looked up, surprised. She had never seen a nun laugh, and it had an oddly cheering effect on her. She already liked Sr. Bernard—very much—and she hoped she might have the chance to get to know her better.

"Well, why not?" Sr. Bernard went on. "If you are agreeable, Elsie, you'll take the general aptitude test today so that we might uncover your deficiencies, if you have any, that is," she said gently. "Once we know where you may be lacking, you might use this information in the procurement and employ of a reputable tutor. Might I further suggest one of our own sisters—to my mind, our Sister Sebastian would be perfect—to help you over the Christmas break, as it *is* nearly six weeks long. Much can be accomplished in that time for those who apply themselves," she said earnestly. "At the end of the break, you can take the official entrance exam, and if you pass, I'll allow you to begin at the winter term in January. Would this be agreeable?" she asked, looking first at Elsie and then at Henrietta.

Elsie opened her mouth to protest this plan, but Henrietta spoke first.

"Yes, that sounds very wise, Sister Bernard," Henrietta said quickly. "Thank you ever so much."

Sr. Bernard acknowledged Henrietta with a nod, but she looked at Elsie now, obviously wanting her to speak for herself. Sensing this as well, Elsie again opened her mouth to speak, yet nothing but a gurgled gasp erupted, so she merely nodded her head instead. Apparently taking that as a yes, Sr. Bernard gave her a quick smile and began to look through various drawers for the test. Not finding it, she stood, her rosary beads clacking, to look in the hutch of shelving off to the right of the desk, each box labeled with the names of various departments. She flipped through several stacks of paper, but still not finding it, let out a deep sigh and excused herself to go look for it in an adjoining office.

"Here we are! We were nearly undone then, weren't we?" Sr. Bernard said with an odd touch of gaiety to her voice, as she reentered the room now. "Ready, Miss Von Harmon?" she asked, to which Elsie gave a slight nod. "Just through there, then," she said, gesturing toward a small room off the registrar's office. "You may sit the test in there. Mrs. Howard, I invite you to remain and wait, or perhaps make use of the library? Your sister will need approximately two hours' time," she added, moving toward the little room, seemingly eager to begin. "I trust you'll be all right on your own?"

"Yes, of course," Henrietta said, standing up now as well. "Thank you, Sister."

Elsie rose slowly and tried to breathe deeply, but her breath was shallow and fast, as if she couldn't get enough air. She suddenly felt panicky. Henrietta seemed to sense her distress, thankfully, and reached out and took her hand. She squeezed it softly and then suddenly gently embraced her. "Don't worry, Elsie. You'll be brilliant," she whispered. "You're better than you think." She pulled away, then, and moved to the door, giving a little wave as she exited.

Elsie watched her go and desperately hoped that her sister was right.

Chapter 5

By the time Henrietta returned to Mundelein, it was nearly dark, though it was only four in the afternoon.

While Elsie had toiled at taking her test, Henrietta had directed Fritz to drive her to the Edgewater Beach Hotel, where she had afternoon tea for one. She wished she had said yes to Julia's suggestion that she accompany them to Mundelein when Henrietta had telephoned her yesterday to inquire more about the college. Henrietta had declined her offer at the time, thinking that it might make Elsie more uncomfortable than she already was, but as Henrietta sat by herself at a table facing the lake, she wished she had said otherwise, as she would have liked a long chat with Julia, having truly come to love her as a sister.

And there was so very much they could have talked about, especially now that she was a married woman. Not that she wished to reveal anything intimate about her and Clive, but rather she wanted to know more about Randolph and his beastly behavior toward her. She knew she couldn't really do anything about it, as Julia herself had said, but perhaps she could think of a way to help. She supposed, however, that even if Julia were here, she would be uncommunicative on this subject, anyway, as she was very skilled, Henrietta had observed, at directing the conversation away from herself.

Well, Henrietta thought, selecting a cucumber sandwich from the little three-tiered tray in front of her, she could also have asked her more about her days at Castle Linley with Clive and Linley and Wallace, hoping for a different perspective on those childhood days than what Clive had already told her while there on their honeymoon trip. Or maybe she should bring up Clive's days in the war, though she doubted Julia knew any more than she did herself. He was so moody these days, and, well . . . unsettled in his mind. Alcott's death was weighing heavily on him. Perhaps she should mention to Julia his suspicion—or should she say preoccupation?—that Alcott's death was not necessarily an accident. But to what end? No, she resolved, she would just have to wait it out. He would soon forget it once he took up his duties at Linley Standard, she supposed.

She looked at her wristwatch and was surprised that so much time had already passed, so she signaled the waiter for the bill and waited for him to bring her her things. She prayed that the test had gone well for Elsie and that this might be a real option for her, not just a whimsical fantasy. She admitted that as they had walked around the campus, she wouldn't have minded being a student there herself, but that was obviously not an option for her. And it felt good, to be honest, that for once Elsie was the one getting something instead of her.

Elsie, as it turned out, was ready and waiting for her when Fritz pulled up and parked in the circle near the Skyscraper building. As Henrietta hurried up the Skyscraper's steps, she found Elsie and Sr. Bernard already in the lobby, Elsie smiling sheepishly. Sr. Bernard explained that given the situation, they would attempt to score the test as quickly as possible and would let them know the results by post, hopefully in the next few days, so that arrangements with a tutor could be made accordingly, if needed. She had wished them well, then, and patted Elsie on the arm before they turned to go, saying that she very much wished that Elsie would be able to join their little community.

All the way back to Palmer Square, Henrietta grinned at Elsie's

excited recitation of the various test questions, saying that it wasn't
so bad after all, that it was a trifle fun, actually, answering all the
problems. She was pretty sure, she said, that she had done passably
well on the language and history sections, but she was sure she had
failed the mathematics and the sciences.

"Oh, Henrietta," she said wistfully. "Do you think I'll get in? I so
want to, you know. I didn't think I did, but I do."

"Of course you'll get in," Henrietta said, taking her hand and giving
it a squeeze before letting them rest together on the seat. "You've
begun, and that's all that matters."

When they finally reached Palmer Square, it was the dinner hour,
and Elsie begged Henrietta to stay with them. She was sure Cook, or
Chef, rather, wouldn't mind, she urged; there was always too much,
anyway. Henrietta paused to think. She hadn't expected their inquiries at Mundelein to take so long. In truth, she was eager to get back
to Clive and Highbury, but she was overcome with guilt at being so
rarely with her family, of always saying no to them. Reluctantly, then,
she agreed to stay and put on a false smile as she followed the now
ecstatic Elsie up the steps.

Once inside, Henrietta paused in the front hall to telephone
Highbury before going in to greet them all. Billings, of course,
answered, and she asked him if she might speak with Mr. Howard.
When Clive eventually came on the line, she could tell he had been
worried, but he was obliging of her wish to stay a bit longer, saying
"of course it's all right, darling." She detected something disquieting
in his voice, however, that she just couldn't place. Perhaps it was
something in the line; they were unused to speaking to each other
on the telephone, and indeed it felt strange to hear his voice come
through. But it seemed more than that. He sounded subdued, but
that was to be expected, was it not? Guiltily, she hoped it wasn't due
to worry over her being out longer than expected. Well, perhaps it
would be nice for him to dine alone with his mother? she had suggested, and he had absently agreed, saying, "Yes, by all means you
should stay." Henrietta hung up the receiver, disconcerted, but she

was determined to try to shake it off for the time she was with her family, which she knew would not be too difficult, as they were all constantly vying for her attention anyway.

For the whole of the meal (which she found to be surprisingly tasty) and later when they had adjourned to the parlor, Henrietta consciously tried to steer the conversation toward noninflammatory subjects, which was not easy given the fact that she could not ever predict which subjects would inflame Ma at any given moment. Henrietta decided that long descriptions of Castle Linley, and England in general, were probably safe enough topics and so proceeded with such, though taking care to periodically glance over at Ma every so often, as if watching an unsteady boiler for signs of eruption.

Castle Linley, Henrietta was now explaining, much to the boys' disappointment, was not a castle at all, but rather a large estate house. That comment, however, unfortunately prompted Jimmy to innocently ask if Castle Linley was anywhere near Phillips Ex-ter, followed by another question, which was why they had to go away at all, and was it something bad they had done?

"Of course not, Jimmy," Henrietta said, pulling him onto her lap, where she sat on the settee, nervously looking over at Ma as she did so, sensing they had just been flung into stormy waters. "It's not meant to be a punishment," she said, looking at all of them uneasily. "It's a great honor, actually," she said somewhat weakly.

"Honor? To get sent away like poor Eugene?" Eddie scoffed. "It's not fair, Hen! We don't want to go!"

"Well, you'll all be together," Henrietta tried to say encouragingly, though in truth the thought of little Jimmy so far from home tore at her heart. "Phillips Exeter is perhaps the finest school in the country," she continued, trying to repeat Clive's words to her. "It's very, very expensive and difficult to get into. Grandfather went through a lot of trouble on your behalf."

Ma snorted in the corner. "Don't be fooled," she sneered. "It isn't for the benefit of any of you, it's all for him. He just wants to control you, as he does everyone. Look what he did with John and Gerard and Archibald," Ma said, reeling off the names of her brothers. "Look how they turned out. Still bowing down to him."

Henrietta contemplated this, concluding that while Uncle John did seem rather obliging, she did not view Gerard as being particularly submissive, but she decided not to say so.

"I'm the only one who wouldn't let him control me, and now he seeks to punish me this way. To take you from me and turn you against me, too. How can you not see his cruelty, Henrietta?" Ma asked angrily, shifting her focus from all of them to just her, as if she were somehow responsible.

"Ma! He's not trying to be cruel to you!" Henrietta retorted. "I know it must seem that way to you, and I admit he has been fierce in the past, but not everything has you at its center. You must see that, don't you? I honestly think he is trying to do the best for the boys. Educate them well so that they have the best prospects in life. Isn't that a wonderful thing? Something that was impossible for us such a short time ago! Instead of feeling downcast, we should be celebrating our good fortune," she suggested uneasily, looking around at them all and hoping she could convince them of something she didn't necessarily feel.

"Yes," Elsie put in hesitantly. "I think Hen's right. It's a chance for you all to make something of yourselves," she said, looking at her brothers in turn.

"Are you two really that blind?" Ma asked bitterly. "There are plenty of schools here! Why ship them off? It's only to punish me, I'm telling you!"

"I admit I don't understand it all, Ma," Henrietta sighed. "He has some notion about Phillips Exeter. That 'all Exley men go there' or some such thing. I'm sure there will be many advantages."

"But they're not Exleys!" Ma shouted.

"I know that as well as anyone, Ma," Henrietta said tiredly. "But that's not the case in Grandfather's eyes. Who knows?" she said, trying to give Eddie and Herbie an enthusiastic smile. "Perhaps it will be the making of you."

Eddie turned away, but Herbie hesitantly returned Henrietta's smile. He was always the softer of the two boys that were so close in age. He was an old soul, wise beyond his twelve years. Henrietta had only been six years old when her two siblings, Rita and Albert, had died of the flu—Rita was just two years old and Albert barely one. But she knew Ma had a picture of them in her top drawer. Occasionally over the years, Henrietta would sneak into the room and take it out to look at it. She had long ago determined that they looked a lot like Herbie, with the same sandy-brown hair with big, light-brown eyes, making them resemble innocent fawns.

"I don't mind going," Herbie said to Henrietta. "I'd like to learn more. St. Sylvester's is a good enough school, but it's been rough, hasn't it, Ed?" he asked, moving slightly in an attempt to catch Eddie's eye, his brother's face downturned. "You know, after . . ." he shot a nervous glance at Ma, "after Pa." He looked again at Ma, and seeing that she didn't react, tentatively went on, softly. "Kids, and the teachers too, never treated us the same after that. You know that, Eddie," he said almost pleadingly. "That's why you're always getting in fights, I reckon. First, we was poor, and now we're rich. You'd think that would put us in a good spot with kids, but they're even more cruel now." He paused. "This way we can start over, Ed," he went on. "Think about it. We'll miss home, of course," he said, throwing yet another glance at Ma. "But we'll be okay." He looked up at Henrietta, obviously seeking her approval.

Henrietta's heart swelled at his little speech, and she thought she might embrace him. Before she could, however, he spoke again.

"And you, Jim, bet you'll be the very best first year there is. We'll look after you; don't you worry none."

Jimmy, clearly not as impressed with Herbie's exhortation as Henrietta was, did not respond at all, but instead wriggled all the way back on the settee, further squeezing himself between Henrietta and Elsie until he could barely be seen. Henrietta felt his hand go to his pocket, where she knew he kept his blanket, or perhaps a remnant of it, having been forbidden by Nanny to carry it about any more.

Could a little boy who still needed a blanket survive an austere boarding school out east? Henrietta wondered uneasily. If she were honest with herself, it didn't feel right, but what could she do? She was already treading on thin ice with Grandfather over asking Mr. Hennessey to walk her down the aisle instead of him and now regarding her interference with Elsie. Nor did she feel she could bother Clive with such a thing just at the moment when he had so many other things on his mind. There seemed nothing for it but to go along with the plan, at least for now. Maybe Clive was right when he had told her about it months ago. Maybe it would indeed be good for them, especially given Ma's somewhat neglect of them.

"Herbie's right, Jim," she tried to say sternly now. "You've got to be a big boy. Show Donny how it's done."

"I'll go, Jimmy! I want to go where Gene is!" Donny said, looking up from where he was meticulously arranging his lead soldiers on the wood floor. Doris sat beside him, patiently handing him new recruits, one by one, to line up.

"Eugene isn't at Phillips, you dunce," chided Eddie. "He's at military school, remember?"

"Why can't I go, Hen?" Donny pleaded, ignoring his brother. "I don't wanna stay here with Nanny! She's mean, and she's fat!"

"Donny!" Elsie exclaimed. "For shame!"

"Well, she is!" Donny rebutted. "Ain't she, Dowis?"

Doris did not respond, but merely nodded, her thumb in her mouth.

"Can't you come with us to Phillips Ex-ter, Elsie?" Jimmy squeaked from his cave between his two sisters.

"I'm afraid not, Jimbo," Elsie said, shifting so that she could tousle his hair.

"Why?"

"Yeah, why don't you have to go to school?" Eddie asked.

Henrietta saw Elsie's face blanch now that the attention was on her and the corresponding look of panic she shot at her.

"As a matter of fact," Henrietta said evenly, "Elsie's thinking of going to school, too, to college."

Ma seemed finally to rouse from the apparent stupor that she had been in and looked at the two of them sharply. "College? What nonsense is this now, Elsie? You go to college?"

"I know, Ma. I . . . I probably won't even get in," Elsie said, again shifting and this time absently taking one of Jimmy's hands in hers as she did so.

"I suppose this was your idea, wasn't it?" Ma accused Henrietta. "Well, you can put such silly thoughts out of your head right now, girl," she said to Elsie bitterly. "Your grandfather will never go for that, believe me. Women are only good for one thing in his eyes."

"I'm sure you're right, Ma," Elsie said, rubbing Jimmy's hand. "I . . . I didn't think it would work out. It was just a stupid thought."

"No, it isn't!" Henrietta exclaimed. "As a matter of fact, Elsie's already applied. She will probably need some tutoring, but we'll find out next week."

"Applied? Applied where?" Ma asked. Her eyes narrowed. "That's where you've been all afternoon isn't it?" she snapped. "Told me you were shopping!"

"Well, I didn't exactly say that, Ma . . ." Elsie murmured.

"It's Mundelein College. It's a new women's school. It's Catholic, very respectable," Henrietta answered.

Ma snorted. "A women's college?! For what? So you can become a secretary or a teacher? You're not smart enough for that."

"Ow!" Jimmy cried out. "You're hurting me, Els!" Jimmy said, pulling his hand from Elsie's.

"Well, I probably won't go anyway, Ma," Elsie repeated, her voice shaky. "It's not worth making a fuss."

"Elsie!" Henrietta exclaimed. How could she so quickly give in? "She's going, Ma, and that's that. How dare you say that about Elsie? Don't you remember what Pa always said? That Elsie got the brains? Well, it's true! She's the smartest one of us, and she's going!"

"Don't speak of him!" Ma roared. "And that goes for you too," she said, pointing a finger at Herbie, who cowered in response.

"Henrietta," Elsie said pleadingly. "You . . . you can't say for sure that I'll get in, so let's just leave it for now . . ."

"Elsie! I can't understand you! Don't listen to Ma!" Henrietta retorted.

"No, of course not. Why would anyone listen to me?" Ma shouted. "Well, it doesn't matter. Your grandfather will be livid. You haven't got a chance in hell of getting around the likes of him."

"As a matter of fact, I've already spoken with him," Henrietta said pertly.

"And?"

"He was against the idea, of course, but he doesn't own Elsie. I informed him that I will fund her education if he won't."

"So high-and-mighty, aren't you? You love lording it over us, don't you? Well, you do what you want, but you'll be wasting your time," she said to Elsie. "You'll just have to get married in the end, and that will be the end of that. And speaking of . . . why haven't I seen Stanley around lately? Answer me that. Hope you don't mean to put on airs like this one," she said, nodding toward Henrietta.

Henrietta slowly extricated herself from beside Jimmy's warm little body and stood up. "I should be going, actually," she said, which resulted in various moans of disappointment.

"Oh, Hen!" exclaimed Jimmy, pulling on her dress from where he still sat. "Don't go! Can't you stay overnight? You can share my bed!"

"No, I'm afraid not!" she said, trying to muster up a cheerful smile for him that she certainly didn't feel. "What would Nanny say?"

"Prol-ally something not nice," Jimmy said with a small voice, which made Henrietta chuckle dispite the situation.

"No, I imagine not."

Doris got up from her perch on the floor and came to her, her hands outstretched. She was too old to be picked up, but Henrietta did anyway. The little girl laid her head on Henrietta's shoulder and wrapped her arms around her neck. Henrietta felt close to tears, but she pushed them down. Donny followed his twin over and stood in front of her.

"Don't go, Hen!" he said, looking up at her.

"Well, of course she's going to go," Ma said bitterly, interrupting the tender scene. "She always does. Don't you all see that pattern by now? Soon as anything gets too uncomfortable, up she gets and goes."

"Yes, Ma. That's me. Always running away from my troubles," Henrietta retorted bitterly. She had managed to keep her patience all night, but she knew she was near her limit. And Elsie's maddening behavior threatened to push her over the edge. She set Doris down. "Good bye, you lot," she said looking at all of her siblings in turn and flashing them what she hoped was a convincing smile.

"I suspect that Antonia might ask you for Thanksgiving, so you can start thinking up an excuse now," Henrietta said to Ma, throwing her a glance. "But if you won't come, maybe you'll let these."

Not waiting for a reply, Henrietta turned and walked into the front hall, where no servant was waiting for her with her hat and coat. Where was Karl? Henrietta wondered in exasperation and after waiting several moments, went into the cloak room herself to extract her things. Elsie followed her and stood silently in the doorway.

"You really should speak to Karl or Mrs. Schmidt," Henrietta said, irritated, as she pinned on her hat. "Grandfather would be furious if he saw this laxness. What are you paying them for? You're too soft!"

"You've changed," Elsie said quietly, watching her older sister.

"Well, I had to, Elsie. We all have to change!"

"Hen, don't be mad at me!" Elsie whispered.

Henrietta let out a deep sigh, sympathy taking the place of her peaking frustration. "I'm not mad, Els, but you can't always let Ma treat you like that. You've got to stand up for yourself more. Don't let her bully you!"

"I know. But I don't let her bully me, usually. Honest."

"It doesn't seem like that to me," Henrietta said, slipping into her coat now.

"You don't have to live here day in and day out, like you said before," Elsie said feebly.

"Well, I used to, and I never put up with that."

"And look where that got you," Elsie said quietly. "In a perpetual fight with Ma, lying and sneaking around the city? I don't like ill feelings, Hen. Sometimes there's another way to deal with Ma."

"Like just giving in to her?" Henrietta said, brushing past her en route to the front hall.

"No . . ." Elsie said, following her. "It's just that . . . half the time she doesn't mean what she says, anyway," she said in a low voice. "Or remember, for that matter. She's getting worse, you know, Hen, about remembering things—"

"Look, Elsie," Henrietta said, pausing by the front door. "Can't you see what Ma is doing? And she's just as prejudiced as Grandfather, which is so maddening since she claims to hate him so much. A secretary or a teacher? It's infuriating!"

"I don't know, Hen. What . . . what do you want me to be?"

"It's not about what *I* want!" Henrietta whispered fiercely. "It's what *you* want. Don't you see that?" she said, her hand on the doorknob.

"Hen! Don't go away mad!"

"I'm not mad, Elsie," she sighed. "Listen, I'm willing to help you with this new plan, but maybe this isn't what you really want, and that's perfectly agreeable to me. Please don't do this to please me. I was just trying to help you, trying to give you some choices."

"Elsie!" came Ma's shout from the parlor. She obviously thought Henrietta had already gone. "Where are you? I need the pills!"

Elsie looked at Henrietta then with such a sad, defeated countenance that Henrietta's annoyance with her melted away completely. She reached out and embraced her sister tightly. She could never stay mad with Elsie for long, even when they were little girls; she always felt too sorry for her in the end. "I'm sorry, Elsie," she said, letting out a deep breath. "You're right, of course. I'm too hotheaded for my own good at times."

"Elsie! Where are you!" Ma shouted, louder this time.

"You'd better go," Henrietta whispered and planted a quick kiss on Elsie's cheek. Elsie squeezed her hand and, after hesitating a few moments, turned back toward the front parlor. Henrietta watched her go and slipped out the door, all the more determined to get Elsie out of that house.

Chapter 6

By the time the Daimler rolled up in front of Highbury, it was well past nine o'clock. Surely Clive would still be up, Henrietta assumed, but she wondered what mood she would find him in. While she was eager to tell him all about Mundelein, she knew he had planned to spend the day going through his father's study, which might have been difficult for him. She tried, on the long drive home from the city, to concentrate on how she might help him, but in truth her mind kept wandering back to Elsie, preoccupied with her frustration with her. She could be so maddeningly submissive! It made perfect sense why she had been seduced by the likes of Lieutenant Barnes-Smith. She wondered why Stanley had not found this particular feature of Elsie's attractive, since he was ordinarily so bossy, but perhaps his new relationship with Rose was telling. Rose was anything but submissive, so maybe that's what he preferred—to be led about. But why go over all that again in her mind? Clearly, Stanley was out of the picture now. Henrietta could feel it in her bones that Mundelein was the perfect place for Elsie to be, if she would only make even the slightest effort toward it, and she desperately hoped that all the work and trouble she had gone through to get her there was not going to be sabotaged by Elsie herself!

As he took her hat and coat, Billings informed her that Mr.

Howard and Mrs. Howard were in the drawing room and awaited her presence, if quite convenient.

"Thank you, Billings," she said as she patted her hair into place, thinking about how strange it was to hear Clive referred to as "Mr. Howard" rather than Mister Clive or even Inspector Howard. She would have liked to have gone upstairs to change, but not wishing to delay any longer, she instead made her way into the drawing room.

Clive rose to greet her. It was so lovely to see him, and she could not help feeling a fresh surge of love for him. They had rarely been apart since their wedding day, but she knew that would come to an end soon, if indeed it hadn't already.

"You're quite late," Clive said abruptly, a cognac in hand and his face troubled.

"Yes, I know, darling; forgive me," she said as she approached the two of them and sat beside Antonia on the settee. Clive sat down again as well, and Henrietta noted with sadness that he sat in the chair normally occupied by his mother, leaving Alcott's vacant.

"Hello, Antonia," she said, leaning over and giving her a quick kiss, smelling her familiar Chanel perfume as she did so. "It's been rather a long day. The tour of Mundelein took longer than expected, and then they wanted Elsie to take a test. It's a lovely campus—you should both see it. It was . . ." She broke off here, realizing that she was talking too fast and that neither of them seemed particularly interested. "Well, we can save that for another time," she said more slowly. "It's just that once I got back to Palmer Square, they all wanted me to stay, of course. And I haven't really had much of a chance to catch up since the wedding, just that one day last week when I went to drop off the souvenirs and to have a chat with Elsie." She glanced at Antonia, hoping for some sort of show of support, but Antonia was looking at the fire. "So I thought I should stay. I hope I haven't worried you," she said, looking up at Clive.

"Well, how are they all, then?" Clive asked. He didn't slur his words, but Henrietta wondered how many cognacs he had had. "Miserable as usual?"

Henrietta's eyebrows shot up and then furrowed deeply. Something was obviously wrong. Clive would never stoop to disparaging her family, especially in front of his mother, who already needed little encouragement in that department.

"They're fine, thank you," Henrietta answered stiffly, both parts piqued and worried, as she carefully folded her hands in her lap.

An odd silence fell upon them, then, until Antonia finally stirred herself. "Shall I ring for some tea?" she asked without the whiff of delight Henrietta expected she might have heard in her voice after Clive's comment. "It sounds positively beastly outside."

In fact, just as Fritz was coming into Winnetka, the rain that had been threatening all day began to lash down, the wind howling beside it and turning it to sleet.

"Yes, that would be nice, thank you. I'm chilled through," Henrietta answered gratefully.

"I'll stick to cognac, if you don't mind," Clive said. Henrietta was about to suggest that perhaps he had had enough, but she refrained.

Without a sound, Antonia stood up to pull the servants' cord, and when Billings dutifully appeared, she asked him to bring tea for two. The three of them again were left in silence, Henrietta feeling more and more uncomfortable by the minute, until she ventured to ask, "How has your day been, Antonia? Where is Aunt Lavinia?"

"She went up early. She's departing at the end of the week, so she wanted some extra rest."

"Oh, I see. Well, it was nice of her to come, wasn't it? At a time like this? I mean, even though it's a time like this." She glanced over at Clive, but he seemed not to be listening. Now *he* was staring into the fire. Something was definitely wrong.

"How . . . how was your day, dearest?" she asked him. "Did you get much done?" she asked hesitantly.

"Yes, I suppose," Clive answered irritably. "Enough, anyway."

"Is . . . is everything all right, Clive?"

She wished they could be alone, so she could really get to the bottom of what was bothering him, but as it was, she would just have to speak in front of Antonia and get used to it. "You seem so . . . so upset . . ."

Clive's head snapped up to look at her, and his eyes flashed. "Well, my father just died, so perhaps I might be excused!" he said angrily.

Henrietta was stunned. She had never heard him take that tone with her, even on the night they had argued at Castle Linley.

As if to conveniently break the tension, James entered the room, then, carrying a large tea tray. Carefully he approached the little group, the low table between them being his obvious destination. As it happened, however, his foot must have somehow caught on the edge of the thick rug, and without warning, he catapulted forward, causing both Henrietta and Antonia to call out in alarm. James somehow managed to right himself before he toppled to the ground, but he lost his grip on the tray, and it came down with an enormous bang on the table, with much of the crockery flying from the tray and shattering on the hard floor beyond the rug. Both Henrietta and Antonia jumped, but Clive actually leaped from the chair, bracing his arms over his head for a moment and loudly crying out his alarm.

"Good God, man!" he shouted at the unfortunate James, who was himself scrambling to stand up properly.

Billings rushed in at the sound of the crash and hurried forward. "Has anyone been injured?" he asked, looking at the women quickly and then giving James a deep frown.

Antonia shook her head. "No, we're quite all right, Billings."

"I'm very sorry, madam. Very sorry, indeed. Get yourself together, man," he hissed at James. "Clean this up immediately. I'll see to you later."

James, who was probably not much older than her younger brother, Eugene, Henrietta guessed, looked as if he might cry, his face crimson now. James had never been a favorite of Henrietta's, but she felt sorry for him just the same and had to resist the urge to help him as he quickly began collecting the shattered bits of china. "I'm very sorry. So sorry, madam . . ." he muttered to no one in particular.

"It's all right, James. It was just an accident," Antonia said stiffly, standing up and taking Billings's hand to help her over the broken bits of glass.

"In case you may have forgotten, *I* am the master of this house now!" Clive snapped at James, giving his mother a snide look. Henrietta saw his jaw clench, and she could see that he was trembling, though he tried to hide it. "In which case, you may direct your apologies to *me*. And your wages will be docked."

"Yes, of course, sir," Billings answered for James. "Yes. Allow me, sir. Perhaps you might be more comfortable in the study or the morning room while we settle this away," he said with an obsequious gesture.

"Yes, I think so, Billings," Antonia said calmly, though her face was dark and furious. "We will retire to the study."

"Very good, madam," he said with a bow and hurried to the other side of the room to open the pocket doors. Antonia stiffly followed him, walking past Clive as she did so but not condescending to look at him.

Henrietta stood hesitating, not knowing what to do next. She wanted to approach Clive, but she was afraid of what his reaction might be. He stood looking at the floor, ignoring her, so, giving him a last look, she walked past him too, and followed Antonia into the other room. Billings was already bustling about the study, hastily lighting lamps and poking the existing low fire into more robust flames. When he retired, Antonia moved to stand before the fireplace. Only once did she glance at Henrietta, but her face remained grim. Henrietta did not think she had ever seen her this angry. Quietly Henrietta sat down in one of the chairs, trying to think of what to say to either of them.

When Clive finally entered the room, Antonia lost no time in addressing him. "How dare you," she hissed. "Don't you *ever* speak to me that way, especially in front of the servants," she continued, her voice that of cold steel.

"I wasn't actually addressing you," he said angrily. Unexpectedly then, he let out a deep sigh and rubbed his forehead wearily. "Forgive me, Mother," he said, walking toward her now. "I'm not myself. I . . . I . . . I'm easily startled at times."

Henrietta saw Antonia's face falter a little, but she remained aloof. "Be that as it may, such behavior is inexcusable. Your father never lost his composure. You might remember that. If you are to be *master* of this house."

Henrietta drew in a breath and expected Clive to throw back a retort, his jaw clenching again, but instead he stiffly tilted his head in acknowledgement. "Please, sit down, Mother," he said, clearly making an effort to control his voice. "Would you like a sherry?" he asked politely.

"No, thank you. I'm going up now. It would seem the two of you have much to say to each other," she said coldly. "I believe I'm in the way."

Henrietta opened her mouth to entreat her to stay, but no words came out, and Antonia quickly brushed past her, anyway.

"Good-night," she said without looking back at them as she disappeared from the room.

Clive watched her go, and then catching Henrietta's worried, accusatory look, shockingly threw his cognac glass into the fireplace, shattering it. Billings appeared in the doorway within moments, and even his normally immovable face looked concerned. Henrietta gestured for him to stay where he was. He looked at her and then at Clive, his eyes quickly ascertaining the situation, and then silently retreated.

Henrietta stood, nervously wringing her hands, wondering what she should do, as she looked at her husband, his arms outstretched on the stone mantle, his head bowed.

"Well," he finally spoke, "don't you want to go up, too?"

Henrietta took a deep breath, walked toward him, and tentatively wrapped her arms around him from behind. His body remained stiff for several moments before she felt him relax into her arms. A flood of relief running through her, she leaned her head against his back as she held him. "Clive, darling, what's wrong?"

Clive remained silent, still bracing himself against the mantel. "So many things," he finally said hoarsely.

"Won't you please tell me?" Henrietta entreated. "It was the noise, wasn't it? It reminds you—"

"I hate myself for it," he whispered. He turned toward her now but didn't meet her eye. "I hate that I'm still that weak . . ."

"You can't blame yourself, Clive! The war was horrible. I wish you'd tell me more about it, but I don't wish to distress you."

"No, best just to leave it." He sighed. "I'll have to apologize to James tomorrow. And to Mother."

"But that's not the only thing, is it? You were upset before that . . . when I came in." She touched his arm and looked up into his troubled hazel eyes. "Is it because I was late?" she asked, hardly believing that he would be so mean in his expectation of her.

He closed his eyes. "No, darling," he said, a heavy breath escaping. "I'm sorry if it seemed that way. I never wish to limit you. I trust you completely," he said, running his finger along the side of her face. Henrietta thought that an odd comment, but she let it go.

"What is it then?" she asked softly.

Clive stared at her for a few moments and abruptly ran his hand through his hair. "I'm pretty sure Father was having an affair," he said quietly.

"An affair?" Henrietta murmured, never guessing that *this* could be what was troubling him. "There must be some mistake, Clive," she said gently. He was obviously getting worse, she worried. First, he believed his father had been murdered and now that he had been carrying on with another woman . . .

"I only wish it was."

"Why . . . why do you think this?" Henrietta tried to ask gently.

Clive hesitated for a moment and then pulled a letter out of his inside jacket pocket. "Here," he said, handing it to her. "Read this. I found it in Father's things this afternoon."

Henrietta took the letter and unfolded it. The paper was thin and of poor quality.

Howard,

It is our anniversary again and time for our usual arrangement. You'd better have the gift ready. I got your note about meeting, and I'm not too happy. I'll let you know when and where. If you're thinking of ending our relationship, don't. You are mine forever. Never forget that.

Susan

Henrietta's brow furrowed as she read it several times before looking across to Clive, who had in the meantime poured himself a new brandy. It certainly was an odd missive, but it did not have the flavor of a love affair to it.

"Hmmm . . . it's very peculiar," she began, looking it over again. "It doesn't sound like a lover, though, Clive. It sounds more like a . . . like a business transaction, not that that makes it any better."

"Yes, I'm aware of that."

"Besides the fact that it is signed 'Susan,' it doesn't seem to be terribly feminine. The language is not very romantic—for a love note, that is."

"Maybe it's a disguise; maybe they agreed ahead of time to write in such a way to avoid suspicion."

"Perhaps, but why would she sign her name? Why not use a nickname?"

"Maybe it is. After all, she addresses it to 'Howard' not 'Alcott.'"

"Hmmm . . . I see what you mean. The language is also rather crude, but perhaps that is part of the ruse as well. It is hardly the speech of a refined woman."

"Well, maybe she isn't," Clive said, gripping his glass tightly.

"No, maybe not," Henrietta said quietly. "The paper is cheap, too."

"Yes, I noticed."

She walked toward him and handed the note back. "Where did you find it?"

"Tucked under a larger stack of correspondence, under the blotter, as if to hide it."

"Were there others?"

"I haven't found any yet, but I haven't gotten through everything. That's another thing," he said, taking a large drink of his brandy. "His affairs appear to be very much out of order. I started to go through his account book, and it seems like he has very little personal cash, which can't be. I must be missing something or not reading it correctly. I get the feeling that something has gone terribly wrong. And then I found this letter—which speaks of their 'anniversary' and 'a gift.' It's not hard to put two and two together. If this were an outside case and not my father, I think I'd have already come to the obvious conclusion." He paused as if to take it all in. "Was he really *paying* a woman to be his companion?" he reasoned haltingly. "I simply can't believe it; and yet, what other conclusion can I draw?"

"It does sound bad," Henrietta admitted. "But perhaps there's some other explanation?"

"I can't think of what it would be . . ."

"Maybe she's someone from his past that he . . . he agreed to help? Or someone that saw him in a compromising position?"

"And is blackmailing him?" Clive said incredulously. "Impossible. You heard everyone at the funeral. 'A pillar of society,' 'a man of his word,' 'honest, true, upright,'—I could go on and on."

"Yes, but that doesn't mean he didn't once make a mistake, Clive."

"He wasn't the type that would cower to a blackmailer."

She let out a deep breath, thinking. "Well, perhaps not. Maybe it really is just a love affair. Your parents don't . . . didn't . . . seem overly affectionate . . ." she said tentatively. "Is it possible?"

"I guess anything's possible, but I just can't believe it of him."

"What about asking your mother . . . in a roundabout sort of way, I mean."

"Never! She's very fragile right now," he said, pouring himself a new glass of cognac.

Henrietta turned this over in her mind. It's true that Antonia seemed to be truly grieving Alcott, and yet she had not given in to excessive sadness or displays of emotion. The servants were looking to her for direction, she had told Henrietta after the funeral. It was her duty to be strong in light of the current crisis, as the smooth running of the household depended on it. Women, she had said, had to be stronger than men much of the time, and Henrietta was inclined to agree with her, at least on that score.

"Yes, darling," Henrietta said gingerly, "but your mother is very much a woman of the world. She's no blushing violet. Perhaps she could easily shed some light on this."

"Maybe . . ." he said reluctantly. "But not yet. I want to try to get to the bottom of this without involving her."

"But why? What good would it do now?"

"I just want to know."

"Are you sure?"

Clive sighed. "Well, if nothing else, I still need to go through the rest of his things. Maybe I'll find something more."

Henrietta didn't know what to say to this. There was clearly nothing more that could be done at this point, and she felt her body correspondingly begin to droop. It had been a terribly long day. She just barely managed to stifle a yawn.

Clive looked over at her as if really seeing her now. "Go up, darling," he said tiredly. "You must be fagged. You haven't even had a chance to tell me what happened with Elsie. I've been frightfully selfish. I'm sorry. And I'm sorry about tonight. I behaved very badly."

Henrietta let his apology go, not wishing to return to the subject, but she was worried about him. She could tell that he was still restless and upset. She did not want to leave him alone, and yet she was, in truth, thoroughly exhausted. "I don't mind sitting up with you," she offered.

"No, I'll just finish this," he said, holding up his nearly empty glass.

"Bring it with you," she suggested.

"No, I'd like to think for a moment . . ."

"Well, if you're sure," she said, walking over to him. She kissed his chin and let her hand brush against his chest. "Good-night, then."

—

Clive stood looking into the fire, wondering what to do next. There were no leads, no clues. He was convinced now more than ever that something untoward had happened to his father, and he meant to get to the bottom of it. He was conscious of the fact, however, that no one else shared this belief, even Henrietta, he suspected, and especially Captain Callahan, to whom he had paid an unannounced visit just a few days ago.

When Henrietta had gone into the city last week to see her family, Clive had decided, on the spur of the moment to drive over to the Winnetka Police Station under the guise of reintroducing himself. He had technically already met Captain Callahan, the chief of police, after the pursuit of Jack Fletcher, but his interaction with him that night had been brief. Clive's original impression had not been, truth be told, particularly favorable, but he hoped that perhaps he was wrong about the chief, that the failed capture of Fletcher was due to bad luck and not his seemingly inept handling of the situation.

Unfortunately, it was an impression not greatly improved upon as Clive took a seat across the desk from him, having secured an immediate audience with Captain Callahan by virtue of mentioning to the desk sergeant that he was a former detective inspector of the Chicago Police. Having then been begrudgingly escorted back to the chief's office and seated accordingly, Clive took his time assessing the man.

His office and his uniform were impeccable, which said much, but he was more rotund than Clive thought a chief, or any officer of the law, really, should be. His gleaming gold buttons were indeed straining as he leaned back confidently in his chair, looking pleasantly at Clive as if this were a social call and idly drumming his fingers. He had gray hair and a thick gray mustache, and his eyes lacked the piercing quality so useful in interrogating subjects or evaluating evidence, Clive thought. In fact, he possessed a jolly sort of absentmindedness, which might be welcome at a family Christmas party, for example, but not as the chief investigator on, say, a murder case. He reminded

Clive of . . . well, of his father in a way, which thoroughly unsettled him. Angrily he chided himself to stop seeing ghosts in every corner.

He forced his thoughts back to the man in front of him, disgustedly wondering how he could possibly become the chief of police, especially in so affluent an area like Winnetka, and bitterly put it down to the usual politics. Even Clancy, his own bumbling sergeant back in Chicago, could have run the department better than he suspected Callahan could. But perhaps he was getting ahead of himself. Perhaps there was more to the chief than met the eye. This hopeful ember of thought, however, gradually diminished once Clive got around to talking about his father's accident. Casually, Clive had found a way of asking if there had been any investigation of his father's death.

"Investigation?" the chief asked with a pleasant smile, as if Clive had just asked something silly or imbecilic. "No, there was no investigation," he said patiently, as if explaining something to a child. "No need, you see. Simple accident is all it was."

"But how can you be sure?"

"Sure of what?"

"Sure that it was an accident."

Captain Callahan looked at him and blinked lazily. "I don't quite follow."

"Look, sir, it just seems odd that my father was seen talking to two unidentified men on the platform, the same platform he's managed to stand on for years without falling, I might add, before he slips and falls to his death before an oncoming train. Do you not find that rather extraordinary?"

This seemed to perplex the chief, and he sat for a few moments as if to decipher it. "Are you suggesting he may have taken his own life?" the chief said in a low voice, leaning slightly toward Clive as he said it.

"Of course not!" Clive said irritably, though it was the second time someone had suggested this explanation in as many days, a fact which he uncomfortably tucked away to reexamine later. "I'm suggesting that he may have been murdered, man!"

"Murdered?" the chief asked, mystified, and then unexpectedly chuckled. "No, Mr. Howard. It wasn't a murder. Of that we can be sure."

"How?"

"Why, isn't it obvious?"

"No, it's not! Were there any witnesses? Surely someone must have seen something. What about these two men my father's chauffer saw him talking to? Were they identified?"

Captain Callahan looked at him blankly.

"It had just recently snowed, as I understand," Clive went on. "Was there any sign of a struggle that could have been read in the footprints or markings on the platform? What about the station master? Did you question him?"

"Look, Mr. Howard, there hasn't been a murder in Winnetka for over twenty years," the chief said defensively.

"That has absolutely no bearing on this case."

"But this isn't a 'case,' you see. Let's not go looking for something that doesn't exist, shall we? Not good for business."

With that comment, Clive thought he saw the first sign of wherewithal in Captain Callahan's eye. So that was it. He was tied to the business owners . . . or someone else, some other entity, perhaps?

"Look, Mr. Howard," the rotund chief said, leaning towards him across his desk. "We're all very sorry about your father, but it was an *accident*. Quite open and shut. We know what you city cops are like. Suspicious of everything that moves, but it doesn't work that way here. Not everything is suspicious, if you understand my meaning."

"Yes, I understand perfectly," Clive said slowly, not breaking eye contact even for a second.

"I'll wish you good morning then," the chief said pleasantly. "Nice of you to stop by. Davis!" he shouted out loudly.

"Yes, sir?" came an irritated voice, in a normal volume, which suggested the speaker was very nearby. Clive turned his head to see a man indeed seated very near the chief's office behind what looked to be the smallest desk Clive had ever seen. Clive thought his bedside table might be bigger. It was just wide enough to hold a typewriter, a desk lamp, and a telephone. Davis wearily stood up and took the few steps required to reach his superior's office. He looked to be a solid young man, his own height, with intelligent, piercing eyes and a black stubble growing across his firm jawline. He was dressed only in a shirt and suspenders and wore no tie. Clive noted that he would never have allowed Clancy to appear this slovenly. Davis was sizing him up as well, he could tell.

"This is my sergeant, Detective Frank Davis," Captain Callahan explained. "Like to keep him close, as you see, heh-heh. Good man is Davis."

The two stared at each other, Clive wondering if he were perhaps the brains behind the department.

"Show Mr. Howard out, won't you?" the chief said pleasantly, leaning back in his chair again.

"Yes, sir. This way, Mr. Howard," Davis said plainly, gesturing toward the hallway.

"Good day, Captain," Clive said as he stood now. "Thank you for seeing me. It was enlightening," he said with a scowl.

"Glad to be of service, glad to be of service," the chief almost hummed as Clive followed Davis down the hallways toward the front of the station. As soon as they were out of earshot of the chief's office, however, Clive ventured to speak to Davis as they made their way down the corridor.

"Listen, Davis," he said in a low voice, "you must have heard what I said. You must see that there's a chance this wasn't a mere accident."

Davis stopped walking and turned toward him now, Clive detecting the faintest glimmer of acknowledgement in Davis's eye.

"Anything's possible, Mr. Howard," Davis suggested coolly.

"Look, I don't want to get you in trouble, but you'll keep me informed of any new developments?" Clive asked softly, pulling his card out from inside his jacket and handing it to Davis.

Davis perused it and casually put it in his shirt pocket. "I will," he said plainly. "But don't expect much to develop," he said, inclining his head at the chief's office.

"How can I get a hold of you? Privately, that is," Clive asked, his eyes inadvertently darting back down the hallway. "Do you have a card?"

"No, I don't," Davis answered, seeming amused. "Probably wouldn't carry them if I did. But you can find me most nights at The Trophy Room."

Clive gave him a quizzical look.

"It's a bar on Elm."

"Got it," Clive said appreciatively and placed his hat on his head. He made his way around the front counter and crossed the lobby, feeling a little bit of hope that he might have at last found an ally. He had hoped for that in the chief, but he would take what he could get. And if his guess was correct, Davis probably ran circles around Callahan.

Clive drained his glass and wandered over to his father's desk, shrouded in darkness along the far wall. He let his fingers rifle through the various stacks of paper he had gone through earlier today. He must be missing something, he thought again. If his father had really been having an affair, someone must have known about it. But who? John Exley? No, too close to his mother, Clive decided. A confession to John Exley would have been teetering too close for comfort. His mind then alighted on the image of Bennett, his father's best friend and colleague at the firm. Would he have confided in him? Clive wondered. He recalled how Bennett had not been able to look him in the eye the whole day of the funeral. He had assumed it was due to grief, but maybe it was due to something else? Clive turned this theory over and over in his brain as he began to pace and found it more of a real possibility with each turn.

Yes, perhaps Bennett could offer some sort of explanation, he mused. It seemed very likely that Bennett would know something of his father's personal life, having spent more time with him than probably any other person, including Antonia. Why had he not considered this before? And perhaps Bennett also suspected foul play?

Clive's mind seized on this possibility, and a bit of a frenzy overcame him, perhaps marginally fueled by having had too much to drink. It became clear to him that he needed to speak to Bennett at the first possible opportunity—nay, immediately, he suddenly decided. He strode back over to his father's desk and roughly pulled opened the top drawer, where he thought he remembered seeing his father's address book earlier this afternoon. Easily, he found the book and began flipping through the pages until he found Bennett's telephone number. Without a thought to the lateness of the hour, he asked the operator to put the call through, not even really sure what he would say. After an infernal number of rings and just as Clive was about to hang up, Bennett finally answered.

"Yes? Hello?" a scratchy, sleep-filled voice asked. "Who is this?"

"Sidney Bennett?" Clive asked.

"Yes. Who is this?" Bennett repeated, a little bit of fear in his voice.

"Bennett, this is Clive Howard. Sorry to disturb you so late."

"Clive? What is it? Is anything wrong?" Bennett asked, the worry in his voice very clear now.

"Yes, there is something wrong, I believe. I've just discovered something unusual."

"Such as?" Bennett asked unsteadily.

"I know about Susan," Clive said quietly.

There was silence on the line for several moments before Bennett finally spoke.

"Leave it, Clive," he said, his voice crisp and chill. "Don't get involved," he added and then hung up.

Chapter 7

"Have you finished the exercises I gave you last night?" Sr. Sebastian asked gently.

"Yes, Sister. Well, I tried," Elsie said, bowing her head as she sat side by side next to the young, frail nun in the little library of Philomena Hall. Sr. Sebastian was as thin as a will-o-wisp and very pale, so much so that upon first meeting her, Elsie had been afraid that she might collapse at any moment, so weak did she appear.

"Difficult, were they?" Sr. Sebastian asked with an encouraging smile.

"A bit," Elsie said, looking at her. As always, she became distracted by how paper-thin Sr. Sebastian's skin was; it was almost transparent, and Elsie could see some of her tiny veins beneath. If she stared at them long enough, they began to form themselves into patterns. Today she saw what looked like a snowflake.

Elsie shook herself now and looked back at her paper. Unfortunately, the patterns there were harder to unearth. She gave Sr. Sebastian another glance. She was certainly not how she envisioned a math and science teacher should look. A math teacher, in *her* mind at least, should be big and hearty and hard-edged, like the numbers being dealt with. Sr. Sebastian, by her appearance, should have taught something light and ethereal, like handwriting, Elsie thought. And yet, she was proving a skilled math tutor.

"Well, never mind," Sr. Sebastian said. "'Great works are performed not by strength, but by perseverance.' Isn't that true?"

"Proverbs?" Elsie guessed. It was a sort of game that had already sprung up between the two of them that had at first disconcertedly reminded her of . . . well, she wasn't going to think of him!

"Samuel Johnson," Sr. Sebastian said with a laugh. "But it never hurts to throw a prayer or two into the mix," she said, giving her the slightest of winks.

Elsie returned the smile and made a mental note that she would try harder to pray more often. She knew she needed it, and yet ever since the whole affair with Harrison, she had admittedly lost her way a bit. Except for when she had resorted to praying the rosary each night so that she might not be pregnant with Harrison's child, she just couldn't of late bring herself to ask for God's help and mercy. It wasn't a laziness or a lack of faith; the truth was that she didn't feel she deserved God's love. She knew that was wrong, but she couldn't seem to see around it. She tried here and there to pray, but it seemed empty and rote now.

In just the short time that she had been here among the sisters, however, she had already observed that whenever the sisters mentioned God or prayer, it seemed to have a lightness to it, even a happiness, rather than being something dull or fearful. Their faith effused their whole being; they were never separate from it. Theirs seemed a freeing sort of faith, not repressive, which was utterly new to Elsie, and which seemed, on the whole, contradictory, considering the vows and therefore the restrictions they lived under. They seemed different from the nuns she had known in the past, as if they were perhaps a more . . . enlightened? wiser? . . . version of any she had previously studied under.

At any rate, Elsie had already begun to feel oddly comforted here at Mundelein, almost at peace, though her studies were indeed rigorous. This was especially true in Sr. Bernard's presence, in particular, though she didn't often get an opportunity to be near her. When she was, Sr. Bernard exuded a warmth, a patience, and a gentleness that Elsie was desperately attracted to. Sr. Bernard was always encouraging and never cross, it seemed, nor was Sr. Sebastian, really. Elsie found it quite remarkable that they seemed genuinely more interested in her mind than in following rules and catechism. She was still terrified of many things, particularly her grandfather and the Exleys, and Ma, to a certain extent, and even of failing here at this thing she was beginning to want more than ever, but for the first time in a long time she felt hopeful. For what exactly, she wasn't sure, but she felt it nonetheless.

Thanksgiving had come and gone without exception. Henrietta had not come to them, which was as expected. She had to stay at Highbury, she explained, as Mrs. Howard was insisting on having the usual family dinner, something about wanting to carry on as normal despite Alcott's absence. From what Henrietta had related in a short letter on beautiful, thick, ecru stationary with her new monogram— HHE—it had been a quiet affair, just the three of them. Antonia had not extended an invitation to the Von Harmons, as Henrietta had thought she might, which was just as well. Alternately, Mr. Exley had tried to force them all to come to Gerard and Dorothy's, but Ma had put her foot down and insisted that they remain home alone as a family, especially as the boys would soon be "ripped from me," is how she had put it. Mr. Exley had oddly given in to Ma, but not without commenting that Christmas would be a different story.

This was the Von Harmon's first Thanksgiving in their new home on Palmer Square, but Elsie wasn't exactly looking forward to the food. Now that they had a cook, Elsie's previous affection for food had ironically diminished considerably, resulting in a significant amount of weight lost. The cook that Grandfather had installed had trained under a distinctly notable chef in Paris, so that all of the food prepared by him seemed foreign and unnatural, at least to the Von Harmons, anyway. Too fancy by far. But what would you expect of a male cook? Elsie had thought more than once and wondered if he was inflicted on them by Grandfather as yet another punishment, for what infraction she wasn't sure—perhaps that they had even been born in the first place. At any rate, it seemed unnatural to have a man in the kitchen, checking the ovens, briskly stirring batters and ordering Odelia about.

Only Doris and Donny were prepared lighter fare and were fed upstairs in the nursery, and more than once Elsie had longed for the plain ham and cheese sandwiches she saw going past her on a tray on their way up the stairs. Meanwhile, the rest of them were given things like *foie gras* or *bouillabaisse* or *coq au vin*. Elsie knew it was wickedly wrong, but sometimes she simply longed for a plate of Ma's hash.

Martha Exley, having herself grown up in luxury, had not the slightest idea of how to cook when she married Leslie Von Harmon, but all the time she had spent as a lonely little girl hanging about in the kitchens of the Exley mansion had at least come in handy for something. She remembered enough basics from watching the old cook at the Exley manor to imitate some of her recipes and had likewise learned much from the neighbors who came and went over the years in the apartments around them in the city. This, plus the fact that she had no money for expensive ingredients, ultimately informed her limited menu selections over the years.

Their Thanksgiving dinner, however, had not been as bad as Elsie had thought it might be. Apparently, the cook—or Chef, as he insisted on being called—had deemed it acceptable for the meal to have a decidedly American flavor, considering the occasion, and had left off any of his usual French influences.

Afterward, Elsie had tried to organize a game of charades, but after a few halfhearted attempts, it had broken up rather early. She tried not to think of last Thanksgiving when Stanley had come over and had kept them all laughing.

—

"Elsie? Elsie, are you quite with me?" Sr. Sebastian was saying now in her very thin voice. "I think we should work on geometry for a bit."

"Oh, sorry, Sister!" Elsie exclaimed and resolved, again, to try to keep her mind from wandering. "Must we?" she asked, trying to stifle a groan.

"Your test showed it to be your weakest subject, I'm afraid. But that just so happens to be my specialty," she said, smiling kindly. "Come along, let's begin. That's the best way."

The two spent the next hour and a half working methodically through pages of problems until Elsie thought she couldn't think straight any longer. It was painfully tiring, and yet she felt a certain thrill when even just a small fraction of the angles and secants and degrees began to make a bit of sense.

"I think this would be a good time for a rest," Sr. Sebastian said, interrupting her work as Elsie tried and failed to discreetly rub her eye.

"I think so," Elsie agreed, now stifling a yawn and stretching. She got up early every day and took the trolley across town, refusing to let Karl drive her. Having a chauffeur was something she thought she'd never get used to.

"Why don't you take a walk outdoors," Sr. Sebastian suggested. "Or perhaps you'd like to have a look at the room you'll have next term."

"You mean *if* I'm here next term, Sister."

"Nonsense! Don't be so pessimistic! You're making wonderful progress. I'm sure you'll pass the entrance exam with flying colors."

Elsie felt her stomach clench at these words. She did feel as though she was making progress, but she also saw, with a certain amount of awe, and excitement, actually, how much more there was to learn. Even Sr. Bernard, the last time she had seen her, had hinted that she thought she would be admitted for winter term if she kept on as she had begun. If she somehow was admitted, however, Elsie still wasn't convinced that she should stay here in the dorms. It didn't make sense to her, as Palmer Square was only across town—but Henrietta was insistent that she not remain in the Von Harmon house, that she have a complete break from that lonely environment and Ma's discouraging comments and live among other young women.

"As a matter of fact, I believe Melody may still be up there yet. She hasn't yet left for break," said Sr. Sebastian. "She's one of the last to leave, I think."

"Who's Melody?"

"Why, Melody would be your roommate, as I understand it. Didn't Sister Bernard mention that?"

Roommate? Quickly Elsie tried to remember everything Sr. Bernard had said the day that she and Henrietta had toured the grounds, and for the life of her, she could not recall the mention of roommates. But she did remember now that when they had toured Philomena and Piper Halls, they had only seen rooms with two or even three beds, so that made sense. Somehow, however, it had not registered that she would have to share a room with a stranger, the thought of which filled her with her all-too-familiar feelings of dread.

Sr. Sebastian rose from the desk where they were seated, her rosary beads barely clacking against her paper-like body, and gestured for Elsie to follow her. Elsie sighed. For a moment she considered insisting on a walk outside instead, but in truth, she didn't feel like going out in the cold, and she supposed she would have to meet this girl at some point, if Henrietta got her way, as usual, and forced her to live here.

As she followed Sr. Sebastian up the wide, beautifully carved walnut staircase leading up to the dormitory, Elsie tried to rein in her anxiety, remembering that she had resolved to try to be more like Hen—braver and more impetuous. She studied the swirling patterns of the William Morris wallpaper as they climbed, trying to distract herself, and glanced at the various paintings hung on the walls, all of them dwarfed by a large portrait by van Dyck of Jesus crucified with Mary and St. John standing, heads bowed, at the foot of the cross. It did little to quell Elsie's nervousness, but the refracted, colorful light from the large Tiffany stained-glass window on the first landing, on the other hand, did much to calm her. It was like walking through a rainbow, and Elsie held out her hand to touch it, the rainbow appearing on her hand now.

When they reached the top floor, Sr. Sebastian led her down the hallway to the very last room, the door of which stood slightly ajar. Sr. Sebastian rapped gently on it and called out, "Miss Merriweather?"

"Is that you, Sister Sebastian?" called a sprightly voice, and within seconds, a matching face appeared at the door. "You don't have to knock, Sister!" the girl said. "I was just packing. Who's this? New recruit?" the girl, apparently Melody, said with an oddly melodic lilt to her voice.

"It is, we hope. This is Elsie Von Harmon. Miss Von Harmon, Miss Melody Merriweather. She may be joining you next term," Sr. Sebastian explained and gestured toward the interior of Melody's room.

"So you finally found me someone! Just when I thought I was to be left high and dry after all! My old roommate left after only a week!" Melody explained to Elsie. "I hope it wasn't me! But I don't think so. She was terribly homesick, you see. Anyway, pleased to meet you," she said, thrusting out her hand toward Elsie. She was a girl her own height with blonde hair, green eyes, and a very trim figure. She was dressed smartly in a red dress with tiny white polka dots with a wide white collar, and she gave off an air of happy gaiety.

Timidly, Elsie shook her hand. "Pleased to meet you, too," she tried to say confidently.

"Charmed, I'm sure," Melody said. "Well, why don't you come in, then? Look around, seeing as this is to be your home away from home, as I call it," she said, opening the door widely and stepping aside.

"Well, it's not for sure . . ." Elsie tried to say, stepping inside the bright, cheerful room.

"What do you mean it's not for sure?" Melody asked.

Before Elsie could explain, however, Sr. Sebastian interrupted. "I'll leave the two of you to get acquainted," she said, removing a tiny watch on a thin silver fob from under her habit and studying it. "Come back down in a half hour, Elsie, and we'll resume." She gave them both a smile and then disappeared down the hallway, her rosary beads clacking softly at her side.

"So, where you from?" Melody asked, making no effort to hide the fact that she was looking her up and down.

"From Chicago, actually," Elsie said, blushing.

"Chicago?"

"Yes, Palmer Square. Or Logan Square, really. That area, anyway," Elsie murmured.

"Never heard of it. But that's not saying much. I don't really know my way around yet. Guess you don't have far to go, then!" she laughed.

"No . . . no, not really. It was my sister's idea that I stay here. If I'm admitted, that is."

"Not admitted yet? That doesn't make any sense. Why are you here, then?"

"I . . . I'm a bit behind, you might say. Sister Sebastian is tutoring me for now . . ." Elsie broke off here, not sure what else to say.

"Oh, you'll get in," Melody said cheerfully. "They need the tuition, you see. Not that it's not a spiffing sort of place. Top-notch, my pops says."

Elsie didn't know what to say to this, so she merely nodded her head. "Where . . . where are *you* from?" she asked, trying to begin again at being sociable.

"Merriweather, Wisconsin. Same as my last name. They named the town after us. Well, not us, really, but my grandfather."

"Oh! . . . Imagine that! . . . Is it far?"

"About two hundred miles. Near Mineral Point. Ever hear of it?

Elsie shook her head. "Sorry," she murmured.

"Oh, don't worry. It's just a little place, really."

"Was . . . was this your first term here?" Elsie asked, trying again.

"Oh, yeah. My first. Going home tomorrow, though, for break. Everyone else has already flown the coop," she laughed.

"Oh, I see. Did you . . . like it?

"Like what?"

"Mundelein. Do you like it here?"

"Sure I do! I was awfully homesick at first, that's the truth, but now it's ever so much fun. Sister Bernard is a dream, and there's loads of dances at Loyola! Tons of them, in fact! The boys there are dreamy, not like the farm boys in Merriweather."

"What are you studying?"

"I'm not really sure. Home economics, I think. This is all my father's idea. He wants all of his kids—there's three of us—to be educated, you see. Not for any good reason, really. Just wants the prestige of it. Freddy's off at Notre Dame, but he's just going to be running the family business, so Mom says it's a waste of money, but Pops says it'll be good for him to learn whatever new business stuff is out there. I got sent here, as you see," she said with a curtsey, "and Bunny's still at home."

"Bunny?"

"Bunny's my kid sister. Her real name is Bonnie, but we call her Bunny or Bunny Bonnie or Bun Bon 'cause of all the pet rabbits she had as a kid. Pops finally made her get rid of them all. All but one, but then it died, too."

"Oh . . ." was all Elsie could manage before Melody began speaking again.

"So we're all getting educated, and we all get a brand-new car when we graduate."

"Oh!" Elsie said again.

"I'm getting a Hudson 8; that's my plan anyway," she said, flopping on the bed.

"You must be very well off," Elsie said and instantly regretted it, remembering too late the injunctions of both Mrs. Hutchings, her failed lady's companion, and Aunt Agatha about proper topics of conversation—the source or amount of one's financial resources being strictly off limits. Melody, however, did not seem to care or even notice her *faux pas*.

"Pops used to be a bootlegger," Melody whispered with a giggle. "Though I'm not supposed to say that. But it's true. That's how he made his money. Well, sort of. My grandpa came over from Wales, I think, where they're all miners. So he mined around in Wisconsin for a few years until he found a lead mine. Struck it big, you see, and became a mine owner. But then most of the money got lost in the Depression, so Pops started making and selling liquor to make the family money back. Now that it's legal, it's easier to do. I'm not supposed to tell anyone, though, so mum's the word," she said with a wink. "What's your pops do?" she asked.

"He's dead, I'm afraid. But he used to work in a motorcycle factory."

"You don't say! Freddy had a motorcycle for a while before Pops made him get rid of it. That's where the car idea came in. It was really just a way to get Freddy to give up 'that wild contraption,' as Pops used to call it. But then I said, 'Well, if he gets one, so should I!' and Pops says, 'You're right, Mel. Fair is fair,' and then he said that I would have one too if I graduated. So here I am."

Elsie smiled at her. She liked her already.

"Have a beau?" Melody asked.

"Well, not really," Elsie said, blushing, simultaneously shocked and amused by Melody's boldness.

"Aha! But I can see you're not a stranger to love, are you?" she teased. "I myself—" She broke off at an unexpected sound coming from the hallway. "Who could that be?" she mumbled and quickly got up off the bed and strode to where the door still stood slightly ajar, Sr. Sebastian not having closed it all the way. She thrust her head out and peered down the hallway.

"Oh, it's just you," she said.

A man appeared in the doorway, carrying some short boards under one arm and a bag of tools in the other.

"It's just Gunther," Melody said, turning to where Elsie still sat. "Hey, Gunther, this here's a new girl. Name's Elsie."

Gunther nodded in her direction. "Hello," he said politely.

Elsie was surprised to see a man on the upper floors, but as she studied him from where she stood behind Melody, she found him quite unthreatening. He was of average height with a shock of thick blond hair that didn't seem to have been combed in a while and a blond mustache across his upper lip. It was hard to guess his age. His eyes had tiny creases in the corners, but they were bright despite the gold-rimmed glasses he wore, and he seemed boyish and young. He turned his eyes from her back to Melody. "I am here to fix back landing," he explained. "The top step wobbles. Unless I will be disturbing you. Should I come back?"

Elsie had suspected from his name that he might be German, and his accent now confirmed it.

"Oh, you're all right," Melody said. "Won't bother us none, will he, Els?"

"No, but I should get going back downstairs, anyway," Elsie said with a faint smile at Gunther. "Sister Sebastian will be waiting."

Gunther nodded and continued on his way, and Melody popped her head back into the room. "He's the custodian," she explained to Elsie. "You don't have to worry about him. He's really quiet. Keeps to himself. Nice enough, though. If you need anything, just ask him. He can fix or find anything you might need."

"Well, it was nice meeting you, Melody," Elsie said, not sure if she should shake her hand again. "Hopefully, we'll be roommates," she said, venturing a shy smile.

"Roommates? Best friends, I'd say!" she said as Elsie stepped out into the hall. "See you in 1936!" she laughed. "Watch your step there!" she said and then popped back into her room, leaving Elsie to make her way toward where Gunther was already working, laying out his tools.

"Sorry," she said, gingerly stepping over his project.

"It is all right," he said, rising quickly and taking her hand to help her past. His hand was very calloused, something she hadn't felt since she had held her father's hand as a little girl.

"Thank you," she said as she stepped across.

"You are new?" he asked, his eyes kind.

"I . . . well, I'm hoping to be. I'm . . . I have to pass the test first."

"Ah. Good luck to you, then. But I feel you will," he said, bending over to continue arranging his tools.

Why did everyone have more confidence in her than she did herself? Elsie wondered, as she stood watching him. And why did Gunther seem so familiar?

He looked up at her again. "So I will say 'welcome' to you now. You will like it here," he said, giving her another smile, though it oddly seemed a little sad. "The Sisters are kind. The girls, too."

"Thank you," she said and felt a lightness well up inside of her as she made her way down the staircase, so much so that she was tempted to skip down them, but she made herself refrain, of course.

She could not help feeling a little like Alice must have when she tumbled down the rabbit hole into the strange new world of Wonderland. But rather than wanting to get back home, which had been the unfortunate preoccupation of poor Alice, Elsie found herself never wanting to leave. And unlike Alice's experience, this new world was not one of nonsense, but instead made perfect sense and put her at her ease, for once. It was her other reality, the one filled with Ma and Grandfather and Aunt Agatha, that had her racing about amongst the mad hatters and the awful Queen of Hearts, playing games she knew she could never win. Elsie hoped that this was not really a dream, as poor Alice's adventure had been. But if it did indeed prove to be, she hoped it was one from which she would never awake.

Chapter 8

Clive sat stiffly at the head of the board room table, listening to each of his father's—now his—department heads report on the state of Linley Standard.

It was enormously grueling, not only because it was painfully dull, but also because his mind was absorbed with thinking about his father's affairs and the cryptic conversation he had had with Bennett on the telephone. It was Clive's first day reporting for duty at the office, and as much as he was looking for an opportunity to corner Bennett, he was thwarted in this scheme by a steady stream of employees and staff coming to express their condolences and to offer any help in his transition to the helm. Clive, though genuinely touched by their efforts, tried to rush through their sentiments as best he could without seeming obvious, but to no avail. He had thus been occupied all the way up until this current late morning meeting, which had been called to order expressly for Clive's benefit so that he might have a clear picture of where the company stood.

Linley Standard had begun humbly enough as a supplier of auto parts for the emerging Detroit and Chicago automakers that had sprung up about thirty years ago. Their biggest clients were Checker Motors, the Woods Motor Vehicle Company, Thomas B. Jeffery and Co. and, of course, the Cunningham Car Company, which is where

Randolph Cunningham had entered the scene and been introduced to the lovely, young Julia. Alcott had expanded into some of the foreign markets as well, Mercedes Benz and Daimler, to name a couple. Alcott, as Oldrich Exley had stated at his funeral, had proved himself at least a decent man of business, but his true passion, those closest to him knew, lay in the importing and selling of luxury cars, which made the company *some* money, but not as much as did the efforts of men like Sidney Bennett, installed early on by Mr. Hewitt, who wisely diversified early into steel, railroads, and even loans, which consequently had grown the company threefold and had allowed them to weather the Depression, if not easily, than certainly ably.

Indeed, Sidney Bennett was really the brains behind Linley Standard and had had a major role in running much of it through the years, allowing Alcott to remain as its figurehead leader in the eyes of Wall Street and the world beyond, though the board had always suspected the truth. The two men had been happy with the arrangement and had actually become quite close over the years, though they were of different backgrounds and temperaments completely.

Sidney Bennett had been born into poverty but had graduated from Harvard Law School and was noticed by Theodore Hewitt early in his career. Bennett had a razor-sharp mind for the law and for business it turned out, though he alternatively had a quiet disposition and was a man of few words. Shortly after Alcott's wedding to Hewitt's daughter and their installment in Chicago, Hewitt had hired Bennett to help run Linley Standard, as he had promised Alcott he would do. Roughly the same age, the two men had worked out any class prejudices they might have had for each other and very quickly settled into a routine, deciding early on upon a façade to put forward to the stockholders.

So earlier this year when Alcott announced the subject of retiring, though he was only sixty-two, the board, fearing what an announcement of that sort would do to the stock price, was thrown into a panic and insisted that Clive be named Alcott's successor when the time came. Knowing Clive as he did, Alcott seemed reluctant to enforce this condition, but when the board pressed, he argued duty and responsibility until he wrested the required promise from Clive, which satisfied the board for the time being. Most of them were privately skeptical about Clive's ability to run the company, but they knew that naming him as president would quell any jitters the stockholders might have. Anyway, it was a problem they assumed they would not have to deal with for quite some time, especially if they could keep Alcott from retiring.

And then Alcott tragically died.

"Wasn't it damned odd?" many on the board had asked. It was as if Alcott had *known* of his impending death, they mused, and there was more than one whisper of scandal subsequently floating through the halls of Linley Standard immediately following the "accident." "Could Mr. Howard have taken his own life?" some postulated in hushed tones. Most of the staff could not, would not, believe this, however. "Why, Mr. Howard had everything to live for, hadn't he? No sign of any outward trouble at home or otherwise! No, it was simply the way of life, wasn't it?" they reasoned, commenting that life was often stranger than fiction, was it not? No one, however, was fiercer in the squashing of said rumors than Bennett himself, who perhaps alone knew the truth.

Clive had spent the whole of the morning's meeting thus watching Bennett, hoping to catch his eye and wondering just how much he really knew.

The morning after his cryptic midnight call, Clive attempted to telephone Bennett again, but Bennett had not answered, nor had any servant. Clive tried to remember what Bennett's living situation was, whether he was married or not, whether he maintained a house in the city with staff or if he managed on his own. Annoyingly, he realized he knew very little of Bennett's personal life, only that he was his father's right-hand man at the firm.

Not being able to reach him by telephone, Clive contemplated driving to his address to confront him. It was a Saturday, and Henrietta had planned a day-long shopping trip in the city with Julia and Elsie, saying that besides the veritable mountain of Christmas gifts that had to be procured, Elsie needed to be fitted for a new wardrobe before going off to school, that is if he could bear to be parted from her, considering how upset he had been last night. Privately, Clive was of the opinion that a shopping trip for a new college wardrobe for Elsie was a bit pre-mature, not to say optimistic, but he encouraged Henrietta to go, nonetheless. After all, he had some investigation of his own to do. Therefore, he had kissed her good-bye with only the faintest of reservations, reminding her to be careful.

Just to be on the safe side, however, he had a private word with Fritz before they left, instructing him to keep his eyes open and to never be too far from them. Fritz manfully accepted this injunction, though afterward Clive wondered just how much protection Fritz, in his advanced years, could realistically offer. Still, he consoled himself with the fact that he would at least be watching and could call for help if needed. Henrietta, for her part, laughed at Clive's warnings to be careful and playfully kissed him on the cheek, saying that she could take care of herself. Clive was not so sure, but he forced his anxiety into the background, reminding himself of his earlier promises to her.

As soon as she was out of sight, his mind eagerly returned to the question of Bennett, and whether or not it would be wise to drive to his house in the city and try to confront him. He would much rather speak with him privately, rather than at the office, but before he could completely decide on the logistics of such a move, Antonia suddenly burst into the study, saying that his attention was needed immediately in the upstairs gallery.

Clive put down the telephone receiver he had just picked up and sighed. His mother had not been at breakfast, and he knew what he now had to do. He had behaved very badly to her last night, and he was anxious to apologize. "Mother," he said, rising from where he sat behind his father's desk. "I need to beg your pardon for last night. I . . . I wasn't myself. I'm sorry for all those things I said. I was shamefully wrong, of course. Can you forgive me?"

Antonia merely stared at him, unmoving.

"Mother, please," he said.

"Very well, Clive," she said crisply. "Let's speak no more of it, but you hurt me very deeply. You've much to learn if you're truly to be the 'master' here."

"Mother, forget I said that," he said with a groan. "I didn't mean it."

"Well, you can come be master of the house just now upstairs. Your attention is required urgently in the gallery!"

Clive sighed. "Are you sure it's not something Billings can sort out?" he asked tentatively. "It's just that I'm rather busy going through Father's things," he said, gesturing at the stacks of papers in front of him. "As you asked me to."

"No, Clive! It's not something Billings can sort out. Would I be here if it was? Stop treating me like a child!"

Clive could tell by the lines on her face that she was very near some sort of hysterics and that he was treading on thin ice. He had seen her get this way with his father at times, and he had no wish to repeat last night's folly.

"Very well. Of course I'll come with you, Mother," he said, stifling another groan. He made his way out from behind the desk and followed her across the room. As they climbed the staircase in silence, he wondered what it could possibly be. "Can't you just tell me what the matter is?" he asked. "Why the mystery?"

"No, you have to see for yourself."

The "back gallery" was more a long, low hallway than a room. It boasted an intricately coiffed plaster ceiling and walls done up in a rich red flock, upon which hung an extraordinary number of master works of art—another of Alcott's passions—many of which had been pilfered from Linley Castle over the years. Antonia marched swiftly to the very end of the gallery.

"There!" she said, pointing furiously to one of the paintings.

Clive looked at the painting and could see nothing untoward. It was a work by a lesser known American impressionist, Joseph Raphael.

"Yes?" Clive asked, confused, peering at the painting carefully. "I don't understand, Mother. It doesn't appear to be damaged—"

"It's not damaged! It's not supposed to be there! It's the wrong one!"

"What do you mean, the wrong one?"

"The Levitan is supposed to be in that spot, but as you can see, it's gone!"

Clive in truth did not know if this was correct, but he was inclined to believe her. His mind raced to the series of thefts that had occurred in the last months at the hands of Jack Fletcher and even Henrietta's brother, Eugene, but he did not think either of them responsible for a theft of this magnitude. His mind then jumped to a worse suspicion—hadn't this Susan woman asked for a gift? he remembered, his stomach roiling. But had his father really just lifted an exceptionally valuable painting from the wall and given it to her, or sold it and given her the money? Or had he needed the money himself? Clive wondered, thinking of the dangerously low balances in his father's accounts.

"Do you think it was that awful chauffeur?" Antonia asked, her eyes blazing. "It must have been! Clive, I insist you call the police! That painting was worth thousands!"

"Yes, Mother, I'm aware of that. But somehow, I don't think it was Fletcher . . . I think . . ." but Clive broke off there. Obviously, he could not elaborate on any theories that may involve his father's mistress. "Let me investigate. Maybe there's a simple explanation."

"A simple explanation!" Antonia almost shouted. "I can't imagine what that would be, Clive!"

"Perhaps a servant damaged it," he suggested, "and they put a different one there until it could be repaired. Perhaps Billings took it into his mind to have it cleaned. It could be any number of things. It's damned difficult to just up and steal a painting."

Antonia did not respond but seemed perhaps to be considering Clive's words; she stood staring at the imposter painting, clearly still distraught.

"Mother," Clive said tentatively, "was everything all right between you and father? You know, were you . . . how shall I put it? Was everything on the level, as it were?"

"What a singular question, Clive," Antonia said sharply, turning to him. "Yes, of course everything was 'on the level' between us, if I understand you correctly. But what on earth does that have to do with this missing painting?"

"Forgive me, Mother, I . . . things just don't make sense lately, is all. Father's affairs seem not perfectly in order—"

"Clive," she said, exasperatedly. "I really must interject. You are positively driving yourself *mad*." She said this last word as a bit of a hiss. "I acknowledge that you . . . you suffered in the war and that you were a bit . . . addled afterward. Anyone would be, of course, darling, after what you endured, but you must be strong now." She sighed. "I know you think of yourself as the police detective, but all of that is behind you now," she continued patronizingly. "I refuse to allow myself or your father's memory, for that matter, to be subjugated to these . . . these mad theories of yours. There has been no foul play, and the sooner you recognize this, the sooner you will find some peace. I don't mean to be beastly, darling, but you're wrong in this. Quite wrong! You know you are. Please give this up, for all our sakes," she urged. "If you must investigate something, investigate this painting!" she said, her irritation returning as she glanced back at the gallery wall.

Clive rubbed his brow wearily. Obviously she now thought him unbalanced. "Yes, Mother, of course you're right," he managed to get out through gritted teeth, resolving to watch what he said in front of her in future. "Let me ask Billings a few questions, and if I'm not satisfied with the answers he provides I will call in the police."

"Do I have your word?"

"Yes, you have my word."

She left him, then, and instead of spending the afternoon looking for Sidney Bennett as he had intended, he spent it querying Billings, who admitted easily that yes, Mr. Howard—the late Mr. Howard, that is—had instructed him to remove the painting, wrap it securely, and deliver it to a Mr. Kennicott, J. Arthur Kennicott, that is, an art dealer in Lake Forest who had agreed to buy it with the purpose of reselling it to another collector he was in contact with in another part of the country. Yes, Billings staidly responded to Clive's question, he had indeed been paid at the time of transfer. He had been instructed to wait, Billings explained, while Mr. Kennicott painstakingly counted out exactly ten thousand dollars in front of him, wrote a receipt, and neatly stacked the cash in a small attaché case, which Billings then promptly delivered—the case of money and the receipt—to Mr. Howard not two hours later. No, he could not say why Mr. Kennicott paid Mr. Howard in cash rather than a check, though he could think of several reasons which no doubt had probably already crossed Mr. Clive's mind. No, Billings said, he did not know what had become of the money after that, though he assumed that Mr. Howard had put it in the safe in the wall, which was hidden, everyone knew, behind a picture of an English hunting scene hanging behind Mr. Howard's desk.

"Did you not think to tell me of this before, Billings?" Clive asked, irritated.

"No, sir. Why would I, sir?" Billings answered emotionlessly. "Do you expect me to relate to you all of Mr. Howard's instructions to me spanning the course of his lifetime?"

"That's very close to impudence, Billings," Clive snapped.

"I'm very sorry, sir, to be sure."

Clive sighed. "I suppose you have a point, however."

"Will that be all, sir?" Billings asked blankly, his facial muscles immovable.

"Yes, that will be all," Clive said, and once Billings had exited the room, he sat at the desk and buried his face in his hands, knowing as he did—having found the key and looked through the safe yesterday—that it was empty.

The meeting had just been adjourned, Clive's briefing now finished and a temporary plan of action in hand for most of the department heads, many of whom paused to shake Clive's hand once more before they returned to their respective offices. Bennett was not among them, however, and was almost out the door before Clive called to him.

"A word, Mr. Bennett."

Clive saw him stiffen and turn back, shifting his black portfolio under his arm. Clive's request to speak to Bennett seemed to signal everyone else to leave directly, then, and Clive finally found himself alone at last with Sidney Bennett.

"You didn't really think I would let this drop, did you?" Clive asked him, leaning back in his chair at the head of the table.

Bennett gave a halfhearted shrug and looked at him steadily. He was a short man, though he held himself erect. His hair was trimmed short and graying, though Clive, once upon a time, had known it to be brown. His bluish-gray eyes had deep creases in the corners, an obvious by-product of the work and stress of his life thus far, but there was a tired sort of kindness to be found in them too. He did not at all appear to be what one would conjure up as an example of an aggressive Wall Street lawyer, though he did have the reputation of being uncommonly sharp. As he stood looking at Clive now, his normally placid, controlled face was one of concern and worry.

"I had hoped you might leave well enough alone," he said thoughtfully.

"Tell me about Susan."

"It's not what you think—"

"Try me."

Bennett cleared his throat and stepped closer. "Listen, Clive. I've known . . . knew . . . your father for many years. I've watched you grow up, if only from afar. I know a great many things about your father and your . . . your family," he said carefully. "Nothing good can come from opening this up. I beg you—"

"How long did it go on?" Clive asked tightly.

Bennett sighed audibly and paused, as if deciding. Finally, he uttered, "From the very beginning, I believe."

Clive swallowed hard, the blow crushing. Their whole married life? "Who is she? Where do I find her?"

"She?"

"Was she blackmailing him?"

"Clive . . . I think there's been some mistake," Bennett said, confused. "There's no woman involved."

Clive banged his fist on the table. "Damn it, man! Don't lie to me!"

Bennett's face grew red, his own ire apparent now. "I'm not lying," he said testily.

Clive wrenched his father's illicit letter from his inner jacket pocket and tossed it down the table toward where Bennett stood. "How do you explain this, then?" he asked angrily.

Slowly Bennett reached for the letter, unfolded it and skimmed it, his face blanching as he did. "Where did you find this?" he asked, looking up at Clive.

"That is not the relevant question that should have first come to mind," Clive answered. "It implies much. So start explaining."

"I thought I collected them all," Bennett murmured, as he carefully set the letter back down on the table, his hand noticeably trembling a bit. He looked over his shoulder at the closed door of the conference room and then turned back to face Clive. "Yes, I'm pretty sure this Susan, as it says, was getting money from him," Bennett said in a low tone. "But it isn't a woman. It's a man who goes by the name of Susan, and I'm fairly certain he's part of the mob," he said quietly.

Clive felt the hair on the back of his neck rise up a little bit at this revelation. Of course! For a split second he allowed himself to feel the relief of knowing that his father was not involved in a love affair, but that bastion of relief was instantly overwhelmed by a much worse realization. *Jesus Christ! The mob? And for how long? From the beginning*, Bennett had just said. Clive felt an uncharacteristic sense of panic, which he fought to control before it got the better of him.

"They killed him, didn't they?" he asked, wanting to be vindicated in his theory, but desperately not wanting it to be true.

Bennett nodded slowly.

Clive let out the deep breath he hadn't realized he'd been holding. "What happened?" he demanded.

"I don't know all of it, Clive, and that's the truth. God knows I'd tell you if I knew."

"Like you have so far, you mean," Clive snapped.

"If you must know, I was afraid, Clive. Already things have been happening . . . awful things . . ." he whispered.

Clive took a deep breath, trying to control his frantic pulse and his need for more information. "Let's take a step back. Let's start at the beginning. Was he being blackmailed? Or was it simple extortion?"

"I'm not sure. One of them, I'm guessing."

"But what would anyone have over him to use for blackmail?" Clive asked, looking at him acutely.

Bennett shrugged. "I don't know."

Clive observed that he shifted slightly as he said this and wondered if he was telling him the truth. "You said this has been going on 'from the beginning,'" he said slowly. "What does that mean?"

Bennett sighed and gripped the back of one of the chairs at the thick, wooden conference table and leaned against it. "I don't know all the details," he began, "but I think it started shortly after he came here, to Chicago I mean. I had no idea back then what was going on. As the years went on, though, I started to wonder, but it was only this last year that Alcott confided bits of it to me. Well, not really. More like hints."

"Hints? Nothing concrete?" Clive asked impatiently.

"As far as I could make out, he was in the habit of paying a certain sum of money to these characters—let's just call them the mob— much to his own detriment. As far as I know, he only ever used his personal salary."

This would explain the low totals in his father's account books, Clive reasoned and felt a resultant fresh wave of fury.

"So what changed? Did he decide to challenge them? Is that why they killed him?" Clive demanded.

"I don't know everything," Bennett said nervously. "Alcott told me that he didn't want to tell me everything, that it would be too dangerous. But he did show me some of the letters. All I know is that recently this Susan was suddenly demanding a very large payment and that Alcott had a plan to end this whole ridiculous affair," he explained.

"Explain what happened that day. As far as you know. The day he died."

Bennett paused, thinking back. "He was to meet with someone at the train station—"

"On the platform?" Clive interrupted.

"I . . . I believe so."

Clive rubbed his eyes, irritated at the thought of how foolish that had been.

"How do you know this?"

"I was there."

"You were there? Good God, man, why haven't you said so before now?" Clive stood up and began to pace. "You're a witness! Why haven't you gone to the police?" he cried.

"I can explain—"

"No, wait. Go back to the beginning. What the hell happened?"

"Like I said," Bennett began again calmly, "Alcott's plan was to meet these 'ruffians,' as he called them. He intended to give them only half of the money they were demanding, and I was supposed to watch from the other end of the platform so that I could be a witness to the transaction. Then we were going to follow them in my car . . . try to get an address or a license number. Alcott thought that if he had some sort of evidence, he could go to the police."

"That's the worst plan I've ever heard of! It doesn't make an ounce of sense. What would giving them only a fraction of their payment serve? And then *following* them?"

Bennett shrugged uneasily. "I tried to tell him. I tried to tell him that the whole thing was acutely foolhardy. But he was insistent."

"So what happened?"

"I don't think Alcott foresaw that they would actually look in the case. They must have realized that it wasn't all there, and then . . . then a scuffle of sorts ensued, I guess you could say. The train was coming, but they didn't move away from the edge. I didn't actually see it all . . ."

"Even though you were there expressly to be watching?"

Bennett looked away at the accusation. "Yes, I . . . I know," he said grimly. "But it happened so fast. One minute they were arguing and the next I saw Alcott fall . . ." He paused here, as if reliving the scene again in his mind, his face contorting. "Hysteria broke out then . . . I ran down the platform toward him, but by then a crowd was gathering."

"What about the two men?"

"I . . . I lost sight of them, I suppose . . ." Bennett said absently.

"Did you at least get a good look at them? Could you identify them?"

"No," Bennett sighed. "I didn't."

"Damn it! Wasn't that the whole point of planting you there? To get a good look at them?"

"Yes, I'm aware of that!" Bennett said angrily. "Their collars were turned up, and their hats were pulled down. It was nearly impossible to see their faces."

"Did you go after them?"

"And leave your father?"

Clive had to admit he probably would have done the same, though he felt sure his father's death must have been instantaneous. "But why didn't you go to the police?"

"I meant to, Clive," Bennett said uneasily, looking at him furtively. "I think I was in shock at first . . . seeing him die before my eyes. I just didn't think . . ."

Clive was silent for a moment as he tried to assess the situation in a calculating manner without letting emotion cloud his mind. How could his father have put up with this for so many years? he wondered, waffling between pity for him and annoyance, even anger. How could he have mishandled his affairs so badly? How could he have put himself—all of them, probably—in danger for so many years? It was just so confoundedly stupid—the whole ridiculous plan. He couldn't believe it. In fact, this whole story had a flavor of egregious unbelievability to it.

And then another thought occurred to him, his stomach clenching. Perhaps this was all a ruse on Bennett's part. He desperately wanted to believe Bennett, for more reasons than one, considering that the whole of Linley Standard was in his hands, but he had to carefully consider the facts. Bennett's excuse about not going to the police was downright feeble, and he was definitely holding back information, he could tell.

"Hmmm," Clive said tightly. "As a lawyer, you are no doubt aware of how suspect this all sounds." He stared at him now, but Bennett held his gaze, not a trace of fear in it. "I'm thinking," Clive went on smoothly, "that maybe you were in on it." He paused here, watching Bennett's face for a reaction. The resultant dark look of fury surprised him.

"I'll ignore that insult for the moment and put it down to grief—a momentary lapse of reason," Bennett said slowly, his eyes flashing. "But I never want to hear you accuse me ever again."

Clive was tempted to lash back, but he forced himself to remain calm.

"Well, I find some of your answers very singular," he said, still not breaking his gaze. "What did you mean then when you said you thought you had collected all the letters?" Clive asked coolly. "That suggests a great many things. What should I make of that?"

"You do me a gross disservice, Clive," Bennett said thinly.

"Answer the question."

"Yes. All right, yes. I did go to Highbury—to tell your mother myself how Alcott had died. I . . . I didn't want the police to tell her. Didn't she mention that?" Bennett peered up at him, but Clive did not move a muscle except the clenching of his jaw.

"No, she did not. Go on."

"And, yes, I did go into Alcott's study and look for all the letters, just in case—"

"Just in case of what?" Clive interrupted. "In case there was an investigation, which there should have been?"

"No! Not that. It was in case . . . in case Antonia found them. I didn't want her to come to the conclusion you so easily did. I sought to spare her that pain."

Antonia? Was he in the habit of calling his mother by her Christian name? he wondered before he swatted this away to concentrate on the bigger question, namely Bennett's possible involvement in the murder. So far everything he had said was flimsy, to be sure, but remotely plausible, he supposed. Damn it! he fumed. There was more to this. Something he wasn't seeing . . .

"All right," Clive continued evenly, "let's say you really were in shock initially, which prevented you from telling the police that your business partner had just been murdered. Let's go with that for a moment. But then what? Why not go the next day, or the day after that? Why keep quiet?"

Bennett sighed. "I meant to. But I . . . I was afraid," he said quietly. "Terrified, actually. They must have seen me there at the station. Someone must have followed me, or they somehow knew who I was . . ." Bennet drifted off here, as if thinking.

"Yes? And?"

Bennett looked back at him and then continued. "While I was still trying to figure out what to do, I came home the next night and found a rock through my window. I wanted to think it was just an accident or that it had just been some kids. I convinced myself of this eventually, but then about a week later, my tires were slashed. And then last night . . . the night you called, I came home and found my dog dead. His throat had been cut," he said quietly. Bennett looked up at him now, his normally placid eyes containing a hint of fear for the first time in this conversation. "They're obviously watching me, and they want me to know it. Though if they want me dead, why don't they just do it?" he asked hoarsely. Awkwardly, he cleared his throat. "Whoever these men are, Clive," he went on, dryly, "they're very dangerous. And I don't think they're through yet."

Clive's mind immediately went to Henrietta, even at this moment roaming somewhere around the city with Julia and Elsie, with only the somewhat elderly Fritz to watch over them. He felt a sudden, desperate urge to dash out of the office and find her, but he refrained, trying to convince himself that he was overreacting, though he was aware of the fact that he had already broken into a thin sweat. He looked at Bennett, standing before him with his hands thrust awkwardly in his pockets. His mind was lingering on the brink of fear. He tried to bring it back and instead concentrate on what was before him.

"Listen, Bennett," he said, clearing his throat. "You're right. If they meant to kill you, you'd probably be dead by now."

"That's hardly comforting."

Clive let this pass. "They want something else."

"The missing cash?" Bennett offered.

"Probably. Any idea where it is?"

Bennett looked at him, puzzled. "You haven't found it?"

Clive shook his head, studying him. Something still wasn't sitting well. "Maybe he never had it," he said, deciding to test him.

"But I know he did. He sold that painting."

So he knew about the painting, too.

"It's not in the safe behind his desk?" Bennett suggested.

Did everyone know about his father's blasted "secret" safe? Clive thought disgustedly. "No, it's not," he answered. Again he considered Bennett's story. A rock through the window, tires slashed? Come on! he thought suspiciously, this was the stuff of comic books. But what reason would Bennett have to lie? The man seemed genuinely upset, truly frightened. And yet . . .

"Have you ever been in the house before? I mean, without my father being there?" Clive asked.

Bennett's previously distraught face became rigid now, clearly angered again. Slowly he removed his hands from his pockets, gathered up his black portfolio, and stiffly slung it under his arm. "You have nothing to gain by following that line of thought, Clive," he said finally. "But if you persist in distrusting me, then so be it. I was your father's closest business associate—nay, friend—and I remain so, despite what you might think. We are not enemies in unraveling the mess we find your father's affairs in. You can disparage me all you want, but I warn you, you should tread lightly. You're probably being watched as well."

Without waiting for Clive's response, Bennett turned and walked out of the room. Clive thought of calling him back, but there was nothing left to say. Angrily, he pounded the table with his fist, which served, if nothing else, to hide his trembling.

Chapter 9

Elsie stood uncomfortably next to Aunt Agatha at the annual Exley winter ball, dressed in a beautiful blue silk evening dress. It was a Worth creation and flattered her shape as much as any dress could, but the fact that it stopped at the bust, leaving her shoulders and arms bare, unfortunately drew unwanted attention to Elsie's propensity to stand with rounded posture unless perpetually reminded. Elsie couldn't help it, however; she had never gone about in such a revealing dress before, and it made her feel decidedly risqué and self-conscious, causing her to try to compensate by hunching herself forward even more than she normally did. Despairingly, she wondered if Aunt Agatha had chosen this dress for a reason . . . an immodest dress for an immodest girl, or something like that, and her face burned doubly with shame.

In fact, Agatha Exley had chosen Elsie's gown for its color, hoping it would accent what she considered Elsie's best feature, her very blue eyes, and for its obvious fashion statement. A Worth gown would be recognized by all the mamas in the room as an immediate mark of not just wealth, which they could all claim, but excessive wealth.

Oldrich Exley, her father-in-law, had recently paid Agatha a visit in which he expressed to her the need to get Elsie married, and married well, and that she should step up her efforts. Agatha had then dared to bring up the current rather obvious obstacle to the plan, which was, of course, Elsie's intent to become educated, saying that perhaps they should wait to see where that might lead, but Mr. Exely had snarled and said, "Certainly not!" He was allowing Henrietta and Elsie to briefly indulge in this fantasy, he had said, convinced that it would come to nothing; he was sure of it. Agatha had then timidly suggested that perhaps a bit of time was wanting, anyway, as she had heard unpleasant whisperings among the gilded set as to Elsie's predilection for a certain lieutenant. Alice Stewart's name was then usually also mentioned in these same whisperings, and the fact that their two names occupied the same conversation could not help but tarnish Elsie, even if just a little. Mr. Exely had emitted a type of frustrated growl, then, and told Agatha to "get on with it!"

And so Agatha had dutifully tried to "get on with it." Not only had she chosen a beautiful gown and an exquisite rope of diamonds to wind about Elsie's neck, she had also had her dirty-blonde hair curled and twisted into the latest fashion and was determined to stick next to her for the whole of the evening, though she dearly would have rather spent it gossiping with her bosom friends from the club, particularly Antonia. But Antonia wasn't there, anyway, having begged off this year, saying she just wasn't up for it, and Agatha could understand why. They all missed Alcott terribly; their foursome was no more. John, her husband, felt his loss keenly and had been in an absolute slump since Alcott's death.

Still, this evening called for merriment and festivity, and Agatha, never one to shy from duty, bravely bucked herself up. She only wished they were standing closer to the food. When she had months ago agreed to take Elsie under her wing to introduce her to society, she had no idea that it would be so taxing! With two sons already satisfactorily married, it had been years since she had had to worry about all of these details.

She looked over at Elsie now, unattractively shifting her weight and picking at the fabric of her velvet gloves. Her weight, Agatha noticed, was noticeably less these days, though she would still be considered a bit thickset. Perhaps Elsie had decided after all to employ the vigorous exercises illustrated in the *Method of Calisthenics for Young Ladies* booklet that Agatha had slid across the table toward her at tea one afternoon. Elsie's face had turned beet-red as she had picked it up and looked it over, but she had not outright rejected it, just politely slipped it into her handbag. Neither of them had had the good manners to mention it again, but perhaps Elsie was employing its directives after all.

Agatha positively quivered at the thought that Elsie had so nearly slipped from her fingers into the arms of Barnes-Smith. She had been as shocked as anyone; hadn't she repeatedly warned her away from him? She had tried to question Elsie about it not long after she had returned from her respite at the Cunningham's, but the girl had remained characteristically silent. Agatha had eventually given up trying to extract information about it and allowed herself to simply be glad that Elsie had so narrowly escaped a disaster, which Agatha felt sure she herself would have been blamed for, and to leave it at that.

Chaperoning Elsie and schooling her in the ways of higher society was certainly proving to be more intricate and time-consuming than she had first imagined, but it oddly gave Agatha a sense of purpose she hadn't felt in quite some time. Like a shepherdess, perhaps, is how she saw herself, with Elsie being her flock of one. But for this one incident of wandering from the fold, Agatha reflected that Elsie was usually a rather easy sheep to tend, all things considered. That's why it was hard to understand Elsie's current desire to go to college, of all things. It was preposterous, to be sure; what would a girl need with an education? She had to admire the pluck it had taken Elsie to voice this, and yet it seemed so terribly out of character for the normally docile Elsie that Agatha had begun to suspect that perhaps it had never really been Elsie's idea at all. This had more the flavor to it of the sister, Henrietta. And if that were true, perhaps Father Exley was right in that this was a fantasy that would soon fizzle out.

At any rate, Agatha had seen the wisdom of Oldrich Exley's desire for Elsie to be married sooner rather than later. She was already eighteen, certainly old enough. She herself had been only seventeen when she became engaged to John Exley, and it had not done her any harm. Therefore, she had stepped up her efforts. She had tried in the past to scold, and lately she had tried friendly persuasion, but nothing seemed to have the desired effect. What was wrong with the girl? she ruminated with a sigh. After all, she had been brought up from the dregs of society into a world of privilege and promise; what more could she want? Granted, she was not the beauty that Henrietta was, but she wasn't bad. And she was quiet and reserved, obliging; that would go far. At least she *had* been, anyway, but lately Elsie did not respond to her in quite the same subservient way as she had previously done. She seemed different somehow after the incident with Barnes-Smith, more sullen and depressed, as if she carried around a heavy burden now. Only in the last couple of weeks, since she had begun her tutoring at that school, had she brightened.

Agatha prided herself on her ability to recognize "affairs of the heart" as she called them. It was quite an extraordinary exception, really, that she had not earlier detected the extent of Elsie's crush on either the lieutenant or on that Stanley Dubowski, for that matter, and put down this failure in her normally acute assessment of any persons around her that might think themselves or, in fact, to actually *be* in love, as a sort of bizarre aberration. Yes, she had begrudgingly admitted to herself, she had failed, nearly tragically, to realize the depth of Elsie's attachment, but she happily knew the remedy for such angst—another love affair, of course!—which fit the current plan perfectly. Affairs of the heart such as Elsie had found herself embroiled in were fleeting at best, she knew, and easily mended. No harm done, or not much anyway. Surely Elsie had not been "interfered with" as the whisperings had hinted at, Agatha told herself, looking over at Elsie once again now and studying her carefully. A girl like Elsie would never submit to such advances, she was sure, though plenty of young women seemed to these days. What was the world coming to? she had exasperated more than once to the ladies of the club in hushed tones. Victoria Braithwaite blamed the war, and Agatha was inclined to agree. After that had come the flappers—women smoking, drinking openly, and engaging in sexual relations outside of marriage! Surely, she knew one or two women who had succumbed to their baser desires before their wedding night, but only when they were engaged, or very nearly so, anyway . . . No, not Elsie. She could not believe it of her. She would snap out of her malaise soon, she was sure of it.

She looked distractedly around the room for Phoenicia Burnham, who had agreed to pressure her son, Garfield, to dance with Elsie for at least one dance. Where was he?!

"Are you having a good time, dear?" Agatha asked Elsie sweetly, turning her attention back to her charge. "Perhaps you should not fidget with your gloves," she added, knitting her own hands together. "That is what children do."

"Yes, Aunt Agatha," Elsie said dully, standing up straight.

Then, as if on cue, Garfield Burnham waddled up, puffing slightly, causing Agatha to breathe a sigh of relief—at last, he had appeared! She could have sworn she heard Elsie groan, but she ignored it.

"May I have the next dance?" he asked Elsie breathlessly in a monotone voice, as if he had memorized this line.

Elsie considered the man—a boy, really—before her, and knew he had of course been put up to asking her. She wanted nothing more but to run from the room, but she instead forced herself to put her hand in his and be led to the dance floor. Garfield Burnham was not much taller than she, and to say that he was merely "portly" would be a kindness. He had tight, curly black hair, heavily greased in an attempt to part it down the middle. He had tiny, black eyes set above puffy cheeks that peered at her from behind his spectacles. What was peculiar about him was not the fact that he lacked even a shred of conversational skills, but rather that his beefy fingers on her back had a way of indenting themselves into her flesh, even through the fabric of her dress. He appeared to be completely unconscious of this as he spoke blandly of the weather or what his mother thought of this or that. Was he really not aware of what he was doing or how distasteful it might be to her?

Elsie gritted her teeth and resolved to endure the dance, though she desperately wanted to cry. Not because of Garfield's thick fingers pressing into her, really, but because Aunt Agatha, and indeed all of the old biddies standing near her aunt now, seemed so approving and pleased for her that she had been asked to dance at all, even though it was only by the likes of someone such as Garfield Burnham. Is that all the better they thought she could do? Was a dolt such as Garfield really to be her destiny? She knew that it was wicked to judge him so quickly, but she couldn't help it. And she could tell that neither was he particularly enamored of her. He was merely obliging his mother, she suspected, just as she was obliging Aunt Agatha.

Never had she been so relieved for a dance to end. Garfield dutifully returned her to Aunt Agatha, who stood on the edge of the crowd looking out, probably wondering where all the men were that she had cajoled into dancing with her miserable self.

Elsie hated these parties now. All those many years in which they had been poor, she had longed to live a fairy-tale life such as this. They had gone from poor to rich in the space of an instant, but like all fairy tales, there had been a price to pay. She felt fraudulent and almost immoral most of the time, as if they had somehow sold themselves to Rumpelstiltskin or to the devil himself. She hadn't minded their old life, not really, though the times when Doris and Donny had cried themselves to sleep at night from hunger had been terrible, she had to admit. But to be put on display for any random man, rich enough to play the game, to pluck and do with her what he may, seemed repulsive—more than repulsive, actually. Why couldn't she be left alone?

Aunt Agatha had increased her attentions to her lately, taking her to more theater productions, operas, and ballets than she had ever done in the past. So many times, she had tried to beg off, saying that it was essential that she stay home and study for her upcoming entrance exam, but it had fallen on deaf ears. It was almost as if Aunt Agatha hoped she would fail. But that was ungenerous, thought Elsie. In truth, she knew that Aunt Agatha had been very kind to her. And she believed that her aunt actually did like her, but she couldn't help but sometimes remember that she was merely following Grandfather's commands.

So it was that she was forced into attending many such galas as this one, the Christmas season bringing even more opportunities to mix with the gilded set, prompting her to get up very early in the morning each day, the only free time left to her to study. In this way, she tried to imagine she wasn't too far from the life the Sisters at Mundelein themselves led, getting up early to pray and to work. Indeed, she had gotten the idea from them and took strength from their example. In fact, she was inspired by them to perhaps take a different step, and a radical one, at that.

She looked up now and saw another man approaching her with a slow, confident pace that unnerved her. It was Lloyd Aston, whom she had met several times before at various gatherings. She never knew quite what to make of Mr. Aston, as he seemed aloof most of the time, usually greeting her, if not warmly, then at least politely. If they ever happened to be seated next to each other at a dinner, he seemed perfectly able to make charming small talk, but nothing more.

Elsie supposed he could be called handsome. He was taller than most, with ginger hair and a sharp, angular face. His brown eyes looked her over, lingering just briefly on her very bare chest, before he then turned to Aunt Agatha and politely greeted her.

"May I have this dance, Miss Von Harmon?" he asked casually, turning back to Elsie now, his voice rich with superiority. "Or are you engaged for this next one?" Elsie couldn't be sure, but she thought he emphasized the word "engaged" a bit too heavily. Was it a reference to Harrison? She wanted to dash from the room, but she forced herself to count to five in her mind.

"No, I'm not, Mr. Aston," she made herself say. She desperately wanted to spurt out some witty retort, but she couldn't think of anything. She felt Aunt Agatha's hand on her back then, and she knew what she was supposed to say. "I'd be happy to dance with you," she said in a low voice and placed her hand lightly in his. He gripped it with surprising strength for one who acted so languidly most of the time and led her to the dance floor.

As the waltz began, neither of them spoke, which increased Elsie's agitation immensely.

"I haven't seen you in quite some time," he said finally, peering down at her.

"No . . . I've not been well."

"Yes, I heard something along those lines," he said with a sly grin.

Elsie felt her stomach clench. Did everyone on the North Shore know of her stupidity?

"Oh, you've nothing to worry about with me," he said, obviously sensing her discomfort, as his hand moved down just a fraction of an inch on her back. "I like a girl with a bit of spunk," he said into her ear.

"I . . . I think you are mistaken, Mr. Aston," Elsie said quietly, not looking at him and instead staring straight ahead at the other couples swirling about them.

Lloyd Aston chuckled. "Oh, I think not. I'm a pretty good judge of character. And I think I've got you pretty well pegged, Elsie . . . am I allowed to call you Elsie?"

Elsie's face grew very warm at his suggestiveness. It didn't really matter to her if he called her Elsie, but she was conscious of the lack of respect it implied. Not only that, but she knew Aunt Agatha would highly disapprove. Before she could answer, however, he went on.

"The truth is, I think we could be rather good together. Have a spot of fun and all that. Away from all of this malarkey," he said, nodding his head toward the opulence of the room. "You're quite pretty, in your own way, do you know that?" he asked, looking into her eyes in a way that disturbingly called up Harrison to her mind. Hadn't he said something just like that?

"I . . . I think you must be teasing me, Mr. Aston. And it's very unkind," Elsie said, forcing herself to look at him for a moment before averting her eyes again.

"Well, perhaps I am," he chuckled. "Thought you wouldn't mind a bit of teasing, you being that sort of girl," he said wickedly.

Stunned, Elsie made a move to break away from him, but he held her tight.

"Oh, no you don't. No escaping just yet."

"I'm feeling ill," Elsie insisted. "I'd like to sit down now, if you don't mind."

"Come, come. You and I have a lot in common," he said, spinning her.

Elsie found herself getting angry. "Please stop, Mr. Aston. Stop toying with me. It's cruel."

"Oh, I'm not toying with you, Elsie. I'm very much in earnest."

"And please don't . . . don't call me Elsie. It's . . . it's presumptuous," she managed to say boldly.

Lloyd let out a little laugh. "As you wish, then, *Miss* Von Harmon," he said finally as he gave her hand a tight squeeze. "But you can't fool me. I know all about girls like you."

"Ow! You're hurting me!" she exclaimed, though she was careful to keep her tone hushed.

"Oh, I *am* sorry," he said, though he waited a few moments before relaxing his grip.

Elsie did not look at him.

"Let me make it up to you," he said, grinning. The dance had ended then, and he began to lead her back to her party. "Tell you what, how about tomorrow? The aquarium? Are you free?"

"No, I'm not," she said crisply. "Thank you, anyway."

They had reached Aunt Agatha now, who stood watching hopefully, a full glass of champagne in her hand.

"I was just asking Miss Von Harmon if she would like to accompany me to the aquarium tomorrow, Mrs. Exley," Lloyd said loudly.

"Oh! What a splendid idea!" Agatha exclaimed. "Elsie would love to go, wouldn't you, Elsie?"

"Well, I . . . no, I have some studying to do, Aunt Agatha . . . my test is the very next day." Elsie tried to plead with her eyes, but Agatha seemed determined to ignore her.

"Nonsense!" Agatha exclaimed, frowning at Elsie. "She'd be happy to, Mr. Aston," she said, smiling up at Lloyd sweetly.

"Excellent. One o'clock?"

"Certainly!" Agatha twittered, smiling broadly.

"Until then, Miss Von Harmon," he said, bowing slightly to her and giving her an obnoxious wink before sauntering away. Elsie watched him wander toward another group of young people and join them. He said something to all of them, and they responded with laughter, one or two of them looking over at her now. Humiliated, Elsie turned her back to them.

"Elsie! What do you think you're doing! Saying that you'd rather stay home and study than entertain Lloyd Aston? Have I not taught you better than that?" she hissed. "Fine and good if you were trying to be coy, but use some other excuse—you had a recital to attend or some such thing. Men don't want wives who are educated. Or clever, for that matter. You can be clever, of course, but the trick is to not let them know that. They need to feel they are superior, you see."

Elsie was rather sure Lloyd Aston did not need any help in that department. "But I don't like him," Elsie complained.

"Why ever not? He's polite, handsome, and very wealthy. He was at Harvard with my Clifton, who tells me he wouldn't be surprised if he became a senator one day. He's apparently a very brilliant lawyer. You should feel flattered by his attention, Elsie! What's wrong with you, girl?"

Elsie sighed. She supposed Aunt Agatha would never really understand her. She hardly did herself. She had tried to tell Aunt Agatha about her studies and about all of the rich girls at Mundelein, thinking that would impress her, but she merely poo-pooed it as a passing . . . what would you call it? she asked—a hobby, until she was suitably married. But why did she have to get married? Elsie wondered for the hundredth time. While it had certainly always been her most cherished dream to fall in love and belong to someone, to be someone's wife, her dalliances with love had twice gone rather badly, and she couldn't help but think that the ship of love had sailed without her. Besides, who would want her now? Only the worst sort of men; men like Lloyd Aston who perhaps knew of her disgrace and sought to use it against her for their pleasure. It made her feel sick inside.

She tightly gripped the champagne glass that Agatha had thrust at her and thought about what her future really held. Despite Henrietta's disparaging comments about being a teacher, she had begun to think that she might actually be happy in that. Indeed, the thought that she could be looked up to and respected in that way was almost dizzying to her and filled her with a deep sort of longing, almost an ache. She longed to be truly useful, and what better way than to teach others what she so enjoyed learning herself?

She had tentatively mentioned this notion to Sr. Bernard one afternoon after she had finished with her lessons, and not only had Sr. Bernard not laughed, but she had been very encouraging and had urged Elsie to pray about it. Elsie had taken Sr. Bernard's advice to heart and had indeed begun praying more intently about her future and about possibly becoming a teacher. And so it was that as she knelt with the sisters in their chapel, her mind had sometimes even gone one step further. An idea had come upon her which she had hardly dared to look at first, but one which was nonetheless gaining a hold on her heart. It was the realization that perhaps she had a vocation, a calling to take Holy Orders and become a nun. It had seemed outrageous at first, ludicrous, even loathsome in a way, but then it had changed. Then it became an intriguing thought, an interesting one, and then a very desirable one. And just lately she was beginning to feel that it was perfect, actually, and when she allowed herself to pull it out and examine it, it made her tremble now at the beauty of it. Yes, she would have to give up a husband and a family, but a marriage born of true love and not convenience—nay opportunity—seemed impossible anyway. And she correspondingly saw, with shocking clarity, that it was a perfect way to escape having to marry someone like Lloyd or Garfield or any of the others the Exley's flung at her. Instead, she would be allowed to gloriously spend her life studying and teaching, maybe even tending a garden somewhere. What more could she ask for? And as for children, why—she would be surrounded by children as a teacher. She would try to see them as her own. The idea had definitely gained on her these last few weeks, seeming to be the perfect solution to all of her woes, but which made evenings such as tonight and dates to the aquarium not only ridiculous, but likewise a colossal waste of time.

But she didn't dare tell anyone. No one, she knew, would understand her in this, even and especially Henrietta. No, it was a secret that she must keep to herself, at least for now. Sr. Bernard had advised her to pray, and so she did. Her quiet presence among the sisters had not gone unnoticed, it seemed, as Sr. Bernard had just recently kindly invited her to attend evening vespers with them after her studies were finished, and she sometimes even stayed to say the rosary with them, which gave her much comfort.

"You will go with Lloyd Aston tomorrow, Elsie," Aunt Agatha sniffed. "There is no reason not to."

"Yes, Aunt Agatha," Elsie agreed reluctantly, knowing there was no way out of it, and quickly gulped the rest of her champagne, likewise knowing, hoping, actually, that her days of drinking something so luxurious were limited indeed.

Chapter 10

Henrietta stood at a low table in the library at Highbury wrapping gifts. She had finished all of her shopping, or hoped she had, anyway, just yesterday with Julia. They had made a last trip downtown to Marshall Fields and had luncheoned at the Walnut Room. Henrietta already knew what she wanted to get Clive, delighting in the fact that she had money to spend on real Christmas gifts for the first time in her life, but she had needed help when it came to selecting something for Antonia. In the end, she had selected a beautiful Cartier broach, which Julia said her mother would be sure to love. Henrietta hoped so.

She had always known that living at Highbury was going to take some getting used to after they returned from their honeymoon, but Alcott's death had made it all the more difficult and confusing. As the unfortunate incident in the drawing room the other night with James indicated, no one was sure of their roles now, and the three of them were almost daily trying to balance the power between them. And to add to this, in the last week or so, Antonia's previously subdued, grieving manner had given way to a sullen irritability that at times reminded Henrietta of Ma, actually. Antonia, when she was with them, usually sat quietly, her lips drawn together tightly, but every so often a fierceness burst forth from her, revealing the still-raw wound beneath.

The turning point in her behavior seemed to have been the discovery of the missing painting, the story of which Clive had, of course, already shared with Henrietta. Since then, Antonia had become critical in the extreme of everyone around her, especially Clive, whom she saw as not acting fast enough in regard to the whereabouts of the painting and the subsequent apprehension of a culprit. It was the fixation point upon which her grief seemed to gather. Henrietta had suggested to Clive that it might be best simply to tell Antonia what he had discovered, that Alcott had sold the painting for the needed cash and leave it at that. But Clive was of the opinion that his mother would persist further and that it would open a whole barrage of questions, most of which he wasn't in a position to answer at this point. Better to keep her in the dark, he had said, at least for now, but that meant he had to endure constant hints as to his incompetence as well as threats of calling the police herself.

But if she was critical of Clive for his slowness in this matter, she was equally critical of his haste in others, at least as she saw it. When he had recently, for example, brought up the topic of making some much-needed changes to Highbury over breakfast with her one morning, Antonia had balked, saying that there was certainly no need to change anything at all. Clive had then gone on to point out that, among other things, the servants' rooms above the auto-garage had not been updated in years, describing to her the squalid details that he and Henrietta had observed when questioning Virgil about old Helen's missing ring this past summer. Reluctantly, Antonia had agreed that, yes, something must be done there, if that's what he meant by changes, but she had then infuriatingly circled back to his previous, idiotic declaration of wanting to be master of the house. It was all he could do, he later told Henrietta, to remain calm at that point, but he had done it, reminding his mother that the whole reason he had agreed to give up being a detective was to devote himself to Highbury, as both she and his father had so desperately wanted. Updating the servants' quarters was hardly playing "master of the house," he had allowed himself to retort, to which she had advised him to watch his tone. Rather than continue this line of discussion, Clive had shifted subjects to one he assumed would breach no arguments, that being the obvious dismissal of his father's valet, Carter, who had been in Alcott's employ since he had arrived in America to wed Antonia. Indeed, he had brought Carter with him from Castle Linley.

"I'll speak to Carter this week," Clive had said. "Make sure his references are in order and get him sorted."

"What are you talking about?" Antonia had asked with such acrimony that it caused Clive to look up at her over the newspaper he had casually picked up. "You can't do that, Clive!"

"Why not?" he said, refolding the newspaper now. "You don't mean to keep him on, do you?"

"Of course, I do!"

"As what?" Clive asked, truly puzzled. "We can't demote him to footman, and we can't give him Billings's job—"

"I assumed he would become your valet," Antonia said crisply.

"Not this again. I told you, Mother, I don't want a valet! And, anyway, isn't he past sixty?"

"Exactly why we can't turn him out! How can you be so heartless?"

Clive was taken aback by his mother's strong reaction; he had not expected it at all. Indeed, he thought she might be grateful to be finally rid of the man, his dour countenance never very welcoming over the years. In truth, he had never understood his father's continued employment and, worse, his over-reliance on Carter. In Clive's mind, he was adequate at best and hopelessly dull—his thin graying hair greased and combed back neatly. Growing up, Clive had neither liked nor disliked Carter. He had always just been there, smelling faintly of camphor oil and always attempting to shoo him and Julia away when Father wasn't looking.

Before Clive could think of what exactly to say to his mother, she informed him coolly that she would not "turn Carter out of this house" and threatened to give him the cottage if Clive did not continue to employ him. Clive recognized this as a particularly low blow, as she knew how special the cottage was to Henrietta and him, having spent their first few nights of wedded bliss there. Also, Clive knew that Henrietta had some silly idea of giving the cottage to Edna and Virgil, should they ever get themselves engaged, though why a perfectly nice girl like Edna should ever cast her hat at the likes of Virgil was beyond him. But that was a different story. In the end, he had agreed to reconsider Carter's position and had curtly excused himself from the breakfast table.

When he related the whole of the story to Henrietta later in their private sitting room, she advised him to take on Carter. After all, she said, what harm would there be, really? Carter didn't seem a bad sort, and, besides, it would be good to let Antonia busy herself somewhat with the servants to take her mind off her grief and possibly the missing painting, of which they never ceased to hear. Clive smiled at this and slyly accused her of selfishly wanting to keep Carter on so that she might have the cottage for her own devices. She laughed at this but added that perhaps keeping Carter served another purpose. Perhaps he knew more than he was saying about Alcott's untimely end.

"What I don't understand is why your father would have entrusted the selling of the painting to Billings and not Carter. Don't you think that odd?" Henrietta asked him.

"I suppose because Billings might have more wherewithal in those types of matters."

"Did you at least question Carter?"

"Of course, I've questioned Carter," Clive said with a roll of his eyes. "He claims he knows nothing about the selling of any painting or Susan or any 'disagreeable activities' is what I think he said. Says Father seemed a bit out of sorts the day he . . . was murdered, but nothing too unusual. Said that after he finished dressing him for the morning, Father wanted a minute or two to himself before going down, which was not his usual habit. Couldn't tell me anything else, said he didn't know what all of this signified, anyway."

"Do you think he's holding back?"

"No, I don't think so. He's a crotchety old git. A bit doddering, to be honest. I don't know what the devil I'm going to do with him. Why on earth would Mother want to keep him on?"

"Maybe it's just familiarity? Maybe he reminds her of Alcott, makes him seem less gone somehow?" Henrietta offered.

Clive inclined his head in thoughtful acknowledgment while he puffed his pipe, a cloud of smoke encircling him now.

"Have you gotten any further with Bennett?" she asked. Clive had also told her all that Bennett had revealed to him that day in the boardroom and the fact that after going through the last of his father's things in his study, he had indeed found his personal accounts drained these many years. He did not find any more incriminating letters, however, nor had he found the supposed missing money, the half of the ten thousand dollars from the sale of the painting that Alcott had not, according to Bennett, anyway, turned over to this Susan and his thugs.

Henrietta had been initially prone to believe that perhaps it had been Bennett himself who had taken the money. Even after Alcott's death, perhaps. After all, she suggested, hadn't he admitted to being in the house?

Clive looked at her, his eyes keen with pleasure. "Yes, actually, that crossed my mind too." He grinned at her. "You're becoming quite the detective, darling," he said, and Henrietta blushed with pride. "We certainly can't rule it out," he went on, "but if that were true, why wouldn't Bennett have lied and just said that Father gave Susan the whole of the money?"

Henrietta paused as if to think. "I'm not sure," she said finally. "But I still think it might have been him. Or he's somehow involved, anyway."

"Maybe," Clive answered thoughtfully.

"Maybe you just don't want to believe that of Bennett," she suggested softly.

Clive considered this and realized that what Henrietta said was true. There was a part of him that didn't want to believe Bennett was lying, that he wanted him to be telling the truth. He thought through their conversation one more time. No, Bennett had seemed genuinely afraid of someone or something.

"Clive, don't you think that perhaps you should go to the police at this point? You mentioned that Detective . . . Davis, was it? He might be worth talking to."

"You sound unattractively like my mother, hounding me to go to the police about the bloody painting."

"But you have evidence now that Alcott was a victim of at least extortion and very probably murder."

"I don't really have any hard evidence at this point. It's all circumstantial."

"You've got the note; that's real!"

"Yes, but it's not enough. And anyway, what's Davis to do at this point that I'm not already doing?" Clive asked, though he could not help but remember what Bennett had said about them probably being watched. His eyes shifted to the window, but all was dark without. Privately, he worried that these criminals might just reappear to claim the rest of what they considered to be their money. But then again, perhaps they had decided to cut their losses and run. After all, they had no claim on him personally. Surely, whoever they were, they wouldn't be so stupid as to attempt to extort money from a detective.

"I don't know," Henrietta answered, "but if you're not careful, your mother will fulfill her threats and go to the police herself."

Clive sighed. Henrietta was right. His mother was growing more and more impatient each day, but he would just try to stay one step ahead of her.

As it turned out, however, Clive was not the only object of Antonia's criticisms, which Henrietta, to her dismay, had unfortunately discovered. Antonia, in her grief, had become rather short with Henrietta as well and daily seemed to find something to critique regarding her dress, hair, language, or even how she spent her free time. Her underhanded remarks lacked bite, however, and Henrietta was usually able to swat her reproofs away without sustaining too much of a sting, having grown up with Ma, after all. Her solution was to try to simply stay out of Antonia's way as much as possible, which wasn't too difficult, as Antonia spent a great deal of time in the morning room catching up on correspondence, of which there was much after the funeral. Likewise, as the chairwoman of several committees at the club, Antonia bravely continued to fulfill her various duties, despite her personal grief, by attending the required meetings and functions, but she did not linger afterwards as she had previously been wont to do. These days, she returned promptly and then spent the afternoons attempting to read or receiving visitors, sometimes Agatha Exley, but usually Julia, who was making more appearances of late, though Henrietta wondered at what price, being under the cruel thumb of Randolph as she was. Henrietta much preferred Julia's visits to Agatha's, as with Agatha, the conversation tended to inevitably veer to the uncomfortable topic of Elsie if Henrietta was somehow present. It had become apparent rather quickly that Agatha now saw Henrietta as a sort of adversary who was consciously attempting to wrest control of her pet project.

There was once, however, when Henrietta had come directly under fire, and it was made worse by the fact that not only had she not predicted the weapon Antonia would choose to use, but that she had also not seen it coming. It occurred one afternoon during which she happened to be sitting with Antonia, privately, having tea. Antonia had begun what seemed to be a pleasant *tête-à-tête* by expressing to Henrietta how very glad she was that she was here amongst them now. Henrietta was not sure if this was really true, but she decided to take it on face value for the moment. Antonia had then taken the opportunity to share that just that morning she had received a letter from Lady Linley at Castle Linley, who had written to say that Wallace's wife, Amalie, had had another boy and that they had named him Alcott Alban Montague Howard. Antonia had related this last bit of news with small tears in her eyes. While she was very touched by her nephew's gesture, she had said, as she looked across at Henrietta, dabbing each eye with her handkerchief, grateful, to be sure, that they had honored Alcott in this way, she had rather hoped that she and Clive might have someday chosen that name for their own son.

Antonia had then looked questioningly at Henrietta and asked if there might be anything they wished to announce? Any news in that department? Not that she wished to pry of course, but it would be such joyful news following Alcott's death to know that his legacy would continue. Was there any problem, anything she might be able to advise on? Antonia had asked, which Henrietta slowly realized was not only a criticism of her clearly un-pregnant state but also one which she saw as being somehow Henrietta's fault, as if it were due to some deficiency in her.

Henrietta was cut to the quick, stunned at how Antonia had somehow found a way in to her most vulnerable spot and discovered the best way to wound her. She sat in silence as Antonia went on to say, with shockingly no trace of shame on her pallid cheeks, that it was quite normal to be hesitant about marital union, but that one got used to it eventually and that it was indeed her Christian duty to submit to her husband. At this, Henrietta's feelings of guilt and incompetency gave way to extreme outrage, and she struggled to hold in the many angry retorts that were filling her mind. How dare Antonia suggest such things! She wished she could describe her wildly passionate nights of lovemaking with Clive, but of course that would be grossly inappropriate. Instead, she cleared her throat as she slowly stood up and managed to reply that, "No, there is no announcement just yet," and then excused herself from the tea table.

As provoked and offended as she was by the injustice of Antonia's snide accusations, they had indeed hit the mark, and all of Henrietta's old worries and fears of inadequacy began to surface. Indeed, Henrietta had almost been in tears later that night in their wing, when she had told Clive about the conversation she had had that day with Antonia and her feelings of failure in not producing a child for him.

Clive's response was to put his arms around her and hold her close.

"You mustn't mind Mother," he said, looking down at her. "She's not herself just at the moment."

"Yes, I know that, but maybe she's right. Maybe there's something wrong with me," Henrietta said in a low voice.

Clive surprised her by laughing loudly. "There's absolutely nothing wrong with you, darling. And anyway, what need have I of a child when I have you?" he said with a grin. He paused for a moment and added, "That sounds rather wrong, doesn't it?" He laughed again, but Henrietta did not join in.

"Henrietta," he said more seriously now, "I told you before our wedding that I have all I will ever want or need in this life as long as I have you. Frankly, I don't care if we ever have a child. Perhaps it would be for the best. Save the bugger all this worry," he said, looking around the room wryly. "And, anyway, perhaps I'm a little gun-shy. After what happened with Catherine. I couldn't bear it if I lost you, Henrietta," he said, caressing her cheek. "No child is worth losing you." He looked lovingly into her eyes and then bent down and brushed her lips with his.

His words calmed and soothed her, and she felt herself responding to his tender affection, slowly at first, and then more eagerly as he kissed her thoroughly. Despite wanting to hold on to them and nurse them, Henrietta's worries and self-doubt slid away at Clive's touch, and she felt herself respond to his efforts. He never failed to elicit an unexplainable passion in her, and she did not offer any resistance as he slowly untied her silk robe and slipped his hands inside to feel the softness of her breasts beneath.

"Nothing underneath?" he said with an arched eyebrow. "How naughty," he said with a grin.

"I was planning on taking a bath," she responded with her own arched eyebrow. "I'm sure Edna has it all ready."

"I think it can wait," he said, bending to kiss her cheek, her neck, and then her chest, as she felt herself tense with anticipation, wanting him to continue downward. He stopped, however, before he reached any of her parts that were already beginning to tingle and instead returned to her full lips. As his tongue found its way to hers, she felt a corresponding flush of desire. Her heart was beating fast as he tugged her robe off without even breaking his kiss. Once it fell away, he bent to kiss first one shoulder and then the other. She stood before him now, naked except her lace panties, and desiring his touch so much that she almost trembled. He brushed the back of his hand lazily across her breasts and gazed into her eyes.

"I love you so much, Henrietta," he whispered as he pulled her to him and kissed her deeply, running his hands down her back until they reached her buttocks. Splaying his hands across them, he pressed them against his hardened state, kissing her desperately until Henrietta felt the moist place between her legs ache. He released her, then, both of them breathing heavily, and with a knowing smile, he took her hand and led her to their bed, attempting to undo his tie with the other as he pulled her.

When they reached their darkened room, Clive swiftly turned and again pulled her to him, clutching her waist and showering her neck with kisses, causing Henrietta let out a little moan. Clive began to fumble to undo his trousers, then, while her hands moved to unbutton his shirt. She paused after opening only two, however, to kiss his bare chest, delightfully breathing in the scent of him, which never failed to arouse her. Hurriedly, he attempted to unbutton the rest of the shirt himself, but he grew frustrated within moments and instead yanked it over his head, popping off any remaining buttons in the process.

Finally free now, he took her face gently in his hands and kissed her waiting lips. Slowly he lay down on the bed, as if, having achieved near mutual nakedness, he wanted to exchange their frantic pace for something more relaxed and sensuous. He pulled her on top of him, resting her buttocks on his lower regions and placing his hands on her hips as he gazed at her, his face full of expectant desire. He paused for a moment, as if trying to take her all in, before his hands traveled to her upturned breasts, quivering in front of him, and he softly began to caress them. Henrietta closed her eyes in pleasure at his touch and let out a soft moan.

No matter how many times they made love, Henrietta couldn't get enough of him. Her stomach still clenched when he walked into a room, and her face still brightened when she looked upon him. He was an exceptionally gifted lover, and each time she gave herself to him completely, never holding anything back. She bent to kiss him, her breasts pressed against his chest as he ran his hands down her back, gripping her buttocks and tugging at her bottom lip with his teeth before abandoning her lips altogether and covering her chest with kisses until she groaned.

Without warning, he shifted his weight with one quick action, gently spilling her onto the pillows as he rolled and poised himself above her. He tenderly kissed her lips, his tongue furtively probing hers until it moved to her breasts, erect with pleasure. He continued downward until he got to her panties and then kissed them, too. She wanted him to pull them off, but he instead slowly, tortuously, made his way back up her body, kissing her as he went until he reached her trembling lips, which bit at his when they hovered near. She felt his hand grasp hers above her head, his fingers lacing themselves between hers as he kissed her slowly, deeply. He released her hand, then, and she felt it resurface on her leg, traveling up her inner thigh until he reached her panties. She let out a deep groan when his fingers deftly found their way under them.

"Oh, Clive," she said, beginning to feel more desperate as he began to caress her there, kissing her neck and then her nipples until she began to squirm under him, her breath coming in short bursts until she didn't think she could stand it any longer. "Clive, please," she murmured.

Sensing her need, as he always did, he tugged off her panties and fitted himself between her legs. He braced himself on his arms, his hands cradling her head, as he looked at her with such intense love she felt she might unravel right there. She reached up and took his cheek in her hand. Many times, he had told her that he was afraid of the love he had for her, and she knew what he meant, for, in truth, she felt the same. There was a longing deep within her to be connected to him . . . to be one with him . . . to *belong* to him, and perhaps that was wrong, but she didn't care.

Steadily he looked at her, his face a mix of love and raw desire, and he held her gaze as he slowly entered her now. He did not look away or close his eyes but continued to look at her as he began to move inside of her, gently at first and then harder. She, too, stared into his hazel eyes, until the intensity of the love she felt for him caused her finally to look away as he began to thrust harder.

"God, I love you, Henrietta," he said, his voice catching. With one hand he reached down and began to caress her again between her legs even as he thrust on top of her, her passion rising until she again began to twist under him. Her urgency was desperate now, and she lost control, no longer being able to contain it. She began to shudder, pleasure ripping through her, and she loudly cried out his name.

With furious intensity, he began to thrust in earnest, pounding her as she still gripped his back, letting the residual waves of pleasure to wash over her until he likewise shuddered and released inside of her. Breathing deeply and trembling, he began to kiss her all over . . . her arms, her chest, her neck, her head . . . and ending with her lips, which he kissed softly and tenderly. Breaking his kiss, but remaining so close that his lips still brushed against hers, he whispered, "Don't ever leave me."

"No, never," she whispered back.

He kissed her one last time and rolled off of her, brushing her tousled hair with his hand as he did so. Once on his back, she kissed his mangled shoulder in return and laid her head on his chest, nestling into him.

She felt a deep sense of peace. Even her previously disparaging thoughts of Antonia were gone for the moment, replaced by simple pity. Of course, Antonia was bound to say things she didn't really mean. And anyway, Henrietta thought, holding Clive tighter, she had *him*, and she felt his utter, complete love of her constantly and basked in the glow of that knowledge.

They remained in each other's arms for a long time before Clive spoke, startling her a bit as she thought he had gone to sleep.

"What can I get you for your birthday, my darling?" he said, running his finger along her arm. Henrietta felt herself smile. She had the fortune, or misfortune, perhaps, of having a birthday on New Year's Eve. When he was still alive, her father had always tried to make it an occasion, but since then, it had come and gone like most holidays, with very little fanfare.

"Oh, Clive, what could I possibly ask for? You've already given me everything I could ever want," she said into his chest.

"Well, I have a few ideas, but I want to know if you want to do something special, especially as it's New Year's Eve. Leave it to you to be born on such an awkward day."

"Beast!" she said, giving him a little pinch. "As if I could help it."

"Minx!" he said, kissing her hair.

"Well, what do you normally do on New Year's Eve? I can only imagine. Some gala ball or something—at which I'm sure your mother expects us. And don't you think we should include your mother, speaking of?"

"As it happens, Mother's rather conveniently informed me this morning that she's decided to take Aunt Lavinia and Uncle Harry up on their invitation to spend the holiday with them on Long Island. So you see, we have the house to ourselves," he said, letting out a small chuckle. "Not that we don't already, really."

Henrietta raised up her head to look at him. "Why is she leaving? Is it because of us?"

"Who knows what Mother is thinking," Clive sighed. "I think she just wants to get away. Christmas will be hard enough, but it has to be gotten through. It'll be just as depressing as Thanksgiving was with just the three of us, only now Randolph and Julia will be added into the mix—as if it couldn't get worse."

"Clive! At least there are the boys. That will be fun, I expect. And, anyway, it's Christmas. There has to be something redeeming about it."

"Darling, one does not use the word 'fun,' one says 'amusing' or 'entertaining,'" he said, slipping into an English accent.

"Snob!" she said, pulling his chest hair.

"Besides, you don't know Randolph as I do. There's nothing 'fun' about him."

"Weren't we talking about New Year's Eve? And my birthday?"

"Indeed," he said, running his finger along her shouder again. "As it happens you were pretty close to the mark when you said 'gala ball' just now. Every year, it's the Penningtons' Ball. It was the highlight of the year for my parents and John and Agatha Exley, but perhaps she wants to have a reason to escape it this year, thus the proposed trip to New York. Anyway, her mind's made up, so there will be no changing it. You should know that by now. No doubt we'll be invited to the Penningtons' as well, but, as it's your birthday, I'll let you choose."

Henrietta absently ran her hand across his chest, deliberating.

"Would it be terribly wicked of me to not choose the Penningtons?" she asked, looking up at him tentatively.

"God, no. It would be heavenly to have a reason not to go."

"So the true motive behind your birthday gift is revealed. Not as generous as I had first thought. Nor gallant, Inspector."

Clive let out a loud laugh. "That's not true! You know I worship you, but don't push your luck! Come on. What's it to be? I can hardly wait to see what you come up with. A night in the cottage? A party with the servants in the stables? Gin rummy in the library, I think I once heard you mention . . ."

Henrietta smiled and pinched him.

"Ow!" Clive said, rubbing the spot on his arm. "Why is it that you have a propensity to pinch me? I put it down to having too many brothers."

"You deserve it!" Henrietta retorted.

"Well, what's it to be, then? Or should I surprise you?"

Henrietta thought for only a moment, as it hadn't taken long to come up with an idea. It was a place she had always aspired to go to. "*I'll* choose, thank you very much. And I choose the Aragon Ballroom!"

"The Aragon?" he said, surprised. "Darling, if it's dancing you want, we could go to the Drake or the Palmer House. Even the Burgess Club. The Aragon's rather beneath us, don't you think?" he asked, somewhat seriously.

"Again—snob!" she said, laughing. "It's a beautiful place, so says everyone. I've always wanted to go to there, but I never had something nice enough to wear. But now I do! Please, Clive," she asked with a little pout in her voice. "You said it was my choice."

"Well, I suppose so," he said, tucking his chin to his chest to look down at her.

"And can I ask Lucy and Gwen? And maybe Elsie would want to go, too . . ."

"Ugh!" he said, flopping his free arm onto the pillows. "I should have just surprised you."

"Shall I take that as a yes?" she asked, a smile on her face now as she put a hand on his thigh and slowly lowered it.

With surprising alacrity, he suddenly rolled on top of her again, causing her to shriek in surprise. "You win," he said, kissing her neck and then her ear. "The Aragon it shall be."

Henrietta took a deep breath to dispel her wandering thoughts and reached for the last family gift to be wrapped—Eugene's. He was due home from Fishburne soon—on Christmas Eve, actually—if there was no delay in his transportation. She was unsure how to feel about his return. A part of her was anxious to see him, but she hoped he would be pleasant company, for all of their sakes, especially as it had been decided that she and Clive would spend Christmas Eve in Palmer Square with them and Christmas Day at Highbury with Antonia and Julia and Randolph. In the many months that he had been away, they had still to receive one letter from him, which did not bode well.

Henrietta sighed as she wrapped up the leather gloves she had bought him and hoped that he could somehow find his own path. Absently, she placed the gift into the basket she had procured to hold all of the gifts, save hers to Clive, which she hid upstairs in her dressing room and which they had agreed to exchange on Christmas Eve night in their own suite of rooms. Henrietta had even had Billings bring up a little tree for their sitting room, and Clive had been genuinely charmed with the homemade snowflake ornaments Henrietta had fashioned from snipping ordinary white paper with a scissors. She had then added the finishing touch, which was a garland made from popcorn and cranberries. The rest of the house was of course dripping in elegant Christmas decorations of gold and silver and holly, with several Christmas trees placed throughout, the largest being the one in the drawing room, where it had been set up and decorated by the staff on the first Sunday of Advent.

The basket also held gifts for the Hennesseys—a new hat for Mrs. Hennessey and a new navy cardigan for Mr. Hennessey, complete with a hamper packed with many goodies and savory treats—some prepared by Mary and some store-bought from Marshall Field's downtown. Before heading over to the Von Harmon's for their Christmas Eve gathering, Clive and Henrietta planned to stop off at Poor Pete's to spend an hour, distributing their gifts to the Hennesseys and perhaps indulging in a glass of Mr. Hennessey's better sherry—the stuff that rarely came out except at holidays. Henrietta was looking forward to seeing them again, as they had been like her pseudo parents for so long, but if she were honest, a part of her dreaded having to hear about their daughter, Winifred, who had been married these fifteen years and was only now pregnant with her first child! The Hennesseys, having given up hope for a grandchild many years ago, were overjoyed of course and were planning a trip out east in the spring for the happy event, or so Elsie had written to her when she was still in England. Henrietta was glad for them, but she more than once had to fight down a stray feeling or two of self-pity or doubt.

In truth, between the visit to the Hennesseys' and having to spend the evening with her family, she was not looking forward to much of Christmas Eve at all, despite the fact that she had chastised Clive in bed for feeling the very same way about having to spend Christmas Day in the company of Randolph. Upon closer inspection, she supposed it wasn't entirely true that she wasn't looking forward to Christmas Eve—she would certainly enjoy seeing Elsie and the little ones and passing out presents; it was just that one could never predict what Ma or Eugene might say or do. She prayed that if nothing else, they wouldn't say anything harsh to Clive, who had already been so patient and generous with them, though they never seemed to acknowledge that, much less be grateful to him.

Henrietta took a step back and surveyed her work, her hands on her hips. Not bad for one afternoon, she thought. She was pretty sure she had remembered everyone—everyone except the servants, of course. Henrietta had wanted to get them all something, but Julia informed her that Antonia would see to that and that it wasn't really her place to give them gifts. "Not even Edna?" she had asked, and then Julia had said that yes, it was acceptable to give one's lady's maid a small token. Henrietta had selected a small black handbag for Edna, which she hoped she would like. Unbeknownst to anyone else, however, she planned to tuck a twenty-dollar bill inside it. She smiled to herself as she pulled out the last of the red tissue paper to wrap it, thinking how excited Edna would be to get it. She attached a small red bow and turned it over in her hands, observing it with mild disapproval before setting it in the basket too. Clearly, she was no expert at "wrapping things up" and smiled at the unintentional pun.

She wished she could be of more help to Clive on the case before them regarding Alcott, if it could even be called that, but between helping Elsie and avoiding Antonia, her attention was divided.

She did have a theory, though, that she hadn't yet dared to pose to Clive. It was just that, well, perhaps his father really had had a mistress. What else had become of the money? She was sure Clive would reject this theory outright, possibly even be offended by it, and privately she had to agree that Alcott did not seem the sort, but then again, everyone was fallible and anything was possible.

Chapter 11

Elsie, her arm wrapped tightly through that of Lloyd Aston's, walked with fascination through the Pacific Coast Gallery at the Shedd Aquarium. She had never been to the new aquarium, and she was delighted with what she saw, despite the company. Lloyd had punctually arrived at John and Agatha Exley's mansion in Lake Forest, dressed impeccably, as usual, and had tea with the three of them before escorting Elsie in his Auburn Boattail Speedster all the way to the city, with the understanding that he would return her at the end of their engagement to the house on Palmer Square so that she could study for her "silly test," as Aunt Agatha had said with a forced sort of chuckle. Elsie had gritted her teeth at this disparaging comment, and several others as well, but thought of little else on the drive down to the city. She had been studying feverishly these last weeks, which had thrown Aunt Agatha definitely out of sorts. Elsie wished she could have returned to Palmer Square for the few days leading up to the big test, where Ma would have left her blissfully alone to either study in one of the many empty rooms or to make her way, unbothered, to the library. Instead she had done the best she could despite Aunt Agatha dragging her out to various functions at what seemed an absurdly desperate pace.

And though Elsie had spent the whole of the drive to the city fretting over the test—as well as having the disagreeable task of having to make small talk with Lloyd Aston—she was admittedly very pleasantly distracted by the wonders she saw all around her now at the Shedd Aquarium, the beautiful art deco metalwork stunning her with its beauty as much as the sea creatures. Looking at it closely, she couldn't help but be reminded of Mundelein's marvelous Skyscraper building. Could they have had the same architect? she wondered, but then quickly chastised herself. Not everything related back to Mundelein, for heaven's sake!

"Are you bored?" Lloyd asked, startling Elsie from her thoughts. "It's frightfully dull, isn't it? Just a bunch of fish swimming around."

"No, not at all, Mr. Aston—"

"Don't you think you might call me Lloyd?" he interrupted her.

"Lloyd, then," she said reluctantly. "I'm not bored at all. It's lovely. My mind is, well, it's on other things, perhaps," she murmured. She again tried to gently withdraw her arm from his, but he held it tightly as he guided her to the next tank.

She wished she could think of something more to say, or that she could be clever in these situations, like Henrietta, but she couldn't think of anything. Well, actually, she could. Many thoughts and questions were all there in her mind, but she lacked the ability to get them out smoothly. Her responses were generally slow and stuttered, as she often put her words through a sort of mental filter first. She had been doing it since she was a child. It was as if she had to translate everything from one language into another. She had thought about this quite often, actually, especially during her days as she sat sewing in Mr. Dubala's shop, wondering why she was the way she was and what was potentially wrong with her. She suspected she "had brains," as Pa had always said, but no one would know it from the way she spoke. Her own theory was that her vocabulary was too big for her own good. She had been reading anything she could get her hands on since she was four years old, when letters had one day magically arranged themselves into words for her. All at once she had somehow been able to read. From that moment on, she began to read voraciously, starting with the Bible, the only book they owned. Words had begun to collect in her mind, and stayed, almost unbeknownst to her. It wasn't until she got to school that she realized her way of speaking was foreign to other kids her age, and she began to be teased mercilessly as a know-it-all and a smarty-pants. This horrified poor Elsie, who sought only to blend into the background and learn, not to be singled out in any way for special attention, even by a teacher. She had thus quickly realized that in order to avoid unwanted attention, she needed to curb her use of words and had consequently formulated a rudimentary system in which she translated "big words" into normal, common, everyday speech. But it was not a perfect system in that it took longer than it should have, which meant that usually the person talking to her assumed she had nothing at all to say or that she was merely stupid and would quickly talk over her. On most occasions, she did not have the energy or the courage to correct their first impressions. What did it matter what anyone thought of her, anyway?

"Here's a good one," Lloyd was saying now, reading the dark-bronze plaque on the wall next to a large tank. "Apparently called a 'piranha.' Says it can devour whatever is in its path in a matter of moments. I say, that's impressive. Look at those teeth."

Elsie peered into the murky water and spotted the fish, sitting on the bottom of the tank as if in wait for something to swim by, its razor-sharp teeth jutting out from its lower jaw. It looked fierce and had an almost cunning look to it.

"It's horrible," Elsie finally said, stepping back.

Lloyd grinned. "Let's try the next one," he said, leading her to the adjoining room, which was labeled South America. Again, they aimlessly wandered from tank to tank until they came upon a particularly large one filled with what looked like a variety of fish. Elsie read the plaque and discovered that it was a tank representing the Amazon. Eagerly she peered in and was amazed at the silvery flashes of scales darting past, some of them thrillingly close to the glass. She tried to look past them after a few moments to the rocks at the back, where she could make out some creatures hiding in crevices. She wished Donny and Doris could see this. Why had she never thought to take them?

She bent to get a better look and was startled when she suddenly felt Lloyd's hand on her lower back. Her whole body stiffened, and she could not help but let out a little gasp when she felt it travel lower to her behind. Quickly she stood up straight and took a step back, looking around the gallery. To her surprise, she found that they were all alone. Indeed, it was late when they had arrived, and as they were making their way from gallery to gallery, they were met with crowds going in the opposite direction, slowly moving toward the exits now that it was so close to closing time. They were like fish themselves, swimming upstream.

Elsie worriedly observed that there was no one left in this particular gallery except a guard at the other doorway. She caught his eye, but he just grinned at Lloyd instead and turned his back to them. She felt a resultant, unexplainable sense of panic, though she tried to tell herself that she was being irrational. After all, what could possibly happen in so public a place? As if in answer, Lloyd stepped toward her and swiftly kissed her, pressing her up against the glass as he did so.

Disgust and then real panic coursed through her, and she pushed him away. "Stop!" she managed to say in a voice louder than she had intended. Horrible memories of Harrison flooded her mind, and she found it difficult to breathe.

"Come now, Elsie. You don't have to play the nice girl with me," Lloyd said, amused. "I thought you were all for a spot of fun. Been a little bit naughty is what I've heard, and I like that."

"I . . . I don't know what you mean," she said breathlessly.

"Oh, I think you do. Though you play the innocent charmingly well. Part of the ruse, I imagine. Come on," he whispered, leaning closer to her. "I've got a penthouse near here. I know you want to," he said, kissing her again, harder this time.

Desperate, Elsie balled her hands into fists and pushed at his chest with all her might. "How dare you!" she whispered fiercely, when her lips finally broke free of his.

Lloyd hovered dangerously near her for several moments, his face clouded with anger as if considering his next move. Mercifully, he stepped back. "Fine," he growled, "be that way." He looked down at her as he adjusted his tie. "I'm surprised at you, really," he said, coolly. "The plain ones are usually more willing to play along."

Elsie, her face flushed, felt she might cry at his stinging words and bit her lip. "I'd like to go home now."

"You can't be serious, my dear. We've only just arrived," Lloyd said incredulously.

Elsie was herself incredulous that he assumed she would still want to spend the rest of the afternoon and evening with him as if nothing had happened.

"I'm . . . I'm not well. Please," she said looking up into his face.

"Listen, Elsie," he said brusquely, "I'm not a bit serious as regards any sort of future with you, and I daresay you feel the same. But if we are to be thrown together in this way from time to time, we might make the most of it, you know."

Elsie was so stunned by this admission that she couldn't think of a single thing to say in return.

Lloyd continued to stare at her expectantly and then let out a sigh. "Very well, I'll drive you home."

"I . . . I could take the trolley," Elsie suggested, actually feeling sick to her stomach. "I think I'd prefer it, actually."

"Oh, no you don't. That would never do," he said bitterly. "I'd never hear the end of it. No, I'll take you."

Elsie stared at him with a mix of fear and hatred, wondering how she could escape from him. "If you insist," she managed finally. "But I want you to take me to Mundelein College. I'd . . . I have some things to do there before I go home."

She fully expected him to refuse, but instead he just shrugged. "I don't care where I take you, so long as I can be rid of you for the evening," he drawled. "You're hopelessly dull, do you know that?"

Elsie bit back her tears on the ride north, having to first direct him to drive up Sheridan Road to Rogers Park, as he claimed he had never heard of Mundelein College before, though she knew she had mentioned it to him at the Exley's ball. She didn't know why she had asked him to take her to Mundelein, but the thought of returning to the cold house on Palmer Square filled her with melancholy and even a bit of panic. She couldn't face Ma right now, or even worse, an empty front parlor and hoped that . . . well, she didn't know what she hoped for in going to Mundelein. She wasn't sure if she would be able to find Sr. Bernard, but as they got closer, her desire to find and talk to her mentor overwhelmed her.

Elsie sat as far as possible from Lloyd, planting herself practically up against the door, and was grateful that he remained silent, even though it was horribly uncomfortable. A light snow had fallen while they had been in the aquarium, which seemed a strange contrast to the tropical waters they had just observed. Normally Elsie would have relished the snow, but at the moment she was in no mood to enjoy it. Finally, she saw the college ahead and breathed a sigh of relief.

"It's just there," she said, pointing to Philomena Hall as Lloyd pulled into the circle.

"This it?" he asked, peering out the window.

Elsie wanted nothing more but to flee from the car now that she was so close. She put her hand on the door handle to get out, but before she could open it, Lloyd reached across and held her arm back. His face was very close to hers, and he remained there as she tried to push herself as far back into the seat as possible before he finally slid back. He looked at her with a grin.

"What do you take me for, Elsie? I'll get the door for you." He got out then, a blast of cold air coming in as he did so. Elsie tried to control her breathing as she obediently sat in her seat and waited as he slowly strode around the back of the car.

She looked out the front window to distract herself. It was well past four o'clock and the sun was already nearly gone, but she could still see a figure she thought was Gunther, bundled up and shoveling the front steps of Philomena, his back to her. Finally, Lloyd appeared and put his hand on the handle, holding it there and seeming to enjoy the power he held as he stared down at Elsie, who sat looking up at him, eagerly waiting to be released. With a grin, he finally opened the door.

As soon as he did so, Elsie popped out so quickly that she almost lost her footing on the slippery drive. Lloyd caught her arm and steadied her.

"Careful, there," he said, patronizingly. Elsie righted herself, Lloyd taking the opportunity to wrap his arm through hers again. "I'll be sure to mention to the Exleys when I see them on Saturday next that you were feeling a bit under the weather and had to cut our outing short, shall I?" he said, bending near. "I'm sure your dear Aunt Agatha will be rather concerned."

"No, I'm perfectly fine," Elsie said worriedly.

"But you're not, you see. You distinctly told me you were ill," he said, his gaze steely. "Here. Allow me to escort you in," he said, gesturing toward the mansion.

"No, I'm fine. I'll just go in now," she said, trying to remove her arm from his.

"Not at all," he said, grasping her arm tighter and leading her down the walk. As they approached the front steps of the mansion, Gunther looked up and stepped aside as they passed. When they reached the beautiful stone porch, Lloyd finally released her arm and stood looking at her. Elsie looked down at the ground and then back up at him, wondering why he didn't just go.

"Thank you, Mr. Aston," she finally said. "I enjoyed the aquarium."

"Aren't you going to ask me in?" he said, nodding his head at the door.

"I'm afraid I can't. No . . . no men are allowed . . ."

"My, that's convenient, isn't it," he said, derisively, looking around as he did so. "Well, I'll say good-night, then." Slowly, he bent as if to kiss her cheek, but at the last moment he turned his head and kissed her on the mouth instead. Elsie stiffened when she felt his tongue thrusting against her lips, but she clenched her teeth shut. She tried to pull away, but he held her tight for several moments before he roughly let go of her. Horrified, Elsie wanted to wipe her mouth, but she refrained.

"So long, *Miss* Von Harmon," he said, smugly. "I suspect I'll see you on New Year's Eve at the Penningtons', if not before." With a grin he turned and walked down the steps, giving Gunther, who was still standing in the shadows, a wink as he did so.

Elsie briefly caught Gunther's embarrassed eye before she turned toward the door, discreetly wiping her mouth. To her surprise and despair, however, the door appeared to be locked. She hadn't considered that Philomena would be closed, but that made sense, as the college was officially closed for Christmas and all of the girls, including Melody, had finally left. She was close to tears as she pushed on the handle again to no avail. Could she do nothing right? she thought miserably.

"Here, let me," came a voice from behind her. It was Gunther. "It sticks sometimes in winter. I keep meaning to fix it." Elsie stood aside, and Gunther gripped the handle firmly and pushed the door with his shoulder. With a loud click, it opened heavily. "Here, come in, you are shivering," he said. "It is cold, yes?"

Elsie stepped into the warm foyer and felt an almost immediate sense of peace. She began to unwrap while Gunther shut the door behind her with a sharp shove. She let out a deep breath. The parlor off to the right of the foyer was dark except for a few low table lamps burning. There was no fire in the grate.

"I am sorry," Gunther said, following her gaze to the fireplace, as he removed his fogged spectacles. "I did not know anyone was coming. Sister did not say."

"No, you weren't to know. I . . . I decided just now to come. Unexpectedly, you see. I . . . I was hoping I might study a little bit. My entrance exam is tomorrow," she said, her voice dropping off.

"Here, then, let me take your coat," he said, reaching for it. "Come," he said once she had reluctantly given it to him. He draped it over his arm and walked past her. "Come to the kitchen. It is warmer there."

"Oh, that's all right!" Elsie tried to say, but Gunther didn't stop walking. Elsie saw no choice but to follow him. They walked down a short hallway and passed through a swinging door into a marvelously old Victorian kitchen, which Elsie didn't recall seeing on her initial tour of the grounds with Henrietta. The floor was tiled in tiny black-and-white hexagons, and the room as a whole was very bright and clean. The walls were tiled in white as well, though midway up there was a row of rectangular blue-and-white tiles depicting old world scenes such as old sailing ships, Dutch windmills, thatched cottages, and peasants bent over in the fields. In the middle of the room stood a large pine table, which obviously served as a workstation, with a multitude of copper pots and utensils hanging above it. Even the mullioned windows were tall and narrow in an antiquated style.

Gunther hung her coat on a hook near the back door and took off his own things, hanging them next to hers. Beneath his coat he was wearing baggy trousers and a thick gray sweater, the sleeves of which, Elsie noticed, were a bit frayed. She could easily mend those, she thought to herself as she watched him walk toward the stove.

"You need some tea, I am thinking, or you will not get warm. Sit," he said, carefully putting his glasses back on. "You like tea, yes?"

Elsie nodded as if in a daze and made a move to sit down before she remembered herself and stopped. "Oh, please don't bother on my account!" she said. "I'm fine. Really. I'll just sit in the library for a little bit if you don't mind."

"It is no bother," he said, smiling, as he filled the kettle now with water from an old-fashioned-looking pump. "I was going to make some, anyway. Sit," he said again.

After a moment of indecision, Elsie obeyed him and pulled out a chair.

Gunther opened one of the cupboards. "I think there are some biscuits somewhere," he said. "Just do not tell Sr. Alphonse."

"Who's Sr. Alphonse?"

"She works in kitchen here. But I help her sometimes, so she will not mind, I do not think," he said, removing a tin. He opened the lid

and put the container on the table in front of her. He turned back
to the stove, then, lighting it for the kettle, Elsie studying him as he
did so. He was just a little taller than she, with thick, blond, wavy
hair and broad shoulders. His eyes, she observed, were the palest
blue she had ever seen. They were like a slice of the sky. Unlike the
first time she had seen him outside Melody's room, he now had a
close-cropped beard as well as a mustache. Again, she found it hard
to guess his age.

"Do . . . do you need some help?" she asked him.

He turned to her with a smile. "No. I am doing it." While the
kettle heated, he opened a blue-and-white canister with a windmill
on the front and scooped out some tea, which he added to a teapot.
Then he reached into a cupboard and found the sugar bowl and a
small brown creamer, which he slowly filled with milk. All of his
actions, Elsie observed, were unhurried and patient. When he was
finished, he came over and sat across from her, reaching for one of
the gingerbread cookies as he did so. It struck her that he seemed
very un-servant-like, though Elsie supposed that he wasn't actually
a servant. Aunt Agatha, she felt certain, would surely not approve of
her sitting with servants, especially a male servant. For herself, Elsie
normally felt uncomfortable sitting with *any* sort of stranger, male
or otherwise, except for someone like Karl, of course, but there was
something very nonthreatening about Gunther. He still reminded
her of someone . . . perhaps one of their neighbors at their old shabby
apartment on Armitage.

"I am from Germany," he said to her now. "You were wondering,
no?"

Elsie blushed a little. "Well, yes."

The kettle began to boil, so he stood to pour the water into a
teapot, covered it with a cozy, and brought it to the table with one
cup, which he set before her.

"Aren't you having any?" Elsie asked before she realized what she
was saying.

"Do you wish me to?" he asked with a smile, and she suddenly felt she might cry, though she didn't know why. Perhaps it was his kindness in offering to sit with her.

"Well, yes," she muttered. "If you . . . if you want to, that is. Aren't you cold from being outside too?"

"I am used to cold," he said, the corners of his eyes crinkling. "But, yes, I will sit with you for little while," he said, reaching for another cup.

"Is it . . . is it cold in Germany?" she asked and immediately chastised herself for asking such a stupid question. Of course, it was cold in Germany!

Gunther didn't seem to think it stupid, however, and answered it eagerly. "Yes, very cold in winter. Like here."

"What is it like there?" she asked, but again regretted it, realizing that it might be painful for him to talk about, given the war and all. "I mean . . . what was it like before the war . . . or . . . Oh! I'm sorry! I'm always saying the wrong thing!" Her face was crimson now.

"It is not wrong to ask about my country. I like to talk about it," he said encouragingly. "It is nice to remember it. Parts of it."

Elsie smiled a little and was grateful when he continued on, as if sensing, perhaps, her discomfort and wanting to put her at her ease.

"We lived just outside of Heidelberg. Near university. My mother kept what I think you would call a boardinghouse. Rented rooms. She was born and raised in England."

"That's why you speak such good English," Elsie observed.

"Thank you," he said with a deferential nod, adjusting his spectacles again.

"What about your father? Is he English too?"

Gunther took the cozy off the pot and poured the tea into their mugs through a tiny strainer. "No, he was German. He died. The war. He was an officer under the Kaiser. My parents met before the war. My father was often in England on business. He met my mother there. They moved to Heidelberg, and then the war came. It was terrible for them to be from opposite sides. They loved each other very much."

"Oh, I'm sorry. My father died too."

"I am very sorry," he said, and it struck Elsie that he seemed to really mean it.

Elsie put her hands around the steaming cup, allowing it to warm her fingers. "Did you . . . did you fight too? In the war?" she asked, blowing on her tea.

Gunther let out an unexpected laugh, causing her to almost spill the contents of her cup. "Fight in the war? I was only boy then. About eight or nine. How old do you think I am?"

Elsie shrugged, but she couldn't help but smile at the look on his face.

"I was born in 1907," he added.

Elsie did a quick calculation and realized he was only twenty-eight. He looked and seemed so much older!

"Germany is very beautiful," he said. "Especially the south, Bavaria, where the family of my father is from. But much of the country is depressed."

"Is that why you came here?"

Gunther hesitated. "In a way," he finally said.

"Oh, I'm sorry!" Elsie exclaimed. "I didn't mean to pry."

"Things are very bad there just now. There was not much left for us, and I agreed to . . . help a friend. So I came here, to Chicago. It has been almost seven months. As you can see, I found work as *verwahrer*. Custodian? I think you call it," he said after a moment's pause.

"Is . . . is that what you did in Germany too? Elsie asked, curious.

"No," he said, his eyes sad. "I was a teacher."

"A teacher?" Elsie exclaimed. "How wonderful! You must be very . . . very clever," she said, feeling her self-consciousness creep up again. Awkwardly, she took a sip of her tea, which was finally cooling off a little.

Gunther laughed. "I do not say clever, but there is a great need of teachers . . . and of schools. I was teaching at very low level. Teaching little ones to read and write while I studied at university for final degree. But then things happened that I did not anticipate, and we . . . we left. Now I work here," he said, gesturing around the room with his hand.

"Who is 'we'?" Elsie asked. "Your mother?"

Again, Gunther hesitated just a moment, and a shadow seemed to cross his face. "Yes, she came with me."

"But can't you be a teacher here, too?" Elsie asked.

"Maybe in time. But for now, I do not have proper papers. And I . . . I might have to go back."

"Oh," Elsie said, trying for a moment to imagine what his life had been like. Bombs going off, no food, people dying. "Do you . . . do you have any siblings?" she asked, trying to think of something innocuous.

"No, just me," he said and took a large drink of his tea and avoided her eyes. There was obviously more to his story, but it might be painful, she realized, for him to talk about. No doubt he had lost other family members or friends in the war.

A silence ensued then for several moments, during which Elsie chided herself for not being able to think of anything else to say. Perhaps she should just go to the library now—

"And how about you? Do you have family?" Gunther suddenly asked, as if he, too, were trying to think of something to say.

"Oh, yes," Elsie said gratefully. "I . . . I live with my mother and my brothers and sister in . . ." she was about to say Palmer Square, but instead she said Logan Square. "There's eight of us," she said. "But my older sister is married now," Elsie said, thinking how strange that still sounded and decided to leave out the part about her being fabulously wealthy. She wanted to explain about Eugene and the boys being sent to boarding school, but she stopped herself. She hated flaunting her new wealth and avoided it whenever possible. It was better to just remain silent, as usual.

"Eight children?" Gunther exclaimed. "Then you are blessed!"

Blessed? No one had ever put it that way before. Usually it was seen as some sort of curse or misfortune to have been saddled with so many mouths to feed. Also, it struck her as strange that he had said something vaguely religious.

"Are you Catholic?" she asked before she could stop herself. "Oh, sorry. I mean—"

"No, I am a Lutheran. But do not either tell this to Sr. Bernard," he whispered and gave her a little wink, which caused her to unexpectedly laugh. Quickly, she covered her mouth with her hand, embarrassed.

"What will you study? When you come here, I mean?" he asked her now.

"I don't know really," she said with a small shrug.

"Well, what is it you like most to do?"

"Read, I suppose," she said with a blush.

"Ah! A student of literature, then, yes?"

A smile escaped despite her best efforts.

"What have you read?" he asked, intrigued.

"Well, not much, really. I . . . I haven't had a very good education. I had to quit school to . . . to work."

"Me too," he said with a sympathetic smile as he gestured around the room. "What was your work?" he asked.

"I was a seamstress."

"So was my mother. In a way," he said with a smile. "Before things changed." He took a drink of his tea. "Well, you must have *some* favorites," he said, looking back up at her.

Elsie wasn't sure what to say. She tried to think of something simplistic, something a girl should say, but she couldn't think. Her "filter" was apparently not working at the moment.

"I . . . I like Charles Dickens," she finally said tentatively, deciding at the last minute that it would take longer to fabricate something than to just tell the truth. She looked up at him again. He just sat there, studying her face expectantly, as if waiting for her to go on.

"And Jane Austen," she offered weakly.

He nodded again. "Who else?"

She paused to think. Normally someone would have spoken over her by now, but Gunther seemed genuinely curious as to what her answer would be. "Well . . . I . . . I quite like Wordsworth and Keats. And, well, Shakespeare, of course," she said and looked at him nervously.

"What is your favorite of his?" he asked, his blue eyes exceptionally bright.

"Of . . . of Shakespeare?"

Gunther's eyes crinkled. "Yes, of Shakespeare."

Elsie considered. She should probably say something like *King Lear* or *Hamlet*, but she decided again to be honest. "*A Midsummer Night's Dream*," she said hesitantly.

"Me, as well!"

"You've . . . you've read Shakespeare?" she asked.

"Some. Yes," he answered, apparently not feeling any sort of slight that could have been construed from her question. "I have read some. Not as much as I would have liked. It was hard to get books. When I got to university, it was easier, but . . . then I did not have so much time." His voice drifted off. "But Sister Bernard is kind," he continued, brightly. "She lets me borrow any of the books I want here. She . . . she makes exceptions. For many things," he said in a more serious tone.

"What do *you* like to read?" Elsie asked, working up her courage.

"Well, Shakespeare is good, yes," he said, giving her a smile. "Of the English poets, I admire Tennyson very much, thanks to my mother. My favorites would be Rilke and Schiller, though, I am thinking. And Garborg. I also like some of the Russians, despite the war," he said wryly. "Tolstoy and Dostoevsky, Pushkin. You know them?"

Elsie blushed red. "No, I haven't . . . I have so much to learn. I know that," she said, twisting her hands under the table.

"But that is exciting, no?" he asked, his eyes bright. "To have so much ahead? So much to look forward to? It does not matter so much what is behind, does it?" he asked kindly. "Just what is ahead."

Again, she felt a warmth run through her, and she began to relax more. His face was so open, so . . . so encouraging, she decided. "Yes, I suppose you're right," she said, not being able to help yet another smile from escaping.

"Anyway, they are all of them there," he said, nodding his head in the direction of the little library at the front of the mansion. "Or at Loyola. They have very big library."

"I'll look for them," she said. Neither of them said anything then, and it suddenly occurred to Elsie that she should go. Her tea was long gone, and though she would have loved to keep talking about books, or anything, really, she worried that she had kept him too long and that he probably still had more shoveling yet to do. She wanted to offer to help him, but she knew it was inappropriate, and that even so, he would probably refuse her help. The scene with Lloyd came back into her mind as she stood up, as if she had somehow been under a sort of spell that was broken now, causing her to once again don her heavy coat of worries.

She walked to the sink to rinse her cup and place it in the waiting enamel tray.

"You . . . you won't say anything to Sister Bernard, will you?" she asked, looking at the sink.

"Say anything? About what?" he asked.

"You know, about Mr. Aston dropping me off . . . about what he did . . ." she said, still not facing him and feeling her face burn at the memory of his kiss on the doorstep and, worse, at his behavior at the aquarium.

"Are you liking this man?" he asked softly.

"Lloyd?" she asked, turning toward him now. "I mean, Mr. Aston? No, of course I don't!"

"Then why do you spend time in his company?" he asked.

"I . . . I don't know, really. My aunt wants me to. So does my grandfather."

"Why?"

"Because he's wealthy, I suppose. Powerful. Something like that, anyway." She attempted a little smile but was unsuccessful.

"And so you are running."

She looked up at him quickly, shocked by the accuracy of his words.

"There is more than one way of being trapped. This I know of," he said patiently. "You are pawn in someone else's game, yes?"

Elsie's breath caught in her throat. He looked at her expectantly, and all she could do was stare at him before then giving him the slightest of nods.

"You must learn to play this game better than they," he said gently.

Elsie felt her heart beat a little faster, stunned that Henrietta had said nearly the same thing to her. Perhaps she should tell him about her latest idea to become a nun, she thought, but then changed her mind. No, it was her secret just for now, and she wanted to hold onto it. Besides, being a Lutheran, he probably wouldn't understand.

"I . . . I should get going I suppose," she said. "Thank you for the tea . . . and for talking."

"The way out is that way," he said nodding toward the front of the mansion.

"Oh, I was hoping to study a bit, if that's still all right. Or . . . or do you want me to go now?"

"No," he said, a smile erupting on his face. "I do not wish for you to go. I mean the library. The books. They are your escape."

She paused, her heart still beating abnormally fast. "What do you mean?"

"They can help you move from one world to another. Even for few hours. This is true, yes?"

Elsie just stared at him, unable to respond, though she desperately wanted to. "I suppose so," was all she could manage to get out. "Good-night."

"Good-night, Miss Von Harmon," he said.

"Can't you . . . can't you call me Elsie?"

He looked at her for several long moments before saying, "If you wish, yes. Elsie."

Elsie hurriedly left the room and made her way into the library, which was dark. She switched on a light, and leaned against a desk, her thoughts swirling. She wondered what Gunther had actually meant by what he had said just now. She had discovered long ago how to use books to escape her reality. And yet, where had that really gotten her, besides giving her a few hours of pleasure? A misguided vision of what love was supposed to be, for one thing. A longing for a Mr. Darcy or a George Knightley, but all she seemed to find in real life were variations of Mr. Wickham and John Willoughby, the worst sort of rogues. And if Gunther had actually been referring to an education as a means of escape, she pondered . . . well, that, too, was limited. Even with an education, she knew she would still be expected to marry—and someone probably not of her own choosing, it was seeming—and to have children, reducing all of her studies to be merely for her own entertainment or perhaps drawing room amusement, not to be put to any real use.

She stood up straight and walked to the wall of books before her, running her finger aimlessly along their spines. No matter which way she looked at it, entering the convent seemed her best option. There was a time when she had envisioned having a family, as she was in truth quite maternal, more so than Henrietta had ever been. Elsie knew that Henrietta had a soft spot for Jimmy, but that was about it. She had always preferred to be out making the money for them, while Elsie had been the one at home with them, caring for them and hearing their little sadnesses and joys. She had always thought that she would make a good mother, but she wasn't so sure it was worth the current price. Better to not marry at all than to have to settle for second-rate love or "pleasant companionship," as Aunt Agatha often referred to it, or worse, an abusive husband. As a nun she would be giving up love, yes, and a family, but it would at least be worth something. It was a noble, higher calling, which not even her grandfather would be able to dispute. He wouldn't dare deny her entrance to Holy Orders, would he? She thought not. And when she became a teacher, her classrooms full of children would be her family, and her lover would be Christ. She would "play the game" for a time, she decided, as both Henrietta and now Gunther were advising her to do, but she only had the courage to do so because she felt she held the trump card, her hand involuntarily moving to the tiny crucifix she had begun to wear around her neck. No, this was the way out; she was certain of it.

Chapter 12

"So I suppose congratulations are in order," Eugene said, holding up his glass of champagne to the assembled family. "You really did it, eh, Hen? Sorry I wasn't there for it."

"Thank you, Eugene," Henrietta said politely, not failing to notice that though dinner had only just begun, Eugene already appeared a little tipsy. Henrietta had to admit that he cut a very handsome figure in his dress uniform and close-cropped dark hair, weighed down with hair cream and parted severely down the left side of his head. He sported a mustache, or tried to anyway, it being of the rather faint sort, at least so far. He seemed so grown up now, a young man, for all intents and purposes, Henrietta thought. Military school had definitely helped him to mature, to become disciplined. He was able to hold his tongue now. Likewise, he had learned some manners, and his edges had been smoothed out a bit. But though he was so far this evening comporting himself appropriately, Henrietta sensed that an anger still brewed deep within him; he had simply learned to control it better. Or so she hoped.

It was Christmas Eve, and Henrietta and Clive had arrived at the Von Harmon house in Palmer Square not an hour ago, to the great delight of all of the children. Even Ma seemed surprisingly in a happy mood for once. Perhaps it was Eugene being home, or perhaps it was simply the joyousness of the holiday.

Ma had had an argument earlier in the week with the cook—or the chef, rather—in which she insisted that he prepare a simple ham dinner for their Christmas Eve feast and not some "foreign nonsense." He had balked, of course, saying that he had planned to serve goose, and was so insulted that in the end he had threatened to leave over it. Martha had fired back "good riddance!" and marched out of the kitchen, leaving the chef fuming. He had reportedly kicked the pail in the storage room so hard that it had come unhinged and had stormed out of the house, French expletives flying from his lips. Though it had all the drama of being the end of his tenure there, it proved merely to have been only an interlude, as after several hours, the errant chef returned, wordlessly stepping back into the kitchen and putting his apron back on, smelling only vaguely of alcohol.

In the end, he had agreed to make the offending "ham" dinner, saying that the goose would instead grace the servants' table, seeing as he had already bought it and had it hanging in the larder. As for the Von Harmons' feast, he had had the last laugh, as he had retaliated by preparing a whole piglet, rather than just a ham, with his characteristic flair. Martha had been shocked when Karl carried the pig to the table, complete with its head still attached and an apple in its mouth. Martha resolved to fire the chef the very next day, Christmas or no, but when Clive said he was very impressed indeed and that he hadn't had something this delicious since he had been in Paris several years ago, she was given pause.

At Clive's mention of Paris, Eugene again perked up. "You wouldn't believe the talk at Fishburne," Eugene said, looking around the table eagerly. "My CO says that Hitler passing the Nuremburg Laws is just the first step. He says war is inevitable in Europe."

Henrietta looked over at him, impressed that he was at all versed in current events. He had never been this way before. They always knew he was clever, but he was usually sullen and withdrawn. This seemed a new creation before her, and she watched him warily.

"Surely that can't be," Elsie said, concerned.

"It's true, isn't it, Clive?" Eugene asked.

"There have been a lot of grumblings, yes," Clive said seriously. "I know the English are nervous about Hitler violating the Treaty of Versailles with his new conscription. And it doesn't look good in Italy and Spain these days. Indeed, Spain seems on the brink of civil war."

"Well, if there is a war, we won't be involved again, will we?" Elsie asked.

"I hope so!" Eddie pitched in. "But I hope they hold off until I can go."

"Edward! Never say that," Ma reprimanded him, which resulted in him momentarily scowling into his plate.

"Yes, it's wicked to hope for war, Eddie," Elsie added.

"Ah, gee," he said, looking down at his plate now and pushing his food around.

"Don't be so hard on Eddie," Eugene said flippantly, leaning back, a wine glass in hand. "I wouldn't mind giving the Krauts a once-over," he said, looking at Clive as if for encouragement. "I've only a year left at Fishburne, and then I'm joining up. I'll be a first lieutenant before long."

"Eugene!" Ma said. "How can you say that? You don't want to be a soldier, do you?"

"Can't stop me, Ma," he said wryly.

"Why can't I go to Fishburne like Gene?" Eddie interrupted. "I'd rather go there than Phillips Exeter any day."

"Now you're talking, Eddie. Phillips is a waste of time. Maybe I should have a word with Gramps," Eugene offered with a little laugh.

"Never refer to my father as 'Gramps,'" Ma said stiffly.

"I don't think you're in a position to negotiate anything, Eugene," Henrietta put in quietly, noting that Herbie, meanwhile, had said very little. She knew he did not want to go anywhere at all, and her heart went out to him and Jimmy, who was also listening with wide eyes.

"Yes, and don't be in haste to be in the fray," Clive advised, shooting Eugene a glance.

"No disrespect, Clive, but it would be different this time. At least that's what Colonel Ferguson says. No saps stuck in a muddy trench waiting for the whistle to go over the top. New technologies coming out all the time. You should see the planes we've got now. Tanks too! Better guns, ships," he said, his excitement growing. "It would be over before you know it. And we'd show the Krauts a thing or two. Teach them to stay in line. That's what they need."

"You're forgetting, though, Eugene, that the Germans and the Soviets more than likely have the very same technology," he said steadily. "It wouldn't be over quickly, I'm sure. Every generation makes that mistake in thinking."

Eugene let out a little laugh. "I doubt it, Clive! Again, no disrespect, but you've been out of it for a while. Things are different. We'd lick 'em quick. And they deserve it!"

Clive felt himself bristle, but he kept it in check. He had seen Eugene's reaction to war a hundred times before. He had lived it. His generation had been full of cocky pups, too, wanting to taste blood and thinking it was all going to be a lark. As much as he wished Eugene to learn a lesson and come down a peg, he did not wish the gruesomeness of war on anyone. He hated to think what another world war would mean.

"Perhaps we should change the subject, eh?" Clive said, forcing himself to be congenial. "This is not the topic for Christmas Eve! Doris," he said looking down the table toward where the twins sat, boosted on a stack of books, "what are you hoping for from Santa Claus?" He gave her a wink, and she smiled shyly. She seemed afraid to answer.

"She wants a dolly," Donny answered for her. "Don't you, Dowis?" he asked her, and she nodded to him. "And I want a twain!" Donny said, excitedly.

Clive smiled, and he felt Henrietta grasp his hand under the table. "How about you, Jimmy?" he asked, as he threaded his fingers through Henrietta's.

Jimmy shrugged with a lopsided grin. "I don't know," he said tentatively. "I want to be surprised!"

"Well," said Henrietta, "I hope you like what we got you!"

"Oh, Ma!" Jimmy whined, looking down the table at her. "Can't we open presents now? I don't want any more dinner!"

"Yes, can we? Can we?" exclaimed Doris and Donny, wriggling in their chairs so much that the towers of books upon which they sat threatened to topple.

"Not until after dessert," she shushed them and signaled Karl to bring it in, which turned out to be what the chef had instructed Karl to announce as "*bouche de Noel,*" or "a Yule log," he said deferentially to Mrs. Von Harmon. It looked decidedly unappetizing, causing several shrieks and much giggling from the children before it was cut into and distributed and discovered, to their delight, to be really made of chocolate sponge cake and cream.

Finally, it was time to adjourn to the parlor where presents were orderly passed out but then wildly opened. Even Ma actually laughed, either due to the occasion or to the several glasses of sherry she had already consumed. Henrietta, a bit on edge through the whole of dinner, also began to relax a little. She hadn't been sure how the evening was going to unfold with Ma and Eugene in the same room and had feared what Clive might have to witness. She adored him for the effort he was putting in to try to be one of the family and felt that it was the best present he could have given her. And to her great relief, everyone seemed to be so far behaving. There was only Elsie's odd request for a prayer before dinner had begun, which was awkward, as they were not, if truth be told, in the habit of regularly doing so.

Several times Henrietta had caught Elsie's eye and smiled. She had not had any time alone with her to ask about her studies, not wanting to bring it up at dinner in front of Ma, but Elsie seemed happy, if not a little quiet. Perhaps she was reflecting, Henrietta mused, as she herself was, on how different this Christmas was than all the other sad ones that had come before.

Everyone seemed pleased with the gifts Henrietta and Clive had brought, the wind-up tin racing cars they had given Jimmy being a favorite, even Herbie and Eddie begging to have a turn with them. Ma, too, seemed genuinely happy with the *faux*-fur lap rug they had given her. Henrietta watched excitedly as Elsie opened her tiny package. Elsie, her face flushed, predictably exclaimed over the contents, though to Henrietta's ears, her reaction seemed feigned.

"They're clips, Elsie," Henrietta explained as Elsie held the pearl earrings in her hand. "Pearls are so versatile; I thought for sure you'd like them . . ."

"Oh, I do, Henrietta! And Clive!" Elsie said eagerly. "Honestly. I . . . I'm just not sure I'll have the opportunity to really use them in the future . . ."

Henrietta let out a little laugh. "Of course you will!"

"Yes, I'm sure you're right," Elsie added with what seemed a false smile. "How silly of me."

Henrietta was surprised by Ma's gift to her—a tiny book of Elizabeth Barrett Browning's poems, written in beautiful calligraphy—which suggested it had perhaps been purchased with Elsie's help. Clive, in turn, had been given a very good fountain pen, which also seemed to have Elsie's touch upon it.

The presents finished now, Eddie proposed a game of charades, and they all joined in, even Clive, to Henrietta's delight. He claimed to have never played such a game and laughed along with all of them when he had to act out Don Quixote. Eventually this broke up, too, when Herbie unearthed a Christmas record—Gene Autry's "Here Comes Santa Claus"—and put it on the Victrola, which only served to excite the children all the more. It was played a full three times before chaos inevitably broke out, and they began racing through the house with their new toys. Henrietta felt this was their cue to leave, not wanting Clive to have to endure any more than he already had, though in truth, he seemed amused by it all.

Stiffly, they rose to go, to the sad exclamations of Donny and Doris, who begged for them to stay just a little longer. When Henrietta reminded them that Santa Claus could not come until they were sleeping, their wails ended, and they raced each other to the foyer. Jimmy ran, too, but instead of passing them, he slowed and slipped his hand in Clive's, the sight of which caused Henrietta's breath to catch in her throat. She didn't know which was sadder, the fatherless Jimmy or the childless Clive.

Elsie interrupted her in these thoughts, however, by slipping her arm through hers. Henrietta looked over at her. "We didn't get any time to talk," she said to her sister. "Everything all right?"

Elsie squeezed her arm. "Yes. I got the letter yesterday. Sister Bernard has accepted me," she whispered excitedly.

"Oh, Elsie! I'm so glad for you. Why didn't you say? We should have celebrated."

"No!" Elsie whispered urgently. "Not tonight. I don't want to upset Ma. She's in such a rare happy mood. But I just had to tell someone."

"You'll be brilliant," Henrietta said eagerly. "What a lovely Christmas gift."

"Yes, it is, isn't it? I've been praying so much about it. I'm praying for you too, Henrietta."

While Henrietta was grateful, of course, for prayers, it struck her as an odd comment coming from Elsie. Before she could ponder it anymore, however, Karl appeared with their coats, and she and Clive were quickly bundled up. Hugs and kisses were then distributed all around, accompanied by endless exclamations of "Merry Christmas." The three littlest children resumed their restless pushing and pulling, as Clive and Henrietta said their final farewells, reserving the last, of course, for Ma.

"Merry Christmas, Mrs. Von Harmon. Thank you for a lovely evening," Clive said as he offered her his hand. Instead of taking it, however, Henrietta was stunned to see her mother shuffle forward and actually embrace Clive, albeit awkwardly.

"Thank you, Clive," Henrietta heard Ma say in a low sort of grasping tone. "Thank you for bringing Henrietta home for Christmas . . . and for . . ." she paused as if not being able to find the words. "Well, you know what I mean. Thank you."

All of them stood, mesmerized, watching the scene play out, Henrietta the most shocked of all. She felt she might cry at Ma's acceptance, finally, of her choice of husband, and therefore, by extension, her.

"It's me that should thank you, Mrs. Von Harmon," Clive said gently, still holding onto her arms.

"Martha."

"Martha," he said kindly, the corners of his eyes creased with pleasure. He bent and kissed her softly on the cheek. "Merry Christmas."

He and Henrietta looked around once more at all the bright faces and then departed into the freezing air, Henrietta holding onto Clive's arm as they descended the front steps and began walking to where Clive's Alfa Romeo was parked. He still refused to use Fritz's services as much as possible—a habit he knew he would have to break soon. After all, he couldn't employ the man to have him do nothing, and letting him go was out of the question, especially after he had already been wrongly fired once before.

As they walked hurriedly along, Henrietta's eyes burned, either from the frigid air hitting her face or as a result of the touching sentiment of which they had just been a part of. As she leaned into Clive, she couldn't remember a happier Christmas Eve in her whole life. She glanced up at him now, however, hoping to bask in her happiness with him, but his face was unusually hard-set and seemed oddly grim. Perhaps it was the cold, she thought, though he was wrapped well with a muffler, she observed.

"Did you have a good time?" Henrietta asked.

"Yes, very much," Clive answered, not looking at her but glancing over his shoulder instead, as he gripped her more tightly.

"Everything all right, darling?" she asked tentatively, though she had to raise her voice to be heard over the wind.

Clive did not respond, but instead looked over his shoulder again. Henrietta made a move to turn too, to see what was capturing his attention, but Clive pulled her forward, saying, "Don't look back." Alarmed, now, Henrietta saw him put one hand inside his coat and she knew he was reaching for his revolver. She had seen this move before. "I think we're being followed," he said in a low voice as he smoothly pulled out his gun and cocked it.

Fortunately, they had not parked far away, and Clive quickly deposited Henrietta inside the car before racing around to the other side and slipping in. He started the car and pumped the engine for several moments before putting it into gear and pulling out onto Kedzie Avenue.

"Are they following us?" Henrietta asked, her breath vaporizing in front of her, as she turned and peered out the rear window.

"Yes, I think so," Clive said severely, looking in the rearview mirror as he shifted gears.

"The blackmailers? Or rather, the extortionists?" Henrietta asked, turning back around.

"Very probably," Clive muttered, remembering Bennett's words about him being watched. His story was beginning to sound more and more plausible, just as his gut had told him.

There were very few cars on the road at this time of night, especially as it was Christmas Eve, and Clive was able to maneuver easily away from Logan Square. At one point he even ran a red light, and they were very soon zipping up Green Bay Road back to Winnetka. The city behind them now, Clive put the Alfa into high gear with a smooth, almost elegant movement of his wrist, and the car responded beautifully despite the paralyzing temperature without.

When they eventually turned off onto Sheridan, Clive was pretty sure that he had lost whoever had been following them, but it was hardly comforting. Obviously, whoever it was knew all about them and could easily pick up the trail at Highbury. Or communicate with whomever might be stationed there . . .

The house was dark when they finally arrived home. Neither Billings nor James was at the door, and Clive was obliged to use his key, though he was glad of the trouble, as he had left explicit instructions that the house be locked in his absence. The servants had of course been given the night off and were engaged in their own Christmas party below stairs.

Clive was just taking Henrietta's coat for her, playing the role of butler, when Billings himself appeared, looking a bit rosy in the face but inquiring if they were in need of anything. Clive asked if his mother had returned yet from the Cunninghams', to which Billings replied in the affirmative, that she had indeed arrived back hours ago and had since gone up to her rooms. Clive winced at the thought of her sitting alone for hours on Christmas Eve, but he pushed it from his mind and focused on the fact that at least she was home safe. He then asked if all the doors were locked, to which Billings again replied in the affirmative. He relayed that everything was quite in order and then asked if there was anything else that was needed at the moment.

"No, no, if we want anything, we'll get it, Billings. Go back to your party."

"Thank you, sir," Billings said with a bow, albeit a sort of unsteady one. "I trust you had a pleasant evening out."

"We did indeed, Billings, thank you. And Merry Christmas," he said distractedly.

"A Merry Christmas to you, too, sir. And to you, madam," Billings said, bowing slightly again.

"Thank you, Billings," Henrietta answered. "Merry Christmas to you."

Billings having finally departed, Henrietta turned to Clive, smiling slyly. She took hold of his tie and pulled him forward, surprising him. "Come on. Try to forget about it," she said, obviously referring to whomever was following them. "There's nothing to worry about anymore tonight. There's nothing we can do. Don't let it ruin our Christmas." She reached out then and rubbed the back of her hand against his cheek, and he felt some of the coiled tension drain out of him, despite himself.

"Let's go upstairs," she said. "Don't you want to see what I got you? Or are you too tired to open your gifts?"

God, he loved her. She could so easily set aside a very bad situation. But he had to be careful that he didn't let his guard down too far, even for her; he needed to be vigilant. He had made that mistake before.

"You're quite right, darling," he answered, trying to push away his anxiety and taking her hand instead. "Of course I'm not too tired, though I do hope you haven't gone and got me socks or some such dreary thing."

"No, nothing like that," she laughed, pulling him up the steps. "Though it *is* sort of handmade."

"Handmade?" Clive was intrigued. "By you?" he asked, climbing the stairs behind her.

"Well, not exactly—" she broke off here as she stepped onto the landing and came face-to-face with Carter, of all people, who appeared to be coming from the direction of his father and mother's wing of the house. Or, rather his mother's wing, he should say, and he felt a pang of grief all over again.

Carter did not appear flustered in any way by suddenly meeting them on the stairwell, but he seemed to have a hard time meeting Clive's gaze just the same.

"Hello, Carter. Anything wrong?" Clive asked.

"On the contrary, sir; all is well. A Merry Christmas to you," he mumbled and stepped aside for them to pass.

"Aren't you at the party?" Clive asked, a suspicious niggling entering his mind.

"Just making sure all was in order for your return, sir," he said briefly. "I've laid out your things. Would you like me to attend to you now?" he asked, looking condescendingly at Henrietta. Since Clive had officially adopted him as his valet, Carter had not expressed even the slightest bit of gratitude or humility, much to Clive's surprise. He merely went about his business as usual, taking up with him where he had left off with his father. In the process, however, Clive had observed that Carter did not seem as deferential to Henrietta as he should, which annoyed Clive, as it was she whom Carter had to thank for his continued employment—besides his mother, of course. It was almost as if she were in the way of him properly serving his new master. But wasn't Carter already used to having to work around his mother in serving his father? Oh, what did it matter? he sighed. Carter would learn, eventually, he supposed, though he was a bit of an old dog.

"I say, Carter, has anyone stopped round the house while we were out?" Clive asked him.

"No, sir."

"Any letters delivered?"

"None of a personal nature, I don't believe, sir."

"Hmm."

"There was one call that came through on the telephone, though, sir."

"Who was it?"

"A Mr. Bennett, sir, is what Mr. Billings said."

"Any message?"

"None that I know of, sir, though I believe Mrs. Howard spoke to him."

"I see," Clive said and glanced over at Henrietta, who was looking at him impatiently and reminding him that he needed to set this aside for the night. "Well, thank you, Carter. Merry Christmas to you."

"And to you, sir," he said with a slight bow.

Once upstairs in their wing, Clive poured them some cognac while Henrietta skirted off to her dressing room to presumably unearth her gift to him. He took a deep breath, thinking about how close their followers had been. As they had stepped out of the Von Harmons' home, Henrietta still saying good-bye to her family, he had immediately noticed two large men standing in the shadows about three houses down, and his suspicions were further fueled when he glanced back and saw that they were indeed following them.

He gripped his glass tightly as he waited for Henrietta to return. He wasn't sure how much longer he could just sit and wait for the mob to make a move in this bigger game he now found himself—*them*—in.

He closed his eyes and took a large drink of cognac, feeling the comforting burn as it went down, and forcing these thoughts from his mind. It was Christmas Eve, after all, and he wanted to enjoy it with his lovely wife. As if in answer to this, Henrietta then appeared, carrying a wrapped package. Her eager smile was contagious, and he found himself smiling back. The package she held—his gift, presumably—was long and flat, and he was surprisingly more intrigued than he thought he would be. He hadn't received a real gift in a long time. His mother and father, and Julia, of course, always gave him the predictable things—cufflinks, driving gloves, a new tie. But this was clearly different, unusual. Handmade, had she said? He couldn't imagine what it would be.

He, in turn, had placed his gift to her under the tree earlier today. She set his next to it and took the glass of cognac he handed her.

"Who first?" she asked, her eyes bright. Sometimes, like right now, she looked almost like a child, and he had to steady himself, remembering that she was indeed his *wife*.

"You," he said, loving her with his whole heart. Just watching her, knowing that she was his forever, was gift enough. Almost as if she could read his thoughts, she leaned forward and kissed him.

"You're my gift," she whispered. He kissed her back, longing for her, desiring her—the gifts be damned—and lifted his hand to grasp her neck and pull her closer. She moved into him for a few moments, kissing his lips and then his earlobe and then his neck, just above his shirt collar, flushing him with desire for her. Abruptly, she pulled back, laughing. "Not yet, Inspector," she said, grinning. "Gifts first!"

His heart contracted when she called him that, and he felt boyishly giddy, more so than he knew he should. She had an intense power over him; he hated to admit it, but he knew in his heart he would do anything for her. He wished only to make her happy in return for the joy she had brought him.

She had gotten up to retrieve his gift to her—a large square box—and sat down heavily now on the settee next to him.

"What is it?"

"Well, open it!" he laughed.

"Somehow I don't think this is jewelry."

"Does that disappoint you?" he asked, concerned.

"Of course not! I've loved all of the jewelry you've given me, of course, but you've never given me anything but. This shows a little creativity."

"Some women are never pleased," he said with a grin, one eyebrow raised.

"That's not what I said, and you know it, naughty thing."

She began to open the package then, carefully ripping the paper, and exclaimed in joy when she saw the stack of brand-new records. Quickly she flipped through them: Artie Shaw, Benny Goodman, Woody Herman, Tommy Dorsey, and Cab Calloway.

"Oh, Clive! How did you know?"

"Well, I *am* a detective; I notice things, as I keep having to remind you."

"Oh, Clive, they're wonderful! Let's put some of them on, shall we? But, no! First you have to open your gift. It sort of goes with what you just said—about being a detective."

This comment intrigued Clive, but it did not help him to guess. Carefully Henrietta extracted herself from among the discarded wrapping paper all around her, reached for his gift and handed it to him. He tried to feel along its length, but he couldn't guess it. A board of some kind? Finally, giving her a smile, he tore open the paper to discover it was indeed a wooden placard with a wrought-iron bracket cleverly taped under it for hanging. He removed more of the paper to read the words that had been carved into it and embellished with gold paint: *Howard Detective Agency*. Puzzled, he looked at her.

"It's a sign!"

"I see that," he said, looking confused.

"For the detective agency . . . you know . . . like we talked about in England . . ."

Clive found this gift enormously absurd, but he was touched nonetheless. It made him sad, truth be told, but he did not want her to see that. "Ah!" He tried to smile. He turned it over and back and read it again. He broke into a little laugh then, amusement suddenly flooding through him. Her naiveté knew no bounds. As if producing a wooden sign for a . . . what was she calling it? . . . a detective agency? . . . would make it possible for it to be called into existence.

"Don't you like it?" she asked, concerned. "Is it not big enough? I thought it might not be, but the man at the hardware store in town said that if it were bigger, it might be considered 'showy,' I think was how he put it."

"I think," he said, pausing and grinning up at her, "that it's the very best present I have ever received." He leaned forward and kissed her, the sign wedged uncomfortably between them. "Thank you, darling. It's marvelous."

"You can't fool me, Clive," she said when their kiss ended. "You think this is a hopeless dream that's been dashed, don't you? But it isn't dashed! I told you that on the ship. You'll see. Soon you'll be able to run the firm without thinking about it, and then you'll have plenty of time to solve cases. Or, I should say, *we'll* have time. It's a partnership, remember?"

"What am I going to do with you?" Clive asked her with a smile, knowing that remaining a detective was just a fanciful dream. He had realized it the moment he had gotten the telegram in England announcing his father's death, and being home this last month and sorting through the various affairs of Linley Standard, had sadly confirmed it.

"You mean, what are you going to do with *it*? The sign, that is? I thought maybe you could hang it on the side of the garage or the stables. We could clear out a space to set up shop. Or maybe the cottage. We could make it our headquarters . . ."

Clive peered at her through eyes that were growing tired and suspected that she had perhaps had too much to drink. Her suggestions were becoming ludicrous now, and he couldn't help but laugh out loud.

"Why are you laughing?" she asked, a smile on her own lips.

"I'm not. Honestly. I . . . I just love you so much. Come here."

"Is that an order?"

"It is indeed," he said sternly.

"Very well," she said and leaned into him, as he expertly set the sign on the ground beside them as his arms encircled her.

"Merry Christmas, darling," he said, brushing his lips against hers.

"Merry Christmas, Inspector."

Chapter 13

Christmas morning dawned quietly, a heavy stillness blanketing Highbury and the surrounding acreage as the thick snow fell as if in some sort of dream. Clive lay in their massive feather bed, staring out the window and watching the abnormally large, perfect crystals fall without making a sound, mesmerizing him in their silent descent. It reminded him, for a moment, of a similar snow that had fallen in the Argonne Forest during the Meuse-Argonne Offensive, as he lay in a copse with his men, watching the snow fall and thinking back to his boyhood and to Highbury. At dawn Clive had had to give the order, against his better judgement, to mount up and advance toward St. Mihiel, which led them straight into the line of fire, cutting the perfect silence of that snowfall with screams of pain or worse—helpless whimpers, as his men were gunned down all around him. He remembered the crippling anguish he had felt when he had stumbled across the clearing afterward, despairing that such perfectly white, pure snow was now grotesquely stained by the lakes of blood oozing from stray body parts and disfigured men that littered the ground. Even at the time, a part of him knew that there was something inverted there in his mind, that he had been fixated on the snow being violated rather than his whole company destroyed, but he hadn't been able to dislodge it, and for a time it had consumed him.

He closed his eyes to shut out these memories and buried his face in Henrietta's hair, her smell intoxicating him. His fingers lightly traced the contour of her shoulder, but he had no wish to wake her. They had stayed up shamefully late, almost until dawn, but to be fair, it was already quite late by the time they mounted the stairs to their wing.

Clive watched her now as she slept. She was so achingly beautiful, and he still could not believe she was his. She had opened a set of emotions in him that he wasn't sure how to govern. Most of the time he still felt like an excited schoolboy around her, wanting to be with her always and missing her when she was away from him, longing to be near her and wanting to touch her, to lose himself in her completely. At other times, he felt an almost desperate *need* for her, something different than mere desire, as if to fill a hole in him that had been blown open during the war and which had never quite healed properly. His need for her in those moments was fierce. At first he had been afraid that she would shy away from him, perhaps even be afraid, but to his amazement and relief, she did not. She always responded in a way he seemed to need and was equally learning to read his moods. He knew that he really shouldn't succumb to these mood swings, or "bouts of humors," as old Helen would have said, that it wasn't manly, but he couldn't help it some days. He was trying, but there was so much to test him. He still could not believe that it was Christmas and that his father wasn't here. A deep sigh escaped him.

He took a moment to quiet his thoughts and to thank God that he had Henrietta. He felt a deep desire to be a better man if not for his father, then for her. He was relieved and delighted that he was able to bring her so much pleasure, both materialistically and otherwise—at least he hoped he did, especially at night in their bed. He had had only one lover besides Catherine, and that had been a dalliance with an older woman during one of his summers in England. He had been just eighteen, and she was a widow. He had thought himself in love at the time, but he realized later that it had been more lust than anything else. She had taught him things that he had never thought about before, how to please a woman, how to bring her pleasure. Skillfully she had guided him, and he had learned quickly. But he had eventually had to return home, and by the next year he found himself somehow married to Catherine and then off to war. He never told Catherine about Nora, and she never asked if he had had any lovers before her. He knew that Catherine was a virgin, and he had been accordingly gentle with her. He was attracted to her, of course, in a certain way, but after Nora, their lovemaking seemed almost formulaic and dutiful. Catherine had always insisted on having the lights off and preferred, if possible, to keep her nightdress on, merely raising it for him when he wished to fulfill his desires.

Henrietta, on the other hand, was completely different. She seemed to relish their lovemaking as much as he did, and her body responded almost instantly to his touch and his caresses. She was passionate and loving and exciting, and yet she could be tender and almost innocent at times too. Occasionally she still cried when they were finished, both of them naked and spent, the bed coverings lying in a heap on the floor, which Henrietta picked up in the morning, not wanting to scandalize Edna or the chambermaid, and which caused Clive no end of amusement. He could easily read the love in her eyes for him, and it made his heart beat faster every time. He felt fiercely protective and—he couldn't help it—possessive of her, though he trusted her completely. It was other men he had to worry about. He sighed and shifted his weight, as he tried again to piece together the events of last evening. Perhaps it was time to pay Davis another visit. It was getting serious now.

Henrietta stirred beside him and sleepily opened her eyes. She looked out the window and saw the snow and then seemed to remember what day it was. She kissed Clive's mangled shoulder and looked up at him, peace and contentment flooding her face.

"Merry Christmas, darling," Clive said to her.

"It feels like we just said that," she said sleepily.

"And is this the way you greet your husband on Christmas morning?" he laughed, giving her a squeeze.

"You're quite right," she said, raising herself up on her elbow so that her long, auburn hair fell about her shoulders, her nightgown open at the top and revealing the curve of her breasts underneath as she kissed him on the lips. "Merry Christmas, dearest."

She looked up at him for a few moments, watching his eyes and said, "You're thinking about last night, aren't you? About whoever was following us?"

Clive sighed. "No, I'm not."

"Yes, you are. I know you too well now," she said, tapping his chest with her forefinger. "Have you given anymore thought to going to see Davis? It wouldn't hurt, you know."

"Have I told you that you remind me of my mother?" he asked, gazing down at her.

"Too many times, you cruel thing!"

"As a matter of fact, I was thinking along those lines."

"That you're a cruel thing?" Henrietta teased.

Clive let out a short, loud laugh. "No, about going to the police. But maybe it's not yet necessary . . ."

"Oh, good idea!" Henrietta said excitedly. "Yes, let's solve the case ourselves!"

"The case?" he asked, his brow furrowed, not sure if he wanted to think of his father's death as a "case," despite what he had said to the police.

"Yes, the case. It *was* 'The Case of the Murdered Millionaire'—or 'Billionaire,' I'm not sure," she said as an aside. "But now it's become 'The Case of the Missing Money.'"

Clive stared at her, stunned by her flippant audacity in referring to his father's death so lightly. How could she? He wasn't sure how to even respond to such statements when she gave him the tiniest of winks. It completely undid him, and he let out a burst of laughter as the humor of what she had said became apparent.

"Minx! How dare you refer to my father's death in such a way!" he said in a stern voice. He lunged for her then, but she blocked him with a pillow.

He ripped it from her, and she gave a little scream before he rolled on top of her and kissed her passionately, breathing heavily.

She ran her hands down his back. "Is it a sin to make love on Christmas?" she asked.

"I don't know. Let's find out," he murmured, kissing her neck.

"I don't want to have to confess to Father Michaels that I had sexual relations on Christmas."

"So don't. Or tell him your husband demanded it as his marital right."

"Beast!" she said, laughing, as he caressed her breast.

They eventually descended, albeit separately, to have a light breakfast with Antonia. Clive was eager to wish his mother a Merry Christmas, and as Edna somewhat unexpectedly turned up to help Henrietta dress, she felt obliged to let her, though she was sure she had told Edna to take this morning off as well as last night. However, Edna seemed unusually determined to stay, so Henrietta had acquiesced and sent Clive down ahead of her. Besides, it would be a good chance to give her her Christmas present in private.

Edna seemed exceptionally cheerful this morning, despite having to work on Christmas Day, and as she helped Henrietta to arrange her hair, she began to eagerly relate all of the goings on at the servants' Christmas party the night before. Apparently, Mr. McCreanney had gotten rather tipsy and had even asked Mrs. Caldwell to dance before he fell down drunk. Bert and Clem had attempted to rouse him to get him back to his room above the garage, but it had been no use. He wouldn't budge; so in the end, they had propped him in Billings's armchair by the fire and put a blanket on him for the night. Henrietta asked if Carter had been at the party at all, and after taking a moment to recollect, Edna said that she thought he was there for just a little bit, but had gone off on his own. But that wasn't unusual, Edna said. Carter never mixed with the rest of them.

"But, miss, I mean, madam," Edna said, "I've saved the best for last. I wanted to tell you first." She paused and looked excitedly at Henrietta before she burst out, "I'm to be married!"

"Oh, Edna! I'm so happy for you!" Henrietta exclaimed and meant it, despite her personal dislike for her intended. "Virgil's a very lucky man."

Edna's face blushed and her eye's widened. "Oh, it's not Virgil, madam," she said hurriedly.

"It's not?"

"No, miss! It's James!"

"James? What's become of Virgil? How did all of this happen?" Henrietta asked, delightedly curious.

Edna then went on to relate how she had broken it off with Virgil just around the time of Henrietta's wedding, that he had gone on and on that much about losing out on Helen's ring that she had begun to wonder just what he cared more about, the ring or her? She had told him that in fact she didn't want that old ring—it was sure to be bad luck, but he wouldn't listen. "And then when Mr. Billings gave us all the day off in honor of your wedding to Mr. Clive, it was James that asked me to have a soda with him in town after the ceremony," she said, her eyes shining. "So I said yes, and that was the beginning of it all, really. I came to see just how nice James really is. I guess I never noticed with Virgil and Jack always in front of me. I was always thinking that James was a stuck-up snob," Edna laughed. "But he ain't. He just wants to do what's right, he says. And he said it wasn't him that snitched on you going to my birthday party, miss, which I accused him of straightaway," Edna said hurriedly, eager to not only prove her lover's innocence in the matter, but also to show her own loyalty as well. "He says it was Kitty."

Who has conveniently left, Henrietta thought, amused. But what did it matter at this point?

"Anyway, miss, one thing led to another and, well, here we are. We began courtin' you might say," she continued abruptly. "And then last night, he asks me 'fore I went up, the party being pretty well over by then, if he might have a word. He leads me all the way back to the scullery, it being out of the way, as you know, and then he says that he ain't yet got a ring but the festiveness of the night—and maybe some of the drink, if I'm being honest, miss—emboldened him to speak what had been in his heart these many long months—that he loves me and has for ages and ages and that he wants me to marry him."

Henrietta could not help but smile. "And so you said yes?"

"I did, miss! I was quite overcome. He said he would get me a proper ring and that he wants me to meet his mother. But I said I didn't need a silly ring, that a wedding band would be quite enough on the day. We went back out to the kitchen to tell anyone who might still be around, but wouldn't you know it, it was only Mr. McCreanney, passed out in the chair, and Virgil, as my luck would have it, slumped next to him. I must admit, I was a little disappointed, miss, as I wanted to tell someone, and then who comes in but Mrs. Caldwell to make sure all the lights is off. So we told her and she was very pleased but said we would have to inform Mrs. Howard, or Mister Clive, miss—I mean, madam—and she says we should have said it earlier so we could all have had a toast, but then we said it had just happened this second. Well, she said, she couldn't leave us go off without a toast, and it being Christmas Eve, at that, so she went to fetch Mr. Billings, whom she was sure was still up. Everything would have been perfect then, miss, if Virgil hadn't chosen that moment to wake up, all bleary-eyed and puffy. Before I could say anything, James tells him that he's missed out after all and that we two are to be married. Virgil called him 'a low-crawlin', back-stabbin' carrot-top,' which made James frightfully angry, so he called Virgil 'a rat-faced coward.' Virgil jumped up then and punched James in the eye and said that he had no right to take me, and I very much think James was ready to punch him back when Mrs. Caldwell and Billings comes in and says that will be enough of that. 'Come now, Virgil, let bygones be bygones and toast the happy couple,' says Mrs. Caldwell, but Virgil wouldn't and slunk off. It did hurt me a bit, miss, that he wouldn't wish me well, but I see now what he's really all about, and I'm well rid of him." Edna finished here and crossed her arms in front of her.

"Well!" Henrietta said, taking a deep breath and trying to hold in her laughter at the love scene just described. "I had no idea you fancied James! What a Christmas story!" She looked at Edna's eager face and suddenly felt so much older than she, though it wasn't too long ago when she had felt herself a girl on Edna's same level. So much had changed. "Well," Henrietta said again, "I think you've made a good choice, Edna. I hope you will be very happy."

In truth, Henrietta didn't really know much about James, but anyone, in her opinion, was better than Virgil. She had never understood why Edna portended to like Virgil in the first place. She stood up and gave Edna a hug and then gave her her Christmas present. Edna exclaimed over the new handbag, saying that it was much too fine a gift and that she loved it and wait till she showed James.

"There's a little something else inside," Henrietta added, "but you can look later. I should get downstairs now before I'm scolded," she said, wanting an excuse to not be around when Edna discovered the cash.

"Yes, miss, I've kept you much too long! Sorry, miss . . . I mean, madam."

Henrietta went down, then, and found Clive and Antonia. Antonia, despite the day, was dressed elegantly in black and seemed relatively cheerful, all things considered, and wished her a happy Christmas Day. To Henrietta's bemusement, James was in attendance, though he seemed a bit worse for wear and had what looked like the beginnings of a black eye. Henrietta tried to catch his attention so that she could congratulate him, but he did not give her that satisfaction. Also, she wasn't sure it was her place to announce the news and guessed that Antonia might take offense at not being the first to know.

As soon as James left the room, however, Antonia surprised her and made the announcement herself. "But I daresay you already know this, don't you, my dear, as Edna is your maid."

Deflated, Henrietta responded in the affirmative and noted, not for the first time, that Antonia, despite her apparent aloofness, was very well versed in what went on among the servants. It must be her maid, Andrews, she mused, who kept her informed.

The three of them bundled up then and were driven to Sacred Heart for Mass. The old stone church was done up beautifully with greenery and candles everywhere, and for a moment, Henrietta imagined herself back in England. They greeted Fr. Michaels afterward in the vestibule, who commented as he shook Antonia's hand that it was indeed a difficult time of the year for some. Antonia invited him to join them for Christmas dinner back at Highbury, but he politely declined, saying that he was already engaged for the day.

When they returned to the house, they found preparations well underway for the Christmas feast, which Randolph and Julia would be arriving for later in the afternoon. Henrietta was full of excitement and festivity and wished she could help in the kitchen. She desperately wanted to do something, but helping the servants, she knew, was out of the question. Even cards seemed an impossibility without Alcott there to make up a fourth. Tentatively, Henrietta suggested perhaps rummy instead, but Antonia disdainfully shook her head and Clive said no as well, though he gave her a discreet wink. He held out his hand to her to join him on the settee, so she finally sat down next to him and took up a book. She would have preferred to be upstairs alone with him in their sitting room if all they were to do was sit around, as she could have then curled up her legs under her and nestled into Clive. She knew, however, they could not abandon Antonia, so she sat upright, albeit very close to Clive, and tried to concentrate on her new book of poems from Ma, while Clive read the paper and Antonia skimmed the Bible.

A peaceful silence descended upon them, and though Henrietta was happy and content, full of joy of the day, she could not help looking up at the mantel clock every ten minutes. Though she detested Randolph and, like Clive, dreaded having to spend Christmas Day in his company, she found herself eagerly anticipating the Cunninghams' arrival. At least she might have some fun with Julia or Randolph Jr. and Howard. It was more disconcerting than she had expected to not have noisy children about on Christmas.

—

At long last, the Cunninghams arrived, Billings taking their coats and wraps in the foyer, while Christmas greetings and hugs were excitedly exchanged, at least on Julia's part. Randolph crisply kissed the air beside Antonia's cheek and stiffly shook Clive's hand, but when he came to Henrietta, his lips actually touched her cheek and remained there longer than she would have wished. She had the desperate urge to wipe any trace of it away, but she refrained and turned her attention instead to Howard and Randolph, Jr., who were dressed elegantly in navy blue velvet sailor suits and stood shyly behind Julia. It seemed odd to see them without their nanny hovering near.

"Merry Christmas, boys!" Henrietta said to them, bending near. "Did Santa come?" she asked. Both of them managed a nod, but only Howard gave a tiny smile. "What did he bring you?" she encouraged.

Neither of them seemed to know what to say, so Henrietta was about to suggest something when Randolph barked, "Answer!"

"Yes, Aunt Henrietta," Randolph, Jr. said bravely.

"This is exactly what I was talking about, Julia," Randolph growled.

Before his comment could escalate, Antonia interrupted. "Come along, let's go into the drawing room before dinner. I believe Santa Claus left a stocking for each of you here as well."

Henrietta expected them to race ahead, but instead they walked staidly beside the adults and sat stiffly in two chairs, farthest from the fire, only their dangling, twitching stockinged legs revealing any excitement they may have been feeling. Clive stood to pour out drinks from the sideboard while Henrietta and Julia sat next to each other on the settee. Henrietta happily clasped Julia's hand, and Julia reciprocated, though she looked upset.

With a strained smile, Antonia distributed the stockings to each of her grandsons, who politely thanked her and then carefully began to inspect them. They contained mostly sweets—chocolates and gumdrops and licorice pipes—as well as some little metal cars, a miniature top, a bag of marbles and a small India rubber ball. Henrietta expected them to pop some of the sweets into their mouths, or to sneak a few, anyway, and to play with their new toys, but instead they sat stiffly, watching their father.

"I've hidden a surprise for you somewhere in the room as well," Henrietta ventured. "See if you can find it," she said.

Both boys looked from her to their father, who gave them a brief nod, and they slid off the chairs and looked around the room from where they stood, unsure of what to do next.

"Go on, look about," Henrietta encouraged.

Hesitantly, they looked at Julia, who gave them a nod, which prompted them to walk toward the piano at the back of the room for apparently a lack of any other ideas.

"This is what comes from that incompetent nanny," Randolph scoffed as Clive handed him a cognac. "She hovers too much, and now they're as timid as mice. And she's not much better," he said nodding at Julia. He seemed in a foul mood, and Henrietta was already beginning to regret wanting them to come.

"Randolph, they're only little yet. Give them time," Julia said.

"Indeed," said Antonia. "Clive was a quiet thing as a toddler."

"Which he soon made up for!" Julia laughed, a bit of her old self shining through her subdued demeanor, if only for a moment.

"It was running after you that did it," Clive retorted.

Henrietta again looked at the children, who still seemed unable to actually search for the hidden gifts. She contemplated how her own brothers and sister would have torn through the house in a very ungenteel, excited frenzy.

"Do you want a clue?" Henrietta called to them, but Randolph intervened.

"Let them do it on their own!" Randolph commanded disgustedly. "If they can't find a Christmas present on their own, they don't deserve to have one."

"Randolph! It's Christmas Day!" Julia urged. "Let's not have any unpleasantness."

"I'm not being unpleasant. I'm merely observing that they are both trembling sissies."

"Well, if you weren't so hard on them, maybe they wouldn't cower so much!" Julia blurted out, but instantly seemed to regret it.

Randolph glared at her with his small, black eyes and seemed about to say something when Billings interrupted by coming in to announce that dinner was served. The hunt was postponed then, as the children were called back, and everyone made their way into the dining room, Henrietta catching Clive's eye as they went. Christmas at Highbury was not exactly what she had expected.

The dinner itself was an exquisite masterpiece—not only in taste but also in presentation—the footmen bringing out course after course of turkey, goose, pheasant, and fish with all of the accompanying side dishes followed by a rather marvelous-looking dessert. It was a concoction that was actually on fire and which Billings called a "pudding" of some sort. Henrietta had never seen anything like it. Antonia explained that it was the traditional dessert at Linley Castle and that she had decided to have it as usual in honor of Alcott. Indeed, the whole dinner was a copy of what was traditionally served at Linley for the Christmas feast, and one which the Howards had imitated these many long years.

Henrietta thought it a little cruel that the boys were not allowed to eat with them, even on Christmas, and she wondered what would happen should she and Clive ever have children. Surely, she would have some say in the matter, wouldn't she? To not have them at the table at Christmas? She thought back to last night's loud and lively evening at Palmer Square and wondered what Clive had thought of it if this is what he was used to?

"It's lovely to have you here with us, Henrietta," Julia put in, bringing her thoughts back to the present moment.

"Thank you, Julia," Henrietta answered with a genuine smile.

"It must be hard not to spend Christmas with your family. I know it was for me the first time I spent it with Randolph's family. But I hope you will think of us as your family very soon."

"Oh, I already do," Henrietta assured her, looking over at Clive. "And we spent Christmas Eve with them, of course, so that's just as nice."

"And did your mother cook?" Randolph asked, feigning innocence.

Henrietta stared at him, sure that he was teasing her. "No, they have a full staff," she answered coldly.

"Just as well. You'd need a staff to keep up with them all," he said with a grin and looked to Antonia for encouragement. "How many of you are there, did I hear?" he asked Henrietta.

"Eight," she answered curtly.

"Well, I'm sure it was . . . cozy," he said distastefully. "Palmer Square, did you say, Clive? Charming, I'm sure," he said with a grin.

Clive's face looked very dark. He seemed about to say something, but Julia beat him to it.

"And your brother was home from Fishburne, was he not?" she asked genuinely. "I'm sure you were very glad of the visit."

"Yes, it was nice to see him," Henrietta said, happy to address someone other than Randolph. "He's looking very grown up, isn't he, Clive?"

Clive nodded, clearly still upset.

"And the rest of them leave for Phillips soon, eh?" Randolph asked, wresting the conversation back with a slight slur, making Henrietta wonder if he had already been drinking before they arrived. It would explain much. Randolph was a boor at the best of times, but at the moment he was being positively monstrous. "Capital idea. Exley knows what he's about. I'm thinking of sending the boys either there or to Saint Andrews next year, myself. That will make them into men instead of the dribbling babies they currently are."

Henrietta looked down the table to where Julia sat, her face ashen.

Antonia spoke now. "Well, I refused to send my children away. Alcott wanted to, of course, as he had been sent off to Eton. But I find it an outrageous concept. I let Alcott have his way in many things, but not this one." She looked pointedly at Julia, who merely gave her a sad smile in return. "Look at Clive," Antonia went on. "It didn't seem to do him any harm. And he made captain in the war."

"Quite so," Randolph said, looking at Clive appreciatively. "But then again, those were desperate times, were they not? Certain standards forgiven and all of that," he said, taking a last bite of his Christmas pudding. "And then there's your fascination with being a police officer, or a detective . . . or whatever your title was exactly. But I put that down to the effects of the war. Does strange things to the mind, I've read."

"Which you wouldn't know about personally, would you?" Clive asked quietly.

"Some of us had to stay back and run the country, my man. Couldn't all run off to join the squabble like errant school boys."

Henrietta was very afraid that Clive would explode at that, but he remained strangely calm. "Yes, some of us felt differently about 'the squabble,' I suppose. Held to a different set of loyalties. I don't think you'd understand that, Randolph, so I will excuse your ignorant comments."

Randolph sniggered. "No need to get sentimental, Clive. All I'm saying is that I mean to send the boys to boarding school. That's all."

"Randolph, please!" Julia broke in. Henrietta wasn't sure what exactly she was pleading for: the boys not to be sent away or for Randolph to cease his insulting remarks.

"Yes, Randolph," Antonia said sternly, clearly assuming it was the latter, "let's not be disagreeable at Christmas."

"My apologies, of course," he drawled then and gave a nod to Antonia, still flashing his irritating grin.

No one seemed to know what to say after that, however, so Antonia rose stiffly, Julia and Henrietta quietly following, and withdrew to the drawing room, where Randolph Jr. and Howard were brought in to them. There, without the austere presence of their father, the little boys again took up the search for Henrietta's hidden surprises with decidedly much more liveliness than before.

Clive and Randolph remained in the dining room, however, James dutifully distributing the port and cigars. In truth, Clive would have preferred to forgo tradition and follow the ladies into the drawing room to watch his nephews hunt for their gift from Henrietta, but he knew his father would turn in his grave if he abandoned tradition, especially on Christmas Day. He watched Randolph now as he took up his glass of port, hating him. He knew he shouldn't hate anyone on Christmas, but surely God would understand. There was a limit to any man's patience, and Randolph was sorely testing it.

"I hope you're not going to be tedious and be offended, Clive," Randolph said, examining the dark liquid in the large, bulbous glass.

Clive did not respond, but Randolph went on. "Actually, I'd have quite liked to be a detective, I think. But I don't have the skill for it. Sneaking about and such." He grinned at him and lit a cigar. He inhaled deeply until it was properly ignited and then blew out a large puff of smoke. "I'm not surprised you've given it up, though. Getting a bit old now to go dashing after villains and the like, aren't you?"

Clive felt his anger rising with each absurd comment Randolph uttered, and he wasn't sure how much longer he could contain it. Why did Randolph seem to be baiting him? It was as if he purposefully wanted to argue with him.

"It's odd, then," Randolph continued, "about the missing painting."

Clive started a trifle, and his thoughts went from mere annoyance to genuine concern, wondering how he could possibly know about the painting. Quickly he deduced that it must have been Antonia who had told him. Was there to be no end to his mother's interference? he groaned internally.

"What do you mean?" he asked, trying to appear indifferent.

"No secrets here, old boy. Your mother mentioned to me that a rather valuable painting has disappeared from the house. Stolen, apparently. Lucky there's an inspector in the house. Or a former one, anyway. Any suspects?" he asked, peering through squinted eyes as he puffed his cigar. "Was it insured?" he asked casually, flicking some ash into a nearby, waiting receptacle. "But doubtless you've gone over all of this already with the police."

"I have it in hand," Clive said, irritated. This was not to be borne any longer! He was going to have to speak to his mother. He would have to tell her the truth about the painting, that it hadn't been stolen, or God knows who else she would tell. Meanwhile, he wasn't sure how much longer he could be civil to Randolph. He desperately wanted to leave the room, but Randolph reached for the bottle of port.

"I think you've had enough, don't you?" Clive said coolly. "I don't want to keep the ladies waiting. I'm sure they want to open gifts."

Randolph let out a short laugh. "Since when are you tied so tightly, Clive?" Randolph slurred. "She has you whipped, I see," he said, taking a drink.

"That's enough, Randolph."

As if he didn't hear him, Randolph continued, leaning toward Clive confidentially across the table. "How *is* married life? I do envy you there, my man. Doubtless you've kept her busy. No baby, though, yet, by the look of it." He leaned back in his chair with a wide grin. "Better look to it, Clive. It would be a shame if the whole of the Howard fortune fell to me by default." He chuckled. "Unless you're too old for that too. Or is it a war wound?" he asked, taking a puff of cigar. "Wouldn't have to ask me twice. Not with a girl like that. Or was she not quite still 'a girl' when you married?" he sniggered. "You can never tell with the lower classes, can you? They're desperate, you see, which is partially what makes them so attractive."

Fury flooding through him, something snapped inside of Clive. "Leave us, James," he muttered.

"Yes, sir," James responded nervously and picked up his silver tray on the sideboard and hurried from the room.

Randolph's annoying smirk quickly melted then into what seemed to be surprised fear as Clive abruptly stood and swiftly strode toward him. Clive grabbed Randolph by the lapels, roughly pulling him into a standing position, and without further pause or warning, sunk a punch into Randolph's gut, causing him to groan and double over.

"I'm not too old to put you in your place, Cunningham," Clive said, fury racing through him. He pulled Randolph back up to a standing position and put his face very close to his. "I warned you the night before my wedding not to *ever* disparage my wife either to her face, as you've done tonight, or behind her back, as you've done just now."

He hit him again, causing Randolph to double over again in pain. "And that one's for my sister. Don't you dare touch her again. And be grateful that it wasn't in a place where it shows," he snarled. "Your specialty, as I understand. But next time—if there is a next time—I won't be as forgiving," he said, shoving him back into the chair. "You can send your boys away to boarding school or hit your wife or insult my mother at her own table, but it won't give you what you don't have," Clive said, breathing heavily. "It just shows you for what you are—a weak, sniveling bastard. And this is the last time I'm going to say it: stay away from my wife."

Randolph sat cradling his stomach as he scowled up at Clive. "You're insane, Howard," he hissed. "Do you know that? Everyone thinks you are, you know."

His comment stung, but Clive ignored it for the moment. "Merry Christmas," he muttered and walked from the room to join the ladies.

Chapter 14

Elsie felt nervously buoyant, sitting outside of Sr. Bernard's office the day after Christmas, waiting to be called in to discuss her future at Mundelein College.

Almost immediately upon receiving Sr. Bernard's kind letter in which she had informed Elsie that she had most certainly passed the entrance exam with all of the Sisters' deepest congratulations, Elsie had written back her acceptance. In her letter, Sr. Bernard had encouraged Elsie to move her things, at her earliest convenience, to Philomena Hall, where she would in fact be sharing a room with Miss Melody Merriweather, as there was not much time before the new term began. Also, Sr. Bernard had written, Elsie was obliged to come to her office at that time to discuss what her new schedule should be.

Elsie had urgently wanted to go the very same day she had received the letter, but it was already Christmas Eve when she had actually read it, as the missive had sat, lonely, for several days on her desk in her room in Palmer Square while she had been away at the Exleys'. Aunt Agatha had not relented in her attempts to throw her into the company of the usual set of eligible men, Lloyd Aston and Garfield Burnham seeming to still be the front-runners. Elsie had nearly been sick in the bathroom the night she was obliged to attend

Uncle Gerard and Aunt Dorothy's annual Christmas ball, knowing that Lloyd Aston would be there. It was the first time she would be seeing him since the Shedd Aquarium incident, and she wasn't sure what to expect. Wonderfully, however, he had been aloof most of the evening, though she had caught him staring at her more than once, each instance of which she tried her best to ignore. Elsie was pretty sure that Aunt Agatha had also noticed the chilliness between the two of them and was decidedly grumpy for the rest of the evening, despite the copious evergreen boughs draping all of the doorways of the Exley mansion, the dripping candles adorning every mantle and sideboard, and the plentiful eggnog spiked with rum, served in exquisite, cut, red crystal glasses by a core of footmen.

At the end of nearly a full week of merriment and holiday cheer, Aunt Agatha was finally obliged to release Elsie back to Palmer Square for actual Christmas Eve and Christmas Day to spend with her "other family," as she was wont to call the Von Harmons now. Upon parting with her, Aunt Agatha was not the least shy in morosely commenting to Elsie that it seemed she was not to get her Christmas wish this year, which was, of course, for Elsie to have received a proposal of matrimony or, if nothing else, then at least the hint of one. She was decidedly very downcast, especially as she had had it on very good authority—i.e. Victoria Braithwaite—that a proposal might have been forthcoming from one Mr. Aston, and therefore she could not help but speculate that its failure to have been uttered may be put down to something controversial that Elsie may have said or done.

To her credit, Elsie had felt more than a little guilty as she kissed her aunt good-bye and wished her a happy Christmas. Aunt Agatha had merely sighed and said not to lose heart—that they would try again at the New Year's Eve ball at the Penningtons', to which Elsie had decided to say nothing.

So it was with the utmost relief, not to say joy, that Elsie had found Sr. Bernard's letter waiting for her and, surprisingly, another one besides. This second one was from none other than Melody Merriweather herself. Elsie wondered how Melody had gotten her address and assumed it must have been from Sr. Bernard. It proved to be a rather frivolous letter, truth be told, in which Melody went on and on about how her Christmas break was playing out back in her home town of Merriweather, Wisconsin, and, though Elsie obviously knew none of the people about whom Melody was writing, she enjoyed it just the same. She was grateful that if she did have to share a room, that it was to Melody she had been assigned. Melody struck her as the type of person who was easy to get to know; she was so wonderfully outgoing and bubbly and exuded a happy sort of lightness that was contagious. It was so very different from the depressive negativity that she was constantly confronted with at home with Ma.

It was for that very reason in fact that she did not immediately tell Ma about her letters and waited until after Christmas to announce what she knew would be the upsetting news. As expected, Ma reacted as if she were hearing Elsie's plans for the first time and was bitingly critical all over again, which threatened to crush the flicker of joy and hope that had begun to beat in Elsie's breast. Ma accused her of abandoning her, first to the Exleys, which had been bad enough, and now to a school on the other side of the city. What need did she have of going to school anyway? She thought she had raised her to have more sense, she had said, and called her "too big for her britches."

Poor Elsie had no choice but to listen to Ma's rants and more than once escaped to her room to cry, her guilt threatening to overwhelm her. At one dreadful point, she resolved to give it all up, but then she managed to steel herself by remembering Sr. Bernard's calm face and encouraging words, not to mention what would be Henrietta and Julia's disappointment, even anger—at least on Henrietta's part— should she give up before she had even begun. In desperation, she prayed a whole rosary on her knees in her room with the door locked, after which she concluded that she would indeed press on with her plan and that it was too late now to get out of it, anyway, even if she wanted to. Which she didn't.

Having thus come through her trial of doubt, as she began to refer to it in her mind, Elsie did her best after that to ignore Ma. She tried being kind instead, making Ma cups of tea and gently tucking the lap blanket around her that Henrietta had gotten her for Christmas. Dutifully she listened to her complain that very soon she would be left almost completely alone, obviously gathering no comfort from what would be the remaining presence of poor Doris and Donny.

Elsie felt sad about the boys leaving too, especially Jimmy, who seemed almost a baby to her, but she had spent the last months feeling as though she had already lost them, anyway. And it occurred to her eventually that Ma's rages about them going away seemed oddly ironic, as when they had lived in the shabby apartment on Armitage, she had always been moaning that there were too many of them and that they were always underfoot. What difference did it matter to Ma if they all left? she could not help but wonder. She never bothered with any of them half the time, anyway.

Though resolute, or nearly so, anyway, in her decision, Elsie still sometimes felt the need for encouragement and therefore snuck off to her room from time to time to reread her two letters. She was especially drawn to Melody's, in which her new roommate expressed her "deepest hope" that Elsie would be indeed coming to Mundelein next term and that, if so, they would be allowed to be "roomies," as she called them, as she wasn't partial to having her own room—as long as Elsie didn't snore, that is. She had a feeling, Melody wrote, that they were to be "fast friends" and that they would have "loads of jolly times" and "hoped awfully" that Elsie felt the same.

With a sigh, Elsie refolded the letter again and put it back in her top drawer, hoping in her heart that Melody really might become a friend, though she was sure a girl like Melody already had plenty. For her part, Elsie had never been good at making friends. There had been one girl at school, Bessie, whom she had quite liked, but then Elsie had had to leave school to find work, and she had not seen Bessie again. She only lived a few blocks away, really, but Elsie had not had time to seek her out. It was Henrietta, she supposed, who had been the closest thing she had ever had to a friend.

—

As Elsie sat, waiting for Sr. Bernard to descend from the convent on the upper levels, she thought again about Melody's reference to jolly times and worried that she might mean cavorting with Loyola boys, as Melody had already casually mentioned upon their first meeting. As much as Elsie wanted a friend, she sincerely hoped that Melody would not prove a distraction from her studies. Perhaps she should tell her about her desire to enter religious life right away so that Melody would understand where she stood— that she didn't need or want to "cavort." But she just as quickly dismissed this as being a bad idea. Better to keep it a secret for a while longer. After all, she didn't wish to appear a prude, and if she admitted it, she wanted Melody to like her. She had hoped to maybe tell Henrietta at Christmas, but there had not been time. And she wasn't all that sure that Henrietta would approve, anyway. In fact, she was sure she wouldn't.

"Ah, there you are, Elsie. Come in!" said Sr. Bernard, somehow appearing now beside her and interrupting Elsie's thoughts.

Elsie gathered up her handbag and followed Sr. Bernard into her office, which, Elsie had discovered, was not on the first floor, where she had expected it to be, but up on the second floor at the end of a nondescript sort of hallway. Elsie thought this an unusual location for the president of the school, but then again, this seemed appropriate to Sr. Bernard's unusual aura of peace and her, well . . . her holiness—the only way Elsie could think to describe her. Elsie was again surprised when she stepped inside the office to find that it was not done up in a modern art deco style, as were the offices on the first floor, but was instead wonderfully old-fashioned with thick wood paneling, a stained-glass window in place of a clear one, and the vague smell of candle wax, all of which had an immediate calming effect on Elsie. She felt like she had entered a warm cocoon, or even a womb, as though she could easily go to sleep here if she weren't so nervous. The only ornament she observed was a small crucifix that hung on the wall behind the desk, which caught Elsie's eye more than once during the ensuing conversation.

Sr. Bernard gestured for her to sit, and as Elsie perched on a chair, she tried to quell the nervousness that was already returning and thought that perhaps she should have brought Henrietta with her . . . But why? she countered with herself. There was nothing to be nervous about, and she would have to get used to acting on her own.

"A Merry Christmas to you," Sr. Bernard said with a warm smile.

"Merry Christmas, Sister," Elsie said politely.

"There was no need for you to come quite so immediately; tomorrow would have been soon enough. I don't wish to call you from your family."

"Oh, that's all right, Sister. I . . . I'm eager to begin, you see," Elsie said meekly.

"Very well," Sr. Bernard said with another smile. "Then let's take a look," she said, rifling through a large, tidy stack of papers. "Ah. Here we are. Elsie Von Harmon." Sr. Bernard took a moment to glance over the paper before looking back at Elsie and giving her a nod. "You did very well, Elsie," she said. Elsie felt her heart swell. "Very well, indeed."

"Thank you, Sister," Elsie said quietly, twisting the tawny fabric of her gloves. She had tried to dress carefully this morning in a green-and-yellow checked knit dress with a matching hat, wanting to appear proper and suitably studious.

"I took the liberty, given the situation, to put together this schedule for you," Sr. Bernard said, handing her a slip of paper. "It's one class short of a normal load, but you can make that up later."

Elsie took it and eagerly let her eyes dart over it: English, Western Civilization, Geometry, and Home Economics and Deportment. She rejoiced at the first two, but inwardly groaned at the latter two.

"Is there something wrong?" Sr. Bernard asked perceptively.

"Oh, no, Sister! It's just that, well, I was hoping that . . . it's just that I'm not very good at geometry," she fumbled.

"Sister Sebastian was quite impressed with you," Sr. Bernard said, looking down her long nose, past her black glasses, at Elsie, who blushed at the unexpected compliment. "She thinks you have much promise and that you'll do well in Sister Joseph's beginning geometry. Sister Sebastian's very willing to continue tutoring you, if you'd like."

"Thank you, Sister," Elsie responded, thinking that it might be nice to still see the wispy Sr. Sebastian on a regular basis.

Elsie sat staring at her schedule and did not know how to voice her objection to the home economics class, as she supposed this was a class that all the girls looked forward to. But she felt she had had enough lessons in home economy to last a lifetime. Anyone who had been forced to make a watery soup with some limp carrots and potatoes and, if they were lucky, some beef fat, week after week, as she had done in the days of their severe poverty, should probably be excused from having to take such a class, she thought. And on the other end of the spectrum, anyone who had been subjected to the likes of her failed lady's companion, Mrs. Hutchings, or even worse, to Aunt Agatha's machinations, certainly had no need of further instruction in deportment. Also, Elsie thought it not a little incongruous that Mundelein College should require of its young, modern women to take both something as challenging and progressive as chemistry and geometry and philosophy alongside something as frivolous as home economics, but she did not say anything.

"Is it the Western Civilization class?" Sr. Bernard asked. "I know it's not the English."

"Oh, no, Sister. I . . . I suppose I was hoping for something besides home economics, but never mind." She smiled weakly.

Sr. Bernard studied her carefully. "What is it that you wish to do, Elsie? What do you see as your future?"

Elsie was taken aback by the question and furtively racked her brains for an acceptable answer. She guessed that she was supposed to say "married with a family," but she hesitated. She tore her gaze away from her gloves and looked up into Sr. Bernard's calm face. Should she tell her? she thought desperately. A sense of panic surfaced from somewhere, and she felt the familiar difficulty in breathing. Before she could stop herself, however, she blurted out, "I . . . I want to become a nun . . . a sister, like you, Sister." As soon as the words were out, Elsie simultaneously felt a horrible stab of fear as well as a blessed relief to have finally told someone her secret desire. Her leg began to nervously twitch as she looked up expectantly at Sr. Bernard, whose reaction so far was slower in coming than she might have imagined.

"I see," Sr. Bernard said thoughtfully. She smiled at Elsie, though it seemed one of pity, not the one of rapturous thanksgiving that Elsie had perhaps allowed herself to envision on one or more occasion, particularly, for example, when she was forced into the arms of Garfield Burnham on a dance floor or having to make conversation with the likes of Lloyd Aston. Indeed, these fanciful imaginings of what she hoped would be Sr. Bernard's reaction to her announcement had lately kept her mind pleasantly diverted at more than one holiday gathering. But now that she had finally blurted it aloud, it did not seem to be having the desired effect. Indeed, the look on Sr. Bernard's face seemed to instead be one of concern.

And then a terrible consideration entered Elsie's mind—perhaps she wasn't good enough to become a nun! Yes, maybe that was it; maybe that explained Sr. Bernard's somewhat muted reaction. Suddenly she felt horribly embarrassed. But that didn't make sense, she quickly countered with herself. No one was turned away from the nunnery, were they?

"How long have you felt this way?" Sr. Bernard asked, breaking into Elsie's anxious musings, which threatened to blow into a bigger storm in her mind at any moment.

"Not . . . not too long, Sister."

Sr. Bernard nodded thoughtfully. "Well, your faithful presence in chapel is certainly to be admired," she said gently. "You've prayed about your vocation?"

"Oh, yes, Sister! Very much! I . . . I believe this is what God is calling me to! I feel it so strongly—"

"Have you discussed this with your family?"

Elsie bit her lip. "Not yet, Sister. But I will. I . . . I just haven't had a chance . . ."

"I see." Sr. Bernard folded her arms under her habit. "What do you think they will say?"

"I hardly know, Sister," she tried fibbing. "I . . . I suppose they won't be too pleased," she said then, after a moment's pause. "Not everyone, anyway, but . . . no disrespect, Sister," she faltered tentatively, "but . . . what does it matter? Surely it is not for them to interfere in what God wants me to do, is it? Look at all of the saints . . . they . . . they sometimes did not have the support or approval of their families for their chosen path in life. Not that I'm a saint, of course. That's not at all what I meant—"

"No, no one or nothing should come between ourselves and what God wills for us. But it is the discernment of such that is the difficult part. Our families have our best interests in mind, don't forget, and sometimes they can see things that are not quite clear to us."

Elsie's face fell, and she felt herself quickly sliding toward despair at what could only be interpreted as Sr. Bernard's rejection of her.

"That is not to say that you don't have a true vocation, Elsie," she said, throwing her a life preserver. "You must pray more about it and ask God to reveal His true will to you. He will not fail you in this, of that you may be certain. Trust Him."

"Oh, but, Sister! I do! I *do* trust Him. I want to serve Him."

"There is more than one way to serve, Elsie," she said gently.

Elsie felt she might cry. "I know that, Sister, but, I . . . I—" She broke off here. "Is it because I'm not good enough?" she ventured finally, feeling as though she had nothing more to lose.

Sr. Bernard let out a kind little laugh. "Of course you are good enough, Elsie! Do you not know that false humility is a sin?" she said, rising and coming out from behind her desk. She reached down then and held Elsie's face in her hands. "My child, you would be a wonderful sister, and we would rejoice at your choice of us and our way of life. But what I want, or what you want, for that matter, is less important than what God wants. He loves you very much," she said, looking into Elsie's eyes. She straightened up from her bent position, letting go of Elsie and pointing instead to the crucifix. "Reflect that

He would have endured the cross just for you, even if you were the only person on this earth. Contemplate that and try to understand your worth to Him. He cherishes you. So you should cherish you, too."

Elsie could not help that two tears escaped down her cheeks. Quickly she wiped them.

"Religious life is something one embraces, as a lover; it is not something one uses to hide within, nor something one rushes to. The veil is put on with great love, not donned in haste or fear. Do you understand?"

Elsie slowly nodded.

Sr. Bernard let out a little sigh. "Take this year to pray about it. If, after a year, you still feel that God is calling you to this life, then I will allow you to enter the novitiate. Does this not seem fair?" she asked, smiling down at her.

"Oh, thank you, Sister!" Elsie exclaimed, standing up now, and to her surprise, Sr. Bernard embraced her tightly, as if she were a beloved child. It was so much better than Elsie's previous silly imaginings of what would happen when she told Sr. Bernard her plan, and she felt a warmth and a gentleness radiate through her.

When Sr. Bernard finally released her, she held onto Elsie's arms and looked into her eyes. "You have so much love to give, Elsie. Whoever receives it will be very blessed."

Elsie immediately thought of the many children she would teach and love, and she felt her heart expand. Sheepishly, she smiled back. "Thank you, Sister," she said, holding up her new schedule. "I'll work very hard. And I'll pray about it, as you've said."

"Well, now that that is settled," she said, kindly, "why don't you go and unpack your things. And if you see Gunther, tell him that I need to see him regarding a telephone call from Mr. Lasik," she said, a hint of worry appearing in her eyes.

"Yes, Sister."

Though her revelation to Sr. Bernard hadn't gone exactly as she'd planned, Elsie left the Skyscraper feeling happier than she had in a

long time, repeating Sr. Bernard's words over and over to herself in
her mind. For the first time, she felt a little bit free and had to restrain
herself from skipping across the circular drive.

When she entered Philomena Hall, she again felt the usual sense
of peace that somehow emanated from these walls. She looked
around for her trunks, which Karl had deposited here for her earlier
this morning. Normally, move-in day was the only day that fathers
or brothers were allowed upstairs, but not being either of those, Karl
had thankfully been spared that task and had set them in the front
hall instead. If Elsie felt any loss at being accompanied to college by
an old, bent servant rather than a happy, excited family, she did not
consciously notice. She was grateful to be here at all.

As she removed her coat and looked around, she realized Gunther
must have carried her trunks up while she was speaking with Sr.
Bernard. She was anxious to go up and begin unpacking, but she
thought she should look for him first, remembering Sr. Bernard's
message and not wanting to be remiss in the first directive given to
her. She was tempted to shout for him but then remembered that it
was unladylike to raise one's voice and instead proceeded back to the
kitchen where she thought he might be.

Gently she pushed on the swinging door and poked her head
around to indeed find him sitting at the table. She stepped inside
and saw him close a little notebook he had been writing in and set it
by his mug. He looked up at her now.

"Oh, there you are," she said, giving him a smile.

"Were you looking for me?" he asked in a muted tone. He looked
more gaunt than she remembered.

"Thank you for carrying my trunks upstairs. It was you, wasn't it?"

Gunther acknowledged this with a nod. "So you are coming?" he
said with a smile. "I told you."

Elsie grinned back, unable to contain her excitement. "Yes, I . . .
I begin next week. I've just come from Sister's office. Oh! Which
reminds me. She said to tell you that she needs to speak with you.
Something about a telephone call from a Mr. Lasik, I think it was."

A shadow crossed Gunther's face, and he wearily stood up. "I will go to her after I am finished here," he said, slipping the little notebook into a pocket of his waistcoat.

"I . . . I didn't mean to interrupt you," she said, her eyes following his movements. "Were you working on something?"

"It is not important," he said. His mood seemed very different than it had a couple of weeks ago when they had talked of books and a little of his past in Germany in this very room. He had been so open and friendly then; now he seemed closed and distracted and perhaps a little sad.

"Merry Christmas," she said encouragingly.

"Yes, Merry Christmas." He smiled at her, but he still seemed sad, not merry at all.

"Are you . . . are you quite all right?" she asked tentatively.

He looked at her as if surprised by her question. "I am fine," he said not unkindly. "Just little tired perhaps." He reached for his mug and carried it to the counter where he pulled off the tea cozy and filled it with steaming tea. He set it on a tray, already prepared, next to a mug of milk and two plates holding a sandwich and a biscuit each.

"Oh, I'm sorry! I didn't mean to keep you from your lunch," Elsie said hastily.

"It is not mine," he said, his back still to her.

"Oh," Elsie said, puzzled. Who could they be for, then? she wondered. The sisters ate in their own private dining room served by the novitiates, so they couldn't be for them. "Are you taking them to your mother?" she asked, finally coming to the only conclusion that seemed possible. "Would you like me to help?"

"No," he said, turning back to her now, as he picked up the tray. "No, I am doing it. Maybe the door," he said nodding toward the back door.

Elsie quickly moved to open it for him, standing aside as she did so. "Don't you want your coat?" she asked.

"No, I am used to it. It is not far. Good day, Elsie. I will see you here soon, yes?" he asked and managed to give her a smile, despite his strained face.

She nodded and closed the door behind him. As she did so, however, it came to her that if the lunch was not for him and was supposedly for his mother, then why were there two plates? Why not just put two sandwiches on one? she thought as she climbed the back stairs to her new room.

Well, she needn't worry about Gunther and his sandwiches, she told herself, as she opened the door of her room and stepped inside. It was lovely and small, just how she remembered it. She had never felt comfortable in her massive room in Palmer Square. She walked across the worn hook rug that covered most of the wood floor and bent to look out the tiny window carved into the wall between her bed and Melody's. The sight of the lake beyond was wonderfully soothing. She stood up straight, then, turning to observe the room itself. Melody had left her side of the room neat and tidy, and on her side, she saw with gratitude, Gunther had indeed placed her trunks at the end of her bed. She still could not believe that she was really here, and she offered a silent prayer of thanksgiving.

Chapter 15

Clive pulled the car up to the Winnetka Police Station and roughly shoved the gear stick into park, irritated that it had come to this. He again questioned the wisdom of consulting the local nitwits, considering how his previous interview with them had gone, but he felt he had no choice.

His mother's endless badgering the last couple of weeks had come to a head last night when the subject of the whereabouts of the stolen painting had been inconveniently broached by none other than Randolph. After being thrashed by Clive, that gentleman had rejoined the merry party in the drawing room, painfully slinking in a full half hour after Clive had left him doubled over in the dining room, and had made it a point—apparently the only recourse to revenge he had at that moment—to politely inquire of Antonia if they had found the painting, shooting a daggered look at Clive as he did so. That, of course, opened up a torrent from Antonia, who once again began to question Clive and to voice her displeasure at the ineptitude of the Winnetka police force. Did they not take stolen art seriously? she had asked stiffly. Surely, he hadn't run his station in such a way, had he? she had asked Clive.

Clive had pinched the bridge of his nose and reminded her that he had never actually been *in charge* of a station. That that had been the chief's role.

Antonia ignored this clarification, however, and plowed on. They hadn't even sent anyone out to observe or even look for clues! she complained. Isn't that what you call it? she asked. Looking for clues? Nor had they even bothered to telephone or interview her. Randolph then snidely suggested that perhaps Clive had *forgotten* to go to the police, that it had perhaps slipped his mind with all that he had to worry about now at the firm. Antonia looked at Clive sharply and asked him if that were true. *Had* he gone to the police as he said he would? she asked.

"You gave me your word, Clive!" she exclaimed. "Your father never broke his word, you know," she added bitingly.

Clive felt the blow and was about to retort when Randolph spoke again, suggesting that perhaps "poor Clive" might be suffering from some sort of mental relapse, something similar perhaps to what he had experienced when he had returned from the war, despondent—nearly out of his mind, really—didn't they all remember that? Perhaps he needed help, Randolph went on. Or a long rest?

Antonia's previously narrowed eyes turned to a look of deep concern. Yes, she had been worried about him too, she acknowledged. Perhaps he should go see a doctor, she suggested.

Clive could almost feel Randolph's smirk at this preposterous statement, but he refused to look at him and thereby give him the satisfaction. In fact, Clive had to use every ounce of self-possession he had, he later told Henrietta, to control himself from calling Randolph outside to finish what he had started. Though glad that the attention had been shifted away from the whereabouts of the painting, he did not appreciate the fact that it had been maliciously replaced by a discussion regarding what could only be called his sanity and therefore grudgingly brought it back to the painting. In the end, he had assured his mother that he indeed had the case in hand and that he had already planned, he said, to revisit the police in the morning, though he couldn't promise who would be there the day after Christmas.

—

Clive sighed as he turned off the ignition and looked over at Henrietta, who had of course insisted on coming along, and he hadn't had the energy this morning to resist. She was bright and chipper, showing no ill effects of all the vintage wine they had drunk last night, and was annoyingly dressed in a tweed suit with a matching lady's fedora, reminiscent of some Sherlock Holmes novel. She smiled at him now, but all he could manage was to raise an eyebrow as he came around to her side and opened the door for her.

As she elegantly climbed out, her long, shapely legs preceding her, he said sternly, "Listen, I'm doing the talking, all right?" It was more a statement than a question, though to be honest, he wasn't really sure what he was going to say. *His father was being blackmailed? Someone had threatened his father's colleague? Someone followed them two nights ago?* He knew how it looked. He had seen it a hundred times before as a detective. It sounded vague and desperate. "Let's just get this over with, shall we?" he said to Henrietta.

"Oh, Clive, don't be such a wet blanket!" she said.

Wet blanket? Where had she learned to talk like that? he wondered and then remembered what her background really was. He forgot sometimes how poor and uneducated she had been. It surprised him, really. She was wonderfully adept at molding herself to whatever situation arose.

"I know you think this will come to nothing," she went on, "but we have to start somewhere. Remember, we *were* followed two nights ago."

Yes, he did remember, and it was actually the real reason he had made the decision to try again with the police. He could not ignore the potential danger that Henrietta, and perhaps even his mother, might consequently be in, and this time he was taking no chances. As they walked up the three cement steps to the station, he prayed that the chief might be off for the holidays and that perhaps Lieutenant Davis might be in instead, hoping that he wouldn't have to seek him out at his local establishment. What was it called? The Trophy Room? On Elm?

There were not many officers around as Clive and Henrietta stepped through the main doors of the station, but that was to be expected. It was only the day after Christmas, after all—Boxing Day, as his father used to call it.

"Can I help you, sir?" asked a clean-shaven officer behind the counter as he looked up from some papers he was leafing through.

"Yes, I'm here to see Chief Callahan."

"Not here I'm afraid, sir. Off for Christmas."

"I see," Clive said. *So far, so good.*

"I can take your name, sir. Or if it's something urgent-like, you can tell me. Something happen?" he asked, glancing at Henrietta now.

"No, no. It's not urgent," Clive answered. "I'm Clive Howard. I just wanted a word."

"Perhaps we might speak to someone else?" Henrietta put in smoothly, batting her lashes just a bit, Clive noticed. "Is there any chance Sergeant Davis would be in?" Henrietta asked sweetly. "I think that's his name."

The officer looked back and forth between the two of them as if trying to make up his mind before he reluctantly said, "I'll check. You wait here," he mumbled and then disappeared deeper into the station.

"I thought I told you that I'd do the talking," Clive said in an irritated whisper to Henrietta.

"Asking for Sergeant Davis is hardly 'doing the talking,' Clive," Henrietta retorted, just as the officer reappeared.

"Follow me," he said blandly, without any other explanation.

They followed the officer back toward the heart of the station, where they could see Sergeant Davis at his little nightstand of a desk, speaking on the telephone. There were more officers back here, typing or attempting to look busy. As Davis hung up the receiver, his eyes assessing first Clive and then Henrietta, Clive again noticed that Davis was still in shirtsleeves and suspenders and had not shaved in several days, by the look of it.

"Oh, it's you, Howard," Davis said casually, propping his cheek up with his fist as his arm rested on the desk. "To what do I owe this pleasure? I'm sure it's not to wish me a Merry Christmas."

"Indeed no. I'm here about my father's case," Clive said curtly.

"Correct me if my memory is wrong, but there is no case," Davis said, leaning back in his chair now and folding his arms.

"Oh, it really is a case, Sergeant. He really was murdered," Henrietta said seriously, causing Davis to stare at her for what seemed a long time.

"And who would you be? Let me guess, Mrs. Howard, the younger," he said, his eyes running her up and down.

"Yes, I'm Mrs. Clive Howard," she said stiffly, in what sounded to Clive to be a very close imitation of his mother, and despite himself, he was amused. "And we have some information—"

"Look, old man, might we have a word?" Clive interrupted. "Somewhere private? Perhaps we could step into the chief's office?"

"The chief doesn't really like anyone in his office, but I suppose we can make an exception," he said lazily. "Since you are *Mr. Howard.*" He stood up, gesturing them toward the darkened office behind him.

Quickly, Clive proceeded past him, deciding to ignore the insolence. Davis followed them in, switching on the light and shutting the door. He gestured for the Howards to sit on the two available chairs in front of the desk, while he walked around behind. Clive noticed with approval that he did not sit down, however, but leaned against the window, his arms crossed again in front of him. At least he showed respect for his commanding officer by not taking his seat, Clive thought.

"Okay, what is it?" Davis asked in a bored tone.

"Look, several things have surfaced that have led me—us," he said, glancing over at Henrietta, "to believe that there was definitely foul play regarding my father's death."

Davis's eyes flicked. "Such as?"

"Well, for one thing, I've discovered that he was being extorted from. I found a rather damning letter in his study. Someone by the name of Lawrence Susan. Ring a bell?"

Davis shook his head but looked intrigued despite his nonchalance. "Go on."

"Apparently, my father's been the victim of extortion for years. His colleague at work corroborated it."

"Hmmm. Extortion, eh? Any idea why?"

"None."

"What's this colleague's name?"

"Sidney Bennett."

"Go on."

Clive cleared his throat. "Mr. Bennett confessed to me that these extortionists have been demanding money from my father for years, apparently, but that just recently, these thugs, led by this Susan apparently, demanded an unusually exorbitant amount from my father. I'm not sure why. As a result, it seems my father sold a rather valuable painting to raise the money and then had some sort of cocked-up plan to only give half the money to them on the train platform, where he was instructed to meet them, and then follow them."

"On the train platform? Here in Winnetka?"

"Yes," Clive said evenly, trying to keep the irritation from his voice. "Remember? The train platform he 'slipped' from?"

"All right, all right," Davis said, rolling his eyes. "Assuming all of this is true, why only give them half the dough? And why follow them?"

"I don't know," Clive sighed. "It doesn't make any sense to me either, but, then again, my father wasn't really the detective type. I'm not sure he really thought it through."

"I see," Davis mused, "Any idea who they were? Can this Bennett identify them?"

"He says no, that he was too distraught when my father fell in front of the train."

"Fell or pushed?"

Clive raised his eyebrows. "Pushed presumably. It seems the thugs opened the case and discovered that half the money wasn't there. Bennett says there was a 'scuffle,' is how he put it, and the next thing he knew, he saw my father fall."

"So not much to go on."

"Not really."

Davis rubbed his chin. "Seems I'll have to question this Bennett," he said, reaching for a notebook from his back trouser pocket.

"Yes, I thought you would. He's had a couple of nasty instances since then, which you might question him about."

"Like what?"

"Rock through his window. Slashed tires. Dead dog."

"They must have seen him on the platform. That or he's in deeper than we know."

"He may very well be. Apparently, there've been many extortion letters delivered over the years, but upon my father's death, Bennett went to his study and removed them all."

"Why?"

Clive shrugged. "He says so that my mother wouldn't find them and be upset."

Davis looked skeptical. "That was considerate of him. But maybe he just wanted to remove the evidence. Maybe he's a part of it, and the vandalism stories are just made up."

"Maybe," Clive sighed. "But his fear seems real."

Davis scratched a few notes down and then looked up at the two of them, as if considering something. "But why now?" he asked. "Why would you two come in now?" he asked again, looking at them. "Something else must have happened. Something recent."

Clive was very impressed with Davis. He was exceptionally sharp, and he liked the way he thought. Also his procedure was first-rate.

"I'm pretty sure *we're* being followed now," he explained to Davis. "Which Bennett warned me about, actually. I caught their scent Christmas Eve night. We were leaving my mother-in-law's home in Logan Square. We lost them when we headed north, of course."

"Hmmm. Getting more interesting by the minute," Davis said, giving them a grin. "Anything else?"

Clive let out a deep breath. "Only that my mother is threatening to telephone here and report the painting my father sold as stolen. I've confirmed that the butler sold it, legally, in town, but I don't want to tell her that. She has no idea about the extortion or the money or any of this really, and I'd like to keep it that way. At least for now. Meanwhile, she's wondering why you haven't done anything to discover the painting's whereabouts. So currently she's rather irate, hence her threats to telephone. Just thought I'd warn you," he said with a small smile.

"I see," Davis said, flipping the notebook shut as he considered the information before him. "I don't know," he said easily. "I've seen Mrs. Howard about. She doesn't strike me as particularly delicate. She might be able to shed some light on all of this."

Clive shifted uncomfortably. Davis had a point of course, but he couldn't explain not wanting to involve his mother. He felt there was more to this case than even he knew at this point. He felt his father was hiding something along with the money; why else would he have been so cryptic and foolish? And until he knew all the facts, he didn't want his mother's involvement in case he found something particularly damning, like perhaps a mistress after all. "Listen, Sergeant, she's been through a lot recently, and I'd rather spare her if I could. At least for the moment. This is hardly the topic of conversation for a lady," he added, attempting to bluff.

"Hmm," Davis said, sticking out his lower lip as he pondered. "And yet you've involved your lovely wife, here," he said, turning his gaze on Henrietta again and making a point of staring at her legs. "And she's *very* much a lady, from what I can see."

Clive felt the heat rising in his face and was about to respond when Henrietta beat him to it. "Oh, you needn't worry about me, Sergeant Davis," Henrietta said, coolly crossing her legs. "As a detective's wife—"

"Former," Clive interrupted.

"I'm made of sterner stuff than that," she said, flashing Davis a smile. "In fact, we're opening a detective agency. If you hear of any cases, you might send them our way."

Clive closed his eyes and let out a groan as a grin erupted on Davis's face followed by a loud laugh.

"A detective agency, is it?" he asked, amused, looking from one to the other.

"Sergeant, listen—" Clive attempted to say.

"Well, that will come in very handy around here, I'm sure," Davis continued, still grinning. "Since our current caseload is overflowing," he said, gesturing aimlessly around the room. "Or do you mean to compete with us?"

His brow furrowed, Clive shot him a look and gave him a tiny shake of his head, hoping Davis would understand. Thankfully, Davis responded with a little wink of understanding, but he still had a grin spread across his face.

Unfortunately, however, Henrietta spied it too. "I saw that, Sergeant!" Henrietta said crisply. "You think we're joking, but we're very much in earnest, aren't we, Clive?"

Annoyed in the extreme, Clive looked at her, a rebuke ready, but, seeing her innocent eagerness, he instead almost gave in to laughing along with Davis, so absurd was the situation. He bit his lip to hold it in. He would speak to her later about following his direction. If they were indeed to work together, he needed to trust that she would listen to him. Technically, he supposed that she had followed his direction in letting him do most of the talking here today, but she had still found a way to maddeningly interject her own opinion. And despite how charming he found it, it simply wouldn't do.

"Listen, can we just get back to the case?" Clive said in a clipped tone, successfully burying his amusement.

"I suppose we should," Davis said, also sobering and pulling his eyes from Henrietta. "Right. I'll start looking into this. I'll dig up this Bennett and go from there. In the meantime, do you want us to stake some guys outside the house? And I'd like to see this letter you found."

Clive considered for a moment. Staking police outside the house would definitely rouse his mother's notice; plus, he wasn't sure it was completely necessary at this point. "I don't think we need that kind of protection just yet," Clive responded. "But maybe some extra patrol cars in the area. In the meantime, I'll bring the letter by."

"Don't you think you should inform the chief?" Henrietta asked.

"He's off these two weeks," Davis said. "Which isn't such a bad thing," he muttered. "Though I didn't say that," he said looking at both of them and wagging his finger between them.

"Right," said Clive, standing now. "We'll be off. Thanks, Sergeant. I'll let you know if anything else turns up."

"Just one more question," Davis put in, as he came from around the back of the desk. "Where'd the rest of the money go? From the painting?"

Again, Clive looked at him with respect. "I wish I knew. I can't seem to find it or trace it in any of his accounts."

"What about the servants? Didn't you say the butler sold it? What's his name?"

"Mr. Billings," Henrietta answered.

"He wasn't able to shed any light on it?" he asked of Clive.

"None, really. It's damned frustrating. No one seems to know anything."

"Except Bennett," Davis said quietly.

"What about Carter?" Henrietta asked.

"Who's Carter?" Davis asked keenly.

"My father's valet, or, rather, my valet now," Clive answered. "Yes, I've questioned him," he said, flashing Henrietta a look. *Why had she brought up Carter?* "He didn't have much to offer."

"That's odd," Davis mused. "Isn't the valet supposed to know all the intimate secrets of his master? He might be worth me questioning at some point."

"You're welcome to try, but he's a bit of a dull dolt. You won't get much out of him."

"Well, you know what they say, 'the butler did it'—or something like that anyway," he said with a cocky smile.

"This is hardly the time for levity, Sergeant," Clive said, annoyed.

"You're right. My money, no pun intended, is on this Bennett. Just a feeling."

They had reached the front doors, and Davis stood to the side as they passed through, his hands rudely in his trouser pockets. "I'll be in touch," he said, touching one hand to his forehead in a little salute. And though irritated by his sudden flippancy, Clive could not help credit Davis's assessment. He wasn't sure what Bennett's role exactly was in his father's death, but he knew he was holding something back, and he hoped he could get to the bottom of it before it was too late.

Chapter 16

Elsie looked up from the novel she was reading and glanced around her little room at Mundelein, perplexed, having forgotten for a moment where she was. Although she had vowed to give up reading novels after the failed affair with Harrison, she shamefully hadn't had the willpower to do so just yet. Besides, she had told herself, surely she would have to give them up once she took her real vows, so she thought it expedient to read as many as possible now, while she still could.

The room was growing dim. It would be dark soon and nearly time for the vigil. She would have to hurry. As usual, she was in danger of being late; only this time, she couldn't blame Ma for it. It was New Year's Eve, and as she set her book to the side, she couldn't help feel a little guilty about the double deception she was participating in. Surely God would forgive her fibs—or lies, she should have the courage to call them—in exchange for the whole night of prayer, wouldn't He? Was lying for a good cause acceptable? she wondered. Hadn't Henrietta once said as much to Ma?

The girls would be returning from Christmas break soon, and Elsie was eager to fit in. She wasn't officially supposed to be here yet, but since Sr. Bernard had allowed her to bring her things after Christmas, she had gotten permission to spend a couple of nights here this week under the guise of wanting to study. It was so quiet and peaceful here in Philomena Hall, and Elsie tried to remind herself that it wouldn't always be this way. Soon, she imagined, it would be loud and bustling and exciting, which she looked forward to in a certain way as well. In the meantime, she enjoyed walking the grounds and visiting the libraries and reading. She helped herself to some of the food in the kitchen, per Sr. Bernard's instruction, as the dining hall was not open over the break, nor was she allowed in the convent to eat with the Sisters.

Once or twice, she had caught Gunther in the kitchen, and he had each time invited her to have a mug of tea with him. His previous good mood had returned, and she found him so easy to talk to. More than once, she marveled at his ability to speak English as well as he did. She asked him to teach her some German, but he had merely laughed, saying "No one wants to speak German now." He had eventually acquiesced, however, and taught her a couple of words here and there, but mostly he told her stories about his past life in Germany, about his days as a teacher. He never asked her any more about her life, which was fine with her. She didn't want to talk about herself.

She had never met a man who had read so much, and she couldn't help but admire him for it, even though she had barely heard of half the authors he spoke about. His love for words and his little soliloquies regarding love and life were contagious and attractive, and she found herself even seeking him out at times. He always had a smile for her, but he couldn't always linger, as he sometimes had to hurry off to do some job somewhere on the tiny campus.

She rose now and smoothed down her cotton dress, glad that she was not having to don a ball gown of some sort. It felt delicious to be doing something so counter to what everyone else would be participating in tonight. She felt special and, well, holy, at having been invited by Sr. Bernard to attend the Sisters' all-night prayer vigil in their private chapel in the Skyscraper instead of being out celebrating and drinking like the rest of the world, though she did feel guilty about having to lie both to Aunt Agatha and to Henrietta.

She had managed to wriggle out of attending the Penningtons' Ball with the Exleys by repeatedly explaining that she had to attend Henrietta's birthday party. Aunt Agatha was positively fuming and actually at one point threatened to call Grandfather over the matter, but in the end, she had finally given up, perhaps having had second thoughts about the wisdom of admitting her defeat to her father-in-law. She supposed Elsie would have to go to Henrietta's party, Aunt Agatha had said to her, but if it were such an important event, why had Elsie not told her about it sooner? She could have arranged things differently, she had huffed and then whined. Elsie did not say much in answer to her aunt's questions but thanked her profusely and promised to be all the more attentive to her in the new year, though she guessed that that would be a difficult promise to keep.

It had been harder to lie to Henrietta, who was begging her to come out dancing with her and Clive at the Aragon, her especial birthday wish. She could meet her friends from the Marlowe, she had said, but this did not really appeal to Elsie, either. Though if it weren't for the vigil, she *might* have been just a little bit tempted. Clive could be so charming at times, and he had always been kind to her . . .

 But she was determined to attend the vigil, and, anyway, she didn't like the sound of meeting up with Henrietta's friends. What if Rose was there? And worse, Stanley? She shifted uncomfortably and felt her face grow warm. It's not as if she still loved Stanley, it's just that she didn't particularly want to see him, either. She was happy for him, if he had found someone to love, she told herself. Perhaps they could be good friends, she mused, having allowed herself more than once to imagine attending Stan and Rose's wedding, dressed in a full nun's habit of course and giving them her blessing. But what if he read too much into it? What if he assumed she had run to the convent because of their shattered affair?

Oh, this was silly! she told herself as she went down the back stairs that led directly into the kitchen. She had gotten into the habit of using them instead of the front staircase, as the old servants' stairs were nearer to her room. And, anyway, the front was kept dark while the term was not in session. What did it matter what Stanley thought?

As she entered the bright kitchen now, she saw Gunther, again sitting at the table, writing in his little notebook. He looked startled to see her.

"Oh. I did not know you were still here. You are quiet like mouse," he said with a smile, as he closed his book and put it in his pocket.

"Sister said I could," she explained. "I'm . . . I'm attending the vigil with them."

"What vigil?"

"The prayer vigil?"

"Ah. Their night of prayer."

"Yes, they're praying all night for peace for the world."

Gunther gave her a sad, disbelieving sort of smile.

Elsie didn't know what to say next. "Are you . . . are you spending the evening with your mother? Or . . . or going out?" she asked, her eyes reactively darting to the counter where two sandwiches again sat. Did they ever eat any other food? she wondered. "I could make you something sometime," she said tentatively, nodding toward the tray. "Until Sister Alphonse comes back. I'm actually a pretty good cook," she said, blushing slightly. "Then you and your mother wouldn't have to have sandwiches all the time."

Gunther stood up. "No, there is no need. But thank you. I live over behind Piper. The stove is broken there, and I have not had time to be fixing it," he said, running his hand through his hair. "It is easier to make something here and carry it over since I am so much being here."

"Oh. Well, do you want any help?"

"No, but thank you for your kindness," he offered.

Elsie didn't know what else to say, and she was conscious that the vigil would probably be starting any minute. "Well, I have to go," she said.

"I will walk with you," he said. "It is icy, and I need to go there anyway for different matter."

"But what about your dinner?" she asked.

"Oh, that can wait. It is still early," he said with a smile as he reached for his heavy coat and tattered cap. "Go on. Get your coat."

Elsie felt uneasy about taking him from his mother and her dinner, but she could sense he would not be swayed. Obediently, she went to the cloakroom for her coat and joined him at the door, wrapping a thick, woolen scarf around her neck.

"Here, take my arm," he said, leading her down the back stone steps. "It is very icy. I am sorry. I need to scrape again."

"You're only one person," Elsie said, taking his arm and noticing how threadbare was his coat. It looked dirty too. "It seems like too much work for just one person. Can't they hire more people?" she asked.

"Ach! No, I can manage. I like to be busy."

Elsie remained silent on their slow walk across the campus, bending slightly from the wind and watching the cars whip by on Sheridan on their way to some New Year's Eve party or club, slowing as they rounded the curve and then speeding up once they passed. For a brief moment, she wished she was joining Henrietta at the Aragon. Maybe she had made a mistake. After all, how often would she get a chance like that?

"Do you think it's all right to lie for a good cause?" she asked Gunther suddenly.

She felt him stiffen, but perhaps it was in response to a particularly strong gust of wind that almost pushed them backward. Gunther took so long in answering that she thought maybe he hadn't heard her. She was about to repeat the question when he simply said, "Sometimes, yes. Sometimes is necessary. Why?" he asked, and she felt him look at her.

"Oh. No reason," she said, not wanting to confess her sins at this point. Besides, they were nearly to the Skyscraper. Gunther let go of her once they were inside and followed her to the shiny, art deco elevators, removing his cap as they went. There was no one in the lobby at all; in fact, the whole building seemed deserted, and their footsteps sounded unusually distinct as they walked across the lobby. The main lights had been turned off, and only the chrome sconces along the walls were lit, giving off a yellowish glow.

Elsie removed her scarf as they waited awkwardly for one of the elevators to open, but there was no movement. The indicator bar in the half-moon glass above the doors stayed permanently on "L," and in fact no internal machinery could be heard working at all.

Elsie finally turned to look at Gunther, conscious that she was holding him up. "Well, thank you, Gunther. You don't have to wait with me," she said politely.

"I do not mind," he said, looking at the bar, which was still on "L."

"Maybe no one's on duty tonight," Elsie said. "I'll just take the stairs. It will do me good," she said, turning away from the elevator toward the direction of the staircase in the center of the lobby.

"It is fourteen floors! No, I can get it," Gunther offered.

"You don't have to," she said, feeling increasingly guilty at keeping him from his mother and his evening off. She wished he would just leave her.

"It will just take minute," he said and reached to draw the grate open. He pulled, but it appeared to be stuck or locked and wouldn't budge. "This is not how it should be," he said, baffled, and put both hands on the grate now and yanked hard. The grate came free then, the culprit in lodging it stuck apparently being a ragged piece of metal that had somehow broken off and caught on the elevator's frame. They later learned that one of the elevator girls had indeed reported this malfunction to Sr. Francis, the sister in charge of the building's maintenance, but it had somehow not been brought to poor Gunther's attention to fix until this moment, when the ragged piece of metal unfortunately caught him as he yanked the grate loose—and subsequently sliced through his wrist.

"*Autsch!*" Gunther cried loudly, gripping his hand and staring at his wrist, the cuff of his white shirt turning red. His knees buckled, then, and he sank slowly to the ground.

Elsie, not realizing exactly what had happened, hurried over to him and was stunned by the large amount of blood pouring from the wound.

"Oh, Gunther," she panted, feeling terrified and faint, as she crouched beside him, watching his blood gurgling out at an alarming rate.

"*Autsch!* Elsie. Help me!" Gunther stuttered.

Panic filled Elsie, and she raised herself back up onto her feet. "Help!" she cried, looking around frantically. "Help!" she called again, her voice bouncing uselessly off the walls of the abandoned lobby. She looked back at Gunther, still on his knees on the ground and gripping his injured arm, the blood beginning to pool under it now.

"Help!" she called again and began to debate leaving him to go find someone, even if it meant running all the way up to the convent.

At that moment, however, the errant elevator girl appeared from around the corner, smelling distinctly of cigarette smoke. Once she caught sight of the two of them, the ground around them splattered with blood, she froze in place and let out a piercing scream.

"Go get help!" Elsie shouted at her and watched as the girl backed slowly away and then turned and ran, calling back as she went that she would get the guard. Elsie turned her attention back to Gunther, sliding down on her knees as well. Without thinking, she tore off her scarf and wrapped his arm as best she could. Gunther's face was contorted in pain, and he looked ghostly white, as if he might pass out any moment. Even so, he tried after a moment to stand.

"Gunther, no!" she cried. "Just sit still. Help will be here soon."

"I am fine, he said raggedly.

"No, you're not," she said, observing the pain in his face. "It'll be okay, but you just have to wait. Help's coming . . . I can hear them."

And she did hear footsteps pounding down the hall, coming toward them. A moment later, the elevator girl reappeared with a portly security guard who looked as though he may have just recently been woken up, and who stood now, assessing the scene as he nervously pushed his cap toward the back of his head.

"Get that chair!" he shouted to the elevator girl, pointing down the hallway toward a lone chair that had somehow escaped its classroom. The elevator girl took several minutes to comprehend what was being asked of her, but when the guard shouted, "Go on!" she snapped to attention and hurried to get it and dragged it back. The guard gave Elsie a nod, then, and they both took hold of Gunther under his arms and got him up and gingerly placed him in the chair.

"All right, let's see what you've got," he said sternly and began to unwind Elsie's now blood-soaked scarf. He dropped it on the ground and began to inspect the wound. Elsie winced when she saw the deep gash, blood still gurgling forth. How had he cut himself that badly? she wondered, her stomach roiling in panic. All he did was pull the grating back . . .

"You've got to get to the hospital, lad," the guard said grimly. "I'll hafta drive you down to Ravenswood," he said, feeling for his keys in the front trouser pockets of his thick navy uniform pants. "Here, little lady," he said, spotting Gunther's handkerchief hanging out of his shirt pocket and pulling it out. Swiftly, he stuffed it on the wound, causing Gunther to cry out in pain. "Put your hand here," he said to her, ignoring Gunther. "Hold it tight."

"No hospital," Gunther said weakly.

"Sorry, lad, but this is a bad one. It's deep, and you're losing a lot of blood," he said over his shoulder, walking briskly back toward his office, the elevator girl following him like a stray dog. "Be back in a minute."

"Elsie, I do not want to go to hospital," Gunther said, leaning his head back against the wall. "Please . . . I cannot go. Help me."

"Gunther, you have to. It's pretty bad," she said, keeping her eyes on the wound and pressing tight on the handkerchief. The blood was beginning to slow a fraction, but it was seeping through to her fingers now. "If it's your mother you're worried about, I can check in on her," Elsie offered, careful to keep up the pressure.

"No," he said, almost in a panic. "Do . . . do not disturb her. She will be asleep," he said, wincing his eyes closed, as if against the pain. Suddenly he opened them and looked at her. "You go," he said. "You go on to your vigil. I will be fine. The guard will help me. Please, this is my fault."

"Don't be silly. I'm coming with you," she said, before she had even thought it through.

"But what about this vigil?" he asked.

"Oh, that doesn't matter," she said hurriedly. "It was just a way for me to get out of having to dance."

"A girl who does not like dancing?" he said, closing his eyes again, as his lips curled into a smile. "This is very strange."

The guard reappeared then and, removing the bloody handkerchief and handing it to Elsie to hold, managed to bandage Gunther's wrist with a bit of flimsy gauze. It seemed adequate enough for the moment, but Elsie thought she might have been able to do a better job.

"We need to go now," the guard mumbled, surveying his work. "You might get lucky. It's still early, so it won't be full of New Year's Eve drunks yet. You comin', too?" he asked of Elsie as she crumpled the bloody handkerchief still in her hand and stuffed it into her pocket.

"Yes, of course I'm coming."

"Let's go, then," he said, indicating with his head that she should stand on the other side of Gunther, and together they helped him to stand up.

The drive to Ravenswood Hospital was miraculously short, the guard escorting them into the main lobby, where he deposited the two of them. Elsie was shocked when he almost immediately turned to go, saying that he wasn't really supposed to leave his post and that, anyway, Elsie seemed to have her wits about her enough to handle the situation, didn't she? Elsie could only nod and swallowed hard at being made responsible for this bleeding man.

Gunther sat with his eyes closed, and Elsie wasn't sure he was even conscious. Before long, a harried nurse appeared and pulled back the bandages, saying that he would need stitches right away. Two orderlies appeared, then, and helped him to walk back through a set of doors. Elsie stood up to follow, but the harried nurse held out her hand to stop her.

"Who are you?" she asked crisply, though her eyes looked tired. A large mole sat near the corner of her upper lip, and Elsie tried not to stare at it.

"I'm . . . I'm his friend . . ." Elsie faltered, not knowing what else to call him.

"You wait here. Shouldn't take long," she said, pointing back toward the chairs lined up against the wall.

Her knees shaking a little, Elsie sat down and tried to sort out her many thoughts. Desperately she prayed that Gunther would be okay. Surely, he hadn't lost too much blood, had he? And what would Sr. Bernard think when she didn't turn up at the vigil? She hoped she wouldn't think that she had frivolously changed her mind and gone to some party . . .

Elsie promptly scolded herself, then, for only being worried about herself! What about Gunther's poor mother? she thought, and envisioned the undelivered sandwiches sitting lonely on the counter. His mother would be terribly worried! If only she could telephone someone—but who? She was pretty sure that there would be nobody at the Mundelein switchboard at this point. Henrietta was already out, she was sure, so who else? For a moment, she considered telephoning home. Maybe Karl could come over, but to do what? More than likely he would bungle it anyway. Her only consolation was that the security guard would eventually have to let one of the sisters know what had happened, and then hopefully they would have the wherewithal to let Gunther's mother know where he was.

Relieved a bit now that there was some sort of plan in place, even if it was only in her mind, she spent first some time looking around her at the plain white walls and then at the staff as they hurried to and fro. As time ticked on, more and more people were brought in, either by friends and relatives or by ambulance—some of them, it seemed, quite severe. Elsie moved to the chair farthest away from the doors and tried to close her eyes to pray, but it was terribly hard to concentrate.

After what seemed to be hours, she felt a tap on the arm. It was the same nurse from before. Quickly Elsie opened her eyes wide, realizing that she must have fallen asleep. "Yes?" she asked, sitting up straight and trying to discreetly rub her eyes.

"Are you with Mr. Stockel?" the nurse asked.

Mr. Stockel? "You mean Gunther?" Elsie asked, embarrassed that she didn't even know his last name.

"The German guy with the slit wrist?"

"Yes!" Elsie said hurriedly. "Is he all right?"

"Yeah, he's all right. But we're going to keep him in. He's lost a lot of blood, and he has a small fever. You want to see him?"

Elsie's stomach clenched. *A fever? Keep him overnight?* "Yes . . . yes, I want to see him."

"Come on, then," she said, gesturing with her hand. They passed through the main doorway, the doors swinging closed behind them, and Elsie was hit with the strong smell of antiseptic. The nurse turned immediately to her right and began climbing the stairs that were there. "Elevator's broke," she said. Elsie furrowed her brow at how odd a coincidence this was. She felt like she was in a dream.

The nurse stopped on the third floor and began walking quickly down the darkened hallway, Elsie struggling to keep up. "Any idea why he did it?" the nurse asked routinely, not even looking at Elsie.

"Did what?"

"Slit his wrist."

Slit his wrist? Elsie pondered. Slit his wrist! "Oh, no!" she said, realizing what the nurse meant. "No, I was there when it happened," she went on in a rush, bending toward the nurse as they hurriedly walked, trying to get the nurse to look at her. The nurse did not oblige but kept her eyes focused on the end of the hallway. "No, he . . . he pulled on the elevator grate," Elsie went on. "It was stuck, you see, and when he pulled, it came loose, and something cut him. It was terrible!" Elsie said.

The nurse did not respond but stopped outside a door behind which Gunther apparently was. Only now did she turn and look at Elsie, her eyes quickly assessing her.

"That's what he said too. Stories seem to match. Didn't really look like a suicide, but we have to ask." Elsie didn't know whether to be relieved or angry. The nurse nodded her head toward the door. "He's a little daffy; we gave him something for the pain. He was asleep when I left him, but you can go in if you want." With that, she turned on her heel and made her way back down the hallway, stopping half-way to enter a different room.

Elsie stood outside the room for a moment and took a deep breath before rapping gently on the door with her knuckles. There was no answer from within, and she had no wish to wake him by knocking louder, so she quietly pushed open the door. She gasped a little when she saw him, lying in the hospital bed, his arm thickly bandaged. The room was dark except for the warm glow given off by a small bedside lamp. His eyes were closed, and he lay so per-fectly still that he looked to be dead. Still standing in the doorway, Elsie could not help but peer through the darkness to see if his chest was indeed rising and falling. When she saw that it was, she breathed a sigh of relief and made her way closer to the bed. As she approached, he opened his eyes, then, and looked at her. He seemed surprised, almost alarmed, by the sight of her and stirred restlessly.

"Gunther," Elsie said quietly, wanting to calm him. "It's just me, Elsie. Elsie Von Harmon."

His face relaxed into a smile, then, and he closed his eyes. "That is not a just," he said, which did not make sense to Elsie. Maybe he really was delirious.

"How are you?" she asked. "Are you in pain?"

He looked awful, she thought, as she peered at him close up. His face was flushed, and his breathing was shallow. Why did he seem so ill? It was just a cut, after all. Maybe he had already been sick with something else?

He opened his eyes. "Not much. You should go now," he said. "You do not have to stay here with me."

"No, I'll sit with you," she said and tried to smile, laying her coat on the end of his bed.

"But what about vigil?" he asked.

"We've already been through this," she reminded him. "It doesn't matter. It was just a silly thing for me to escape from my ridiculous aunt."

Gunther opened his eyes wide then and tried to sit up. "I must go now," he said, looking around the room wildly. "Please. I must go back."

"Gunther, no. You're not well," she said eagerly. "You have to stay, the nurse said. You have a fever."

"Ach. No. I must go!" he said, swinging his legs off the bed as he sat up.

"Gunther, no!" Elsie said. "The nurse will be back, and you'll be in trouble. You can't leave like this!"

"I cannot leave her there. She does not know where I am!"

"I'll go and tell them in a little bit. Anyway, I'm sure the security guard will have told the sisters by now," Elsie said calmly, hoping this were true. "They'll make sure she is okay." She saw that he was hesitating. He was beginning to sway, and she ventured to press on his shoulders, trying to do so by only using two fingers from each hand. "That's it," she said. "Just lie back." He relaxed his body and allowed himself to lie back down.

"You will make sure, yes?" he asked, his voice raspy. "That the Sisters go to her?"

"Yes, of course I will," she said, gingerly pulling up the blanket for him and trying not to look at his chest as she did so. His eyes followed hers for a moment before he closed them in what seemed to be exhaustion.

Relieved that she had gotten him back into bed and further wanting him to drift into a deeper sleep, she looked around for a chair that she could sit on. She saw one on the other side of the bed, but that part of the room was dark. Quietly, she made her way around and bent to pick it up to carry it around to the other side where there was more light. As she did so, however, she saw that someone, probably one of the nurses, had set his coat there. Elsie picked it up to move it, and his little notebook fell to the ground. She bent to retrieve it, looking over at him, but his eyes were still closed. She set the coat on top of hers at the end of the bed and then carried the chair around. She sat down on it, the notebook still in her hands, and wondered what to do next.

Elsie took the opportunity to study his face. It was a fine, angular face with a high forehead. She hadn't noticed how long his eyelashes were and that they were almost blond. His mustache and beard were neatly trimmed. He looked a lot younger with his eyes closed and his spectacles removed. Someone had removed them and folded them neatly on his bedside table.

Unexpectedly, he opened his eyes again, startling her, as he turned to look at her. "Tell me something about yourself," he said.

Elsie didn't know what to say. Did he think she was someone else? "I . . . I don't know what you want to know."

"Anything," he said "It will help me to be going back to sleep. I am restless," he said, looking up at the ceiling. "*Bitte.* Please."

"Well . . . what do you want to know?" she asked tentatively.

"Anything. Tell me about your life as a little girl."

She furrowed her brow, studying him, as if trying to decide whether she should really share any of her childhood memories with him . . . if she trusted him enough. He looked at her again, his sky-blue eyes patient and waiting. She sighed deeply and slowly began by telling him a story about her father and how he once rescued a cat for her. It was her earliest memory; she was probably no more than four, she said. Gunther listened, a small smile on his face as he closed his eyes again. She could see that he was drifting in and out, so she kept going, telling him all about their miserable poverty and how her father had eventually killed himself and what Ma was like now. As she said this last bit, she looked down at her hands and realized she was still holding his notebook.

She looked back at him to see if he were yet sleeping, but he was not. He was looking at her, his eyes heavy and kind. "What else?" he asked, and she felt oddly encouraged to go on. She had never really told anyone her whole story before, and she found she was enjoying it in some strange way. She went on, then, to talk about how Henrietta had met Clive and how they had been reunited with her mother's wealthy family and how things were finally so much better for them.

"Are they?" he asked tiredly. She could see that he was struggling to stay awake, but she was eager to tell the rest of her story, though she felt horribly selfish at wanting to go on. The whole point had been to put him to sleep! Perhaps if she sat quietly, he would drift off. . .

He closed his eyes and breathed deeply for a few moments before opening them again. "Are they?" he asked, looking at her again.

"Are they what?" she asked.

"*Ist es jetzt besser für dich?*"

She did not understand him. He kept lapsing into German; perhaps he was delirious.

"Are you happy?" he asked.

"Yes, of course I'm happy," she said, startled by this question.

"Then why do you wish to *flucht*? Escape?" he asked, his eyes closing again.

Elsie was stunned by this. How did he know? But then she remembered the very first conversation she had had with him in which he had told her that she must learn to play the game better than they and that through books lay her escape. How had she forgotten this?

She paused, trying to think how to answer. Should she tell him her secret? What would it matter? she finally decided. He probably wouldn't remember any of this tomorrow anyway. "I . . . I don't want to get married," she said hesitantly. "Not to any of them," she said.

"No?" he said, turning toward her now and watching her with his pale blue eyes.

"No," she said, leaning toward him a little, conspiratorially. "I . . . I'm going to become a sister."

"You are already a sister," he said, blinking slowly.

"No, a nun, I mean. I'm going to enter the convent," she tried to say proudly, but it came out sounding hollow and dry. He was the first person she had told, besides Sr. Bernard, of course, and it again wasn't unfolding the way she had imagined it would.

He turned his head away and closed his eyes. "*Es tut mir leid*—I am sorry," he said, his voice cracking. He drifted off then, leaving Elsie to wonder if his apology was for succumbing to sleep or regret for her announcement. Well, she reasoned, if it was regret, what had she expected? He was a Lutheran, she remembered, so he wouldn't understand. Not many would, she knew. It was just something she was going to have to get used to. Well, at least she would be pleasing God, and that was all that mattered, she told herself.

She could hear Gunther's deep breathing now, and she sensed that he was finally asleep. She shifted in the hard chair and felt uneasy that she had revealed so much about herself. Well, she thought, pulling at her blouse to adjust it, hopefully he really wouldn't remember anything of what she had said. Her eyes traveled to the notebook still in her hands. She was pretty sure this was the same notebook she had often seen him writing in in the kitchen of Philomena.

She looked over at him, still asleep, and then back at the notebook. She knew she shouldn't read it, but she longed to see what he kept in it. Besides, she reasoned, she had just told him so much about her life. Wasn't it fair for her to have a little look?

Carefully, holding the book on its side, she flipped the pages quickly through her fingers to see if anything interesting revealed itself, at least in the margins. Nothing surprising jumped out at her, however, so she gave herself permission to open it a little more . . .

It looked like it was just notes.

She glanced over at Gunther. Would it be terrible if she read some of it? she wondered. Well, what would it matter? And what else was she to do? She supposed she should eventually go back to the college,

but she did not wish to leave just yet and not without saying good-
bye. And, honestly, there was nothing for her to do back at Mundelein
except go to bed, and it wasn't even yet ten o'clock. She supposed she
could sit here and say the rosary as a way of still fulfilling the vigil,
albeit remotely. The more she pondered it, the more she thought that
it was a wonderful idea, actually. But the notebook lay hot in her
hands. She compromised with herself, finally, that she would read a
little of Gunther's writings and *then* say the rosary.

Happy with her decision, she opened it up to the first page, holding her breath, but let it quickly out when she disappointingly saw
that most of it was written in German. She could make out the date
on the first page, which was *12, April 1930.* It looked like a journal
entry maybe, just a few lines of writing. She flipped to the next pages,
all in German as well, with various dates, until about a quarter into
the book, where she caught something in English: *I must write more
in English. To learn.*

After that there seemed to be a mix of German and English entries.
The bits in English were not that interesting really. Just notes about
what he had done on a particular day. *Had coffee in town. Weather
sunny.* Or *Kinder worked hard today. Rolf learned to write name and
can follow in class much better.* One entry dated *3 Juli 1931* caught
her eye. *Fraulein Klinkhammer left very dear package with us, and
we are in chaos. Mother is very upset. Anna cries night and day. It is
impossible to work.*

This was followed by lengthier accounts in German for many
more days. Elsie made out a name, Anna, in some of them. Who
is Anna? she wondered. He said he had no sisters . . . Maybe his
wife? She looked over at Gunther's hand but she saw no ring. A
sweetheart? There was not another English entry until much later.
It was longer, and Elsie guessed that he had learned more English
at this point. It was dated *11 Juni 1933*—about a year and a half ago.
*Fraulein Klinkhammer is nowhere to be found. I am determined to
find her. I have only one letter. Mother wants me to the authorities go,
but I cannot do that to her. She would never survive.* This was followed

by a quote: *"When you love someone, you love the person as they are, and not as you'd like them to be." Tolstoy*

Elsie was not that familiar with Tolstoy's work beyond knowing that he wrote *War and Peace,* but she liked this phrase very much. She was pretty sure Gunther had mentioned Tolstoy before as being one of his favorites. She read on, looking for more, though she was beginning to feel uneasy about reading what was obviously so private a journal.

The next entry in English was dated *8 April 1935. Forever, the passage stretches. Both Mother and Anna are sick. I try to tend them as best I can. The food is wretched, mostly rotten. Yesterday, for orange, I traded my pocket watch. It was worth it to see Anna's face light up. She is so beautiful. Worse than pit in my stomach is one deep in my heart. I am grateful to have brought a few books. They are my only solace. I find comfort in writing bits of them in English here for practicing. Schiller comes to mind this day: "It is not flesh and blood, but heart which makes us fathers and sons."*

Next came a very short entry from a couple of days later. *10 April 1935. Mother is worse. I ask ship's doctor to come and tend her. He is kind but there are many sick, and I have no money to pay for extra. I am* überwältigt *with worry.*

The entries that followed were dated intermittently with much space between and were long, long tracks in German. Elsie turned many pages until she finally came to an entry that was written in English again. It was dated *7 Mai 1935. I am grateful to find job, finally, in Chicago. I have neglect my writings, but now that we have warm place to stay and work, I will be finding time to scratch some things down. My heart is still heavy with grief, but Anna helps me. Sr. Bernard is kind, but she does not approve of Anna living with me. I must find another place for her, but it is difficult. She does not understand why we cannot live as we were before, but all of that is changed now.* Again, this one was followed by a quote: *"To love a person is to learn the song that is in their heart and to sing it to them when they have forgotten." -Garborg*

Elsie had not heard of Garborg either, but she was particularly struck by the beauty of these words, which caused a sort of an ache to well up in her heart. She looked over at Gunther, wondering desperately who Anna was and what other secrets he might be hiding. His eyes fluttered, as if he were aware of her scrutiny, but they did not open. She waited, watching him, until he settled and then let her eyes wander back to the notebook. *15 Mai 1935. I have found a place for Anna. Parting from her was very painful, but I tell her to try her best and work hard. Someday we will be together, I tell her. All this time I have not had chance to be looking for Fraulein Klinkhammer. She is not at the address on her last letter. Where to look now, I have no idea. America is much bigger than I imagine, and so is Chicago. It could be she is no longer even here. I despair that I might never see her again.*

The next several months of entries consisted mostly of descriptions of his work at Mundelein. Elsie read them at first, noting that his English was slowly improving, but got quickly bored and could not help letting her eyes dart ahead to find any entries that had Anna or Fraulein Klinkhammer in them. Finally, she found one: *22 Juni 1935. The girls have left the school, and I am missing their* schwätzerei. *Chatter? I learn much from them. It is quiet and lonely and even sisters I do not see often; they stay in their tower. I spend most of nights reading. I have almost given up finding Fraulein Klinkhammer. She seems to have disappeared. Perhaps she is dead. Sometimes I sneak Anna here to be with me, but I do not wish to* gefährden *my place. She wants to be with me more, but when I ask her, she says she is content where she is. I pray this is true.*

Elsie was quite shocked by this revelation, truth be told, but she was beyond being able to stop reading. Did he live in sin with this woman? Is that who the other sandwich had been for? She glanced up at him now, but he was still deeply asleep, so she went on. Disappointingly, however, the next several pages of entries that followed seemed to only consist of notes regarding various projects he worked on over the summer around the campus. There were a few translations that she enjoyed reading, but most of the summer months were uninteresting.

Not until fall was there another entry in which Anna was mentioned. *13 September 1935. Anna has been ill again. She has had another fit. Mr. Lasik has told me of his concern for her and that if it continues, she will have to leave their home. I understand this, but I do not know what to do. I have had to ask Sr. Bernard, and she has said she will help me. It is more important than ever to find Fraulein Klinkhammer. I must be trying harder. But the girls have returned now, and they have many small demands. Oh, Anna. How I do so love you, but you are a heavy care around mine heart.*

Elsie bit her lip and kept reading. *29 Oktober 1935. This time of year is always melancholy for me. It is of course the time when Fraulein Klinkhammer—Liesel—first came to us. Still no word. "We need, in love, to practice only this: letting each other go. For holding on comes easily; we do not need to learn it." -Rilke*

Elsie paused here. What did this quote mean? Was it Liesel he really loved? She didn't understand.

"Anna," Gunther moaned now, causing Elsie to jump. It was as if he knew she were reading about her! With her heart beating very fast in her chest, Elsie waited again to see if he would wake, but he did not. Elsie was feeling slightly sick to her stomach and ashamed that she had read his intimate jottings, but yet, like a mystery unfolding, she felt compelled to see how it ended. She was very near the end, she knew. Giving him one last glance, she opened the notebook again and saw that indeed, there was only one entry left and that it was very recent. *23, Dezember 1935. Something new in my heart is awakening, something which I did not expect ever to feel again. Having met her, I cannot cease to think of her, though my case, I know, is without hope. I have nothing to offer but my heart, which is little enough according to this world's measure. If only that I could wrap my arms around her and say what is in my heart. I wish that I were better poet that I might do her justice. Only in Schiller, sweet Schiller, can I find something remotely close:*

"Is it possible never to have known something, never to have missed

it in its absence—and a few moments later to live in and for that single experience alone? Can a single moment make a man so different from himself? It would be just as impossible for me to return to the joys and wishes of yesterday morning as it would for me to return to the games of childhood, now that I have seen that object, now that her image dwells here—and I have this living, overpowering feeling within me: from now on you can love nothing other than her, and in this world nothing else will ever have any effect on you.

"Perhaps all the dragons in our lives are princesses who are only waiting to see us act, just once, with beauty and courage. Perhaps everything that frightens us is, in its deepest essence, something helpless that wants our love."

That was all. Elsie sighed, closing the book. Whoever this Anna is, he must love her very much, she mused. She had never read Rilke or Schiller or Garborg before, but their words connected to something deep within her, and she found herself reading them all again, and still one more time. And at the very back of the journal, she discovered, were pages of what seemed to be Gunther's own attempts at poetry, some in English and some in German. Of the ones she could read, she noted that they were all about love or loss in one capacity or other. Elsie thought them very beautiful in their own right. She was moved by their simple, honest, raw emotion and was taken off guard when they awoke in her a matching sort of longing, one that she recognized as having been with her for as far back as she could remember. It was a feeling that often frightened her, as it did now in the dark hospital room, and she struggled to repress it, as she always did. She fought the old familiar ache of wanting to be loved, truly loved, and instead tried to envision herself in the arms of Christ.

She looked over at Gunther again now, wondering what kind of man he really was. She saw him so differently now than she had before, the contents of his notebook revealing much. With his beard and tousled hair, which was even matted in some places, he could have been mistaken for a vagrant. His shoulders, peeking out from beneath the thin hospital blanket he lay under, were likewise very broad, with a deep scar running across his chest, visible despite the thick blond hair it hid within. His strong physical appearance contrasted so sharply with what his writings revealed to be inside—a deep kindness and compassion, a softness, even. He was obviously one who felt very deeply . . . felt the beauty of poetry and words as she did. She knew he loved to read, but his notebook had revealed something else again. It was practically a crime, Elsie thought forlornly, that he spent his day shoveling snow and fixing stairs and stoves, she thought, when he should be a . . . well, if not a writer then certainly a teacher, as he once had been.

And who was it that he had in mind, she wondered, as he had copied out Schiller's words—*Something new in my heart is awakening . . . I cannot cease to think of her . . . If only that I could wrap my arms around her . . .* Who is *she*? she wondered. Did he mean Anna? Or Fraulein Klinkhammer, whom he had once let slip and called "Liesel?" Or someone else, perhaps? A stray thought came into her mind then, that perhaps he meant . . . No, it couldn't be, she resolved and pushed it from her mind.

Oh, what did it matter? she told herself as she sighed again deeply, and quietly lay the book on top of his coat. She wished that she knew more about him, about the secrets of his past, but more than anything else she wished with all her heart that she could help him somehow. Help him to find this Fraulein Klinkhammer whom he so desperately sought. He seemed so ragged and forlorn, despite having a mother to care for him. But she had no idea how to even begin to help him, except to pray for him. She closed her eyes, then, determined to begin the rosary that she had promised she would say after she allowed herself to read his notebook. She did not get very far, however, before she, too, fell asleep, keeping a very different vigil than the one she had envisioned.

Chapter 17

Henrietta had nearly forgotten how much fun it was to go dancing as Clive neatly spun her around the room. As a little girl, when her father still worked at Schwinn, they would sometimes listen to WGN's broadcasts from the Aragon on their old radio. Even Ma seemed to enjoy it. Henrietta had always dreamed of one day going to the Aragon to dance, but by the time she was old enough, Leslie Von Harmon had killed himself, and then she had been thrust into the working world and was always too busy. Even if she could have somehow found the time, she had never had anything nice enough to wear to meet the Aragon's dress code. And when she had gotten the job as a taxi dancer at the Promenade, the Aragon's dirty little cousin, dancing had soured then a little bit for her, as it had taken on the more distinct flavor of work.

But now inside the Aragon's lush interior—built to look like the courtyard of a Spanish palace with crystal chandeliers, rounded arches and balconies and even a terra-cotta ceiling—in the arms of her dashing husband as they danced to "I'm in the Mood for Love," it did not feel like work at all, but almost like heaven. Dressed in a silver silk satin Chanel gown with an intricately beaded bodice, she was now wealthy enough to gain entrance even to the likes of the Drake or the Palmer House or the Burgess Club, where Clive had asked her to marry him—or re-asked, she should say. Next to those exclusive, glittering giants, even the grand Aragon paled. But here she was, even still, and she loved Clive for indulging her. He had insisted on wearing white tie, as he would have at the Drake, and he chatted charmingly with Lucy and Gwen, her friends from her days at the Marlowe, throughout the evening as if he were entertaining the Earl and Countess of Ashforth, say, in the ballroom at Linley Castle.

When Henrietta had telephoned Lucy just before Christmas to suggest that they all spend New Year's Eve together at the Aragon, Lucy had initially told her no, that the three of them had to work, she was almost certain. But after all of about ten minutes, Lucy had rang her back to say that, though she couldn't speak for Rose, of course, she and Gwen would most certainly try to at least get out of part of their shifts and come, saying that, after all, they might never get a chance like this again. Henrietta was delighted with this—a wonderful birthday gift, she had exclaimed, and promised to buy them drinks for the evening.

The only blight on the evening was that Elsie wasn't there. Henrietta had asked her half a dozen times, but each time, Elsie had declined and said she felt obliged to attend the Penningtons' Ball with Uncle John and Aunt Agatha. Henrietta supposed Elsie was right in doing so, but she would have dearly liked to have spent time with her in this setting. It would have been good for her, Henrietta thought, particularly as it seemed like Elsie was becoming even more quiet and withdrawn. Henrietta sensed there was something Elsie wasn't telling her. Perhaps she was still pining for Harrison? She had tried drawing Elsie into a conversation on Christmas Eve, but she had been reticent, and later, when Henrietta had mentioned coming out with her and Clive for New Year's Eve, she had very quickly said no.

Unfortunately, however, Eugene had overheard her asking Elsie to the Aragon and had boldly expressed his desire to tag along with her and Clive in Elsie's stead. Henrietta had internally balked at the idea, but she could think of no satisfactory excuse to dissuade him, especially as she had just invited Elsie. Clive had intervened, then, and politely said that by all means he should accompany them. She supposed she should be grateful for Clive's gallantry, but she was not too happy to be spending an evening out with Eugene. He certainly seemed more mature, almost pleasant, even, but there was still an unpredictability to him that made Henrietta uncomfortable.

As it was, Eugene thankfully split off from them as soon as they reached the Aragon. He was standing now at the bar, talking with several men, Henrietta noticed with a wince and quickly looked away. She had hoped that military school might cure him of his sexual irregularity, but he had seemed as effeminate as ever when they had spent the evening with him on Christmas Eve. She tried hard to ignore it, but she noticed tonight, for example, he had yet to even dance one dance when all the other soldiers present seemed to be tripping over themselves to dance with any available woman.

"I'm in the Mood for Love" came to an end, and Clive accordingly attempted to lead her back to the table where Lucy and Gwen were sitting, unable to publicly dance with each other, of course, but allowing their hands to graze against each other every so often under the tablecloth. They still wore their "wedding" rings, Henrietta noticed. She supposed she was being hypocritical in not condemning Lucy and Gwen for their deviant relationship with each other, while doing so with Eugene, but somehow it just seemed different. The lesbians at the Marlowe had been her friends and protectors, having in truth saved her life. She had been shocked at first to discover what they got up to at their dressing room parties after the shows, but she had grown to rely on them, with Lucy, Gwen, and Rose becoming her particular friends. Well, Rose *had* been a friend before she had taken up with Stanley, anyway.

The crowd was very thick, and Clive was having a difficult time wending his way through, having to pause to wait for someone to move or to shift to the side and often narrowly avoiding a drink being sloshed over the side of a glass grasped loosely by the person in front of him. Henrietta stood, waiting, facing Clive's broad, strong back, and she wished she could slip her hands around him from behind and hold him.

Instead she heard a voice very near her ear say, "Hello, Henrietta."

She quickly turned to look and was surprised to see none other than Stanley Dubowski! And Rose, too, standing quietly at his side.

"Stan!" Henrietta said and embraced him. Stan did not fully return the embrace, but stood stiffly, looking uncomfortable, his face red.

At Henrietta's exclamation, Clive turned around, too, and spotting Stan, broke into a wide grin as he held his hand out to him. "Well, hello, Stan!" Clive said in his deep, resonant voice. Henrietta was silently grateful that he had remembered not to call him "the pipsqueak."

"How are you, old boy? Fancy meeting you here!"

"We had no idea you'd be here—did we, Rose?" Stan squeaked out, turning to Rose now. Rose shook her head and held Henrietta's gaze for only a moment before looking away.

"Sorry about your dad, Clive," Stan offered.

"Thank you," Clive responded genuinely. "It was quite a shock."

"I'll say. Guess you didn't get to go to all those great places on your honeymoon, huh?" he asked Henrietta.

"There'll be another time," Henrietta said with a small smile, as she put her hand in Clive's, a gesture which, though inconspicuous, Stan's eyes seemed to observe all the same.

"How's Elsie?" he croaked out.

"Very well. It's kind of you to ask."

"When's her wedding? Or was it already?"

"Haven't you heard?" Henrietta asked, puzzled, as she shot a glance at Rose. "It was . . . it was called off. She's decided to go to college now."

"College?"

"Yes, Mundelein College? On Sheridan Road?"

"Never heard of it."

He paused for several moments, rubbing his chin as he took in this information.

"Gee whiz, Hen, college?" he said, lapsing into his old familiarity. "What happened to the lieutenant?"

"Stan!" Rose exclaimed, finally speaking.

"Sorry!" he said, defensively. "I was just wondering. Seems sudden is all."

An awkward silence descended upon them, then, despite the band striking up the next song, "My Romance."

"Did she break it off? Or him?" Stan asked in a louder voice now, to be heard above the band.

"Stan!" Rose exclaimed again, this time stamping her foot a little.

Henrietta bit her lip and was about to respond when Clive beat her to it. "Did we mention that Henrietta's brother Eugene is back from Fishburne?" he asked him, patting Stan on the back.

"Is he?" Stan asked.

"As a matter of fact, he's here with us tonight," Henrietta said, grateful yet again to Clive. "He's over by the bar, I think. Why don't you go find him?" she suggested loudly.

"I think I just might," Stan said, seeming eager for a way to extract himself from the present company. "Come on, Rose," he said to her.

Rose shot him a dirty look and said, "I think I'll just powder my nose."

"I'll come with you," Henrietta volunteered, though Rose looked anything but pleased at this suggestion.

"Well, then, I'll come along with *you*," Clive said, putting his hand on Stan's shoulder. "If you don't mind, that is."

"Well, suit yourself, I guess," Stan said unenthusiastically.

Henrietta watched the two of them disappear into the crowd and then turned toward where Rose had been standing, but Rose had already left the spot and was making her way to the ladies' lounge.

Henrietta called after her. "Rose!"

Rose either didn't hear her or was choosing to ignore her because she kept walking.

"Rose!" Henrietta called again, attempting to follow her and having to squeeze her way through the throng of bodies in order to do so. "Rose!" she called again.

Perhaps because they were no longer as close to the dance floor now and therefore away from the main crush of the crowd or because Rose decided to finally address her, she came to a halt and slowly turned back toward Henrietta.

"What?" she asked, annoyed.

"What are you doing?" Henrietta asked, having reached her now.

"I already said. Powdering my nose."

"You know what I'm talking about, Rose. Don't play dumb. Why on earth arc you dating a *man*? And why Stanley? You knew he was my sister's. How could you?"

"Listen, *Gumdrop*, it's none of your affair. Just leave it, why don't you!"

"Well, I rather think it *is* my affair, as you put it!" Henrietta said hotly. "Imagine my surprise when, on my wedding trip, I receive a letter from Elsie in which she describes seeing you kiss Stan outside the electrics! What were you doing?" She paused, her eyes flashing before they eventually relented a bit. "I thought we were friends, Rose," she said in a softer tone. "After all that happened at the Marlowe?"

Rose's own eyes were large as they held Henrietta's. She seemed about to retort, but instead let out a deep sigh. "I'm sorry," she said and suddenly burst into tears.

Of all things, Henrietta was certainly not expecting this particular reaction and stood stunned for a moment before she instinctively moved close to Rose. She was about to put her hand on Rose's shoulder, but Rose seemed to sense this and pulled away before she did so.

"I didn't plan it this way," Rose mumbled. "Well, not exactly, anyway," she said, hurriedly wiping her eyes now. "I didn't realize at first that he was your sister's beau. I . . . I was trying to get away from some man— at your wedding, actually. He wouldn't leave me alone, so I asked Stan to intervene. I didn't have any intentions of stealing him away, if that's what you want to call it, but then I ran into him again at the electrics and, well, I could see he didn't really care for Elsie . . . "

Henrietta took a deep breath at this and held in the retort that was on the tip of her lips. She forced herself to be rational, admitting to herself that ultimately it was she herself who was to blame in trying to get Stan and Elsie together in the first place. "But I thought you were . . . like Gwen and Lucy," Henrietta interjected. "That you wanted to be with *women*," she said in a low voice, looking around surreptitiously as she said it. "What about Libby Shoemacher?" Henrietta asked, referring to her friend, Polly's, sister, the girl Neptune had presumably raped and tortured before killing her. "I thought you loved her," Henrietta whispered.

"I did love her," Rose whispered back fiercely. "But I . . . aw, forget it," Rose said disgustedly. "You wouldn't understand."

"Yes, I will!" Henrietta urged. "Lucy said something about you experimenting. Is that what you're doing? With Stan, I mean? Or was Libby the experiment?"

Rose studied Henrietta and let out a deep breath. "You have no idea what my life is like."

Henrietta wasn't sure what to say to that, so she remained silent.

"Look, it's all right for you. I know you started out rough, just like us, but you lucked out. You landed on your feet," she said, nodding toward Clive, whom they could just make out, standing at the bar with Stan and Eugene. "In spades. But there's no escape for me if I follow my heart. And I've got to escape, Henrietta. I've got to get away from my ol' man."

She paused here and took a cigarette case from her handbag. With slightly trembling hands, she extracted a cigarette from it and lit it, inhaling deeply.

"It would be one thing if it were just me, but it's not," she said, exhaling a large cloud of smoke through her nostrils. "It's my brother, Billy, I've got to think of, too. He's backward, you see. And my ol' man has lately started beating him when he can. He won't beat a woman, strangely enough, so he doesn't touch me, but now he beats Billy in my place. Don't know why. Never used to. And Billy just takes it," she said, wiping a few fresh tears. "I've got to marry someone and get out of this," she said imploringly, looking up at Henrietta. "I can fake it well enough. I have all my life. I'll just lie back and think of Libby when I have to. Pump out a few kids, and no one's the wiser." She inhaled deeply. "Look. Stan's a dope; I know that," she said, exhaling. "But he's got a good heart. We could both do worse. I'm sorry about Elsie, but someone else will come along for her—let's face it, especially with all that money now from gramps. I plan to marry Stan if he asks me, which I think he might. Maybe even tonight," she said with a sad grin.

"So . . . so you're just going to lie to him?" Henrietta asked, incredulous. Stan had certainly been a constant irritant in her life, but she did not wish to see him hurt and, in truth, thought he deserved better than this. Unfortunately, however, she had seen this scenario play out many times before. How many women married men they didn't love, or only thought they loved? And both her mother and Julia proved that it didn't matter what their social status was.

"If I have to, yes," Rose said, her eyes narrowing as she inhaled again. "He'll be none the wiser, believe me. I'll treat him right, if that's what you're worried about. Look, sweets. Don't blow this for me."

"There you two are!" exclaimed Lucy, as she and Gwen came up behind them suddenly. Rose took her handkerchief and wiped her eyes again.

"Made up, then, have you?" Gwen asked, looking from one to the other.

Rose nodded, but she looked up at Henrietta as if for confirmation.

Henrietta gave a short nod in response. In the end, she couldn't help but feel sorry for Rose. She didn't really blame her for the bad situation she found herself in, but she needed to think about it more. Still, it wouldn't do to continue to hold a grudge, especially on New Year's Eve and her birthday. She gave Rose a weak smile and held out her hand to her. Rose took it and held it for just a moment before she let go.

"About time," Lucy said, looping her arm through Henrietta's as Gwen looped hers through Rose's.

"Come on," Gwen said. "Let's check our faces. You're a mess, Rose," she said and steered them into the ladies' room.

"But *was* it the lieutenant?" Stan asked Clive where they stood at the bar next to Eugene.

"Who broke it off?" Clive asked, eyeing him over a glass of Scotch.

"Yeah. Or was it Elsie?" Stan asked nervously.

"Actually, it was my sister who stopped it in the end. They were planning to elope, but thankfully Julia intervened in time to stop them."

"Gee whiz," Stan said with a low whistle. "Was she cut up?"

"Elsie? Quite, as I understand it," Clive said, taking a drink of his Scotch and observing Eugene out of the corner of his eye.

Eugene, obviously in the dark as to the recent goings on at Palmer Square, held a face that looked sullen and ugly as the bits and pieces of what had occurred with his sister in his absence trickled down to him. "Weren't *you* supposed to be her beau?" he asked Stan now.

"Well, sort of, I guess," Stan answered, shifting uncomfortably.

"Why'd you go for her, anyway? I never understood that. Thought it was Henrietta you were always panting after. For a couple of years, wasn't it? Following her all around town?"

Clive cleared his throat, and Stan colored beet-red. "All right, Gene. Enough already," Stan said, annoyed.

"Hard to compete with the likes of this one, though, eh?" Eugene continued, nodding his head toward Clive with a snigger. "Still, why'd ya dump Elsie?"

"I . . . I didn't dump her. Not exactly," Stan said hotly. "'S'pose she lost interest after she met the lieutenant, and, well, I was helping Rose; she was in distress, you see, and, well, one thing led to another and, gee Eugene, you're blamin' the wrong guy. I'm just as much the victim here, you know." Stan gripped his glass of beer. "And I don't so much like your tone."

"Calm down, Stan. Just messing with you," Eugene said, taking a long drink of his whiskey. "But I'll tell you one thing. I mean to look up this Barnes-Smith. Fucking bastard. I have a long memory, and I'll give him what he's got coming. If he so much as laid a finger on her, I'm going to kill him."

"Well, you'll have a hard time of it. He was reassigned to a regiment in Oregon State," Clive put in. He did not particularly like the way this conversation was going and sought to change the subject. "Anyway, how do you find Fishburne?" he asked. "Have you come across a Major Conlon? I knew him in the war; damned fined officer. Heard he went to Fishburne after."

"Since neither of you two were man enough to defend my sister's honor," Eugene slurred, ignoring Clive, "I'll have to do it."

"Hey!" Stan said.

"Retract that, Eugene," Clive commanded. "I was not even in the country when this unfortunate affair occurred."

"Sorry," Eugene muttered, peering through his cigarette smoke at Clive as he said it.

"Furthermore—"

Clive stopped abruptly when he felt a tap on his shoulder and turned to see a waiter standing expectantly beside him. The man leaned toward him now and said, "Mr. Clive Howard?"

"Yes?" Clive asked curiously, wondering how the man knew his name.

"Your wife is in need of your assistance out back, sir," the waiter went on. "Said she needed some air and would you attend her?"

"Take me to her," Clive said quickly. "I'll be back in a moment," he said to Eugene and Stan.

"What is it?" Stan asked eagerly.

"Nothing," Clive said, calling back over his shoulder. "Henrietta needs some air out back," he shouted as he followed the waiter through the crowd on the main floor to the back doors, feeling more and more uneasy with every step. Something wasn't right. If she did need a breath of cool air, why wouldn't she have gone out front? Why the back alley, where it seemed he was being led?

Instinctively he reached for his revolver and cursed when he remembered that he had left it at Highbury. His tuxedo was so close-fitting that it prevented him from tucking the gun inside his jacket where he normally kept it without it noticeably bulging out. He had tried placing it there anyway before they had left the house, but Henrietta had spotted it immediately and asked him for once to leave it behind, as she didn't wish to feel it against her chest as they danced. He had been reluctant to do so, not wanting to travel into the city, of all places, without it, but Henrietta had begged, saying that it was her birthday, and New Year's Eve at that. Surely nothing would happen tonight! He had indulged her, of course, but now he cursed, feeling naked and vulnerable without it. Nervously, he craned his neck to see the table where Lucy and Gwen had been sitting, but they were gone as well. Clive's sense of unease increased.

When they finally reached the back doors, the waiter paused and indicated with his head that he should go through. "Just through there, sir," he said and quickly disappeared.

Clive stepped out into the freezing night air, the wind imme-diately stinging his eyes and making them water. He looked quickly around the back lot he found himself in but saw Henrietta nowhere. He felt himself begin to panic, doubly so when two large men wrapped in great coats emerged noiselessly from a small gap between the building across the lot and the wall of the Lawrence "L" station. Another man followed, smaller and thinner. Clive peered through the darkness, his heart racing as he sickeningly recognized him.

He should have known, he groaned inwardly, and immediately thought of Henrietta. Where was she? He prayed she was still inside and that this was merely a trap to get him alone outside. Quickly he looked to his right, toward Winthrop, but no one was in sight on this freezing New Year's Eve. Calling out would be of no avail, he realized, his fists flexing, especially with the trains rumbling by.

As Neptune slowly approached, his hands tucked casually in the pockets of his coat. Clive struggled to control the fear and rage, which were fighting at that moment for dominion within him. His breath was coming more rapidly now, though he concentrated on keeping it hidden from the men in front of him.

"Inspector Howard," Neptune said coolly. "Fancy meetin' you here. Been wantin' to speak to you for a very long time now, but yer always hidin' up north nowadays," he said, slowly assessing him. "Carlos, here, thinks it's cause yer scared."

Carlos grinned. Clive instantly recognized him as being one of Neptune's goons from the Marlowe and wondered what had become of Vic. Vic had been Neptune's right-hand man, acting as both bodyguard and even impersonator when needed. The police had not caught him the night they took Neptune into custody. He seemed to have disappeared, and it was rumored that he had left the country. Obviously, Carlos had been promoted to Vic's previous position. Clive did not recognize the other goon, but he was as big and beefy as Carlos. Looking at him, Clive's fingers itched.

"What do you want?" Clive asked cooly, though even as he asked it, he sensed this was much bigger than Neptune's bizarre obsession with Henrietta. Somehow he now knew that Neptune was likewise responsible for his father's death.

"That's obvious, ain't it? I want my money."

"What money?" Clive asked, deciding to play dumb.

"Come on, Inspector. Don't fuck with me. I don't have time for yer bullshit. You know what I mean. I'm skippin' the country, maybe permanent, and I'm collectin' on all my accounts."

"I don't know how my father got involved in this, but you've got nothing on me. I'll not be extorted from," he snapped.

"Oh, I think you will."

"You killed him, didn't you?" Clive seethed, stepping closer to him.

"That was just an accident, wasn't it, boys?" Neptune said with a grin, briefly looking over his shoulder at his goons. "That wasn't supposed to happen; not exactly good business to do in the source of the dough," he said with a wheezy laugh that made Clive want to punch him right then. "Didn't expect him to try to cheat us. Never had before. Some pushing and shoving may have occurred and well . . .

It just happened, I guess. He really shouldn't have tried to double-cross us," he said with a shrug. "It was his own fault."

Clive's mind flooded with rage at Neptune's casual reference to killing his father. As if his father had just been some unfortunate piece of garbage that had gotten in their way that day. A good man's life ended for something so senseless.

"Fuck you," Clive spit out.

"Now, now," Neptune said merrily, obviously enjoying Clive's fury. "Where's those nice manners you got?" He stepped closer to Clive so that his face was very near his, and Clive could smell his putrid breath. "Now you listen to me, Copper. Yer going to get me that money. And then we're done. I disappear, and you never see me again. Understand?"

"How stupid are you?" Clive retorted. "Extorting money from a cop?"

"Stranger things have happened."

"I'm not afraid of you."

"No, but yer little nephews were," he said, an evil smile spreading across his face.

Clive's heart constricted. *His nephews?*

"Do I have yer attention yet?" Neptune chuckled. "Had a little chat, shall we say, with the two of them while they were out playin' in the park. The parks in Glencoe are so much nicer than the ones in Chicago, ain't they, Rodge?" he asked, finally addressing the other goon. "Lotsa trees and bushes to hide in, ain't that right, Carlos?"

Both Carlos and Rodge grunted, like two pigs.

"You're bluffing," Clive said, though he had a sickening fear that he was not.

"Oh, I never bluff. That's for amateurs. Or the police," Neptune said icily. "No, I'm not bluffin'. Spoke myself to little Randolph and Howard. Or, Randy and Howie, is what I called them. Answered me just the same. That's right. I know their names," he said, seeming to enjoy the fear that Clive knew he wasn't hiding well. "Told them I would find them in the night and cut them into little pieces if they weren't good little boys. Should have seen their faces," Neptune said and laughed suddenly.

"You bastard!" Clive roared and leaped toward him, but Rodge stepped between them and pushed Clive backward as easily as if he were swatting at a fly. Clive righted himself, breathing heavily from fear and rage, and tried to quickly ascertain how best to attack. It was obvious that he couldn't win a fight against both Carlos and Rodge unless he were to do something very clever or was incredibly lucky.

"Would have been so easy to just carry them off there and then," Neptune went on. "But I thought I'd be nice and give you one last chance to cough up the dough. Little boys is not my preference, but there's always a first. I'd prefer your little filly, but you always got her hidden away, don't you? Afraid your little cherry is gonna get eaten?" He grinned at Clive savagely. "Who knows? She just might, Inspector. She just might. We follow her sometimes, don't we, boys? Likes to shop in the city, don't she?" He tilted his head and glanced sideways at Clive. "She's escaped me so far, but that only makes me want her all the more," he whispered. "Know what I mean? Just might have to take her anyways, whether you pay up or not."

"Fucking bastard!" Clive shouted, unable to control himself any longer and leaped toward Neptune and grabbed him around the neck. He squeezed with all his might, attempting to choke him. Rodge and Carlos, temporarily stunned by the suddenness of Clive's action, moved quickly now to grab him. They ripped him from Neptune, who dropped limply to the ground, his hands to his throat as he struggled to catch his breath. Carlos managed to grab Clive's arms and wrenched them behind his back while Rodge sunk a fist into Clive's gut, causing him to double over in pain. As Neptune got to his feet, Rodge hit Clive again, this time near his right eye.

Neptune watched as Rodge repeatedly struck Clive over and over about the face and then finally motioned for him to stop. Clive sank to his knees, and Carlos grabbed a chunk of Clive's hair and yanked his head back so that Neptune could address him. Neptune grinned at the sight of him. One eye was already swollen shut, and blood was pouring from his nose. Neptune leaned close so that he was just inches from Clive's face in a mocking reversal of the scene in Humboldt Park over a year ago when the tables had been turned.

Clive's ribs seared in pain, and he felt like he might vomit. Breathing in Neptune's fetid stench as he leaned close nearly pushed him over the edge.

"You ready to listen, yet, Copper?" Neptune hissed. "I was reasonable in the past. But now I'm angry, see, and now yer going to bring me double, understand? I'm uppin' it to twenty thousand dollars. You've got two weeks to cough it up."

"Fuck off," Clive spewed out, trying to wrest himself free.

Rodge kicked him in his bad shoulder, almost as if he knew it was his weak point, causing Clive to cry out.

"I don't have it," he finally managed to utter through his severe pain.

"Well, you'd better find it, then," Neptune snarled. "Shouldn't be hard, should it? Big house, lotsa cars, pretty paintins, big company downtown. Don't cry poor to me. If you don't deliver, we'll take all yer little cherries, simple as that. All three of 'em. The boys I'll sell to the highest bidder—that should raise a pretty penny. But I'll keep the little filly for myself. Till I get tired of her, that is. They usually stop screamin' after a while, and then it's no fun. Then it's time to throw the toy out. You understand, Copper?"

Clive, on fire with pain and rage, still managed to raise his head in response to this and spit in Neptune's face, promptly causing Rodge to kick him again.

This time Clive fell forward, his face scraping against the icy street as he did so. He lay there unable to move and felt himself slipping from consciousness. He could sense Rodge above him, maybe positioning himself to kick him again when he thought he heard the back door of the Aragon bang open. He was able to slightly move his head in that direction, and with his one functioning eye, he could just about make out Eugene and Stan standing there, bewildered.

"Hey!" Stan shouted. "Call for the police!" he said frantically to

Eugene. Eugene paused, apparently needing a moment to take in what was happening before he dashed back inside the Aragon.

Clive tried to shift himself as he saw Stan hesitantly pick up a bottle lying nearby and smash it against the side of the building, but pain seared through him. He watched, helplessly, as Stan approached the group, his outstretched hand trembling slightly with the jagged remnant in his hand. "Get out of here!" he shouted in a shaky voice.

With a smirk, Rodge quickly reached out for Stan, his unexpected swiftness apparently taking Stan by surprise. Rodge was able to grab Stan's wrist, but Stan instinctively twisted and managed to slice a part of Rodge's hand in the process, or maybe it was his wrist. Infuriated, Rodge hit him in the face, causing Stan to drop the glass. Without his weapon, Stan's response was to hunch into his best football stance and lunge at his opponent, impressively pushing him against the wall of the building opposite. Rodge recovered quickly from the shock of it, however, and punched Stan in the gut, while Carlos, who had been idly watching, stepped in now and grabbed Stan from behind.

Meanwhile, Clive struggled, despite his burning pain, to stand and stagger toward the fight. With a fresh burst of adrenaline, he attempted to pull Carlos off of Stan, who was swinging wildly but ineffectively. Clive stuck his foot behind Carlos's leg and pulled at his shoulders, effectively tripping him and causing him to fall. Before Carlos could right himself, Clive kicked him repeatedly in the ribs, as Carlos attempted to roll away from him. Clive may have continued this indefinitely had he not then suddenly remembered Neptune. He looked over his shoulder and saw him standing near a gap between the wall of the "L" station and the building from which he had emerged, like a spider, eagerly watching the scene unfold before him.

"Two weeks," Neptune shouted to him before he turned, then, and slipped through the gap. Clive wanted to go after him, but he knew, in his current state, that he wouldn't be able to follow far. Instead, he left Carlos lying where he was and hit Rodge on the back of the head, distracting him momentarily from Stan, whom he was still fighting.

Rodge turned and swung at *him* now, but Clive managed to sidestep it.

"Stan!" he shouted, as he tried to keep Rodge distracted. "Go after the leader!" he said, nodding his head toward the gap. "It's Neptune."

Mercifully, Stan seemed to comprehend quickly and set off in pursuit through the gap, though Clive assumed Neptune was probably already long gone by now. Carlos had staggered to his feet, and Rodge was coming for him again as well. Clive wasn't sure how much longer he could keep this up and began to contemplate his own escape. Just then, however, Eugene burst forth from the back doors again.

"Cops are coming!" he shouted, and, as if on cue, a siren could be heard in the distance. Both Rodge and Carlos stopped in their tracks, then, and panicked, each one taking off in a different direction. Eugene ran after Carlos, who ran for the gap, and Clive attempted to follow Rodge, who ran toward Winthrop, but his injuries were such that he could barely walk, much less run. By the time he reached the street, Rodge was nowhere in sight. He halted and bent over, putting his hands on his knees, trying to catch his breath.

A police car pulled up, sirens wailing, and Clive could hear several officers banging out of the car. It was only when he heard a familiar voice say, "Oh, it's you, Inspector" that he managed to look up to see his old sergeant, Clancy, smiling dumbly down on him. "Didn't expect to see you roaming the streets on a night like tonight."

Chapter 18

Elsie hesitated before stepping out into the bitter cold, the weather having turned sharply as the new year began, with temperatures dropping dangerously into the single digits. She wrapped a scarf around her head and pulled on her cashmere-lined leather gloves—the only item of luxury she allowed herself—and hurried across the circle toward Philomena Hall. Henrietta and Julia had insisted she bring her fur with her to Mundelein, purchased many months ago on a particularly exhausting shopping trip with Aunt Agatha, who had been suitably horrified when she had turned up for the first time in Lake Forest wearing her sturdy wool coat. Knowing of its existence somewhere in the depths of her dressing room in Palmer Square, Henrietta, and thus Julia, had suggested that it was just the thing to have to dash about to class in. And while Elsie observed that a few girls did indeed wear furs to class, she refused to. Hers was still discretely hanging in her small closet in Philomena, taking up a lot of precious space and still as of yet undisturbed in the tissue that Odelia had packed it in for her on the eve of her departure. She knew Julia and Henrietta would probably be upset if they knew she had not yet used it, but she felt ridiculous in even contemplating wearing it. A wool coat was more than good enough to run across the campus with.

As of just ten minutes ago, Elsie officially completed her first week of classes, and she found, to her delight and relief, that she had enjoyed them very much. She had been so nervous the night before her first day that she had broken out in a rash, which Melody, having since returned from Wisconsin in a bubble of talkativeness and excitement, declared to be hives and had accordingly run to get Sr. Vincent, who happened to be the sister on duty that night. Sr. Vincent was exceedingly old, a small ball of wrinkles, really, who moved about very slowly, and her solution to Elsie's sudden rash was for Elsie to lie quietly on her bed with a cold compress on her forehead. Elsie had not taken much stock in this advice, especially as the girls all told her that this was Sr. Vincent's standard remedy no matter what the medical emergency, but she obeyed anyway, Melody staying by her side and entertaining her with stories of Fred and Bunny and all of the hijinks the three of them had gotten up to over the holidays. They sounded like a wonderful family, Elsie thought at the time, so different from her own.

As it turned out, the next morning she miraculously awoke sans spots, and Melody herself escorted her, arm-in-arm, to her first class, Home Economics, where she sat stiffly at the back of the room, hoping not to attract any notice and taking copious notes, despite the fact that she seemed to already know much of the material, though it was, admittedly, merely the introduction. Still, it had given her confidence to go to the next class, which was Geometry, where she found the material certainly more challenging, but not as overwhelming as she had allowed herself to imagine it might be, thanks to Sr. Sebastian's careful tutoring. She was surprised, actually, that she so far liked Western Civilization the best and wondered if it was because Sr. Ambrose, the professor, was so alive and engaging. And while she had been looking forward to English Literature the most, she found their first reading assignment, *Beowulf*, to be rather difficult and, dare she say, dull, even despite the looming threat of the monster.

The girls, she found, were on the whole quite friendly—another relief. There were a few snooty ones, to be sure, but she was used to that now, having been immersed in the upper strata of society for almost half a year in the company of the Exleys. More than once, she found herself sincerely grateful to have been assigned to room with Melody Merriweather, as she saw how very kind she was despite her famous popularity. For reasons Elsie could not fathom, Melody had taken what seemed to be a genuine liking to her and immediately introduced her all around and invited her to her many social gatherings and outings. And while Elsie was indeed thankful to thus have almost an instant group of friends, she had managed, for the purposes of studying, to muster up the needed courage to resist at least some of Melody's invitations—a feat she was quite proud of, actually, as it was difficult for Elsie to say no to anyone. Melody did not seem offended in the least, however, if Elsie turned down an invitation, and seemed to be content even if the only time they saw each other was late at night before turning in to bed. She had so far twice smuggled some cocoa upstairs to their bedroom to drink while they sat on the side of their beds, reminding Elsie, painfully, of her days of drinking cocoa with Henrietta. But that seemed so very long ago now, almost like another lifetime.

Elsie stepped gingerly along the icy path and made her way up the stone steps of Philomena. The path was not as clear as it normally would be, with Gunther having been restricted by Sr. Bernard from working for one full week after his accident. It had unfortunately snowed once since then, and the novitiates had been asked to clear the paths in his place. Elsie had not seen him since she had slipped from his hospital room in the wee hours of New Year's Day, but she had found, several days later, a tattered copy of Tolstoy's *Family Happiness*, outside her bedroom door with a note that read: "To Elsie, With many thanks. G."

Since the night of the accident, Elsie had asked Sr. Bernard about Gunther's well-being so many times that the last time, yesterday afternoon, if she remembered correctly, Sr. Bernard had not answered, but had simply raised an eyebrow. Elsie concluded then that she was becoming a nuisance and had resolved not to ask her about him anymore. But she was desperate to talk to him. Surely, he was up and about by now? She had so many things to ask him, so many things to say. She had more than once contemplated going to see him as he convalesced, but she wasn't exactly sure where he lived, and she didn't dare snoop around looking, much less ask.

Elsie paused as she stepped into Philomena, stamping her feet on the front mat and instinctively looking around for Gunther, who, of course, was not there. It was just as well, really, as she was supposed to be meeting Melody and her friends in the front parlor under the guise of studying for Western Civilization, though she rather doubted that any studying would actually occur. Already she could hear Melody's tinkling laugh coming from the next room. Elsie began to quickly unwrap and hang her things in the cloakroom. When she emerged, she stopped at the little front desk, which was manned this afternoon by Sr. Joseph.

Now that school was back in session, the sisters rotated the duty of sitting at the front desks of each of the two dormitories, their main object being to serve as chaperones for their young charges and to take down any telephone messages that came through. Though men were not allowed anywhere in the private areas of Philomena or Piper Hall, especially upstairs, Elsie had already heard stories of how, in years past, boys had been snuck in through windows or the back stairs as part of some elaborate ruse thought up by some of the more risqué girls. Melody claimed she had not yet done something so daring but that she wouldn't be opposed if the right situation, or the right "fella," she should say, came along. The girls were allowed to entertain gentleman callers in the parlor only, and said gentlemen were required to sign the guest book at the little front desk, like some quaint leftover from a bygone era.

Elsie wrapped her navy cardigan sweater about herself tighter as she paused at the desk to give Sr. Joseph a smile and to glance at the registrar. Melody, she saw, had not only invited Cynthia Forsythe, as she had said she was going to, but she also appeared to be entertaining Charlie McAllister and Douglas Novak, two Loyola boys who were part of Melody's inner bosom gang. They seemed nice enough boys, Elsie concluded after meeting them for the first time earlier in the week. Melody called them her "chums," though she had already confessed to Elsie on her first night back, during which she had insisted they stay up late and trade secrets, that she had the most terrible crush on Douglas Novak. Melody had then forced Elsie to offer up one of her own "secrets." Elsie didn't dare relate a real one, so she sinfully resorted to fabricating one. After a few minutes of hesitation on Elsie's part, which Melody undoubtedly confused with inner torment, she confessed to once stealing a cake from Cook, which wasn't too far from the truth, as she had once shamefully stolen some raspberry tarts off a tray intended for Doris and Donny before it had been carried up to the nursery.

"Is that all?" Melody had asked, clearly disappointed, and prodded her for something else. Something related to love, she had suggested. But what was Elsie to say to that? She dared not share her real secrets. Though they were probably the same age, Elsie felt immeasurably older than Melody, who seemed wonderfully frivolous and gay. Indeed, Elsie wished that she could be as such, but her "secrets" very much weighed her down and made her feel older than she was. How could she really tell Melody that she had already had not once but two love affairs? And how she was even now being pursued by several society men, Lloyd Aston currently leading the way by having already attempted to telephone her several times since New Year's? And how could she tell Melody, when asked in a whispered giggle if she had ever been kissed, that she had actually gone far beyond kissing—that, in truth, her virtue had been stolen and that she was indeed already ruined? How her only hope—no, *desire*—was to take Holy Orders and become a nun? No, there were many secrets which Elsie felt she had to hold close to her chest, and she instead attempted to play the part of the innocent schoolgirl as best she could. She was trying her best to fit into that role and to this new life, but it was at times very difficult.

She paused outside the parlor now, taking a deep breath and

steeling herself to try to be friendly and gay. These social situations were as frightening to her as walking unprepared into a geometry class, but she knew she had to try.

"There you are!" Melody called out to her as she silently slipped into the room. "We've been waiting ages!"

Melody was perched on the divan in front of the large picture window that looked out over the vast expanse of the lake, the sheer beauty of which could sometimes bring tears to Elsie's eyes. For this reason, Elsie made sure to carefully avert them now and focus instead on her friend.

Melody patted the seat beside her. "I've saved this spot especially for you!" she said. "Douglas, here, has been regaling us with a particularly droll anecdote of how he taught his dog, Jocko, to play dead over Christmas break. It's screamingly funny!" she laughed.

Elsie sat down gingerly next to Melody and bashfully gave a nod to the other girl in the room, Cynthia, who was another of Melody's friends, but she couldn't muster the courage to look at either of the two young men.

"Yes, do go on, Douglas!" encouraged Cynthia. "You'll love this, Elsie!"

"Oh, yes, Douglas is so very entertaining, isn't he?" Charlie said with a grin. "I rather think poor old Jocko really did die, and Douglas here was too dense to notice!"

"What a brute you are, Charlie!" Melody laughed. "That simply can't be true!"

"Yes, if it *is* true, then his ghost is particularly clever, as he jumped up and nipped me right after," Douglas said with a shrug as held up his little finger and winked at Elsie, one dimple showing on his cheek. Elsie had to admit he was awfully handsome, and she could see why Melody liked him. She observed, however, that Melody never made it obvious how she really felt about him and was sometimes, in Elsie's opinion anyway, downright rude to the hapless Douglas. It was clear that Melody was an accomplished flirt, and she in truth reminded Elsie, at times, of Henrietta.

"Yes, we must leave poor Douglas alone. He has such a sad little life that the whole of his Christmas break was spent teaching his little dog tricks. Have you ever heard anything more pathetic?" Charlie said in an aside to Cynthia. "Whereas I spent the whole of my holidays with my aunt and uncle in Los Angeles," he said proudly.

"Ooh! Los Angeles!" Cynthia swooned, turning her attention to him fully. "Did you really, Charlie?"

"I sure did."

"Did you go to Hollywood?"

"We did, as a matter of fact," he said, shooting Douglas a look of triumph.

Douglas merely tucked his hands behind his head and stretched out his legs before him in the most casual way, giving Charlie a grin as he did so. "Well, go on, then," he said, smirking. "We're all enthralled."

"Ooh! Did you see Clark Gable? Or Maybe Gary Cooper?" Cynthia exclaimed.

"Well, can't say that I did. But we did get a smashing tour. Even got to see Irene Dunne's dressing room."

"Imagine!" Cynthia cried.

"I have it in mind to maybe head out there again at some point. I wouldn't mind working in Hollywood. Palm trees all around," Charlie said smoothly. "Sure beats all this snow and ice."

"Is that before or after you get the law degree your father wants?" Douglas put in, drawing his legs up now and crossing them in one fluid motion and resting his chin in his hand as he balanced it on his knee.

"After, of course, old boy. You can come along if you wish. I'm sure there're plenty of jobs for the likes of you—custodian, maybe, or street sweeper."

"I say," Douglas said, ignoring Charlie's jabs, "speaking of Hollywood, we should all go to the pictures this evening. What do you say, girls?"

"Oh, yes!" Cynthia gushed. "Marvelous! Let's!"

"Well, we can't go like this," Melody said to Douglas, inclining her head toward Elsie. "You'd have to come up with a third man."

"Of course I would! What do you take me for?" Douglas asked her.

"An idiot," Charlie put in quickly.

"Say!" Douglas said with pretend hurt. "Better an idiot than a cad— wouldn't you say, girls? Anyway, I just happen to know that Bernie Talbot is dying to see *Captain Blood*, the new Errol Flynn film. In fact, he'd really be rather annoyed if he found out we went and didn't ask him."

"Oh, no!" Elsie said hurriedly, realizing a bit too late that they were trying to compensate for her. She had been thinking about poor Gunther, actually. It had been Charlie's comment about custodians or street sweepers that had started her down that road of thought.

"Don't . . . don't ask him on my account! Though I'm very grateful, to be sure," she said, smiling uncomfortably. "I . . . I can't tonight."

"Why ever not?" Melody asked.

"It's . . . it's just that I promised my mother I'd go and see her."

"Go and see her?" Melody exclaimed. "You just got here!"

"Yes, I know," Elsie said, shifting her weight and, in desperation, stuffing her hands under her thighs. "But . . . I . . . my brothers only left for boarding school just this week, and she's terribly upset. She shouldn't be, I know, but she's . . . she's not been well," she said, pulling her hands back out and trying to fold them on her lap as she had been taught by Mrs. Hutchings. That venerable lady would have been horrified just now at seeing her attempt to sit on them, but Elsie couldn't always remember the right thing to do at any given moment—there were always so many things to consider.

"Oh! I didn't realize!" Melody said. "Then of course you should go. How awful for you, though. It does sound tremendously dull."

"Perhaps we should all come with you?" Cynthia offered unenthusiastically. "We could play cards?"

"Oh, no!" Elsie said hurriedly. "But . . . but thank you," she managed to say.

"I can't say I blame you, Elsie," Charlie put in. "You wouldn't want Douglas here anywhere near civilized society. He's not only an idiot, but he's also a terrible klutz, not to mention a dolt."

"Anything else?" Douglas said wryly.

"Boys!" Melody said. "It's time you left. If we really are going out tonight, then we positively must study now. You'll have to leave," she commanded, pointing stiffly toward the door.

Douglas and Charlie promptly stood up. "Well, we know when we're not wanted!" Charlie exclaimed dramatically.

"You're not!" Melody laughed.

"Have you ever, for the life of you, met girls like this, Dougie?" Charlie said, putting his arm around Douglas.

"As a matter of fact, no. The girls back home are much nicer."

"Well, why don't you go back there, then! The nerve of the two of you!" Cynthia exclaimed.

"Have mercy," Charlie implored, folding his hands together in mock supplication. "Douglas can't go home, remember? Jocko's dead!"

They all laughed at that, and even Elsie couldn't help but smile.

"There's always a wise guy, isn't there?" Douglas asked of no one in particular as they made their way into the foyer. Charlie bent to sign them out while Douglas retrieved their coats.

"Sorry you can't make it, Elsie," Douglas said sincerely, slipping into his. "Maybe next time?"

"Yes, next time."

"Promise?" he said with a grin. She suspected he was being nice to her on Melody's account.

"Yes, promise," she managed to say with a smile. There was a part of her that really would have liked to go with them. She wished she could be as light-hearted and gay. It seemed so easy for them.

"But what am I going to do with Bernie now?" Charlie asked. "He really will be cast low if we don't ask him to come."

"Oh, I'll find someone. Don't worry," Melody said. "Vivian Anderson or Rosalind Chambers, perhaps."

"Not Rosalind," Charlie said. "She never stops talking. We won't hear a minute of the show!"

"Yes, it would be a terrible shame if someone were to talk more than you," Melody tinkled, and everyone laughed again.

"Well, ta-ta, girls!" Douglas said then, tipping the cap he had just thrust upon his head an inch above his sandy hair. "See you later!" he said singingly and stepped out with a flourish.

Cynthia promptly shut the door behind them, leaned against it, and looked over at Melody and Elsie. "Can you believe those two?" she asked with a wide grin. "They're so terribly funny, but I'd never let them know it!"

"Never let them know it?" Melody exclaimed. "You've already made it much too obvious!"

"Well it's *obvious* you're head over heels for Douglas, so I wouldn't act so superior!" Cynthia countered, causing Melody to catch her arm and entwine it with hers. Slowly they made their way back into the parlor.

"Which one do you like?" Cynthia asked Elsie in a low voice, as she stood arm in arm with Melody.

"Oh, don't ask her!" Melody put in. "She's very mysterious. My guess is that she has a lover somewhere, but she won't say. She's a very dark horse, this one, as Pops would say!"

"Ooh! Delicious!" Cynthia whispered loudly, surreptitiously glancing at the front desk to see if Sr. Joseph was listening. Sr. Joseph, however, seemed to be concentrating on writing in something that had the decided look of a grade book to it. "Do tell!" Cynthia begged, looking back at Elsie. "You simply must, Elsie! It's rather mean to keep it all to yourself. Is it a Loyola boy?" she asked eagerly.

Elsie felt her face grow warm. She had no wish of course to talk about love or lovers at all, much less in front of one of the sisters. She was trying hard to adopt an image of purity and virtue.

"Don't be silly," Elsie finally managed to answer. "I'm . . . I'm not in love!" she stammered, as she glanced over to where Sr. Joseph was still bent over her work. "Anyway, aren't we going to study?" she asked, gesturing awkwardly toward the library.

"Oh, leave her alone," Melody said to Cynthia. "It's all right if she wants to have a secret from us," she added, giving Elsie a little wink. "It keeps us guessing! Come on; we'd better get started."

"Aww, we're not really going to study, are we?" Cynthia whined. "It's Friday night!"

Melody gave her a rueful look and let out a little laugh. "Perhaps we'd better give it a miss for tonight, wouldn't you say?" she said, looking at Elsie hopefully. "Seeing as I have to find a date for poor Bernie. Would you mind?" she asked Elsie.

"Oh, no!" Elsie said quickly. "I'm sorry if I've caused you trouble."

"Don't be silly!" Melody exclaimed. "And you should stop apologizing all the time."

"Sorry," Elsie said, and all three of them laughed.

Melody and Cynthia left then, and Elsie slowly gathered up her books. She preferred to be alone, actually—a feeling she found peculiar. She had been pining away for so long at home, wanting company or someone to talk to, and now that she was here, surrounded by people, she often felt the need to be alone. Perhaps it was just a habit she needed to break—like so many others, she thought with a sigh. She wasn't particularly looking forward to seeing Ma tonight, knowing she would be in a bad mood, but she couldn't just abandon her.

She had promised Ma last Sunday, the unfortunate day slated for not only the boys' removal, but also her own, that she would come the following Friday and spend an evening with her.

The boys' leaving had been a terrible farewell scene, of course. Grandfather's man of business, Bernstein, had shown up as scheduled, bright and early, to escort them to the train station and to make sure everything was in order for their journey out east. Eddie had descended from the upper floor of the house, eager and bright, having decided at some point that being sent to boarding school was to be seen as an adventure and was determined to engage it as such. Herbie had followed down the stairs, perceivably pale and withdrawn, but putting a brave face on it, especially in front of Ma. All might have been well if it hadn't been for Jimmy, who not only sniffled his way through breakfast, but also gave in to tears and loud wailings when it was time to board the car. He clung to Ma's skirt and then to Elsie's before Bernstein took matters into his own hands and scolded him for his infantile blubbering. Jimmy had become subdued after that and dutifully allowed himself to be led out to the cars, but sat peeled to the window, staring back at Ma and Elsie, who waved forlornly on the front steps until the car disappeared into the throng of traffic on Kedzie.

Only when they were out of view did Ma break down into sobs, a sight which Elsie had only witnessed a few times in her whole life. Elsie had predicted that Ma might be upset, but her loud wailings took Elsie very much by surprise considering Ma's normal depressed disinterest. Elsie carefully persuaded Ma back into the house and up to her small sitting room, whispering little words of comfort even as she tried not to feel guilty that she, too, would be leaving in a few hours hence. She had confessed to Henrietta the night before, when Henrietta had turned up briefly to say good-bye to her brothers, slipping each of them a small box of goodies and extra spending money, just in case Grandfather did not plan to provide them a monthly allowance, that she could not but help feel that this sad state of affairs was all her fault, really.

Henrietta had told Elsie, in response to her downcast state, that Grandfather's decision to send the boys to boarding school had nothing whatever to do with Elsie's behavior, that it was a plan set in motion long before her affair with Harrison had ever happened. Her theory was that Grandfather was just using her unfortunate situation with the lieutenant as a means of making her feel responsible and to thus further control her, as Ma, actually, had warned them. Elsie supposed she believed Henrietta, but it brought her little real comfort.

She tried to repeat Henrietta's words to herself as she rummaged through Ma's top dresser drawer looking for her nerve pills, having deposited Ma in a slump on the love seat in her private sitting room, where she sat flopped over like a wet dishrag. Elsie finally found the pills just as Odelia walked in with a pot of chamomile tea and some small cardamom cakes. Elsie handed Ma a pill, which she willingly swallowed, as she sat up to drink some tea.

Elsie sat down then beside her, watching her, and could not help but feel a little irritated, actually, with Henrietta. Why was she always the one who had to deal with Ma? But as soon as this churlish thought entered her head, Elsie immediately scolded herself for her selfishness, surprised by it in fact and worried. She had never felt irritated with Henrietta before, except perhaps years ago when Henrietta had been working as a hair curler demonstrator at Marshall Fields and had been constantly imploring Elsie to "smarten yourself up."

While she wished that Henrietta could be more on hand to help, she knew that this was unrealistic and that, in truth, Henrietta had done more than her share over the years. Likewise, Henrietta was Clive's wife now, Elsie reminded herself, and she had a whole new life to attend to. Just last night, for example, Henrietta had whispered to her something about how she and Clive suspected that Alcott's death had not been an accident and that Clive had been beaten in an alleyway outside of the Aragon on New Year's Eve. Elsie had been thoroughly shocked by this news. How was Henrietta always getting herself involved in some sort of mystery or danger? she wondered nervously and supposed it came from marrying a detective. She had been about to relate her own strange New Year's Eve affair, but just as she was beginning it, Jimmy had wandered in and distracted them. Well, that was probably for the best, she reasoned later. Best to keep all that to herself.

No, looking after Ma was definitely her job now, Elsie sighed, as she offered to get Ma her magazine. She sat with her for some time, herself reading Trollope's *The Way We Live Now,* having decided that Trollope might be safer than Jane Austen in his ability, or lack thereof, rather, to conjure up extreme romantic notions, until Ma dropped off to sleep. Quietly, then, Elsie got up and finished packing the last of her things. About an hour later, Karl came up to her room to tell her that it was time to go and to carry any last items down to the car. Ma had not emerged from her room at all, so Elsie went back up to say good-bye.

Ma lazily opened her eyes as Elsie knelt in front of her, resting her hand on Ma's knee as she had done as a little girl. Whether Ma was still partially asleep or just momentarily disoriented, Elsie wasn't sure, but she seemed to not fully grasp that this was Elsie's farewell. Perhaps she was already so used to her leaving to go to Aunt Agatha's that she was confusing it with that. Elsie had expected perhaps some tears on Ma's part—maybe not as many as she had cried for the boys, but maybe a few? Crushingly, however, none seemed to be had, and indeed, they somehow found their way to Elsie's eyes instead.

"Leavin' now, are you?" Ma croaked out, shifting her weight in the chair.

"Yes. Good-bye, Ma," Elsie said, still on her knees in front of her mother. Elsie reached for her hand and squeezed it before Ma pulled it away.

"When you comin' back?" Ma asked.

"I thought I'd come back and see you on Friday, remember? And have a little game of rummy?"

"Yes, all right," Ma said with a dismissive nod.

"I'll try hard, Ma," Elsie said pleadingly.

"All right then."

"At school, I mean."

Ma looked momentarily puzzled, but merely waved her hand listlessly. "Best get going then. Tell Odelia to come up."

Elsie rose unsteadily, tears blurring her vision as she stood awkwardly in front of her mother. This was not how she envisioned her departure, the beginning of her new life, to go. "Well, bye, Ma," she said, wiping her tears with the back of her hand, and hurried downstairs.

And if Elsie felt sorry for herself as Karl slowly pulled away from the house on Palmer Square, no one on the steps to wave good-bye, she soon forgot it upon her arrival at Mundelein. She had spent the Thanksgiving and Christmas breaks hovering between her two worlds—well, three, really, if she counted Aunt Agatha and the Exleys, and she was tired of it. She longed to be part, fully part, of just one world, and she had most definitely chosen to give her heart to this one, the one before her now—Mundelein, with its studies and the sisters and the girls. She would try to see them as her family now. And though she told herself that she wouldn't mind completely cutting herself off from her family at home—she quickly pushed away a stray image of Doris and Donny that had come to mind—she knew that to do so was unrealistic, even if she wanted to, which, of course, she didn't really. She knew she still had a duty to at least check on them from time to time.

In the confusion and anxiety and thrill of the first week, however, she had nearly forgotten her promise to Ma to return. She had only remembered just this morning when she woke up. It had cast a bit of a cloud over the whole day, but she tried to shake it off. She also had an oddly disquieting feeling she was forgetting something else as well, but she couldn't think of what it could be.

Melody and Cynthia having already gone upstairs now, Elsie stepped into Philomena's foyer and instinctively looked around for Gunther yet again. Why was she always looking for him, expecting him to be close by? she thought, irritated. She supposed it was because she had spent her first weeks here, on and off, with him alone, and it felt odd not to see him about as she had before, running into him occasionally and sharing what they were doing or reading. Though it didn't make a bit of sense, it had almost felt as if this was *their* house, that they were the sole occupants and that all of these people coming and going now were merely visitors. And she was of course desperately worried, despite Sr. Bernard's reassurances, about his injury and how his mother had fared in his absence. Not to mention the cryptic contents of his notebook, which she longed to ask him about. Could he be avoiding her on purpose? she wondered, but she dismissed this as ridiculous. Why would he want to avoid her?

Sr. Joseph looked up at her and smiled, which prompted an idea to suddenly come into Elsie's mind. She had resolved not to pester Sr. Bernard anymore with questions about Gunther, but she had made no such resolution regarding the other sisters, she reasoned with herself.

"Hello, Sister Joseph," Elsie began. "Have you seen Gunther anywhere?" she asked, in what she hoped was a casual voice.

"The custodian?" Sr. Joseph asked.

Elsie nodded.

"I believe he's in the kitchen," Sr. Joseph said, glancing behind her. "Do you need something?"

"*This* kitchen?"Elsie asked, not believing that he was so close . . .

"I believe so. Would you like me to call him?" Sr. Joseph asked kindly.

"Oh, no, Sister. I'll just . . . no, that's all right."

Elsie hurried down the hallway toward the kitchen, afraid that she might already have missed him. Quickly, she pushed through the swinging door and felt an oddly warm surge of relief to see him, finally, calmly sitting at the table.

"Gunther!"

A small smile crept across his face, but he did not speak.

"Are you . . . how are you?" she asked, her eyes dropping to his wrist. It was still bandaged, but it looked dirty and frayed, as though it hadn't been changed in a while. Why hadn't his mother attended it? Perhaps she was infirm, Elsie suddenly reasoned. That would explain much . . .

"Better, thank you," he said, standing up. Slowly he reached for the now familiar notebook that was sitting on the table, Elsie following his movements with her eyes. She wondered what he had written in it since.

"I haven't seen you all week! I . . . I wanted to come check on you, but . . . Sister Bernard said you needed rest . . . and I don't actually know where you live," she said hurriedly.

"No, do not concern yourself," he said earnestly. "You did enough. I . . . I owe you a big debt of thanks, Elsie. Thank you for what you did for me. I am sorry to have been so much trouble. To have spoiled your plans."

"Oh, don't worry about that. I . . . I was happy to . . . I mean, I'm *glad* I was there to help you. It was actually my fault in a way . . . if I hadn't insisted on going to the Vigil, then you—"

"*Unsinn!* Do not say that. Nothing has been your fault."

Elsie didn't know what to say next. There was much she could ask, but she didn't know how. Many times since that night in the hospital, she had speculated about who the woman named Anna was. And she had since scoured the library as well, rifling through an old volume of German poets until she had found at least some of the ones Gunther had copied so that she could read them all again. She even knew a few of them by heart now. She wished she could tell him how beautiful she thought they were, but how could she admit she had read his notebook?

"Thank you for the book," she said, suddenly inspired. "The Tolstoy book."

The strain in his face relaxed. "Ah. Have you read it?" he asked eagerly, as he gripped the back of the chair.

"Yes, I finished it."

"Already?"

Elsie wasn't sure what to make of that comment. "Well, it's not very long. And I'm a fast reader," she added, a little hurt.

"No . . . I did not mean. Forgive me. I am still little mixed up on days. Did you . . . did you like it?"

"I *did* like it," she tried to say convincingly.

In truth, Elsie had liked *Family Happiness* well enough, but she had been startled by how much of it—the first part, anyway— reminded her of Henrietta's story, likening Henrietta of course to the fictional young Mashechka who falls in love with the much older Sergei. The two eventually marry, despite Sergei's misgivings that Masha will soon tire of the quiet, secluded life he desires and will want to explore more of the world, despite her protestations to the contrary. Anxious to keep her happy, Sergei introduces her into society, where Masha indeed shimmers and becomes the darling of the Russian aristocracy.

After Elsie had returned to Mundelein from her vigil at the hospital with Gunther, she convinced herself that he would not remember much of what she had said to him there in the dark. . . or so she hoped. But at about the halfway point in *Family Happiness*, she began to uneasily suspect that perhaps he *had* been cognizant of her words, his choice of story seeming to indicate that he had indeed been aware of all that she had said about her family, though she didn't remember going this deeply into detail regarding Clive and Henrietta's relationship. For one thing, she wasn't privy to it. Thank God she had not mentioned Stanley or Harrison or even Lloyd—though, she uncomfortably remembered, Gunther had already met Lloyd.

Perhaps it was all merely an odd coincidence, she mused. After all, he had told her that he liked to read the Russians. Well, she had thought, as she had continued turning the pages, if he had chosen this particular story based on her own family, at least it was about Henrietta and not her. And it was odd that it was entitled "family happiness" when her family always seemed anything but happy. Doubtless there was a deeper meaning she hadn't yet fathomed.

"Yes? What exactly did you like about it?" he asked her.

Elsie hesitated. What should she say? "Well, the story reminded me a lot of Henrietta, actually. My sister," she added when she saw his look of puzzlement.

"Ah, yes," he said, rubbing his chin now. "I . . . what else?"

"I . . . well, I liked the style of writing, I suppose. He reminds me in a way of Dickens."

"In what way?" he asked curiously.

Why was he asking her all these questions? She would rather talk about his poetry or his journal entries. She tried to think of an acceptable answer to his last question. "The way he describes things, I suppose," she finally answered, hoping to get away with being vague. "But he's much more poetic, I think, than Dickens, isn't he? But the . . . the dialogue was sometimes choppy," she reflected, her brow furrowed as she tried to think back.

"That is probably the translation. It is not a particularly good one, I am afraid."

"Oh. I hadn't thought of that."

"Much of what you read depends on how accurate is the translation, Elsie. Remember this," he said, looking straight into her eyes, as he slowly put the notebook he was still holding into his pocket.

He knows! she suddenly realized, her heart quickening. He knows that I read it! But how could he? she wondered, allowing herself a moment of hope. No . . . he must know, she quickly countered. Why else would he have said such a thing? She should confess right now and apologize, she knew, but she just couldn't make herself.

"I . . ." she began, and though she was looking at the floor, she could feel his eyes on her. She made herself look at him now and was surprised that he did not look angry, exactly, but maybe just sad, or was it fatigue?

"I . . . I should go," she muttered, losing courage. "I can see that you're tired. You should be in bed."

"Elsie, I . . ." he began and then stopped, closing his eyes. He had an odd air of defeat about him. "Yes, you must be tired too, after your first week," he said, slowly opening his eyes again. "Are you staying in? Tonight, I mean."

"I'm going to study for a bit, and afterwards I promised my mother I would go and see her."

Gunther gave a little nod. "I see. Is your—what do you call it?—*chauefer*? to pick you up?"

Elsie blushed. "No, I don't want to bother him. He likes to listen to *The Shadow* in the evenings. I can't bear to ask him to come out, especially when it's so cold. I'm going to take the bus and then walk a little ways. It's been awhile since I have."

"Perhaps I should walk with you," he suggested. "You should not be out alone at night. We can talk."

"About what?" Elsie asked, nervous.

"About whatever you wish. *Family Happiness*, maybe. Or you can tell me about your classes, how you find them." He was looking at her so kindly that she felt an odd desire to embrace him—as a good friend, that is, but she refrained, afraid that it might not be interpreted as such.

"But what about your hand?"

"Ach!" he said, holding it up and looking at it as if he had forgotten about his injury. "It is fine. Cold will not hurt it."

Elsie hesitated. "Well, maybe for just a little ways," she said finally. She liked the idea of not walking alone, actually, and maybe she would find the courage somewhere along the way to ask him about Anna and Fraulein Klinkhammer, seeing as he seemed to know she had read his notebook. And then maybe she could ask him about his poems. "I . . . I can't ask you in, though," she said quietly, her face feeling exceptionally hot. "When we get there, I mean."

"It is fine, yes. I understand. Your mother."

So he *did* remember what she had said, she confirmed, mortified. But why should she feel mortified? she corrected herself. She had said nothing shameful!

"I will see you later, no?" he asked with a smile. "Go now," he said, nodding his head toward the stairs.

Obediently, she made her way up the stairs and reflected on how strange were the methods they had so far employed in revealing a part of themselves to the other—she stealing a glimpse of him from his notebook and he extracting bits of her under the cover of darkness and delirium. She supposed that made them equal somehow and warmed a little at this thought. It made her feel connected to him, as if he were part of her family here now too, along with Melody and Sr. Bernard. He was like . . . a cousin or maybe a brother. Yes, that must be it, she thought contentedly. Like a brother.

Chapter 19

"**F**ind anything?" Clive asked, as he opened the drawer of the nightstand next to his father's bed.

"Not really," Henrietta called from the closet, where she listlessly rifled through Alcott's suits, which still hung neatly in the closet that adjoined the room he had shared with Antonia. "I'm not sure I feel comfortable looking through your father's things, Clive."

"I distinctly remember you saying that you wished to help," Clive responded, not looking back at her but instead opening up another drawer. "Demanded, I think it was, actually."

The swelling in his right eye had finally started to subside, leaving just a deep purplish-yellow smudge beneath it. He had half expected Henrietta to be hysterical when Stan had gone back into the Aragon to fetch her and hurriedly lead her out into the alley where Clive was leaning against a police car, holding a towel against his mouth to stop the blood pouring from his lip. But she hadn't. He had been impressed that she had kept her head and calmly, albeit shakily, asked Clancy what had happened. And then the next thing he knew, he was being driven to Ravenswood Hospital to be checked over. He attempted to protest, saying he was fine, that he had had worse, but Henrietta took the advice of the officers and insisted. As he suspected, several ribs were cracked. The doctor on call wanted him to be admitted for observation, but Clive refused, so they merely taped his ribs and then reluctantly released him.

He spent the next day in bed, with Henrietta hovering around him, bringing him ridiculous things like cocoa, when all he really needed was a stiff drink. He was grateful that his mother was not home to see him like this and hoped his eye would heal before she returned.

With that in mind, he finally dragged himself out of bed on the second day. He needed to act quickly before she returned. As of yet, the only place he had not searched for the missing money—or a hidden account book, a ledger, something!—was in his parents' room. He had mentioned to Antonia his desire to search through his father's personal effects on more than one occasion, but she had refused, saying that there was absolutely nothing "hidden" in their room. And just what was he looking for exactly? she had demanded, which prompted Clive to quickly change the subject.

Still, Clive couldn't rest until he searched the room, especially in light of what had happened at the Aragon, and now that Antonia was in New York, it was the perfect opportunity. Henrietta tried to keep him in bed, but when he explained the urgency, she reluctantly agreed that they should take advantage of the situation—emphasizing *they*. Clive did not have the energy to argue, so they both made their way to his mother's room and slipped inside.

Much as he hated to admit it, Clive suspected his mother was right. Surely, she would have noticed a large pile of money lying around, an attaché case, a box? He knew how it felt to lose a spouse, endlessly going through all of their things looking for something . . . some last trace of them . . . a note of love perhaps? A treasured token? Some communication written before their death that would magically soothe the raw hurt now felt. He knew his mother had probably been through this room a hundred times by now, and yet he needed to see for himself.

Unfortunately, he had so far not found anything, and Henrietta was proving to be not so much of a help, not so eager a participant in

the snooping as she had first seemed, having spent more time looking at the photographs on his mother's bureau than actually searching for something.

"Who's this?" she asked, holding up one of the photos.

Clive looked back over his shoulder, squinting to make out the
image. He had left the lights switched off, not wanting to attract the
servants' attention, but it made it difficult to see. It was still early
afternoon, but the room was dark and gloomy with only a weak
January sun to illuminate it.

"That's me and Julia and Linley and Wallace outside Linley Castle.
Don't you recognize it?" he asked, turning his attention back to the
contents of the drawer he was searching.

"Linley looks so much like you. You could have been mistaken for
brothers," she mused.

"Yes, that's what everyone—"

"Clive! Did you hear that?" Henrietta interrupted with a whisper,
noiselessly setting the photo frame back in place.

Clive paused where he stood in front of an armoire. It was probably Billings or that idiot Carter, he guessed, who seemed to be
perpetually lingering around this wing of the house, like an old dog
waiting for his master to return. It was beyond irritating.

"I think someone's coming," Henrietta whispered again.

Silently, Clive moved to stand in front of her while he swiftly
pulled out his revolver, the only sound being the crisp click of the
hammer as he cocked it. More than likely, it was one of the servants,
but Clive was taking no chances these days. After all, *someone* in the
house had to be communicating with Neptune. Both of them stood,
bracing themselves, as they waited for the intruder to come closer.

Henrietta gasped when the door burst open, and Clive, seeing
who it was, let out a deep groan, lowering his gun as he did so.

"Mother?"

Antonia indeed stood before them in the doorway. "Just what do
you think you're doing?" she asked in a shrill voice, looking from one
to the other. "Put that silly thing away, Clive."

Antonia reached over and switched on the light to observe them more closely. "What are you doing in my room?" she repeated, clearly perturbed.

Clive sighed. "Mother, I can explain."

"Really? Do try," she said crisply.

"Why are you home early? Has something happened?"

"Don't try to change the subject, Clive."

"But *has* something happened?"

"In New York? No." Antonia studied Clive. "As it happens, Billings telephoned me to say that you had been in some sort of accident." Her face looked worried now.

"It was hardly an accident, Mother. Just a scuffle," Clive tried to say casually, privately cursing Billings.

"Is that what you call it? Billings says that the police were involved. Did you not think to telephone me and let me know he was okay?" she asked Henrietta directly now, who had moved from behind Clive.

"I—" Henrietta began.

"Mother, there was nothing to tell. I was attacked in an alleyway, but it wasn't serious. As you can see, I'm fine. I can't believe you came all the way back from New York for this . . . it's ludicrous!" he said, his voice rising.

Antonia stood stiffly observing him before she let out a deep breath, her face crumpling.

"Oh, Clive," she said with real anguish. "I couldn't bear it if I lost you too. I was so very worried. When Billings said it was an accident, I suppose I panicked. He said it wasn't necessary to come home, but I just couldn't stay there . . ."

Clive went to her, then, and embraced her. "Mother, I'm sorry. No real harm has been done. Just some bumps and bruises. Isn't that so, Henrietta?" he said, glancing over at her for help.

"Yes, Antonia. Honestly. He was checked over at the hospital. He just needs to rest," Henrietta said eagerly.

Antonia allowed Clive to hold her for a few more moments before she gathered herself up and pulled away.

"Well," she said, sniffing and looking at both of them as she wiped her eyes, "if you are supposed to be resting, then perhaps you might tell me why you are both snooping about my room?"

"I told you before, Mother," Clive sighed, "I need to go through Father's things."

"Whatever for?" Antonia asked, her previous, irritated tone seeping back into the conversation. "I don't understand this . . . this obsession of yours. There's nothing here, as I assume you've since discovered."

"It's difficult to explain," Clive said uncomfortably. "We're—I'm looking for . . . for—"

"Clues," Henrietta put in.

"Clues?" Antonia asked, her brow furrowed. "Not this again," she sighed, as she carefully set her handbag on the dressing table. "Clive, I insist you see a doctor. I've already had a chat with someone, actually; he's a very good friend of the family. Very discreet. I'm quite sure he can help."

Clive tiredly rubbed his eyes.

"And you," she said, shooting Henrietta a dagger, "I'm disappointed in you, Henrietta. Going along with this nonsense. Clearly, he's unwell. Did you not think what indulging his fantasies might lead to? Total madness," she whispered in a hiss.

"Mother. That's enough. I'm perfectly sane."

"Clive," Henrietta implored. "I think you should tell her."

"Tell me what?" Antonia asked, looking sharply at Clive.

Clive caught Henrietta's eye and saw her give him the slightest nod of encouragement. She was so damningly beautiful . . . He closed his eyes to focus himself, knowing she was right. The time had come. He went to where his mother stood and took her hands in his. "Listen, Mother, there's something I must tell you." He paused here, considering his words. "We know for a certainty that Father's death was not an accident. He was killed. We have proof now," he said as gently as he could, studying her face for what he was sure would be her extreme reaction.

"Clive, please," she said in an unexpectedly calm voice and tried to pull her hands from his, but Clive held them tightly.

"Mother. It's true. I've confronted his killers. They've as much as admitted it. They—"

"Is that what happened?" she interrupted, her voice wavering a bit now as she turned her attention to his bruises. "To you, I mean?" she asked fearfully and pulled one hand free from Clive's grasp and lightly touched the side of his face.

"Come on, let's go downstairs. We'll explain over some tea," he said, putting his arm around her. As he moved to usher her from the room, he shot a glance at Henrietta, and she nodded, knowing what he wanted and went ahead to arrange things with Billings.

Once the tea had been delivered and the three of them were alone, Clive began to relate all he knew about Alcott being a victim of extortion, how he had sold the "missing" painting, presumably for money to pay the mob, as they most certainly could be called, and how it had ultimately led to his death.

Antonia sat resolute, holding her teacup in her hands, staring at the pattern of the Oriental rug as Clive and Henrietta exchanged worried looks.

"Poor Alcott," she whispered. "All those years he had to bear this burden alone. I wish he would have confided in me."

"Yes, I know the feeling. I suppose he felt he couldn't, though," Clive tried to say gently. "That it would put you . . . and us . . . in danger somehow."

Antonia reached up with her handkerchief and wiped her eyes.

"He wasn't completely alone," Clive said in an attempt to comfort her.

"What do you mean by that?" she asked, looking up at him.

"Just that Bennett knew."

"Yes, Bennett," she said quietly.

"He's known all these many years, apparently. And he was there when he died," Clive reminded her.

"Yes, he told me. He came to me that day. But he said that he slipped. That Alcott had lost his footing . . ."

"Obviously, he meant to spare you. And to protect you, perhaps."

A new thought crept into his mind, then. "Has . . . has Bennett been acting or saying anything odd . . . especially lately? To you?"

"Odd? What do you mean by that?" she asked, her voice growing steady.

"Carter told me that Bennett rang here on Christmas Eve. That you spoke to him. I'd forgotten about it until now. What did he want?"

"Really, Clive. I can hardly remember," she said giving him an unexpectedly icy look. "I think it was just to wish us a Merry Christmas—despite the situation, of course. That he had hoped to tell you that at the office but that you hadn't been in. Something like that, I believe. And, anyway, what business is it of yours what Sidney Bennett says to me?" she said, drawing herself up.

"Well, given the situation, I'd say it's very much my business, Mother," he said dryly and wondered why he just couldn't shake the feeling that Bennett was hiding something.

"I still don't understand what you are looking for upstairs among Alcott's things," Antonia said suspiciously.

"Don't you see?" Clive sighed. "Father sold the painting and gave half to these thugs. Now they want the rest. I could raise the money elsewhere—and it looks like I'm going to have to, maybe by selling off some of my personal stock—but where is it, the original stash, that is? What did father do with it? I can't find any trace of it in any of his accounts or the safe. It's just disappeared, and I feel like there's something behind it. Some link to the case somehow."

Antonia looked dubious. "I suppose," she said. "But the bigger problem is the fact that the mob is after *you* now, as well as Bennett, it would seem."

Clive had not related to her how Randolph Jr. and Howard—all of them, really—were now a target for Neptune and his men. It was a detail she did not need to know at this juncture.

"That's what *I* said, Antonia," Henrietta put in, and Antonia gave her a small smile.

"Clive, you've got to go to the police. I positively insist," Antonia said. "If you don't, I will," she threatened.

"Yes, yes. I've been to the police."

"But not since you were roughed up at the Aragon, Clive," Henrietta pointed out.

"Clive!" Antonia wailed.

"I'm waiting for some sort of signal—one of their letters, maybe?— to come through from them as to when and where I'm supposed to meet to hand over the rest of the cash," Clive tried to explain.

"Which you will then report to Sergeant Davis, right?" Henrietta encouraged. "You do have a plan, don't you? One that involves the police? You can't just hand the money over to them. Surely they'll just keep demanding more, or maybe even . . . kill you," she said urgently.

"Yes, of course I have a plan," Clive said flippantly, though in truth it was sketchy at best. "But there's something else that's been bothering me," he said, turning toward Antonia. "Any idea how these notes, or letters, have been finding their way into the house?"

"No," she said slowly, as if considering this for the first time. "None at all."

"What about Carter?" he asked.

"Carter! Carter wouldn't do something like that!" she exclaimed.

Clive narrowed his eyes and studied her. If it wasn't his own mother, he would have guessed that she were hiding something. "Think clearly, Mother. It could have been him. He would be in the perfect position to place letters on Father's desk."

Antonia's response was swift. "How dare you, Clive!" she said hotly. "Carter has been a good and faithful servant all these many years. He came with your father from England; he would never have betrayed him. They were almost like brothers. In fact, I daresay he was probably closer to Carter than even Montague."

Clive did not think this was true. On more than one occasion of his youth, he himself had heard his father disparage Carter, though usually only after a couple glasses of brandy. Obviously his mother was unaware of this, Clive realized. But what good would it do to mention it all now? "Be that as it may, Mother, no man is beyond temptation. Or maybe Carter was delivering the letters under duress. Maybe the mob had something on him and was forcing his hand."

Antonia paused to consider this. "I very much doubt it," she said, her eyebrows raised.

"I've already spoken to him once, but I'll have to question him again," Clive said stiffly.

"Let me do it," Antonia suggested a little more hastily than Clive appreciated. "He might speak to me more than he would to you," she added.

He gave her a skeptical look.

"He's actually quite shy. He might be too intimidated by you to speak to you regarding such matters."

Clive would never have described Carter as "shy," nor did he ever remotely appear "intimidated." Quite the opposite, actually. Were they even talking about the same person?

"As you wish, Mother," Clive said, though he still planned to corner Carter later, but there was no need to tell his mother that.

"So what do we do now?" Henrietta asked.

"We keep looking for the money," Clive said soberly.

Antonia set her tea cup gently on its saucer. "I think I might know where it is."

Clive groaned as he pushed against the door of the cottage, a ripple of pain radiating from his injured ribs. He gave it another shove, this time with his good shoulder, and was relieved when the door finally swung open, creaking loudly as it did so. He shone his flashlight around the interior. They had not been here since their honeymoon night, but upon first glance, it appeared to be as they had left it, though tidied up since, of course, by the servants.

Clive made his way into the darkness, with Henrietta following closely behind. It was little warmer than the frigid air outside, and their breath fogged in front of them. Clive gave the flashlight to Henrietta to hold while he grappled inside his coat for the matches in his suit pocket. He lit one and then bent to light the kerosene lamp on the kitchen table. Antonia had suggested that they wait until morning to search the cottage, especially as it did not have electricity and it was already growing dark when they had first sat down to tea, but Clive wouldn't wait. He was hoping the search would be quick, but he had not foreseen how cold the cottage itself would be and now wondered how far they would actually get, bundled up as they were. He did not really want to take the time to light a fire, but the sight of Henrietta shivering beside him, blowing on her gloved hands, convinced him. Anyway, perhaps it would take longer than he had imagined to conduct the search, and it would be a much more pleasant task if it were warm. He wasn't at all convinced that the money was out here; it seemed a wild goose chase, despite what his mother thought. She had been very closed-mouthed as to why she felt it was out here, saying that it was just a hunch, but his mother, Clive knew, did not operate on "hunches."

He moved toward the big stone fireplace and found a few small logs still sitting in a basket on the hearth. Carefully he stacked them in the grate.

"It's a shame this place is sitting empty, Clive. Someone should live in it." Henrietta said, as she went around lighting more lamps.

"I think Mother mentioned something about giving it to Carter, of all people," Clive said, reaching for the billows that looked old enough to have been from the Civil War. "But I thought you wanted this to be our special place. Isn't that what you said?" He shot her a teasing glance.

"Oh, those were the silly ravings of a young girl on the eve of her wedding," Henrietta said, the cold air frosting her cheeks pink in the most delicious way, as she stood by the old Victrola. "Still," she said, "this place does hold such fond memories for me. It will always be special to me." She walked toward him now and stood in front of him. "If it weren't so cold," she said, kissing his warm lips, which caused an immediate response in his lower regions, "you could take me on the bed. For old time's sake," she whispered. She wrapped her arms around him, which unexpectedly caused a stab of pain to rip through him, and he winced.

"Oh, I'm sorry, darling," she exclaimed, pulling away. "Oh, you poor thing!" she said, and couldn't help laughing a little. "What are we going to do?"

"We'll have to figure that out later," Clive said ruefully, wondering how he could make love to her with cracked ribs. He'd have to be inventive.

The fire had caught now but it was weak. Clive knew that if he didn't add more wood to it, it would die out soon. Henrietta seemed to read his mind.

"I'll go out back and look for some wood," she suggested. "You start snooping around."

"You're sure?" Clive asked. "You're marvelous, darling."

"I keep reminding you that I used to work for a living—quite hard, actually," she called, as she tightened her scarf and made her way back out the door.

Clive removed his bulky coat despite the cold and looked around the cottage. Nothing looked disturbed. Where would his father have stashed something? And why here, in the cottage? And yet his mother had been quite sure. There must be more to that story, he reasoned, but he hadn't had time to drag it out of her.

Where to start? He glanced over at the kitchen, but instinctively he did not think it would be there and instead moved toward the bedroom. He first went to the little desk in the corner, but it had nothing on it but a lamp and only one drawer, which was empty. He went to the bedside table, then, but that was also empty. With great difficulty, he got down on his hands and knees to peer under the bed. Again, nothing. He heard Henrietta come in with the wood and drop it loudly in the basket.

"Need help?" she called out, as he heard her place a few logs on the fire.

"No, you look in the kitchen, would you?" he shouted back, as he gripped the side of the bed to help himself up, trying not to groan as he did so. Slowly, holding his side as he walked, he went to the old bureau and pulled each drawer open. Again, nothing. He sighed. The only other place to look was the armoire in the corner, but that seemed so obvious. Still, he walked over to it and pulled open the doors, peering inside. Of course, there was nothing. Nothing hanging, no box or envelope sitting conveniently on the floor of it. Clive methodically opened all of the side drawers but found nothing there, either, except some old cedar blocks. Almost routinely, he ran his hand quickly along the top shelf and likewise felt nothing, except perhaps something way back in the corner . . . It was probably nothing, he told himself, but his heart skipped a beat just the same. He raised himself up on his tiptoes to stretch for it. The pain that ripped through him as a result was intense, and he involuntarily cried out.

"Are you all right?" Henrietta called from the kitchen.

"I might have found something. Would you help me?" he called back, breathing heavily and hating to ask for help. But he had no choice.

Henrietta was at his side in a moment.

"Back there," he said, looking up at the shelf. Henrietta stretched her full length, but it was too tall for her.

"Just wait a moment," she said, and she ran from the room and returned carrying a chair. "Here," she said, setting it down in front of the armoire. Carefully she stood on it, Clive holding one of her hands to support her. She took a moment to feel around the back of the shelf and then looked down at him with a smile. "Yes, there's something here," she said, proudly pulling out a large, bulging envelope and placing it in Clive's waiting hand.

"Jesus," Clive muttered. "This has got to be it." He held his hand out to her, giving her a quick wink, and once she was safely on the ground, he grasped the envelope firmly, feeling the bulges inside and turning it over to look for any writing, any sort of address. "I think this is it," he repeated, and shoved his thumb under the sealed flap and ripped it open. Eagerly he looked inside and, to his utter delight and disbelief, saw the stacks of green money. But had his father really stored five thousand dollars in a plain envelope and put it on the top shelf of an armoire in the empty cottage at the edge of their property? Despite his elation at finally finding the money, he was not a little annoyed at his father's movements. Anyone could have found it out here! What had he been thinking?

He handed it to Henrietta, who peered inside as well. "Oh, Clive," she murmured, looking back up at him with a smile. As she held it out to him to take back, however, her eye seemed to catch on something else, and she stopped and peered inside again. "There's something else," she said, reaching inside and pulling out what looked to be a smaller envelope. She handed it to him. "Some kind of note maybe?"

Clive examined the thick envelope, his heart speeding up, and quickly opened it to reveal what looked like a long missive in his father's hand, the sight of which unexpectedly caused his eyes to become blurry, and he felt his throat tighten. "My dear boy," he read aloud and then had to stop, surprised by the unexpected emotion he felt. He cleared his throat and began again.

My Dear Boy,

I address this missive, obviously my last, to you, as I have no doubt that it will have been you that has found it. You are quite skilled as a detective, but I never told you that, for which I am now very sorry.

If you are reading this, then something has gone very wrong, and I have departed from this world. No doubt my death will have seemed like an accident to all, except, I suspect, to you, and, of course, Sidney Bennett. By now you will surely have pieced together the fact that I have been the victim of extortion almost from the beginning of my new life on these shores. I should have done something about it long before, but, though it pains me greatly to admit it to you, I am a coward at heart. Still, though I by no means deny this charge, I will say that I acted not out of desire to protect myself all these years, but for fear of what might have happened to you and Julia and my Antonia.

There is much I would write—so many things I wish I would have said to each of you, but time is running short now and my rendezvous quickly approaches. Would that I had had the presence of mind to compose this at my leisure, but it is only now, as the clock quickly ticks down, that I feel compelled to explain myself should all not go satisfactorily. It is my fervent hope, however, that I may return, victorious from my encounter with this villain, and have the deep pleasure of tearing up this missive, welcoming you home with your lovely bride in a few months' time, and having the joy of one day holding in my arms your child, my heir. But if you are reading this, then all has not gone well, and so I shall employ this thin tract, grossly insufficient as it is, to relay to each of you my deep, enduring love.

Clive paused here. When he continued, his voice was husky.

There is not time to explain in great detail all that has happened leading up to this desperate moment, nor is it necessary, I suppose. What is done is done. Try not to judge me too harshly. I believe I have been a victim of those more commonly called the mob. And as abhorrent and as cowardly as it was, I may have been able to continue paying the original thugs who coerced me, though the financial strain was considerable, as I'm sure you're well aware of by now, but things have radically changed in recent months, which have now made it nearly impossible—nay intolerable—to continue. When this new character, this Lawrence Susan, entered the equation, all seemed lost. He seems to know so much about you, and, oddly, Henrietta as well, and I am nearly paralyzed by the violence of his threats and have lain awake night after night dwelling upon them and my miserable situation. And in this way, I have strangely found a new courage. But, no—this is not true. It is not courage that propels me but rather a different type of fear.

I deeply regret selling the Levitan, as it came from Linley Castle, and by selling it and giving the money to these ruffians, it seems as though I foul my ancestral home by association. Still, I could not have raised this amount of cash without stealing funds from Linley Standard, which I was loathe to do, though I admit to you now, Clive, that I was sorely tempted. Selling a painting seemed my only recourse, but now that I am on the brink of handing over this blood money, every cell of my body rebels.

It was my original intention to give this Susan the exorbitant amount that he is demanding as a way of hopefully ending this arrangement once and for all. But now, this very morning, it occurs to me in some miraculous way that this is not the way out. My fevered mind tells me to give them only half of the money in hopes that I may set some sort of trap for them with the rest, possibly with the help of the police. Bennett has more than once begged me to go to the authorities with this, despite the scandal it might cause in the financial world and thus negatively affect the stock price of Linley Standard, but Susan, like his predecessors before him, have promised certain death, and worse, if I do so. And so I have not, though I did once seriously contemplate it.

It was about five years ago, not long after Chief Callahan was hired onto the Winnetka force, that I attended a charity event where he was the guest of honor. I read on the evening's program all about his background and his impeccable record and how he had made a name for himself in Chicago during Prohibition. Assuming he must have much experience in dealing with the mob, I approached him at one point in the evening and presented my situation under the guise of it being a "friend's" problem. If I was concerned that he might see through my ruse, I should not have worried, as not only did he not suspect the truth, but he seemed positively oblivious to the existence of real crime, saying that Winnetka was such a charming town, was it not? Not bothered at all by murder or kidnappings or any of the seedier sides of the underworld. Indeed, he seemed to me almost simpleminded, and I wondered, then, if he had been booted out of the force in Chicago and "promoted" to chief out in our small corner of the world where he would not do any harm. Whatever the case, I knew from that moment that he would be of no help to me, and I was afraid at that time to search farther afield for aid.

Instead, I continued on as I always had until just this morning when I awoke with a new idea in my mind, which is simply that I must stop running, that I must put an end to this. It became eminently clear last night as I lay awake that I have failed across the board—nearly bankrupting Highbury, soiling my honor, disgracing the Linley name, and foolishly putting the ones I most love in this world in danger. Nearly paralyzed with guilt all night and sleeping only in fits, I strangely awoke with a clear sense of what I must do and was encouraged and comforted by the hope that comes from having at least the rudiments of a plan. For this I am extremely grateful, as I have not felt hope for so very long. And if I should perish in the process, then it is more than fitting—I deserve it, and I am not afraid to meet my Maker.

In short, I have decided to call this Susan's bluff, to use a colloquial phrase. I telephoned Bennett very early, and he has agreed to accompany me this morning and to help me, reluctantly you should perhaps know, with my plan. It is simply this: I plan to give Susan and his thugs only half of the money this morning with the promise of delivering the rest at a later date at a place of my choosing, where I can have the police waiting to ambush them. I fear it is too late just now to involve the police, especially considering the chief's reticence of action, but perhaps Bennett and I can get a good look at them and, if we're lucky, a license plate number. I can then submit this information, this evidence, to perhaps the Chicago police, who I hope will aid me in my attempts to convince them of this creature's villainy.

Whatever happens, know that I tried to be brave and to do my duty, albeit late, but hopefully not too late. It further occurs to me that as I attempt to play your role as a detective, that it is damned difficult to fill someone else's shoes, and I now realize, in a very real way, what I am asking of you in the filling of mine. And yet we don't always have the luxury of many choices in life. Mine was not to come to America and help to found Linley Standard, but such was the role I was assigned, and I was happy in it, in the end. My prayer is that you, too, will be happy in it.

Not much more remains to be said, I suppose, except to relay that Bennett was in no way involved in this scheme except by my express urgings that he accompany me this morning. I have never revealed the whole of the mystery to him, though I have on occasion hinted or let things slip, and I daresay he has drawn conclusions very near the truth, knowing Bennett as I do. It is important to relate to you that Sidney Bennett has ever been my most stalwart ally and friend through the years and that you may trust him, as I have done, with your very life. You might be surprised at this, thinking that that role may have been reserved for John Exley, and though John is a very good friend indeed, Sidney and I have been through much. We have grown up together, in a way, and he saved me once when I was about to make a very grave, very foolish mistake. Make a friend of him, Clive, and lean on him, especially in regards to the firm. For Linley Standard is as much Sidney Bennett— more so, actually—than it is, or ever was, me.

Give Julia, my darling girl, my love. She has ever been a bright spot in my life, and I pray she may be happy always despite the unfortunate marriage she finds herself in. For my hand in that, I also bear much regret.

As for Antonia, my dearest wife, tell her how very much I love her. Tell her how sorry I am that I had not time to write a separate missive to her, but my time is nearly out now, and I must soon depart. I would have her know, however, that I never stopped loving her despite her . . . well, let's just leave it at that. She will know what I mean. Tell her that I have always loved her and always will.

I go now to face my extortionists. It gives me great satis-faction to have been able to say good-bye to you, Clive, even in this hurried, unusual way. Know that what I did, I did for Linley. Good-bye, my boy. You were always a good son, and I love you dearly. Be happy with Henrietta, and do your duty.

Your loving father,

Alcott

Clive slowly folded the letter, letting out a deep breath as he did so. He felt Henrietta's comforting hand on his, and he slipped his arm around her, drawing her close to him.

"It's a lovely letter," she whispered in his ear.

All he could do was nod. It was hard to take in every aspect of the letter—there was so much in it, so much that needed deeper reflec-tion. His mind was on fire, racing from point to point, with his emo-tions dragging along behind. Perhaps uppermost in his thoughts, however, was the realization of how very tragic the whole thing was, how senseless his father's death had been. He could not help but think how easily his father's death might have been prevented if Alcott had only waited and shared the burden with him. And how could he, Clive, have not seen what was under his nose all these years? But then again, he had not been privy to his father's financial dealings nor the workings of Linley Standard. But maybe that was his fault too. If he had shown more interest early on . . . he thought bitterly. Damn it! How could his father have been so stupid, so naïve?

To think he could bluff the likes of a mob boss like Neptune? A burst of rage burned in his heart, and he felt a desire to actually murder Neptune—putting him behind bars—as he had already done once in the past—was not enough. But didn't that go against what he purported to stand for since he'd returned from the chaos of the war? Truth, justice, order—all of that?

And what of justice and order? he thought, a new suspicion entering his mind, then. His father's letter, though it was obviously not part of the intent, shone a very telling light on Chief Callahan. Could he somehow be connected, too? Clive wondered. Was he somehow being paid off to look the other way in certain matters? It was certainly in the realm of possibility, Clive thought uneasily, and it would explain the chief's quick dismissal of him. He wondered if Davis was in on it too. He let out almost a groan. The whole thing infuriated him. Neptune wanted the rest of the money; well, he would give him what was coming to him—in spades.

"I would have loved to have found such a letter from my father," Henrietta said, interrupting his thoughts. He stared at her as if he had forgotten she was there and felt a fresh surge of unease. No matter what his promise to her had previously been to involve her in his cases, he would not allow her to be a part of this one. He sought revenge now, and he didn't want her to be anywhere near this.

"Yes, it's a gift," he agreed reluctantly. "It's . . . it's too much to take in all at once," he said, rubbing his brow.

"Will you show it to your mother?"

"I suppose I'll have to at some point. But all I can think about right now is catching these bastards," he said, walking to the window.

"Of course you will, darling."

"Look, Henrietta, there's something I haven't told you about the other night," he said, turning back toward her.

"That Lawrence Susan is Neptune?" she said calmly.

Clive was stunned. "How did you—?"

Henrietta gave a small shrug. "Lawrence, Larry?" she said, looking at him expectantly. "And your father's letter confirmed it. *He seems to know so much about you, and, oddly, Henrietta as well"* she repeated back. "Who else could it be?" she asked, as she wrapped her arms around herself.

"Yes, it's him," Clive sighed. "He was in the alley. I knew he wouldn't give up so easily after Jack escaped, but I didn't think he would go this far."

Henrietta remained silent, deep in thought. "But . . . wait a minute," she said, finally. "None of this makes sense. Your father was extorted from for years . . . so it can't have been Neptune!"

"But it wasn't always Neptune. I think he took over from the original men that had set up the 'contract' with my father. They have rings of 'clients' who pay them, but sometimes the ring is taken over by someone else, usually when a new gang moves in and tries to claim territory. Or they're given to someone as a reward. Neptune somehow must have gotten hold of the ring that includes my father, probably as a way of getting to us personally. His mistake, however, was to tighten the noose."

"I don't understand his obsession with . . . with me," Henrietta faltered.

"I don't either, darling," he said, coming toward her and brushing her cheek with the back of his hand. "But he seems fixated on you, on *us* now."

He saw her bite her bottom lip to stop it trembling, solidifying his decision all the more.

"I wanted to tell you that it was Neptune behind all of this so that you would understand the gravity of the situation. We're all of us in danger—especially you. We must be very, very careful. This isn't the silly case of the 'Millionaire's Missing Money,' or whatever you so charmingly called it," he said, his eyebrow rising. "This is a life-and-death sort of case. Or worse," he said sternly. "Do you understand?"

She slowly nodded, her big, blue eyes looking back at him with so much trust that he wanted to punch a wall.

"This ends here," he said bitterly, and privately resolved that it really would end this time. He meant to kill Neptune, even if he died in the process. At least Henrietta would be free of this torturer, this killer, then, and the beginnings of a plan were forming in his mind. "I give you my word."

"What do you mean to do?" she asked softly, gently linking her hands behind his neck, causing his stomach to clench out of love for her.

"I'll explain later. Come," he said, slipping out of her embrace and catching her hand to give it a quick kiss. "Let's get back to the house with this," he said, holding up the envelope. As he slipped his coat back on, his mind still going over his father's last letter, one line in particular surfaced for him: *I strangely awoke with a clear sense of what I must do and was encouraged and comforted by the hope that comes from having at least the rudiments of a plan.* He reflected on how odd it was that he, too, felt the same, and he was grateful that his father had been allowed to feel at least a glimmer of hope before the end had come for him, Clive knowing as he did that a life without hope was a very hard one to bear.

He glanced across at Henrietta now, who was waiting for him and looking at him with eyes that seemed unmistakably sad. "Henrietta," he said softly, "I'm sorry about your father, too."

Chapter 20

Elsie was surprised to hear the faint knock on her door. Melody had already left for the theater, and she herself was just about to leave for Ma's. She got up from her desk where she had been writing and went to the door, tentatively opening it a crack. She was surprised to see that it was Gunther. Her initial resultant smile, however, faded as she observed his grim demeanor.

"There's someone below to see you. Sister Bernard sent me up to tell you," he said.

"Who is it?" she asked, baffled, and immediately began worrying that it might have something to do with Ma. Maybe she had had another attack of nerves . . .

"He says his name is Lloyd Aston. I believe he was the man who escorted you here before, yes?"

Elsie groaned. "Lloyd Aston?"

Gunther gave her a slight nod. Why was he looking at her that way . . . like she had committed a crime, or something?

"He is dressed well," he added quietly. "Do you perhaps have an engagement?" his German accent sounding very stiff and formal now.

An engagement?

"Oh, no!" she murmured, then, as it all suddenly came back to her. The opera! That was the thing she had forgotten! Aunt Agatha had arranged for her to go tonight with Lloyd, she remembered in a panic. She looked down at her plain cotton skirt and white blouse. It would take her ages to get dressed and do her hair for the opera. She couldn't possibly go . . . but what should she say to Lloyd? And what about Aunt Agatha? She would be furious if she found out she hadn't gone!

Elsie suddenly felt as if all the air had gone out of the space around her, and she began to struggle for breath. She felt so awfully trapped. She put her hand to her chest and tried to breathe deeply. Gunther, ignoring the house rules, entered the room and took her by the arm.

"You are ill?" he asked, with a gentleness that surprised her.

"No, I'm . . . I'm fine," Elsie managed to say, and though she wasn't looking at him, she could feel him studying her. "I'm . . . I'm supposed to go to the opera with him. I must have forgotten," she said, embarrassed, as she took short, clipped breaths. "I'll . . . I'll have to explain. Maybe he'll wait while I get ready."

"You are going to go with him?" Gunther asked incredulously. "What about going to see your mother, as you said?"

Elsie bit her lip. Maybe Ma wouldn't even remember she was supposed to be coming. Or if she did, she would just have to make it up to her some other time. "I'll have to go . . . in the morning, I suppose," Elsie murmured, avoiding looking at him.

"Elsie, perhaps you should not do this," he said quietly. "You are afraid of this man, no?"

"Of course I'm . . . not afraid of him!" Elsie forced herself to say, though she saw by the way he looked at her that he did not believe her.

"Elsie . . ." he said, gazing down at her as she looked up at him.

"I can't let Aunt Agatha down," she said, finally able to take a deep breath now and fill her lungs. "She'd kill me. I have no choice but to go through with this. It's just the way it is," she said, clearing her throat.

"Elsie," he said gently. "You must begin to choose your own path in life, for yourself. *Um deinem herzen zu folgen.* To follow your heart. Not to do always what others tell you to do."

"I . . . I *am* choosing for myself!"

"Are you?" He looked at her with something akin to pity, and she thought she might cry. "I once made this same mistake, Elsie, and now I pay a very dear price for it. Do not put yourself in this man's hands because you might disappoint your . . . your family. He is not good."

"I know that, Gunther!" she exclaimed, louder than she meant, the heat rising in her face. "I know that," she repeated in a hiss. "But I . . . I—"

"Elsie, this path does not lead to happiness," he said, nodding his head slightly toward the door.

"Maybe not everyone is meant for happiness, Gunther. For that kind of happiness, anyway," she said, wiping a stray tear.

"Ach. Elsie. Do you really believe that?"

"Well, yes. I think so, anyway."

"You must have been hurt very deep to feel and say these things," he said quietly. "Yes?"

Elsie felt in real danger of crying then, and her throat felt so tight she could not speak. Instead, she merely gave an almost imperceptible nod.

Both of them jumped when they heard a creak on the stairs and a familiar voice call out, "Elsie?"

Sr. Bernard's towering figure filled the doorway suddenly, her eyes taking in the scene before her, Gunther pulling back the hand that had somehow been holding Elsie's arm. She looked at Elsie's tear-stained face and then back at Gunther.

"Gunther, I asked you to bring Miss Von Harmon downstairs," she said sternly. "Elsie," she went on, "you have a visitor below. Shall I tell him you are unwell?"

"No, Sister," Elsie said, hurriedly taking a handkerchief from her pocket and wiping her face. It was the same handkerchief she had used to try to stop Gunther's blood from flowing on New Year's Eve.

She had since washed and ironed it and had been carrying it around in her pocket, waiting for a chance to return it to him. No, I'll come down," she said quietly. "Here," she said, placing the handkerchief in Gunther's hand, "this is yours."

The sight of Lloyd Aston pacing in the foyer below caused Elsie's breath to again come rapidly as she timidly walked down the stairs toward him. She gripped the beautifully carved wooden railing as she went and tried to calm herself down, her mind reeling after the interlude with Gunther. She could barely make sense of everything they had said to each other, but she couldn't think about it now. Her stomach clenched at the thought of confronting Lloyd. In truth, she *was* a bit afraid of him, but why? It's not as if he had *really* done anything to her . . . not like Harrison, anyway, and yet she wondered if she might be confusing the two of them in her mind. It would certainly explain the nightmares she was having lately, all of them seeming to involve Harrison. In them, she was either running from him or she had died and they were burying her, except that she wasn't really dead. But she could never open her mouth to tell them. In one of them, Stanley had even appeared, asking her why she hadn't told them she was dead and blaming her for everyone being all confused now, saying that flowers had already been ordered and yet here she was, apparently alive.

"There you are!" Lloyd exclaimed, noticing her now as she came down the stairs. He had a smile on his face for a fraction of an instant before it soured. "Why aren't you dressed?" he asked, glancing at his wristwatch. "We're going to be terribly late!"

"I'm sorry, Lloyd," Elsie said, wringing her hands. Sr. Bernard, having followed her down, slipped behind her and resumed her post, unfortunately not far from where they stood. "I . . . I must have forgotten."

"Forgotten?" Lloyd asked derisively. "Didn't your aunt tell you? I tried telephoning you half a dozen times, but no one ever answered," he said, shooting Sr. Bernard a reproachful glance, which, Elsie was glad to observe, seemed to go unnoticed.

"It's bad enough you weren't at the New Year's Eve ball, but now this? It's outrageous!"

"Yes, I'm sorry about that," Elsie said. "I've been busy, you see—"

"Stop blabbering! Go up and get dressed," he said, waving his hand toward the stairs. "I'll wait. We'll miss the first act, but that's not always such a bad thing. Dreadfully dull. No one of any note shows up before the second act, anyway. I had hoped to go somewhere else beforehand, but no matter; we can go after, I suppose. Go on," he urged.

Elsie, her heart beating very hard in her chest, was unsure of what to do next and felt herself dangerously waver. She was mortified to be the center of attention in this way, knowing that Sr. Bernard and Gunther, as well—she could sense that he was standing silently, like a statue, at the top of the stairs—were listening to their every word. It would, perhaps, be easiest if she just gave in and went with Lloyd as he wished and not cause any more fuss, especially as she knew the ramifications of not going would be terrible to endure. But not going to see Ma would be terrible, too, she tried to tell herself, though a part of her knew that some of her hesitation also had to do with not wanting to disappoint Gunther. To look weak in his eyes. Oh, how had she gotten herself in the middle yet again!

"Well, what are you waiting for?" Lloyd quipped.

Something inside of Elsie seemed to crack, then—just a tiny fissure—and she knew that she couldn't make herself go with him, however horrible the consequence would be. It wasn't just a matter of weighing Ma and Gunther's disappointment to be greater than Lloyd's and Aunt Agatha's, not to mention Grandfather's, that had forced her decision to be such, but it was down to something deeper still. Something Gunther had said about choosing for herself that lingered in her mind and which she clung to. In truth, she didn't want to sit alone in a dark opera box with this man—with *any* man, actually—ever again. She had chosen her path, the path of Holy Orders, and it was ridiculous and cowardly that she continued with this pretense. She should have written to Grandfather long before now, she chastised herself, and resolved to do so first thing in the morning. Until, then, however, she had to find a way out of tonight. She would simply have to tell Lloyd that she would not be accompanying him. She took a deep, slow breath and tried to calm her racing heart.

"Mr. Aston . . . Lloyd . . . I'm awfully sorry," she began, faltering slightly, "but I don't think I can go with you tonight, after all. I've made other plans, you see," she went on, haltingly. "I'm very sorry for the trouble I've caused you."

"What other plans?" he asked, and his eyes alighted on Gunther, who was slowly descending now.

"I've got to go see my mother," Elsie answered.

"Your mother?" Lloyd scoffed. "That's rich. So go see her tomorrow."

"She's . . . she's not well," Elsie stammered.

Lloyd startled her by letting out a little chuckle. "Elsie, my dear, you'll eventually have to come up with some other excuse besides illness. Usually, it's you who portends to be ill, but now you're drawing other people into your circle of contagion. It's becoming tiresome in the extreme. Not to mention unconvincing."

"Lloyd, I—"

"Listen, Elsie," he said, annoyed now, "I'm done playing around. I was hoping to do this later, but I have something very particular I'd like to say to you. To ask, that is. In private," he said, glancing again toward where Sr. Bernard sat.

"No, Lloyd," Elsie said, panicking, "that isn't necessary," she said, also glancing over at Sr. Bernard, who maddeningly did not look up.

"I positively insist, Miss Von Harmon. You owe me that much," Lloyd said bitterly.

Elsie stared at him, knowing he wasn't going to leave until she had heard him out.

"Very well," Elsie said resolutely, swallowing hard, her stomach clenching again. She could guess what "question" Lloyd meant to ask her. How had things progressed this quickly? She had hoped to avoid this situation by writing several letters in the morning, thereby ending Lloyd's attentions and those of any others that Aunt Agatha meant to throw at her. But it was too late for that. She would simply have to endure and then refuse what was sure to be his proposal.

"Here," she said, gesturing toward the parlor. "We can talk in there."

Lloyd nodded curtly and strode in ahead of her, grasping his lapels as he did so. As she moved to follow, she perceived the slightest movement behind her, accompanied by a small cough, and turned to see Gunther. She hadn't realized that he had been standing so very near to her during the last part of her exchange with Lloyd. He reached out his hand toward her, but before he could touch her, he pulled it back.

"Elsie," he whispered. "Please . . ."

Elsie could see the concern on his face and found it touching. She wanted to say something to comfort him, to explain what she was about to do and that she had it in hand, but all she could manage was an unconvincing little smile before she turned and followed Lloyd into the parlor and shut the door.

The room itself was dim. Just a few of the lamps had been lit, and the fire was low. Lloyd was standing in front of the fireplace with his back to her, but when she entered, he turned to her, coolly assessing her as he looked her over. She halted under his scrutiny, unable to go any farther. She knew what was coming, but why? She knew her limitations in terms of physical beauty, and the two of them had never had a conversation deeper than the weather or the scores at Arlington, Lloyd having more than a little interest for horse racing. They were so obviously unsuited that she might be tempted to laugh if it weren't so depressing and frightening, actually. They were both obviously ruled by powers stronger than themselves. What else would motivate a man like Lloyd Aston to take this sort of step with a girl like her? Why couldn't she just be left alone?

He gestured for her to come and stand before him. "Come, come. Don't be shy," he said with a smirk. Elsie made her legs move until she was awkwardly standing in front of him. He gestured toward the sofa upon which she had, earlier today, sat with Melody. That frivolous episode seemed ages ago, Elsie reflected sadly. She felt a chill, despite the fire, and wished she had brought down her cardigan. She wrapped her arms protectively around herself.

"I . . . I think I'll stand," she answered softly, rounding her shoulders and waiting for the blow.

Lloyd, still assessing her, extracted a silver cigarette case from inside his jacket pocket and flipped it open. "Listen, Elsie, let's be frank, shall we?" he said, tapping a cigarette on the case, his eyebrow arched as he studied her.

"If you wish," she said quietly, glancing at the fire.

"I expressly asked you to come out with me tonight, as I had something I very much wanted to ask you."

"Yes, so you said before, but—"

"Hear me out," he said, lighting his cigarette now and inhaling deeply. His nostrils flared as a resultant thick cloud poured through them. "I'm to ask you to marry me. Father's wishes. So how about it?" he asked casually through narrowed eyes due to the smoke.

"Oh . . ." Elsie said biting her lip. Though she had guessed that he meant to propose to her, she was nonetheless a bit taken aback by the cavalier nature of its delivery. And yet, what had she been expecting? Roses and poetry? Wild, albeit false, declarations of love? It was better this way, was it not? she tried to tell herself. To approach it for what it was—little more than a business transaction. She supposed she should be grateful to Lloyd for treating it as such, but she found— to her extreme annoyance—that even still, two small tears appeared, unbidden and unexpected, in the corners of her eyes.

Quickly she tried to whisk them away with just her fingertips as she sadly wondered if every marriage proposal that came her way was to be so utterly mean. Was she worth so little? Stan had not really uttered the words to her, but merely hinted that they might be forthcoming, though he had been eager to speak of their future together. And Harrison's had been in the heat of the moment, during the act of love itself, and while she had at first convinced herself that it revealed his deep feeling and passion, she had recently had to admit that it was merely his attempt to trap her. Well, she tried to console herself, this proposal would be the last she would ever receive. This was the last time she would put herself in this position, she thought bitterly, though, in truth, she countered, she had not put herself in it at all— this had been Aunt Agatha and Grandfather's doing. After tonight, she resolved, she really would publicly announce her desire to join the Sisters of the Blessed Virgin Mary, and then maybe she would blessedly be left alone.

"May I take your silence and quaint display of emotion as a yes?" Lloyd said, a slight smirk on his face as he inhaled again.

"I . . . No! Lloyd, I . . . I think there's been some mistake."

"Mistake? Not at all."

"But I don't—"

"Love me? Of course you don't. Why should you? Neither do I love you, but that should hardly stop us," he said casually.

Elsie let a small gasp escape. To say the truth so blatantly . . .

"Consider it a marriage of convenience, if you will," he went on. "You'd be quite free to do as you wished, as long as you played hostess now and again to the extravagant parties I've become so frightfully attached to. Eventually you'd have to produce a brat or two, to please Mama, of course, but it doesn't have to be right away. There are ways around it. One of them being that we abstain altogether, which would be fine by me. I don't find you terribly attractive, and from your reactions to my advances, I suspect you don't find me so either. So you see, it's perfect, really. We can get the codgers off our backs and go about our business just as we have been. You can continue your . . . efforts here . . . if you really want to," he said, looking around the room dismally . . . "and I'll pursue my efforts at the track and with certain lady friends of my acquaintance. What do you say?"

Elsie just stared at him, her mind a speechless blank. Surely he wasn't serious, was he? She had told herself that it was a business transaction, but his brutal candor was difficult to take in.

"But . . . but why me?"

Lloyd laughed. "Surely you're not that naïve, are you?"

"But . . . but you said you didn't need my money," Elsie said hesitatingly.

"Turns out I do, apparently," he said, walking about the room now. "Funny how the threat of being cut off from one's allowance can alter one's feelings—the deeper sort, anyway."

"But there must be another girl with money whom you like better than me," Elsie tried to argue.

Lloyd inhaled again and shrugged. "Quite," he said, exhaling. "There are several women I like more than you, to be exact, but Father's being really rather insistent. Your grandfather, you see, is dangling a very large carrot, one my father feels he simply must get hold of, so I am to be the sacrificial lamb," he said, spreading his hands wide in a flippant manner. "But that doesn't mean we can't fall in love with someone else," he drawled, as his eyes darted ever so briefly toward the foyer and then back to Elsie. "I'd be a terrifically forgiving husband . . . if you returned the favor, that is. But, of course, I'd want my turn now and again," he said, grinning. "You know, to produce the brats. So, what do you say? Come on, Elsie," he said, flicking his ash into an ashtray. "This is becoming a bore now."

Elsie stared at him, repulsed and saddened to her core. How could she ever pledge herself to one such as this? Her old feelings of panic were fighting their way up her chest, but she managed to push them down. She didn't have to give in, she reminded herself.

"Are these the words of a gentleman?" she asked quietly, borrowing in her distress from Jane Austen. It was all she could think of. "Is this how you would propose to me?" she asked, gaining a shard of confidence from them.

"Really, Elsie. How droll," he said, a wicked grin still on his face. "Don't tell me you're holding out for love or some other such nonsense," he said with a little laugh.

"I'll never marry you, Lloyd Aston," she said, her voice becoming stronger. "You . . . you thoroughly repulse me!" she said and took a hesitant step back, astonished by what had just come out of her mouth.

At her bold words, Lloyd's previously amused, flippant face grew taut and fierce. He was angry now, she could see, as he took a step closer to her.

"I wouldn't play the high-and-mighty part with me, my dear," he snarled. "Beggars can hardly be choosers, you know."

"I'm not a beggar," she said firmly, looking him in the eye.

"Very nearly," he said with a snort. "The *nouveau riche* are all the same. No one forgets that you've only recently been scooped up out of the sludge, *Miss* Von Harmon. Your poverty clings to you even now, like an odious vapor. Despite Exley's bribe, you don't see many lined up, do you? God knows *I* wouldn't be if I had any say in the matter."

"And this is how you would choose to win me? By insulting and humiliating me? Why would I ever bind myself to you, to subject myself to your protection and . . . and affection—not love, as you've painfully made clear—when this is how you speak to me in this moment? I'm well aware of my limitations, as you've so gallantly pointed out, but I am not a beggar. As a matter of fact, I'm not going to marry anyone—I'm going to become a nun!" Elsie spewed out, her filter well and truly gone.

Lloyd's face went from a look of fury to one of amusement, which was perhaps even worse to witness. "A nun?" he said with a smirk. "A bit too late for that, so I've heard," he chuckled. "Don't they have certain qualifications—chastity being one?" he said with a raised eyebrow.

The realization of what he was implying took a few moments to sink in, but when it did, she was astonished by the fury she now felt. That her sexual exploits with the lieutenant were obviously not only public knowledge, as her paranoia had led her to believe, but that this man, her intended, had the gross indecency to actually speak of them—nay more than to speak them aloud, but to actually taunt her with them! For the second time in only the space of about twenty minutes, something seemed to crack inside of Elsie, and she swiftly reached out and slapped Lloyd Aston across the face, the sound of her hand cracking his smooth cheek rippling across the parlor.

Stunned at first, he recovered quickly and grabbed her roughly by the arm, causing her to cry out.

"Well, well, well. I knew you had a bit of spunk to you," he said with a grin.

Elsie stared wildly into his eyes, fearing not only him, but what she had just done. She hadn't known she was capable of such a thing. Lloyd was breathing heavily and he leaned toward her, pulling her arm to draw her close. Elsie knew he was about to kiss her, so she pulled back, though he held her tightly. Intuitively, she twisted her arm and yanked and managed to free herself, almost stumbling backward as she did.

"You should go now, I am thinking," said a voice, firm and steady, from the doorway. Elsie, rubbing her wrist, looked over and felt a wave of gratitude to see Gunther standing there. Lloyd looked, too, and stepped back, scowling first at Gunther and then at her.

"Who's this?" Lloyd asked, breathlessly.

"My name is Gunther Stockel," Gunther said steadily.

"A Kraut, eh?" Lloyd said, standing up straight and pulling his waistcoat back into place. "Seems you're always conveniently hovering about, like a faithful dog, aren't you? Looking for scraps, I imagine. Well, there're plenty here, I'd say," he said, nodding his head toward the floor above them. "I wouldn't get any ideas with this one, though, Kraut," he said, looking at Elsie. "You're barking up the wrong tree. And she's a bit cold—for a bitch that is."

"How dare you!" Elsie whispered, both infuriated and ashamed all in one.

Gunther instantly moved across the room and advanced upon Lloyd, grabbing him by the lapels of his jacket and giving him a shake. "Get out of here!" he said fiercely. For a moment Elsie thought he was going to strike him.

"Steady on, Kraut," Lloyd said, roughly pushing Gunther away. "I could have you deported, you know," he growled. He stood, adjusting his tie and slicking back his hair with his hands, which seemed to calm him, and his lips curled up into another smirk. "Don't worry.

I'll show myself out." With irritating slowness, he walked toward the door, but he paused before going through, turning back toward them.

Gunther stepped slightly in front of Elsie.

"By the way, shall I tell dear Aunt Agatha that the wedding bells are not to ring forth?" Lloyd asked with mock sweetness. "Or will you? Should I mention your other plans?" he asked, glancing at Gunther. "I'd love to be a fly on the wall when old Exley hears them. Or do they already know? No? I didn't think so," he said, seeing the fear on her face. He bowed deeply. "Well, good-bye then, Elsie. I'd say that I'll look for news of you in the society pages, but somehow I don't think you'll feature too often," he said with a scowl, his natural facial expression, it seemed, and with that, he finally left the room.

Elsie and Gunther stood motionless until the heavy outer door thudded shut. Upon hearing it close, Elsie let out a tiny moan and burst into sobs. She was keenly aware of Gunther standing next to her, and she felt all the more small and awful that he was witnessing her weakness, but she couldn't have held back the tears even if she wanted to. They had been building for so long now, and they needed to come out. She covered her face with her hands and rounded her shoulders away from him, wishing she could curl up into a ball. She stiffened when she felt his hand on her arm and tried to choke back her tears.

"Elsie . . ." he said gently.

She stood up straighter, then, and attempted to wipe her eyes with her fists. He held out his handkerchief to her. "You'd better have this back," he said with a smile, and she could not help but give a little laugh as she took it.

"I know what you're thinking," she said, looking up at him, as she blew her nose.

"You could not possibly know what it is I am thinking," he said softly and took her hand.

Chapter 21

"Well, what do you think?" Henrietta asked, as she leaned across Sergeant Davis's desk, studying his face carefully.

"You're sure this is where he went?" the detective asked, looking at the letter again. It was the same thin, cheap paper that Clive had handed her weeks ago when he had showed her the letter he had found from Susan in Alcott's study. Only this one read:

Lucky's, Elston & Division, Jun 4, 4.00 p.m. Alone. Susan.

"Yes, I'm sure of it," Henrietta answered.

"And you found this where?" he asked, as he picked up a crumpled pack of cigarettes on his desk and fished around inside it.

"On Clive's bureau!" she said, exasperated.

"Go on," he said, putting what looked to be the last of his cigarettes to his lips and lighting it.

"I've already told you everything!"

"Tell me again," he said, inhaling and blowing a cloud of smoke towards her.

"Look, Sergeant, I'm married to a detective," she said, waving the smoke away, "so I'm aware of all of your little tricks. Can't we just get on with this? We've got to hurry! If I knew it was going to take this long to convince you, I would have come earlier. Or not at all."

Davis grinned crookedly. "Okay, okay. Let me get this straight. Your hubby gets roughed up outside the Aragon by Susan's gang—or Neptune, as you're calling him now—where they demand their missing cash. Howard goes home, miraculously discovers—"

"It wasn't miraculous."

"Miraculously discovers the missing cash from his pops—and a note," he added, his eyes skeptical. "Then a letter arrives on his desk somehow—neither of you has figured out how yet—telling him where and when to meet this Neptune character. He sticks it in his pocket, tells you who it's from and what's in it, but won't give you the details. Says it's too dangerous. You turn on the waterworks; he still won't budge. Next day, you say you've got to go into the city to say good-bye to your brothers who are being shipped off to boarding school. Howard's not too happy to let you go into the city alone. Can't go with you as he's supposed to show up at the family five-and-dime that day, so he proposes that the fat butler escort you, as a what?—protector?" he asked, skeptical again.

"How do you know he's fat?" Henrietta asked, her eyes narrowed.

Davis didn't respond but just looked at her steadily, as if he knew something she didn't. Could he have been spying on them? she mused. That didn't seem likely . . . Oh, what did it matter at this point, anyway? she decided and tried her best to stare back at him.

They continued to look at each other for several moments, both of them refusing to back down. Henrietta could swear he was teasing her; he looked as though he would laugh at any moment, and she had to eventually bite back her own smile that threatened to escape.

"I wouldn't call him fat," she said finally. "Portly, maybe."

"It was a guess," Davis confessed, chuckling a little, as he rubbed his stubbly chin. He was the very flirty type. She had seen it a hundred times before. Once upon a time, she might have even fallen for it . . .

"But you refused his company. Why?" he asked, intrigued.

"I've already told you this. It has no bearing on the case! Billings is the ultimate spy. He knows everything that goes on in that house, and he reports it back to either Clive or Antonia. He's obnoxious."

"So he knows everything that goes on in the house, but he can't explain how these letters are getting in."

"I wouldn't know, Sergeant! I wasn't the one who questioned him."

"Okay, okay." Davis thought for a moment. "So somehow you persuade the hubby—I won't say how—" he said, suggestively looking at her with a raised eyebrow, reminding her shockingly of Clive, "to let you go into the city without the spying butler."

Henrietta bit the inside of her lip at how close he was to the truth, but she managed to keep her face a blank.

"So the chauffer—Fritz, is it?—drives you into the city to Palmer Square," he went on with an annoying grin, "and you visit your family. Anything unusual?"

"With Fritz? Or them?"

"With anything. Isn't this where you picked up the two thugs following you on Christmas Eve?"

"Yes," Henrietta answered slowly, thinking about this.

"See anyone?"

"I don't think so . . ."

"Did you go anywhere else?"

"Really, Sergeant. Again, this has no bearing on the case."

"I'll be the judge of that," he said, leaning back. He inhaled deeply, watching her in what seemed a very inappropriate way.

"Sergeant, are you going to help me or not?"

"I'm getting to it," he said, crushing his cigarette into the overflowing ashtray in front of him. "So this morning, hubby says he's off to the five-and-dime again, but you suspect this is the rendezvous. But you didn't suspect that the day before. Why?"

"Because he didn't take his briefcase today."

"That's it? That's all you have to go on?"

"Yes," she said severely, "it is."

"Right," he said, crossing his arms. "So off he goes, and then you panic. Start to look through his things. And you find this on his bureau," he said, holding up the letter again. "Anything else?"

"No, that's it!" she said impatiently. "Now, let's go!"

"Is he armed?"

Henrietta was a little taken back by the question. "Yes, he always has his revolver on him."

"Except on New Year's Eve at the Aragon?"

"That was my fault."

"So you've said. Because it would interfere with your dancing," he said mockingly.

"Listen, can we get on with this? Perhaps there's someone else here who could help me?" she asked, making a show of looking around.

"All right, all right, sister. Don't go upsetting your apple cart." He opened his desk drawer and riffled through the contents until he found another crumpled package of cigarettes. "This is my spare," he said, glancing over at her as he fished for another cigarette and put it to his lips. He struck a match and lit it. "There's one thing that doesn't quite make sense, though" he said, exhaling.

"What?"

"If this rendezvous is really where Howard went, why would he go it alone? He seems halfway intelligent and an ex-copper to boot. He has to know he's walking into a trap or at least a very bad situation. Why not arrange an escort or a stakeout? He's gone out of his way to bring me into the loop before this. Why not now at the crucial moment?"

"I don't know! The note said 'alone,' so . . . "

Davis let out a laugh.

Why was he laughing at her? She admitted that Clive's decision was reckless. Why indeed had he gone alone? she asked herself for the hundredth time.

"I don't know, Sergeant," she repeated. "It doesn't make any sense. Except that he has some sort of personal vendetta against Neptune.

"He . . . he has a sort of obsession with me—Neptune, that is. Maybe it's to be some sort of one-on-one, like a duel or something."

"Assuming that would really be very stupid on Howard's part. And, anyway, aren't you two supposed to be a team?" he asked, taking a deep drag and then blowing the smoke out thoughtfully. "Why would he leave behind his pretty partner?"

There was a time when Henrietta would have felt the slight Davis was insinuating, but not this time. It was too personal now to Clive, she knew. He was out to get Neptune, and to bring her along with him would not have even been in the realm of possibility in Clive's mind. He had barely been able to handle her coming along to stake out the cottage in Derbyshire in which his cousin Wallace had sat hiding out with his wife and child, she remembered with a small smile. This one, she knew, was out of the question.

"Unless he figured on you finding this and acting on it . . ." Davis muttered, absently twisting the note between his thumb and forefinger.

At his words, a cold realization gripped Henrietta's heart. Was that what this note was? A communication from Clive? Perhaps . . . Could he have trusted her in this way? Was he counting on her to figure it out? To bring along backup? Or was it so that she would know where to look for his body, should it all go wrong? Damn it! Hadn't Clive repeatedly chastised his father's ill-thought-out plan, and yet here he was seeming to engage himself in something equally foolhardy. There must be something more to it, she determined, and she had failed to deduce it!

She stood up hurriedly, the chair scraping against the floor. "I'm leaving, Sergeant, whether you're coming with me or not."

And she meant it. She was prepared to go it alone, having taken precautions yesterday for just such an event. Involving the police had been Lucy's idea, not hers. But she had done that now, Henrietta absolved herself, and if Sergeant Davis chose not to help her, then she would resort to plan B, sketchy though it was.

While it was true that she had gone into the city yesterday to see her brothers off, she had used the opportunity to conduct an additional "errand," one could call it, as Davis had come very close to ferreting out.

Early yesterday morning, she had crept into the study at Highbury to use the telephone, asking the operator to put a call through to Lucy Szweda, LAK-0421. Henrietta anxiously twisted the thick leather cord around her finger as she waited and offered up a silent prayer of thanks when Lucy finally answered, sounding groggy. The girls usually slept in, she knew from experience, from working so late at night.

"Listen, Lucy, it's Henrietta," she said quietly.

"Well, hello, sweets. Bit early, isn't it? Anything wrong?" came Lucy's scratchy voice through the line.

"No, nothing's wrong. Sorry it's so early. Say, you wouldn't have Rose's telephone number, would you?" she asked.

"Rose? What's the gig, gumdrop?" Lucy asked, obviously curious considering the tenuous situation between Henrietta and Rose.

"I need to borrow something from her," Henrietta said in a low tone, hoping Billings wasn't hovering outside the door.

"Borrow something? Like what?"

"Like, her g-u-n," she whispered.

Ever since the letter had appeared in Alcott's—now Clive's—study, Clive had been moody and grim. Henrietta knew that he did not mean to involve her—he had told her as much—but she was uneasy just the same. She had a bad feeling about the whole thing. Considering that Jack had been Neptune's agent and had lived here under the same roof, she didn't think she could be too careful. Who knew where and when Neptune would pop up, or who was working for him? She knew Clive would never give her something like a firearm, nor did she want one, really, but this current situation called for extreme measures. But time was short, she felt, and she hadn't the slightest idea of how or where to procure a gun, though she thought she had seen some shotguns hanging on the back wall of the hardware store where she had gone to have the sign made for Clive's detective agency. It was then that she remembered that Rose had a gun, or at least she had once had one.

Last year, on that dreadful night when Neptune had captured her and Clive, it had been Rose who had produced a gun to hold Neptune's thugs at bay until the police could get there. How or why Rose had procured a pistol no one had ever asked, and Henrietta had put it out of her mind until now.

"Her gun?" Lucy whispered back. "What's happening, Henrietta? Are you in danger?" she asked.

"Not exactly. Look, it's a long story. Can I tell you later? I just need Rose's telephone number."

"They don't have a telephone," Lucy said slowly. "Tell you what, sweets. I'll talk to Rose and ask her to bring it to work later today. We're both on at four. That is, if she still has it—and if she'll agree to lend it to you. You'll have to do some explaining, I'd imagine."

"Oh, I don't want her to have to bring it to work. I'll go to her house and get it . . . if you think she wouldn't mind."

"Better not, sweets. She don't like no one going 'round the house. It's her dad. Bit of an ass, if you know what I mean."

Unfortunately, Henrietta did.

"All right, then. I'll be at the Melody Mill at four. And thanks, Luce."

"Still need us, don't you, gumdrop?" she said, her voice sounding thick with satisfaction, as Henrietta hung up the heavy receiver.

Henrietta had Fritz drive her to Palmer Square later that same day, where she distributed sweets and pocket money to the boys as well as what she hoped was an encouraging speech. Ma was surly and out of sorts, as usual, and Elsie, too, seemed peevish. But maybe it was just her. Henrietta was sad to see the boys go, but she knew there was nothing she could do, and, in truth, she found herself eventually coming around to Clive's point of view over the intervening months, which was that perhaps it wasn't such a bad idea after all.

But even if she wanted to dwell on these many problems at home, she didn't have that luxury at the moment. She sensed, even at that point, that she and Clive were somehow in very grave danger, and it was all she could think of.

She bided her time as best she could, trying to make conversation with Elsie about how the Penningtons' Ball had gone, but Elsie had been oddly evasive regarding it. It had been on the tip of her lips to tell her about seeing Stan and Rose at the Aragon, but then she had thought better of it and had instead told her, in whispers, how Clive had been beaten up in an alley outside. She kept nervously glancing up at the clock on the mantel every few minutes, only half listening to Elsie telling her some story of an injured janitor at Mundelein, until the clock had finally struck 3:30 and she was able to summon Karl to have Fritz bring the car back around. There was a tearful good-bye all around, as Henrietta told them to do well, to uphold the Von Harmon name, such as it was, and that if they were good, she might come and visit them.

Once seated in the back of the Daimler, she instructed Fritz, trying to keep her voice steady, to drive her to the Melody Mill instead of straight home.

"Yes, madam," Fritz answered dully and only once looked in the rearview mirror at her. She was gambling on Fritz not mentioning her side errand to Clive or Antonia, and she hoped the odds were in her favor, as Clive had once told her that a chauffeur, like a valet, had a responsibility to keep certain things private. Henrietta was sure that this referred only to the master of the house, but, she thought, with a wry smile, what was good for the goose . . .

Despite these progressive hopes, however, she still had Fritz drop her off a block down from the Melody Mill on Belmont, not so much to keep Fritz in the dark as to her ultimate destination, but to not draw attention to herself as she entered the dance hall.

She walked briskly down the sidewalk, keeping her head down against the wind, and slipped inside. She stood for a moment to let her eyes get adjusted to the dim interior. Lucy must have been watching for her, though, because she came over right away, calling to Rose as she did so, who, even despite their "friendly chat" on New Year's Eve, approached warily. Henrietta saw that she nervously clutched a black handbag, which Henrietta was pretty sure contained the little pistol. Lucy again asked her what was going on, looking over her shoulder to make sure the owner wasn't in sight, and reminding Henrietta that she didn't have much time to "spill the beans."

Henrietta then gave them a sketchy outline of events, saying that she was pretty sure Clive intended to have a "showdown" of sorts with Neptune and that she wanted to be ready, just in case. Lucy, of course, thought it a very bad idea for Henrietta to go following Clive around, if that was indeed her plan. Henrietta admitted that she honestly didn't know exactly what she intended to do, just that she would feel better if she had something to fall back on, and they could either let her borrow the gun or not. She looked directly at Rose now, who held her gaze. After a few short moments, Rose thrust the bag into Henrietta's hands, saying "Take it."

"Rose!" Lucy exclaimed, as if Rose had broken protocol in not deferring to Lucy for the final decision. "Promise not to do anything foolish," Lucy said, turning her frown from Rose to Henrietta.

"I won't. Honestly," Henrietta said, tucking the bag under her arm. "It's just in case."

"You sure you don't need our help somehow?" Lucy asked. "You know we can be discreet."

"That's a terrible idea," Henrietta said. "But thanks for the offer," she added quickly. "But it just wouldn't work. For one thing, I don't really know what's going to happen."

"Listen, Henrietta," said Rose. "It's none of my business, but shouldn't you tell the cops?"

"Yeah, gumdrop. At least promise us that. Promise you'll go to the cops," Lucy said, grabbing hold of her coat sleeve now as if she wouldn't let go until Henrietta agreed.

Reluctantly, Henrietta promised, though she wasn't at all sure she would keep it.

"Why do you have a gun, anyway?" Henrietta asked Rose, glancing back toward where the owner was watching them now from behind the bar. "Where'd you get it?" she asked in a low tone.

Rose looked uncomfortable. "Let's just say I found it," she said.

"A girl can't be too careful. 'Specially working in joints like this. You should know that."

"Well, thanks," Henrietta said. "I'll get it back to you as soon as I can."

"Yeah, see that you do. I won't be able to sleep as good without it."

Henrietta gave her a puzzled look.

"I sleep with it under my pillow."

Henrietta wondered what horrors Rose hid from at home that required her to sleep with a gun and felt guilty that she was taking her only apparent means of protection. "How's Stan?" she thought to ask.

A wave of something crossed Rose's face, which Henrietta couldn't interpret.

"Fine," Rose said with what seemed a false smile. "We're getting married," she said plainly.

Married? Though Rose had hinted at it at the Aragon, it still took Henrietta by surprise, and she didn't know who she felt sorrier for— Rose or Stan.

"Oh, Rose! That's . . . that's wonderful," she forced herself to say. "I . . . when is the happy day?"

"I think June, though I'm not sure. I'm meeting his family this Sunday."

"Well, I'm . . . I'm so happy for you," Henrietta said.

"No hard feelings, right?" Rose asked.

"No . . . none at all. I hope you'll be happy together," she said and realized she had said "happy" three times already now.

"Listen, dames!" called out the owner. "Youse want a job here or you want to yack?"

Lucy and Rose both jumped. "Gotta go, gumdrop," Lucy said, hurriedly. "You be careful. Take some cops with you. Promise?"

"Yes, all right. Thanks for this, Rose," she said, tapping the handbag. Lucy had already hurried off, but still Rose stood there looking at her despite more grumblings erupting from the back. She seemed to be waiting for something. "It's loaded, right?" Henrietta asked.

Rose nodded. She looked so frail and fragile, as if she were a matchstick that could easily be broken in two, and Henrietta suddenly felt sorry for her. Not knowing what else to do, she leaned forward and kissed her on the cheek. "Good luck," she said, though afterward as she hurried back down the block where the Daimler stood idling, she wondered why she had not said, "Congratulations."

When Henrietta found Neptune's letter, or what she had assumed was Neptune's letter, on Clive's bureau the very next day, she felt doubly relieved that she had had the foresight to get the gun. She had dutifully gone, then, note in hand, to see Sergeant Davis, as she had promised Lucy she would, convincing herself that he counted as "the cops," though she worried that she was losing precious time in doing so. Despite his condescending skepticism during their ensuing conversation, he was quick to follow when she finally stood up, frustrated, to pursue the case on her own.

"Oh, no you don't, sister," Davis said, as he stood up too, and reached for his holster hanging from the corner of his chair. He had said it lightly, but Henrietta did not fail to notice how serious his face was as he took out his pistol, opened the chamber to make sure it was loaded, and snapped it back.

"Come on," he said, as he quickly strode across the office now, roughly grabbing his coat from where it hung by the door. In fact, he walked so quickly down the front steps and then down the street to where his car was parked that she had trouble keeping up with him.

As she climbed up into the car, panting slightly, to sit beside him, she was relieved that she hadn't had to resort to plan B, which she hadn't had time to formulate, anyway. On the other hand, the fact that Davis was accompanying her meant that her fears and suspicions were not unfounded. Her stomach clenching, she patted her handbag yet again. With the gun inside, it was heavier than she was used to.

"What? Riding in front with the help?" Davis said wryly, as he turned the key to the "on" position in the Ford Model A in which they sat. "What will the neighbors think?" he said, as he pushed the "start" button on the floor with his foot and then deftly pulled the choke, succeeding in getting the engine to cough to a start despite the bitter cold both inside and outside of the car.

"You're not amusing, Detective," she said crisply and looked out the window.

It was midafternoon by the time they hit the city, Henrietta feeling more and more anxious the closer they got. What if they were too late? The letter had said 4:00 p.m., and though it was only 3:50 according to Henrietta's wristwatch, when they pulled up outside of what they assumed was Lucky's, it being the only building on the corner of Elston and Division, Henrietta's stomach was a knot of anxiety that they hadn't made it in time. Clive was nowhere to be seen, nor was his Alfa Romeo, but that didn't mean anything. Most probably he had parked it somewhere nearby and walked over. All Henrietta could think about was him lying hurt or dead inside, so that almost before the car was even stopped, she had her fingers on the handle, ready to jump out as soon as she could. As Davis rolled the car to a halt, however, he shot out his arm to stop her.

"Wait! Where do you think you're going?" he asked.

"Come on! We've got to get in there!" Henrietta pleaded, shocked that he did not share her urgency.

"Listen, we're not doing this half-cocked. We can't just go barging in there, guns blazing, looking for Howard."

"Well, why are we here, then? What do you propose to do instead?" she hissed. "Sit here and wait?"

"*You* are going to sit here and wait while I check it out," he said, opening his door smoothly and getting out.

"Oh, no, I'm not!" she protested. "I'm going in with you," she said, leaning across his side of the seat to shout up at him.

"Keep your voice down!" he chastised her as he leaned back in. "And yes, you *are* staying put until I see what's what. We don't even know if your hubby's in there, and if he's not, I don't need him on my ass when he finds out I compromised you." He leaned down to look in at her, the icy wind from the open door biting her legs. She did not fail to see his eyes quickly travel the length of them before he spoke in a low voice. "You wait here. Keep a lookout. Wait for my signal," he said and closed the door as quietly as he could.

Signal? Henrietta thought desperately, watching him draw his gun from a holster inside his jacket. What was the signal?

She watched as Davis disappeared down the side alley running alongside the bar. After only a few moments, however, he reappeared, hesitating in front of the building. There was no use in his trying to peer into the windows, Henrietta saw, as they were shuttered. A battered piece of paper with the word "closed" scrawled across it was visible in one of the windows, haphazardly taped there against its will and forgotten. She saw Davis put one hand on the door handle, the gun in his other, as he tried it. It seemed to open easily. Henrietta watched him step inside and then held her breath, waiting for she knew not what. As the seconds ticked on and nothing happened, she exhaled loudly. Now what? More seconds ticked on into minutes, which felt painfully like hours.

Twice she opened the car door a crack before reluctantly shutting it again. Where could he be? What was happening? she wondered. He must have encountered something, Henrietta reasoned, or he would have returned to the car by now. Perhaps he had been ambushed. If that were true, didn't that mean that Clive must have been apprehended as well? Or worse? she thought desperately, her heart beating faster and faster. The thought of him lying unconscious finally decided it for her, and this time when she opened the door, she allowed her legs to follow.

She crept toward the tavern and was nearly at the door when she heard a gun go off. She froze and instinctively put her hand over her mouth to stifle the scream that was at the back of her throat. She stood, paralyzed, not sure what to do. She was desperate to see if Clive was okay, but she was terrified as well. She waited, listening, until she could stand it no longer. She needed to get in there!

Tentatively, she pushed the door hanging listlessly open, and crept inside. Almost as soon as she entered, another shot was fired, and she crouched low, her head bowed, waiting for some sort of impact. After remaining in that position for what seemed an eternity, she dared to move out of her crouched position, having gratefully ascertained that she was uninjured, and looked quickly around the interior, the noise of the shot still ringing in her ears. She was in what looked to be an abandoned tavern, filthy and run-down, with a few broken barstools huddled near the bar and trash strewn everywhere. A light was coming from a back room, though, and she could hear voices.

Taking a deep breath, Henrietta stood up straight and tried her best to tiptoe toward the door. Walking gingerly and stepping over various items of garbage—an Old Forester whiskey bottle, a battered leather boot, broken glass, and various crumpled newspapers, among other things—she eventually reached the door and stood behind it. After trying to get control of her rapid breathing and getting up her courage to face whatever she might see on the other side, praying one last time that Clive was unharmed, she leaned forward just a little to peer inside.

The first thing she saw was poor Davis, lying on the ground nearby, and she nearly screamed again when she saw that his shirt was full of blood. She could see his face, but his eyes were shut, and she had no way of knowing if he were alive or dead. She waited several moments, her heart racing, as she tried to detect whether his chest was rising and falling, but she couldn't tell. Please God, not Clive too, she thought desperately and bit her lip. Steeling herself, she leaned a little farther to see more of the room through the small opening. For a moment her heart stopped when her eyes rested on another man, lying prone on the ground against the back wall, and again put her hand over her mouth to keep from crying out. But within seconds, she just as quickly deduced that it was not Clive, and almost cried with relief. It must be one of Neptune's goons, she reasoned. He and Davis must have had a shootout . . . but where were Clive and Neptune, then? She moved slightly to the side, hoping to get a better view of the interior of the room when she heard Neptune's voice shout out, "No funny moves, now, Copper."

Henrietta felt an intense pressure in her chest. Just hearing the sound of his voice brought back a flood of terrible memories, and she guessed he was now addressing Clive. He obviously had him! But at least he was alive, she countered with herself . . . or was he? Maybe it was a different cop in there? She had an irrational urge to rush in and had to fight herself to stay put, to think this through.

She looked again at Davis and almost started to see that his eyes were now open and staring at her, as if he were a dead man who had suddenly come alive. His eyes were wide and frantic, as if he were just now realizing where he was and who she was, or maybe he was in terrible pain or shock, she thought in a panic. She needed to go to him, she decided, but almost as if he could read her mind, he gave her a barely perceptible shake of his head.

"I told you to come alone!" she heard Neptune snarl.

"I did come alone," she heard Clive respond and felt a flood of relief wash over her that he really was still alive. Two tears formed in the corners of her eyes. "I swear it," Clive said, his voice tight. "I have no idea who that is."

"Of course you'd say that, wouldn't you, Copper?" she heard Neptune say. "But somehow I believe you." There was a brief pause, and Henrietta tried to hold her breath, hoping he couldn't hear it from beyond the door. "But that can only mean that this dog turning up is either a very odd coincidence," he said coolly, "which I don't believe in, or if I'm right—" his voice sounded like it was getting closer, and Henrietta could see Davis shaking his head more frantically— "he's a pet of Miss Von Harmon herself."

"Run!" Davis croaked out, but before Henrietta could fully comprehend this or even move a fraction, the door whipped open and she was face-to-face with her nemesis. She still had nightmares of Neptune from time to time, of that awful night that he had entrapped her, tied her down . . .

She was finding it difficult to breathe, and though a part of her brain was telling her to run, she simply couldn't make her legs move. She was paralyzed, like a small creature before a snake, and she simply found it impossible to flee. Her heart was pounding in her chest so hard she thought it might erupt at any moment.

Neptune took his time looking her up and down, his sunken gray eyes resting on her breasts for several moments before he looked back at her face.

"Ah, Miss Von Harmon," he said with a chuckle. "The prize itself has arrived! I've been expecting you. Come in, come in," he said, taking a step back and waving her in with his pistol. She could see he had what looked to be Clive's revolver stuffed into the waist of his trousers. Somehow, Henrietta made her legs propel her forward, and she stumbled into the room.

"Henrietta!" Clive exclaimed. "What are you doing here?" His voice was one of dual fury and panic. Henrietta saw his jaw clenching, and never had she seen such fear in his eyes.

"Now, now, before you get into a nasty domestic squabble, she's here at my request, ain't you?" Neptune said, licking his lips as he looked at her, though he still kept the gun pointed at Clive. "Got my note?" he said to her.

"Note?" Henrietta coughed out, the first words she had spoken since the car.

"The note I had left for you."

"That was . . . that was from you?" she rasped, her breath coming in spurts. "I . . . I thought that—"

"That the copper left it for you? How sweet, but no. I guessed he wouldn't bring you or tell you, so I had the note placed there for you to find."

"But . . . how? It was on his bureau . . ." Henrietta whispered.

A sort of rattled cackling erupted from deep in Neptune's chest. "Easy enough. We've done much more elaborate things than that," he wheezed.

"Who?" Henrietta murmured. "Who is it that's working inside with you?" she managed to get out.

"It's Carter, isn't it?" Clive offered bitterly from where he stood across the room.

"Shut up, Copper!" Neptune barked, though he kept his eyes trained on Henrietta. "I'm havin' a conversation with *her*," he said and only briefly glanced over at Clive, the gun still pointed at him, before he turned his attention back to Henrietta.

"Is it . . . *is* it Carter?" she asked hesitantly.

"Naw, it ain't Carter."

"Who then?" Henrietta asked, hoping to keep him talking.

"Some sap named James. 'Footman for the swells' he calls himself," Neptune laughed.

James? How could that be? Henrietta wondered furiously and instantly grieved for poor Edna. James had distinguished himself as a snitch in the past, but helping the mob to extort money or being an accessory to Mr. Howard's death was another thing altogether.

"That can't be true! James would never betray the Howards," Henrietta offered feebly.

"Everyone's got a weakness," Neptune crooned. "It's just a matter of findin' it. Turns out the 'footman for the swells' has an elderly old lady in Cicero. Not hard—stay where you are, Copper!" Neptune barked, fully turning on Clive now, who, Henrietta had observed out of the corner of her eye, had silently tried to creep closer.

"Turns out yer *my* weakness," Neptune said suddenly, licking his lips again and grabbing a lock of Henrietta's hair. "My pretty little filly I've waited so long for. Took so many chances. Morelli said I was an idiot, but look who got the prize in the end," he said, breathing heavily.

Henrietta instinctively pulled back at his touch on her hair, causing him to grip the lock he held all the tighter and give it a hard yank.

"Ow!" Henrietta said, sudden tears coming to the corners of her eyes.

"Let her go!" Clive shouted, taking a step toward Neptune.

Neptune, in response, shot a bullet into the ceiling, causing Henrietta to scream. "I said stay back!" he shouted at Clive.

"Okay, okay," Clive said hurriedly, his hands in the air. "I'm back."

"That's it," Neptune wheezed. "Nice and easy. I don't want to kill you willy-nilly. I want to have some fun with it, which I'm gonna do in a minute. Then you and me is gettin' outta here," he said to Henrietta. "It won't be the same, 'cause you ain't no virgin anymore, but I have things I can do," he cackled again.

Henrietta's heart was racing, and she felt herself succumbing to panic. If only she could get Rose's gun out of her handbag, she thought, suddenly remembering it. Why hadn't she thought to take it out before she came in?

"Come here, Cherry," he said pulling Henrietta by the hair so that she stumbled forward. "I'm gonna call you Cherry from now on. Like that?" he asked her with a wicked grin.

Henrietta did not respond.

"I said, like that?" he repeated, yanking her hair again.

"Yes," she gurgled.

"Stop it!" Clive shouted.

"You have no say in this anymore, Copper, so shut the fuck up!"

Henrietta took the few seconds afforded her by Neptune's distraction to avert her eyes to where Davis lay. His eyes were closed now, and she feared that he might have already died. Frantically she fought the tears that threatened to well up. With his hands still raised, Clive said, "Look, Neptune, or whatever your name really is," his voice filled with more anxiety than Henrietta had ever heard from him, though she could tell he was fighting to sound in control, "we can surely come to some arrangement. Let us go, and you can name any sum. I can easily raise it," he offered eagerly. Henrietta could hear the desperation in his voice, and it cut her to the quick.

"That ain't what you told me before," Neptune said coolly. "Singin' a different tune now, ain't you? Nah, I ain't never lettin' this one go," he said, tugging Henrietta's hair again. "She's mine now," he said, giving her head a little shove as he released her finally and pointed his gun at Clive, gripping it with both hands. "And I can't let you go. You'd never stop chasin' me. Yer just like me, see? Obsessed," he whispered. "We're both obsessed with the filly. That makes us the same, don't it?" he asked with a grin. "No, we got to go now. Rodge!" he shouted suddenly, causing Henrietta to jump.

No one appeared in response to this call, so Neptune turned his head toward the door that Henrietta had come through just a few moments ago, though it seemed like an eternity. "Rodge!" Neptune shouted again.

Still no one appeared.

"Where the fuck is he?" Neptune said irritably. "I tell him to do one fuckin' thing . . ." Neptune moved sideways toward the door. When he reached it, he kept the gun trained on Henrietta, and Clive beyond, and looked out briefly into the darkened tavern. He spun his head back then and snarled, "No funny business, Copper." He took a step backward so that he was half in and half out of the room. "Rodge!" he called into the darkness again.

Instinctively Henrietta knew she had to act. Their only chance was Rose's gun. Quickly she unzipped the handbag, hoping that if she did it fast it would not make as much noise, but it did, and Neptune heard it.

"What was that?" he snapped, turning his eyes toward her.

Before she could answer, a man barged into the room, almost knocking Neptune's gun out of his hand as he did so.

"Cops, boss," the man almost whined. "Fucking cops!"

"You bastard!" Neptune shouted at Clive, his face flushed a deep red with rage. "You double-crossing fucking bastard!" He cocked his gun and aimed it at Clive.

"It wasn't me! I swear it!" Clive said, taking a step back.

"Boss, come on. We've got to get out of here. Shoot him, take the dame, and let's go," Rodge urged, making a move toward Henrietta, presumably to grab her.

"Stay back!" Henrietta said, her voice wavering as she shakily held Rose's gun in her hand. She dropped the handbag she had been holding and gripped the gun with both hands now to try to hold it steady.

"Is that a toy?" Rodge asked, an amused sneer on his face. He had stopped in his tracks at the first sight of the gun, but now he continued toward her. Henrietta took a step back, raising the gun higher until it was aimed straight at Rodge, internally panicking as she realized that she didn't actually know how to use it. Well, it was too late now. Squinting her eyes and bracing her shoulders, she squeezed the trigger. Nothing happened.

"Give me that," Rodge said and lunged for her, stepping over Davis's inert body to get to her. Just as he did so, however, an apparently still-alive Davis managed to raise his leg and weakly kick him, which was enough to catch the goon off-guard and cause him to at least stumble.

"Henrietta!" Clive shouted, holding his hands as if to catch something. Swiftly she understood and tossed him Rose's gun.

Neptune, momentarily distracted by Rodge's stumbling movements and Davis's apparent resurrection, spun toward Clive, but it was too late. Upon catching the gun, Clive instantly cocked it as he ducked low and expertly fired three shots into Neptune's chest, causing him to instantly collapse. He quickly turned the gun on Rodge, then, who had recovered enough to raise his gun at Clive. Before he could fire, however, Clive shot, and Rodge's big body slumped to the ground, causing Henrietta to let out another scream. Both Clive and Henrietta remained frozen for a moment or so after, the reality of what had just happened taking several seconds to sink in, before Clive moved. After a quick glance at Henrietta, frozen with her hands over her mouth, he raised himself up from his crouched position and hurried over to where Neptune lay in a pool of blood and kicked him over with his foot. He was obviously dead, with three holes gouging his chest, but Clive, standing over him, cocked the gun again and, aiming it at Neptune's chest, fired again, causing the body to lift slightly off the ground from the force of it at such close range. "That's for my father," he said, bitterly.

Henrietta could hear Clive's voice speaking, but it was as if it were from a far distance, as if she were in a tunnel and the light at the edges of the room was beginning to close in on her. She felt suddenly weak, as if she could no longer stand . . .

"Henrietta!" she heard Clive shout and then gratefully felt his arms go around her. She sank into his arms and breathed in his scent, as he ferociously deposited kisses on her head. "Darling, are you all right? Are you hurt? You were marvelous," he said in a choking voice. "I'm going to kill you, though, you know. How could you do such a thing?"

Henrietta wanted nothing more than to be held by him, to retreat into him and let him take care of her, but something was niggling in the back of her mind. "Davis," she croaked. Clive released her, then, and they hurried, Henrietta practically crawling, to where Davis lay, his eyes closed.

Henrietta was no nurse, but even she could see that it didn't look good. The wound was on his left side, just under his ribs, and he was losing a lot of blood. She had seen her share of bar fights over the years but had never seen a gunshot wound. There was so much blood pooling around him that she thought she might be sick. She didn't see how he could possibly live through this, and she fought back tears.

"Davis, you bastard," Clive said, his voice thick.

"Oh, sure. Blame me," Davis rasped, his eyes still closed.

Henrietta let out a little cry. "Oh, my God, Clive. Do something. Quickly!"

Clive had already positioned himself on Davis's other side, squatting beside him and putting a finger to his neck to feel his pulse. "Jesus. Hang on, Davis," he said, pressing his hand on the wound. "Where are these goddamned cops they were talking about?" he muttered, looking over his shoulder as if they might appear. Bizarrely, as if on cue, sirens were heard wailing in the distance.

"Davis!" Clive said, lightly slapping him on the face. "Stay with me. Was it you who arranged for the police escort?"

"Of course it was me," Davis muttered, his eyes still closed. "I'm not stupid enough to go into a mob bar alone without backup. Can't speak for others, though," he said, coughing blood now.

"Stay with him," Clive commanded. "Put your hand there," Clive said, indicating the wound. Upon removing his hand, blood began to ooze again. Henrietta felt the vomit rise in the back of her throat, but she forced it down and made herself put her hand on the wet, warm hole in Davis's abdomen. "Harder!" Clive commanded as he rose. "I'll be right back," he said, running through the door, presumably to direct the police.

With her free hand, Henrietta struggled to find her handkerchief in the pocket of her skirt. She finally dug it out and pressed it onto Davis's wound, struggling to hold back her tears. Oh, please don't die, she prayed desperately. It would be all her fault. Her mind was going in so many directions at once. Had Clive really just killed Neptune? she thought next and looked over her shoulder at the lifeless body only a couple of yards from her and felt herself begin to shake. She looked back to Davis now, who was deathly pale and unconscious, his breathing becoming more and more labored. "Come on, Frank," she begged, terrified all over again, her hands full of sticky, red blood. "Hold on."

Chapter 22

Elsie bit her hangnail again, causing a tiny bubble of blood to well up in the corner of her thumb. Instinctively, she sucked it, the familiar metallic taste filling her mouth as she walked among the tropical greenery of the hidden greenhouse on the seventh floor of the Skyscraper. She had nearly forgotten about this place, having only seen it once on her initial tour of the grounds with Henrietta. Sr. Bernard had explained at the time that it was a "living laboratory" for the private use of the botany students. And while it was not officially off limits to other students, its use as a recreational spot was certainly not encouraged, lest any of the plants or specimens be damaged, Sr. Bernard had further explained at the time. In fact, most of the girls didn't even know of its existence.

It had therefore taken Elsie not a little detective work to actually find this small Eden again on her own, but she had eventually been successful and wandered now along the narrow pea-gravel paths between the different shades of vegetation. She hoped no one would mind her merely walking here, and she clasped her hands behind her back lest she give in to the temptation to reach out and touch something alive and growing. She had woken this morning feeling very unsettled and utterly sick to death of the miserable weather, and the greenhouse had somehow come to her mind from almost the first moment she opened her eyes. Normally, she would have pushed away such fanciful thoughts, but today, after a small cup of tea, she decided to seek it out, like a warm, green beacon in a frozen landscape of white and gray.

She sighed heavily and sat down at the feet of a statue of the Virgin Mary, which doubled as a fountain, softly gurgling water and oddly soothing, in the center of the garden. Elsie sat on the low cement wall that surrounded it, tracing the rough grooves of the grout with her finger. She knew she should probably be thinking about what had happened between her and Lloyd last night and how she was going to explain it to Aunt Agatha, but as worrisome as that situation was, something else was pressing on her more.

After Lloyd left last night, Gunther asked her if she still wished to go see her mother and offered to still accompany her. At first, she was inclined to refuse, but he encouraged her, saying it would be good to get some air. She agreed, then, thinking that he might be right, and signed out under Sr. Bernard's watchful eye.

Luckily, they did not have long to wait for a motorbus to come lumbering up Sheridan, but they had to ride along in the dark, the interior bus lights being out of order for some reason. At first, the darkness and the fact that there were so few people sitting near bothered Elsie, but as they rode along in silence, Elsie listening to Gunther's quiet, rhythmic breathing beside her, she welcomed it, and a confessional mood stole over her. It somehow seemed necessary after what he had witnessed between her and Lloyd, as if she needed to explain the situation and herself, and so she began to talk, haltingly at first. But then, as if some sort of stopper had been uncorked, she found herself going on and on. She told him all about Stanley and even Harrison, though she stopped short of actually saying they had had "relations," just that he had . . . well, taken advantage. She had even gone so far as to tell how she had agreed to elope with Harrison, but that Clive's sister and father had intervened. That was before he had died—Alcott, that is.

She stopped here, rather abruptly, not knowing what else to say.

Silence descended upon them again, and she began to fear that she had said too much. Gunther had not said anything at all during her long exposition, and he didn't say anything now, but he gave her hand a long squeeze through their gloves. Elsie could not feel the warmth of his hands, but she at least felt the pressure and somehow knew from that simple gesture that he neither judged nor condemned her. Even when they finally disembarked and began to walk toward Palmer Square, he still did not comment on her story, but instead, mercifully, began talking about all of the strange people who had at times rented rooms from his mother back in Germany, as if he could sense she needed him to talk now.

"It must have been a big house," Elsie said encouragingly, grateful for his perception.

"It was, yes. Very old and rambling. Like big barn with many *geister* . . . ghosts . . . living and dead, in it. Many times," he said, looking over at her, "the lodgers would leave things behind, even very valuable things." He said this last part slowly, deliberately.

Elsie had just been about to ask what type of things, but, looking up, she saw that they had unfortunately already reached the house. She felt self-conscious, then, not knowing what to do, as they had both understood that he would not be coming in, but she felt she could not turn him away now. What was he to do? Simply turn and walk back to the bus stop? She had not thought this far ahead. She contemplated asking him in—he already knew so much about her, what would it matter now if he were likewise exposed to Ma's eccentricities? However, after her heated conversation with Lloyd not an hour ago, she wasn't sure she could endure another confrontation, the chances of which, considering it was Ma, were very high if she were to bring in a stange man. Elsie reluctantly said good-bye to him, then, and was touched by the fact that he did not press to be invited in, nor did he make her feel guilty about it.

"Well good-bye, Gunther," she said awkwardly. "Thank you for walking me home."

"It was my pleasure. I like talking with you."

"I'm sorry . . ." she said, listlessly gesturing at the house behind her.

Gunther gave her a warm smile. "Do not fret on my account. I must go, anyway. *Auf wiedersehen.*"

Just as he was turning to leave, the front door unexpectedly opened to reveal none other than Ma herself standing there. Elsie wondered where Karl might have gotten himself off to . . .

"Elsie? Is that you?" Ma called, peering down at her and wrapping her sweater around herself as she did. "Why are you standing out here in the cold? I've been waiting here for you for ages. Thought you weren't coming. Who's that with you?" she asked, trying to get a better look at Gunther. "Stanley! Is that you?" she asked with so much eagerness that it pained Elsie.

"No, Ma," Elsie explained with a muted sigh. "This is my friend Gunther. He's from the college. He walked me here."

"Don't tell me you walked all the way from Roger's Park?"

"No, we took the bus."

"Well, no use standing out there catching pneumonia. Get in here, if you're coming."

Elsie sighed. She had been so close to escaping inside! She looked over at Gunther now, who surprised her by giving her a little wink, and she felt tempted to laugh at the absurdity of the situation.

"Come on! What are you waiting for?" Ma said, louder this time. Looking at each other one last time, they seemed to come to the same conclusion at the same moment and proceeded up the steps in unison, Elsie bracing herself for what might happen once inside.

As it turned out, they spent a very unusual evening of pleasant domesticity with Ma, with only a few minor embarrassments, the greatest of them being Ma's repeated reference to Gunther as Stanley. Elsie attempted several times to explain to Ma just who Gunther was, but she wasn't sure Ma fully understood. It didn't help when Doris and Donny made a short, excited appearance in the parlor before being whisked off to the nursery for bedtime, and Gunther had somehow produced a sweet for each of them from the depths of his pocket, further reminding Ma, so she said, of Stanley. This *faux pas* aside, however, the evening passed without any further embarrassments, except when Ma suggested they play rummy, of all things!

Gunther seemed to take this suggestion in stride, however, and readily accepted, though he said he didn't know how to play. Elsie managed a small smile, then, and offered to teach him the rules, if he were really serious, that is, about wanting to learn, she said. He accepted her offer and returned her smile, and Elsie found she enjoyed the process of teaching him very much. She liked knowing something he didn't. After they played a few rounds, which he was suspiciously good at, he had revealed that it was similar to a game they played in Germany called *Telefunken*.

When they finally left Palmer Square, later than Elsie had intended, Ma was in a good mood and entreated them to come back soon. At that, Gunther merely looked at Elsie, who blushed at the thought that Ma obviously thought them a couple. She was at a loss for what to say to this, so she simply gave Ma a quick kiss on the cheek and said good-bye.

In silence they walked back toward the bus stop, the frigid air perhaps preventing them from speaking. Before they walked very far, Elsie stopped them.

"I . . . I could have Karl drive us," Elsie shouted over the wind. "I forget sometimes . . ."

"But, as you say, he will miss his radio show . . . *The Shadow*? I think is what you called it?"

"Oh, that's long over by now," Elsie shouted again. "He's probably already in bed."

Though his tattered scarf covered his mouth, she could tell by his crinkled eyes that he was smiling. "I am not one to get a man out of his bed. No, we will leave him to his rest. I like to walk," he said, holding his elbow out to her.

"So do I," Elsie said, taking his arm.

They continued on in silence, bent slightly forward by the piercing wind, until they finally reached the bus stop. Fortunately, they did not have long to wait before a bus came lumbering along.

"I'm sorry about Ma," Elsie said, rubbing her gloved hands together, once they were seated back on the bus, this one being blessed with at least some working interior lights. "She doesn't realize—"

"I understand this," Gunther said with a nod, looking down at his hands.

Elsie meant to use the ride home to ask him about Anna, as, after all, she had already told him everything about herself. Surely he wouldn't mind her asking now after all they had shared this evening.

He caught her off guard, however, and before she could say anything, he asked, still looking at his hands, if she were serious about becoming a nun.

She was taken aback by this, surprised that not only would he bring up such a subject, but that he had apparently remembered all that she had told him that night at the hospital, despite his being in and out of consciousness. Or, if he hadn't, she quickly reasoned, he had probably overheard her say it to Lloyd just this evening. Either way, it reminded her that she must write to her grandfather immediately—first thing in the morning, actually, before he heard it from some other source. Thinking of it all again, now, she began to feel anxious all over, nervous and trapped. She shifted in her seat.

"Do you not wish to talk about it?" he asked, looking at her.

"Oh," she said, realizing she hadn't answered his question. "No . . . I don't mind. But yes, I . . . I *am* serious, as a matter of fact."

"How long have you felt this way?" he asked, still looking at her.

"Well, not long, really. But I am very determined," she added quickly.

"Have you spoken to any of the sisters?"

"I did speak to Sister Bernard, but she said it was too soon. That I must wait a year and then I can join the novitiate."

"Have you told no one else? Your mother, maybe? Or Henrietta?"

"No, not yet . . ."

She turned and looked out the window. How had the conversation turned yet again to be about her? She was determined to reclaim it and abruptly turned back toward him. "Who is—" she began, but he again spoke first.

"Elsie, you are sure?" he asked quietly. "Why is it you wish this life?"

Elsie remained silent, trying to think of how best to craft her answer. How could she explain it to him?

"Elsie, it is not my place to say; I know that. But I think this is *fehler*—mistake."

Elsie gave a little groan. Why did everyone always think she was making a mistake, no matter what she did? That she somehow didn't know her own mind? "I suppose you wouldn't understand," she added, after a few silent moments. "Being a Lutheran," she said quietly, staring at the seat in front of them. She looked over at him, and his face held a puzzled look.

"This has nothing to do with it."

They both sat silent, studying the other.

"Isn't it obvious?" Elsie asked finally, with a little sigh. "I should think after what I told you just tonight and what you saw unfold with Lloyd that it would be more than evident why I want to be a nun."

"Because of two *verblendungen*—infatuations . . . you wish on love to give up altogether?"

Elsie was shocked by his cavalier opinion of something that had affected her so deeply, had changed her irrevocably. "They were more than *infatuations*," she said stiffly. "At least to me."

"Forgive me," he said, sincerely. "I did not mean it this way. I mean . . . you are very young, Elsie. You will of course meet man you will fall in love with. Someone who is worthy of all this love you have to give." He looked over at her now.

Ah, but that was just the thing, Elsie knew, again surprised—but not surprised—at how he had come to the crux of it all, two small tears appearing in the corners of her eyes. She was not worthy of any decent man's love, and that was the sad truth of it. He obviously must not have caught her meaning before, when she had spoken about her affair with Harrison—which was probably a good thing, actually. Why had she told him so much, anyway?

"Maybe it is such that you have met him already," he suggested softly.

"You're teasing me," she said with a small smile. "Surely you don't mean any of the 'society' men I'm thrown together with. They're all the same basic variant of Lloyd Aston. So, no. I don't think so."

Gunther remained silent and looked at the seat in front of them.

Elsie wanted to explain that it was more than that. That even if she could find such a man, one whom she loved and somehow loved her back, she would most likely not be allowed to marry him anyway. She looked up at Gunther, the headlight of a passing car suddenly illuminating his face, and she thought he looked sad. Perhaps he felt sorry for her, but she didn't want him to.

"Gunther, I don't think I have many choices in whom I marry, and I have no desire to marry some rich man who only wants me for the increase it will bring to his bank account. I feel like I'm being sold to the highest bidder," she mumbled in a low, disgusted tone.

"You would be rich, well cared for," Gunther pointed out.

"Yes, in a cage," she said mournfully. "A golden cage is still a cage."

"So you trade one cage for another?" he asked. "The wedding veil for the nun's?"

Elsie bit her lip. "The convent is not a cage!" she said, remembering Sr. Bernard's words about the veil being put on *with great love, not donned in haste or fear*. "I would love to be a sister!"

"Why? I do not understand this."

"Because . . . because I wish to study. To learn. To read and not be stopped. To learn so many things. Like you." She chanced a glance at him to gauge his reaction. "I . . . I'd like to be a teacher. For poor children. I want to help them to learn, too. To help them escape, even if for just a little while, between the pages of a book, as I used to. Why is that so hard to understand?"

Gunther was staring at her with a strange look on his face. Why was he looking at her this way? As if . . .

"But why can you not be teacher *and* wife?" he countered. "Why do you have to be nun to make these dreams come true?"

"Do you really not see?" she asked incredulously, searching his eyes. "I couldn't possibly be a teacher for poor children and be someone's North Shore wife. *That simply isn't done!*" she said in her best imitation of Aunt Agatha, and he obliged her with a small excuse of a smile. "I'll be expected to throw elaborate dinner parties and play the hostess to a lot of snobs. Henrietta might be able to do it, but not me," she said mournfully, leaning her head against the cold glass of the window. "And you heard Lloyd, I'm sure. I'd be expected to *produce a brat or two*. Does that sound appealing to you?"

"Do you not wish to have children?" he asked, concerned.

"Not like that."

Gunther looked down at his hands again.

"I don't have the strength to keep fighting them all, Gunther. This is the easier way. I'm a very weak person. That should be obvious by now," she said sadly.

"You are the least weak person I know, Elsie," he said and took her hand and squeezed it again. This time he held on to it, though, until the bus came to a stop outside Mundelein.

Slowly they walked to Philomena, where they finally parted at the bottom of the steps, Gunther still having to walk over to Piper. Elsie had been mulling over all that she had said on the bus just now, and while she didn't regret anything, she found it disturbingly incomplete, as if she had missed something important. Gunther did not refer to any of it, though, as they parted, merely thanking her for a nice evening. He turned to leave, but she couldn't let him go without saying one last thing. She put her hand on his arm to stop him. He looked back at her, curious.

"It's not just that," she said eagerly. "What I said on the bus. I . . . I do feel as though I have a calling. I . . . I want to serve God."

"But what of love?" he asked so softly she could barely hear him. "Is this not why we were created? To pass on the love that has been given to us?"

Elsie felt unexplainably irritated again. "Why do you keep talking about love?" she asked, a hint of exasperation in her voice now. "There are many types of love," she said hoarsely. "Service is a form of love. Isn't that what God wants of us?" she asked.

"'Mercy is what I require, sayeth the Lord, not obedience.'"

Michelle Cox

Elsie bit her lip, his words shaking her to the core. She knew she couldn't refute the Bible, and, likewise, she was unable to think of something to counter his logic.

"There are many ways to serve God, Elsie," he said with a sad smile.

"I know."

"You need to *entbinden* . . . what is the word? Absolve? . . . yourself. Or you will never be free."

Again, they stared at each other. Elsie tried to dislodge whatever feeling was welling up in her.

"Why do you care so much? Just . . . just leave me be! Weren't you the one who was telling me to choose my own path? Well, let me!"

Gunther looked as though she had struck him. "You are right, of course," he said, taking a step back. "I should not care. I have no right to care. This is not my affair. Forgive me," he said, bending and giving her a small kiss on the cheek. "*Gute nacht.*" He turned then and began to walk briskly across the snowy lawn.

"Gunther!" she called after him, suddenly regretting what she had said, but he did not turn back.

Elsie barely slept all night, so many things going through her mind, bits and pieces floating up to the forefront in no particular order at all. There was something she was missing, she fretted, but she just couldn't figure it out. For what seemed like hours, she pondered Gunther's words about love and service, happiness and mercy. Who was she supposed to have mercy on? she wondered. Him or herself? Or both somehow? But couldn't his biblical quote mean that she should have mercy on all of God's people and thus serve them? As a teacher, for example, who would teach them of God's love and mercy? Didn't that make the most sense? Why did Gunther always make her feel like she was doing something wrong? And why, as she had asked him last night, did he care? What was she to him? she had asked herself over and over through the night. Perhaps it was the poet in him. But surely, as a poet and probably because of what he had been through in the war, he of all people should understand sacrifice. Weren't so many of the poems he had copied about love and loss? Love in some form or another seemed to preoccupy him, almost obsess him, she saw. And then a niggling thought, like a ghost or a sort of ethereal specter, came into existence and hovered near her conscious mind, but she shooed it away before it could take hold.

She tossed and turned, periodically becoming conscious of Melody's light snoring, and felt her irritation at Gunther rise. He had told her to choose her own path, and when she did, he didn't approve! She lay there and tried to explain herself to him over and over in her mind. In each scenario, he frustratingly still did not seem to understand—though, to be honest, sometimes she didn't either. She was starting to not make sense, even to herself. At one point in the night, in desperation, she got up and knelt by her bed to pray, but she kept looking over her shoulder so many times to make sure Melody wasn't disturbed by her actions that she kept losing her concentration. Eventually, she gave up and crawled back in bed, determined to pray there, but she fell asleep before she could finish.

Elsie twisted her hands now, thinking about it all again, and began to pace along the pea-graveled pathways of the greenhouse, trying to find solace in this hidden world. She should have brought *Beowulf* to read here amongst the greenery, she chastised herself, if only to take her mind off her woes.

"I was thinking I would find you here," said a voice, and she spun around, startled, to see none other than Gunther himself in the doorway. She felt immediately embarrassed, as if he could somehow know she had just been thinking of him.

"How did you know I was here?" she asked, baffled as to how he had found her here, when she herself barely knew how she'd gotten there.

"I do not know. It just came to me."

"That's peculiar," she said, wondering if in truth he had followed her.

"I . . ." he said, coming toward her. "I am sorry about last night.

I said things I should not have. Or it is maybe that I did not say enough." He paused here as if searching for the right words. "There is something I need to say to you," he said, his face a mask of anxiety. He looked as though he hadn't slept well either.

Not again! She didn't think she could endure yet another conversation about her misguided desire to join the convent. "Gunther, please. I don't want to talk about it all again," she begged, though she had herself been thinking of nothing else, of course.

"I . . . very well," he said, then, biting his lip and putting his hands behind his back. He strode about for a few moments before roughly sitting down beside her, his arms resting on his knees as he clenched his hands together.

Elsie did not look at him. She was relieved that she had succeeded in stopping him talking about her choices in life, but now what was she to say? What *should* they talk about? Perhaps his injured hand? she wondered, glancing at it out of the corner of her eye.

"Elsie, why do you think I gave you *Family Happiness* to read?" he asked softly, not looking at her.

"I . . . I don't know," she said, surprised by his sudden choice of conversation. "I . . . I wondered, actually. I couldn't help but think there was some purpose to it, some sort of theme you wanted me to take note of?" she asked, looking over at him.

"Yes," he encouraged, looking over at her now too. "Can you . . . do you know what it is?"

Elsie shook her head. "Even if I could name the . . . the themes, I can't imagine what they have to do with me. Poor Masha . . . after the attentions of the prince and . . . and the glittering Russian aristocracy, having to return in the end to her husband, Sergei, and find a sort of happiness in that life . . ." she broke off here, a niggling thought slowly forming on the horizon of her conscious mind. "Is that . . . that what you meant for me to take from it?" she said slowly, her breath catching in her throat. What had he really intended? she wondered.

He opened his mouth to speak, but she continued on.

"I don't understand why it is called *Family Happiness*. It's not happy at all. It's sad," she said, her brow pinched. "Why do you like it?"

"Because it's a redemption story," he answered quietly. "They both get second chance at a deeper sort of happiness,—peace. They find a deeper sort of love."

"And you think that I . . . I am in need of redemption?" Elsie asked, the truth of it cutting her to the quick.

"No, *I* am," he said, turning fully toward her. "Or maybe it is that we both are." He paused. "Elsie, I have not been honest with you, in many ways. I have been a coward. But last night showed me that I must be . . . what is the word? . . . forthright? Honest. To tell you the truth. I had hoped you might guess, but I see now that I must more speak more plainly."

Something in the way he was looking at her now, so desperately, the way she had caught him looking at her even for just a few moments on the bus last night, made her stomach quickly clench into a knot. His words, too, from last night came back to her. *You will of course meet man you will fall in love with . . . Maybe it is such that you have met him already.* How could she have been so stupid? She knew, then, what he was about to say to her and felt herself panic. He couldn't really be—

"Elsie," he said softly, "I think I am in—"

"No! Don't say it! Please don't say it," she begged.

Gunther gave her a look as though she had struck him. "Elsie, I . . ." he began again and swallowed hard. "I care for you—very much," he said hoarsely.

No! she thought wildly. How could this be? she asked herself, searching his sky-blue eyes even as the guilty truth soaked in—that the longing she recognized in his eyes had a reciprocal feeling in her own heart. How long had it been there? And how could she have not seen it before now? But love—if it *was* love— wasn't supposed to happen this way . . .

"I . . . I thought you were my friend . . ." she said haltingly, feeling betrayed not only by him but by herself.

"I *am* your friend."

"I . . . I can't possibly marry you!" she blurted out before she could stop it.

A wave of something crossed Gunther's face before he quickly hid it away. "I am not asking you to marry me," he said gently, looking at her steadily, as if explaining something to a child.

Elsie blushed to the roots of her hair. "No, of course not," she said hurriedly, as a sickening recollection of Anna filled her mind, then, and nearly crushed her.

"I am not speaking of marriage because . . . because you are not ready," he went on, interrupting her thoughts. "I know this. You are much confused, Elsie. There is much hurt in you. And there are things that you . . . that you do not know about me."

"Gunther, I . . ." she began, confusion coursing through her. "I can't—"

"I do not wish to make a . . . complication? But I must speak before you make a choice you cannot change," he said with uncharacteristic hurry. "You must allow me to say that I do care for you. Very much."

Elsie felt herself beginning to tremble, to slip, wanting to give way to the flood of emotion that threatened to drown her. She tried desperately to remember and hold on to all of her resolutions, but she felt them melting away, as if they had been made of cheap, thin paper. They were quickly burning up, being consumed, as she realized, horribly, what a small part of her must have always known—that she cared for him too—very probably loved him.

Without thinking, she raised her finger and put it gently against Gunther's lips. Softly he kissed it, and a resultant electric current immediately coursed through her. He reached up, then, and wrapped her tiny hand in his calloused one and turned it slowly, so that he could brush her palm with his lips.

There was more tenderness, more intimacy, in that small gesture than any she had ever known with the likes of Harrison, and she knew she was becoming untethered, skating farther out to where the ice was very thin. Her heart was pounding in her chest, and she felt as though nothing had ever existed before this moment. He was leaning so very close to her, his lips inches from hers, and she could sense him trembling too. But before she gave in completely, a warning bell went off somewhere in the far corners of her mind, forged perhaps from her many hours of tears over Harrison—and of Stanley, truth be told—and the current spell was sadly broken. Slowly she pulled her hand from his.

"Who is Anna?" she whispered, searching his eyes with her own.

"Anna?" he asked, confused.

"I . . . I read your notebook," she said, though her tongue felt thick in her mouth as she said it. "The night at the hospital. I . . . I thought you knew . . ."

"No, I did not know this," he said, puzzled.

"You called out for her in your sleep." Elsie watched as his face contorted. "Who is she?"

"Ach! Elsie," he groaned. "I meant to tell you. I have wanted to tell you for so long. It is partly what I came here now to tell you. She . . . she's someone I am helping. It is a very long story."

"She lives with you, doesn't she?" Elsie guessed.

Gunther nodded slowly, his eyes closing. "Sometimes," he sighed.

"With . . . with your mother, right?" Elsie asked, the hope in her heart that there was at least the semblance of a chaperone present causing her chest to burn.

"My mother is dead," he said quietly. "She died on the way over."

Elsie felt all the breath go out of her, not realizing she had been holding it in. Dead? she said to herself, trying to take it all in. "You lied?"

"I didn't mean to, it's just that—"

"So it's just the two of you?"

"Yes, but it is not what you are thinking, Elsie," Gunther said the urgency in his voice increasing.

Elsie stood up and thought she might be sick. *Not again.* "Please . . ." she murmured.

"Let me explain," Gunther begged, standing up now, too.

"No!" Elsie almost shouted. "No, I don't want to hear it. Any of it. I can figure it out for myself," she said, backing away from him. "How dare you come to me like this and say these . . . these things when you aren't free? I thought you were different!" she cried, breaking down into sobs.

"Elsie, please," he said, tears in his own eyes now, as he tried to grasp her arms. "You do not understand. Anna is—"

"How dare you," she interrupted, roughly pulling away from him. "How dare you tell me what I am doing is wrong and to try to turn me from it! To what end?

"I am not trying to tell you what you are doing is wrong!"

"Yes, you are! You say that I'm confused and somehow don't know my own mind. That I'm running from one cage to the next, as you put it. And you tell me this—why? So that I will fly into yours? Yours, which is just as tarnished as all the others, it would seem."

"Elsie, you must let me explain—"

"Do you *love* her? No! Don't answer that," she said before he could answer. "I don't want to know."

She began to cry again, and she was overwhelmed with a desperate desire to flee. To be anywhere but here. Suddenly the tropical air felt overwhelming and thick, noxious even. She ran toward the door.

"Elsie, please . . ." Gunther called out.

But Elsie did not stop to listen, and instead hurried through the doors and down the circular staircase to the gleaming floor below. She ran across the hall to the main staircase, gasping for breath as she clasped the chrome railing and feeling utterly sick to her stomach. How had she fallen prey to yet another brute? she wondered, as she ran across the circular drive to escape into her room.

Chapter 23

"Another?" Clive asked Bennett, holding up the decanter of cognac. Bennett gave a tight nod from where he sat in the leather armchair in the study at Highbury, a fire crackling in the large stone fireplace. As Clive poured, he was uncomfortably aware of how reminiscent it was of all the evenings he had spent in here with his father. Outside it was snowing again, coming down heavily.

"So he's dead, then?" Bennett asked, swirling the amber liquid that Clive had just poured into his glass.

"Yes, the bastard's finally dead. I can finally stop looking over my shoulder, or Henrietta's shoulder, I should say," Clive responded, bracing one outstretched arm against the mantle as he gazed at the fire. "Thank God."

He was elated that Neptune, and both of his right-hand men had been shot and killed that night, and he couldn't stop replaying it in his mind, over and over. Watching Neptune fall after he had pumped three shots into him and seeing the look of shock and pain on the bastard's face as he went down slaked a fury inside him that he hadn't fully realized was there.

"Davis going to make it?" Bennett asked, peering up at him.

Clive let out a deep sigh. "Yes, I'm pretty sure. The doctors think he'll be in for a few more weeks, but they're hoping for a full recovery."

—

Davis had indeed survived the shot to his abdomen, the bullet somehow miraculously missing all of his vital organs. Clive and Henrietta had been to see him every day since that fateful night, especially as no family members had so far come forward to visit. The chief had come at least once, blustering his way into Davis's room, and Clive and Henrietta had run into a few other men visiting from the station, but mostly, they observed, he was alone. So far, he had been unconscious each time they visited, but just yesterday, he was awake when they came in.

Henrietta rushed to his side, setting down the flowers she had brought from the florist in town, exclaiming as she did, "Oh, Sergeant Davis, you're finally awake!"

"Don't you think you'd better call me Frank?" he asked with a voice thick and gravelly from underuse. "Considering."

"Yes, I suppose you're right," Henrietta said, her eyes crinkling into a smile as she patted his hand. She looked up at Clive as she did so, who merely arched his eyebrow in response.

"How are you?" Clive asked, clearing his throat, as he stepped closer to the bed.

"Been better," Davis managed.

"I owe you one," Clive said.

"I'd say so."

"You're very lucky, Sergeant Davis," Henrietta said.

"Frank."

"I mean, Frank," she corrected herself. "The doctors can't believe it wasn't a fatal shot."

"Luck of the Irish, I guess," he said with another grin. "On my mother's side."

He closed his eyes, as if even that little bit of conversation had exhausted him. Henrietta looked at Clive and then back at Davis. His eyes fluttered open again after a few moments.

"Sorry," he croaked.

"Don't apologize!" Henrietta said. "You're obviously very weak still. We'll go and let you rest now. Can we bring you anything?"

"Nah," he said, closing his eyes again briefly.

"You're sure?" Henrietta persisted.

"How about a Scotch?" he said, opening his eyes to peer at Clive.

"When you get out," Clive responded. Davis gave a barely perceptible nod and closed his eyes again.

A nurse bustled in, carrying a clipboard braced against her massive chest. "Visiting hours are over, I'm afraid," she said crisply. "Sergeant Davis needs his rest."

"Of course," Henrietta said, giving Davis's hand a squeeze, which caused him to open his eyes again and look at her. "We'll be back tomorrow," she said to him with a smile and made her way quietly out.

"Good-bye, then, old man. Chin up, as they say," Clive said, holding his hat in his hands.

Davis looked to where Clive was standing. "You're lucky you have her," he said, his voice thick.

"Yes, I know," Clive said and ducked out of the room.

"He'll be back at work soon enough, I should imagine," Clive said now to Bennett, shrugging his bad shoulder as he slumped down into the armchair opposite.

"You wish you could join him, don't you?" Bennett asked, observing Clive. "Go back to detective work."

Clive let out a deep sigh. "Is it that obvious?"

Bennett unexpectedly laughed. "It's been obvious since the minute Alcott died, my boy."

At the older man's utterance of "my boy" as he sat in his father's chair, Clive's breath momentarily caught in his throat. He tried to ignore the surreal similarity before him and concentrate on Bennett's words instead. Painfully, Clive tried to consider how much of him grieved his actual father and how much of his grief was for the life he had hoped to take up here with Henrietta—the detective work, the shoring up of Highbury, making a clean slate of things, modernizing. It hadn't fully occurred to him until just this moment, and he didn't know what to say. Part of him was ashamed by this line of thought's very existence.

But at least he had gotten revenge on his father's killers, he repeated to himself yet again. Well, three of them, anyway, he conceded and wondered where the rest of Neptune's gang had scattered to, especially Vic. He was tempted to telephone his former chief in the city, who naturally had ties to the underworld, informants who would know who was afoot and who had jumped town to lay low for a while. But what did it matter? It wasn't his job anymore. It was time once and for all to put that behind him, he told himself. His future sat in front of him in the form of Sidney Bennett. Now that he could truly lay his father to rest, he knew he needed to pour all of his energy into running the firm. It was time.

"So why don't you?" Bennett asked him as he took a drink of Scotch.

"Why don't I what?" Clive asked, perplexed.

"Go back to detective work."

Clive let out a snort and took a drink of his cognac—a big one.

"I'm perfectly serious, Clive," Bennett said, casually crossing his legs. "I've been thinking about it since . . . since Alcott's unfortunate demise. It's obvious you're not suited to running the firm."

"Thanks very much."

"I don't mean you're not competent. Not at all. You are certainly *capable* of running Linley Standard. But your heart isn't in it, is it? I tried to tell this to Alcott, but he wouldn't listen."

Suddenly his father's parting words in the letter in the cottage came back to him, his instruction to listen to and trust Bennett. He mulled over the words once again. *We have grown up together, in a way, and he saved me once when I was about to make a very grave, very foolish mistake. Make a friend of him, Clive.*

"What exactly did you save my father from?" Clive asked abruptly.

Bennett's brow furrowed. "What do you mean?"

"Just that in my father's last letter, the one I found in the cottage, he says that you saved him from making a very grave mistake. What was it?"

"Ah." Bennett said, not looking at him and instead averting his eyes to the fire. After a few moments, he looked back at Clive. "I suppose it doesn't matter now if I tell you."

Clive waited expectantly.

"It was just that your father nearly had an affair," he said quietly.

"Jesus Christ." Clive had had a niggling feeling ever since he had read the letter, but he had hoped it was something else. Like a bad investment perhaps. He gave Bennett a sideways glance. "Who with?"

Bennett sighed. "Does it really matter?"

Clive contemplated this. "How long ago?" he asked instead.

"Years and years ago. Not long after I met him, really. I was surprised at the time that he listened to me, to be frank. He confided in me one night. We had both been drinking. Said he was tempted, that he was thinking of taking it further, that it was common between servants and masters in England."

"Servants?" Clive coughed, his cognac going down the wrong way. "It was a servant?" he asked, quickly running through them in his mind. Who had been with them that long?

"Not . . . not Mary, was it?" Clive asked, thinking that chronologically it had to be either the cook or Mrs. Caldwell, but both prospects seemed ludicrous in the extreme . . .

"It was Helen," Bennett said softly.

"Helen? Helen Schuler?" he scoffed, holding onto a tiny shred of hope that perhaps it was some other Helen, now long since gone.

"Yes, Helen Schuler."

"But that's impossible. She was . . . she was insane!" Clive insisted.

"She wasn't once," Bennett said. "She was gorgeous. No other way to put it. Golden hair, curves, the accent. I would have been tempted too, I'll admit it. I felt sorry for Alcott in a way. It was torture for him for a while, knowing she was just below, in the kitchens, working away. It would have been so easy . . ."

"But wasn't she married? To one of the gardeners or something like that?"

"Yes, Neils was his name.

"Did she . . . did she return his affections . . . my father's, I mean?" Clive asked hesitantly.

"I don't think so. From what I understand, she was devoted to Neils. But at the time, she was sleeping upstairs in the maids' quarters, and Neils was out above the stables with the other gardeners. There were no accommodations for married servants. Alcott could have easily gone up and had his way with her. She was terribly young; wouldn't have put up too much of a fight—not that he was that sort," Bennett said when he saw Clive wince. "Quite the opposite, actually."

"What happened?"

"Apparently, he found her alone one night when he stumbled downstairs after some dinner party. This is what he told me, anyway. Said he tried to kiss her, but she turned her head away. Said it was the 'please' that got him."

"'The please'?"

"She whispered 'please' to him, as in 'please don't', and it utterly unmanned him. Couldn't go through with it. Didn't even touch her. But it didn't stop him obsessing, though."

Clive remained silent, trying to take all of this in. "So where do you come into this?"

"I told you. He confided it all to me in a misguided, drunken state. I tried to talk sense to him. I liked Alcott very much. Loved him, actually, in the end. He was a great man. I . . . managed to persuade him to let her be. It was my idea to have the cottage built, and he agreed to it. He put out a grand announcement, saying that married servants should have their own accommodation, that it was the only decent thing to do, all that sort of thing, but it was really just a way to get her out of the house, out of the line of temptation."

Clive mused this over. "But why? Why would you care if he had an affair? I'm sure half the men you've dealt with over the years have done so."

Bennett shifted uncomfortably. "I was worried it might be bad for business. Especially if Hewitt got a whiff of it. He was fiercely protective of Antonia."

Clive gave him a skeptical look.

"All right," Bennett sighed. "It was for Antonia too. I cared for her. I didn't want to see her hurt. I knew her in New York, you see," he added, not meeting Clive's eye.

Clive wasn't sure how much more he wanted to know. "So that was all there was to it? Nothing really happened?"

"No, nothing happened. I told him to turn to Antonia. Get to know her better. I think, in truth, he was a little afraid of her in the beginning."

Clive smiled. "Everyone's a little afraid of her."

"Seems he did, though, and she was soon pregnant with Julia. Helen got pregnant right around the same time, so that clinched it.

Clive looked up with an arched eyebrow.

"No, you don't have a long-dead half-sister. It was Neils's. That was obvious. Alcott never spoke about it again to me, so I don't know if it was hard to get over Helen or not. He seemed devoted to Antonia after that, however. He did love her, if that's any consolation," Bennett said, looking at him steadily.

"Yes, he said so in the letter. And I do believe he did." He paused, thinking. "Do you think she knows—Mother, I mean—about his . . . his feelings, let's say, for Helen?"

"Why else would she have thought to look for the money in the cottage?" he said, taking a drink of his cognac. "Of course she must have known."

Clive let out a deep breath. It all made sense. It was as though a veil had been removed to illustrate a part of his father's life he hadn't known existed, hadn't even suspected. Slowly he traced the etchings in the crystal glass he held. Something else was bothering him, though. Something else that was in the letter. *Tell her I never stopped loving her despite her*—Despite her what? Clive wondered.

He looked up at Bennett, who was staring into the fire. He supposed Bennett knew what this referred to, but Clive wasn't sure he had the heart right now to hear anything more, especially of a disparaging nature against his mother. He couldn't bear to think of her having an affair. He let it sit for a few moments, trying to drag his mind back to his father or Helen or Neptune or anything, really, rather than the possibility that his mother may have once strayed, or nearly so. It was one thing for his father to be tempted, but not his mother. Unfortunately, despite his effort to the contrary, he began to wonder, almost against his will, who might have caught her eye, and his mind went almost immediately to Carter, the speed with which it did so its own source of irritation. *Could* it have been Carter, though? he wondered. Always sneaking around the upstairs wings, particularly near his mother's rooms? And why else was she so protective of him? He would never have thought it was possible, but perhaps if she had indeed known of Alcott's predilection for . . . for Helen (God, he could barely think it), she might have thought that what was good for the goose was good for the gander? No! Impossible. If something had . . . happened, he preferred to imagine it was someone from their set, someone rich and powerful. Somehow that would make it more palatable than if it had been the old dog, Carter.

"Was it Carter?" Clive finally said aloud, unable to keep it in any longer.

Bennett startled. "Was it Carter what?"

"Was Carter my mother's lover?"

Bennett actually laughed out loud. "Was Carter your mother's lover? God, no. Why would you think that, my boy? If it wasn't so preposterous, I'd be offended. Possibly have to thrash you, actually."

Relief flooded through Clive in a way that embarrassed him. He glanced over again at Bennett, whose brow was wrinkled now as he looked at the fire.

"No, your mother never took a lover," he said quietly. "As far as I know, anyway," he said, clearing his throat and looking back at Clive. "And if she did, it wouldn't have been Carter."

"No, of course not," Clive said, wondering why Bennett suddenly seemed so melancholy. "Forgive me; my mind's a mess."

"Exactly why we should get back to the point," Bennett said, reaching for the decanter after a quick raise of his eyebrows and a corresponding tilt of his head, checking for permission to pour his own.

Clive nodded his assent. "Which is?"

"That you should let me run Linley, as I always have been. You work at being a detective. It's what we both do best. You'll remain the figurehead, of course, just as Alcott was, show up at meetings, et cetera, but I'll concern myself with the day-to-day affairs."

He paused for Clive's response, but Clive remained silent.

"You can be as involved as you want to be," Bennett went on, assuredly. "As time goes on, and you feel you want to take more of a role, then that can easily be arranged and accommodated. I hope you know me well enough by now, Clive, that I wouldn't be suggesting this for any personal gain. But Linley Standard is my life. It's all I know. I never married, never had a family. I just have the firm. We took a hit with the Depression, but we've weathered it better than most. I want to see the day when we're on top again. We'll get there. I know we will. I've diversified so much that we've stayed afloat. But that's not enough. I want us to lead the industry again."

Clive stared at Bennett as he spoke so passionately about the company he himself couldn't care less about, much to his shame. He was sorely tempted to take him up on his offer; it would be like a dream come true for him. But how could he do that to his father, who had been so adamant he take over the reins? He had promised his father that he would do his duty. And was this how he meant to honor that promise? Escape at the first chance that came his way? Clive took a deep drink and realized that Bennett had stopped speaking and was looking at him expectantly.

"Well? What do you think?" Bennett asked.

Clive sighed. "It's an interesting proposal, Bennett, but I don't think I can do that to my father. He wanted me to take over so badly. You know that as much as I do."

"Yes, I know, but maybe it was to alleviate his own sense of guilt. Maybe he was hoping that you'd be the better man of business. I mean him no disrespect, you understand," he said at Clive's quick glance. "Did he tell you he read Greek at Cambridge?"

"Many times," Clive said wryly, swirling his cognac.

"Well, then. He was the perfect English gentleman. He was fiercely loyal to the Linleys, his father, and the estate and all of that. He did what he had to do, did it manfully. But Linley Standard was never really his; it was Hewitt's. And he got in over his head, as we all know now. I wish he would have confided in me sooner," Bennett said, sighing. "It's one of the reasons, I suppose, that Hewitt hired me in the first place, to protect against such things. So if anyone's to blame for this mess, it could be argued that it's me."

"It's hardly your fault, I'm sure, Bennett," Clive responded and grew silent, thinking. He looked at the fire. "But if we're following that thought, why didn't he confide in me? Let me help him?" Clive asked quietly. "I think that's what bothers me the most. That he didn't think to ask me for my help with something I could have actually been of service with." Clive rubbed his forehead despondently.

"I think he was ashamed, Clive," Bennett said gently. "I think he was desperate to get out from under it before you found out."

A log fell then, two charred ends of the main log falling into the grate, the center burned through. Clive stood up slowly and took a poker from the heavy iron stand and pushed them back into the flames, using the time it took as a chance to think. He bent to throw a new log on top, causing sparks to fly up and out. *You may trust him, as I have done, with your very life,* his father had said. Is this what he had meant? If he refused Bennett his offer, he really would have to run the company, and while he was pretty certain he could keep it afloat, he knew he couldn't make it excel, as Bennett could. After all, his own formal education had been sketchy, as he had joined up almost immediately after high school had finished. He regretted now not getting the degree his father had wanted him to. But he had been hotheaded then, eager to join the fray and defend his country and his British cousins. At the time, nothing else seemed to matter. Ah, the folly of youth, he thought, letting out a deep sigh. But he was older now and certainly wiser, and he had the presence of mind to know that a pivotal moment lay before him. He took his time in pondering it before rushing in headlong.

"He was immensely proud of you, you know," Bennett said, interrupting his thoughts. "He used to talk to me sometimes about your work. Said he wouldn't have the stomach for it. But he would tell us parts of your cases, and he would even repeat back bits of your speeches about seeing justice done. He really was very proud."

Clive tightened his grip on his glass and did not look over at Bennett. "That was all just bunk. Don't let it fool you," he said looking at him now. "I was doing it for my own reasons."

"Maybe so, but it doesn't make it any less true. Follow your heart, Clive. You did with that pretty wife of yours and look how that's turned out. Make your father's death mean something."

Clive's throat was very tight. He so wanted to accept Bennett's proposal. And yet, how could he?

"You have a chance to do with your life what you will. Not many people get that chance."

It was the second time he had heard that in so many months. His cousin Wallace, too, had implored him to make his life his own. Again, his mind went back to his father's letter. *Trust Bennett.* All right, he silently resolved, he would do it. As Bennett had pointed out, he could always go back.

He held himself erect and stiffly held his right hand out to Bennett. Quickly Bennett scrambled up and grasped Clive's hand firmly. "Partners?" he asked.

"Yes," Clive answered. "Partners."

It occurred to Clive, then, that just as Bennett had once "saved" his father, he was now saving him too, in a certain way.

"You've made a good choice, Clive," Bennett said, putting his other hand on top of their still clenched hands. "I won't let Linley down."

"I know you won't," Clive said seriously. "But I wouldn't get too comfortable if I were you," he added with a smile. "I'll probably be back before too long, my tail between my legs. I can't imagine there's too much 'justice' to be served up here. Davis is probably bored out of his mind normally."

"Oh, I think you'd be surprised. After all, we've just had theft, extortion, and murder," Bennett said, ticking them off on his fingers. "Seems challenging enough."

"Not according to the chief," Clive said wryly, and wondered just how tightly Chief Callahan was connected, just how deep the corruption there went. He was looking forward to finding out what the chief's reaction was to Davis's involvement in taking down a local crime boss.

"Speaking of justice, what's become of that servant? James Swindon is it?"

"Ah, yes," Clive sighed, coming back to the here and now. "I had him arrested, of course. He confessed under questioning. One of the maids is completely distraught. Seems she was recently engaged to marry him. But that's more Henrietta's problem, or my mother's, than mine." Clive drained his glass. "I confess I was hoping it was someone else."

"Carter, perhaps?"

Clive gave a small shrug and a smile.

"What do you have against Carter, anyway?"

"Nothing really, I suppose. He was a crabby bastard when we were small. Always shooing us away from father. And now . . . I suppose he's just a little too obsequious, if you know what I mean. Always hanging about."

"Isn't that what a servant is supposed to do?" Bennett smiled.

"In my mother's wing of the house?"

A ripple of something crossed Bennett's face, but it disappeared as he drained his glass and set it on the mantelpiece. "I don't think you have anything to worry about there, my boy," Bennett said, the 'my boy' causing Clive's heart to wrench yet again. "I must go. Please give Henrietta and your mother my regards. I'll show myself out." He held his hand out again to Clive, who took it firmly. "You won't regret your decision, Clive. We'll make Linley great again," Bennett said with a wink and strode out.

—

Clive could hardly wait to get Henrietta alone. He was eager to relate to her his conversation with Bennett, knowing she would be pleased. He did not immediately have a chance, however, as they spent the evening with Antonia, who surprised Clive by scolding him for not bringing Bennett in to greet them. She had not seen him since the funeral, she commented, which she thought odd, as before Alcott died, he was always coming and going from the house. She asked what they had talked about, and Clive had vaguely replied, "The firm, mostly."

Clive was not in the mood to get into it with his mother or to hear her opinion about what he and Bennett had privately agreed upon. As far as he was concerned, it wasn't up to her, and she didn't need to know all of the details, at least not yet. As it was, she was talking about returning to New York to stay with her sister again. It had been a mistake to come back, she said; she saw that now. Besides, she went on, she felt the two of them needed some time alone, as their honeymoon had been so abruptly shortened. And Clive, she added, needed to begin going downtown in earnest, if he was quite sure he had finally wrapped up this dreadful business of Alcott's.

Clive had only given her the very briefest of overviews about what had happened during the showdown with Neptune. If they *were* to pursue detective work, having Antonia be privy to what actually went on during their cases would not be a good idea, he decided, so he didn't want to set the precedent now, even if this one had indeed involved his own father . . . if they even had any cases, Clive thought ruefully, thinking again about Callahan, as he sat playing rummy with Henrietta and his mother. They needed a fourth, of course, for bridge, so Antonia had of late condescended to play Henrietta's favorite.

"And how is your sister doing, Henrietta?" Antonia said, as she fanned out her cards carefully and began rearranging them. "She's returned to school, is that not right?" she asked absently.

"Yes, Mundelein College," Henrietta said, laying down a jack. "She's doing well, I think. I haven't spoken to her recently."

"Agatha is quite beside herself. Says Elsie hasn't been to stay with them in ages. Agatha's quite set on an engagement," Antonia said over her cards. "But I'm sure you know all about that. She does go on about it."

Clive watched as Henrietta's brow furrowed. He wanted to smile, but he held it in.

"Really?" Henrietta mused, picking up the top card. After a few moments of hesitation, she discarded it.

Swiftly, Antonia picked it up and placed it carefully in her hand before she laid her cards on the table. "Gin!" she said triumphantly.

Clive tossed his cards onto the table in disgust. "You win, Mother. I quit. I'm going to turn in, I think." He hoped Henrietta would follow. He could not stop looking at her all evening. The curve of her face, the tendril of her auburn hair that hung down, partially concealing her eye. He wanted to reach across and tuck it behind her ear, but he could not do that with his mother sitting there. He felt on fire for his wife, wanting to hold her in his arms, make love to her. He felt freer than he had in months. Free in so many ways.

Later, as they climbed the stairs to their wing, Clive could not resist putting his arms around her from behind. She turned and gave him a kiss on the cheek, entwining her fingers behind his neck. "What's this for, Inspector?"

His insides churned when she called him that in that sultry way of hers that she reserved only for when they were alone. He bent to kiss her, deeply kiss her, there on the staircase. He was pretty sure one of the servants scurried away behind them. Probably Carter, except he was incapable of moving quickly, Clive thought derisively. Well, he didn't care who saw them. The tip of Henrietta's tongue on his caused him to harden, then, and all thoughts of the servants left his mind. His hands traveled down her sides and rested on her hips, gripping the fabric of her dress.

"Come with me," he said. "I have something to tell you."

He couldn't wait to see her face when he told her that her silly idea was coming true after all. He could hardly believe it himself. There was a deep satisfaction in the idea of having his own agency, the more he thought about it. Answerable to no one and able to call the shots as he saw fit. Not having to "look the other way," because of some political situation or other or cowering to the mayor. He hoped to someday get to the bottom of the situation with Chief Callahan, if nothing else. Perhaps that should be his—*their*, he reminded himself—first priority.

Well, at least he had Davis. Or, he hoped he had an ally in him after what they had just been through together. He smiled at the realization of how that had all come about, more or less, because of Henrietta. Many times, he thought about how she had handled the whole thing—eliciting Davis's help, getting a gun from one of those girls from the Marlowe, and then having the inspiration to toss it to him at the crucial moment. It did not fail to impress him, many times over. But more than that, it actually elicited an excitement in him, drove his passion all the more for her. She was incredible, this girl—this woman—and he couldn't wait to ask her to join him. Bennett was now his partner at the firm, but Henrietta would be his partner in the work closest to his heart.

They didn't bother lighting a fire upon entering their little sitting room, but sat on the sofa instead, the fringed lamp in the corner giving off enough of a warm glow for them to see each other. Henrietta sat facing him, her legs tucked up under her so deliciously. Clive sat facing her, his outstretched arm along the back of the sofa so that he could caress her shoulder. "I've something to tell you," he repeated again, smiling.

"So do I," she said softly.

Clive groaned. "If it's about Edna and James, I really don't want to hear it," he said.

"No, it's not about Edna, though there are a few things I need to tell you on that score . . . "

Clive put a finger up to her lips. "Not tonight. Let me guess. Is it about Elsie?" he asked, lowering his finger now.

Henrietta shook her head, her eyes large and almost glistening.

"I think I'm pregnant, Clive," she whispered and held her breath.

Chapter 24

Elsie lay on the bed engulfed in darkness, waiting for dawn. She had lain awake most of the night thinking about what had happened in the greenhouse with Gunther and knowing now what she had to do.

After she had so childishly fled from him, not letting him explain himself, she spent the rest of the day wishing that she had and cursing herself for being so stupid. She had paced endlessly around her room, her sobs finally subsiding, and after washing her face with cold water, she had sought out Melody and remained with her the whole day.

Melody was quite surprised by Elsie's attentiveness—but delighted, so she said, to have Elsie so unusually close. They spent the first part of the afternoon under the pretense of studying, but despite their books laid open in front of them, neither of them read a word. Only once did Melody look at Elsie with narrowed eyes and ask if there was anything wrong, but Elsie had quickly demurred, saying that she was just a little tired and that wasn't studying awfully boring?

For a moment, Elsie feared that she had stepped too far out of character and that Melody might question her further, but she had thankfully just laughed and agreed. Accordingly, then, the two of them frittered away the afternoon, Melody chattering idly while Elsie alternated between sitting on her hands and wringing them under the desk until Melody got up and switched on the radio, saying it was almost time for *The Romance of Helen Trent,* if Elsie didn't mind, that is. Elsie said she of course didn't mind, though she had never listened to a single episode before, which Melody found simply unbelievable. *The Romance of Helen Trent* was truly her very favorite show! she had exclaimed and then declared that Elsie was a very odd duck and that she must have led a very sheltered life indeed.

If Melody was further shocked when Elsie later declared she was not in the mood to study in the evening, as was already her normal habit, she did not reveal it but instead suggested—nay *insisted*—that Elsie come with them to Cabaret Night put on by Charlie's fraternity. She did remember that it was tonight, didn't she? Melody asked as she gave her nails a quick file. When Elsie said that it must have slipped her mind, Melody declared that she simply didn't know what she was going to do with her! She was so awfully forgetful as of late. Anyone might think she was in love or something, she said, winking at her, and Elsie tried not to blush.

Melody had promptly stood up, then, and rifled through Elsie's closet, choosing the dull-green (Didn't she have anything more colorful? They would have to go shopping!) Patou party dress for her to wear and told her to put it on quick. Not wanting to be alone with her thoughts, Elsie saw no choice but to obey, while Melody reminded her that Charlie and Douglas were to perform a scene from *Romeo and Juliet,* with Douglas of course forced to play the part of Juliet. It will be a scream! Melody laughed. Quickly she applied some lipstick to Elsie's full lips and adorned her in her fur, having exclaimed loudly at her discovery of it still in its shell of tissue, and then pulled poor Elsie downstairs with her and across the campus, where they were joined by several other of Melody's many friends until they formed what seemed a small entourage of sorts.

Elsie was glad of the other girls' presence, as it distracted Melody's attention away from her, and she was able to walk along undisturbed. Only once did she look around her as they crossed the campus to

Loyola, wondering if she would see Gunther, which she then just as quickly realized was preposterous. Why would he be just standing out in the cold at the mere chance that she might be walking by at any given time? Of course that made no sense, but many of her thoughts did not make sense tonight.

The boys had saved tables for them up front, and as the girls settled themselves on the wobbly, brown metal folding chairs, Elsie looked around at the badly decorated, wood-paneled room without really seeing it. The boys had put up streamers and set each table with a thick candle and strung some Chinese lanterns around the room. Elsie had no idea what the inside of a cabaret looked like, but she felt pretty sure this was not an accurate imitation. Still, she admired even the little bit of effort that had been put forth.

Once the show began, she tried concentrating on the many acts of "talent," but it was difficult to keep her mind from straying. She did perk up, though, when Charlie and Douglas finally came on, the room erupting in laughter at the sight of Douglas, dressed in a long, pink gown with a matching pointed pink cone of a hat from which a tulle veil hung down and under which flowed a wig of long blond curls. Red rouge had also been smeared on his cheeks—(or was this a natural shade given the poor boy's current circumstance?) as he stumbled, or perhaps was pushed, out onto a balcony, which appeared to have been constructed hastily, by the look of it, out of some wooden boxes stacked on top of each other and hidden by a thick red curtain, or perhaps it was someone's bedspread. Cheers were alternately heard when Charlie entered stage left, dressed as Romeo, a wooden sword hanging at his side.

Melody leaned forward and whispered to the girls seated at her table that each year the two lowest-standing freshmen in the Delta Sigs were forced to perform an act of the upperclassmen's choosing for the annual talent show, *and,* Melody giggled, guess who had managed to finish last this term? The girls laughed at that, which resulted in many loud exclamations of "Hush!" from the rest of the crowd as the act began.

JULIET *(Douglas): Well, do not swear. Although I joy in thee,*
I have no joy of this contract tonight.
It is too rash, too unadvised, too sudden;
Too like the lightning, which doth cease to be
Ere one can say "it lightens." Sweet, good night!
This bud of love, by summer's ripening breath,
May prove a beauteous flower when next we meet.
Good night, good night! As sweet repose and rest
Come to thy heart as that within my breast!

ROMEO *(Charlie): O, wilt thou leave me so unsatisfied?*

JULIET *(Douglas): What satisfaction canst thou have tonight?*

ROMEO *(Charlie): The exchange of thy love's faithful vow for*
mine.

JULIET *(Douglas): I gave thee mine before thou didst request it.*
And yet I would it were to give again.

ROMEO *(Charlie): Wouldst thou withdraw it? For what pur-*
pose, love?

Here the touching scene was unfortunately cut short, as Douglas, in his exuberance, leaned a little too far over the edge of his precarious tower, which caused him and the whole stack of boxes to tumble forward in a horrible crash, causing shrieks of laughter and not a few of fear from the crowd. Charlie and Douglas, both laughing, jumped up then, and took a deep bow, Douglas's veiled cone and wig falling off as he did so, causing another round of shrieks from the crowd.

Later the boys claimed that it had truly been an accident, but Melody did not cease to accuse them of ruining their own set on purpose so that they wouldn't have to continue with their very badly performed—would it be too far from the truth to say, perhaps even odious? she suggested—love scene. It probably was for the best, really, she had consoled them, as it was a terrible offense to the genius of Shakespeare. "*Romeo and Juliet* is simply ruined for me forever!" she exclaimed through her coy smile.

Elsie surprised herself by laughing with all the rest of them as they walked back to Philomena Hall, though Charlie and Douglas's dialogue during the scene had somehow disturbed her, despite the comic performance. Was everything going to be a constant reminder of her woes? she asked herself.

Once back at the hall, Elsie separated from Melody and the girls, leaving them downstairs in the parlor as she climbed the back stairs . . . not without a quick look in the kitchen . . . and sought the sanctuary of her room. She shrugged off her heavy fur and got undressed and slipped into bed, knowing that she could no longer escape the thoughts that she had been running from all day. What was she to do? she wondered fretfully for the hundredth time that day, as she curled up on her side. What was she to make of Gunther?

He had told her that he cared for her very much, having stopped just short of saying that he loved her, but she had only to think of his lips on the palm of her hand and the look of agony in his eyes to know the truth. He didn't need to say it for Elsie to know it to be true. She finally recognized in someone else, for the first time, really, what had so long been in her own heart, and her stomach clenched at the thought of it.

One by one, she thought back to all the encounters she had had with him, all of the conversations. He was unlike any other man she had ever met, so much so that she had barely thought of him as a *man* at all . . . more like a friend. That was her first mistake, she decided—not seeing him as a man. She supposed this was because he had not sought to gain anything from her, as all the men in her life—well, except her father—had done, even going all the way back to Mr. Dubala in his dusty shop, breathing heavily and hovering over her as she had sat mending. No, Gunther had never tried to put a claim on her, even as he told her how much he cared for her, she realized, her skin prickling.

And what of *love*? she thought now, turning restlessly onto her other side. Wasn't that different too? The way he always spoke about it, as if nothing else on earth, or heaven, for that matter, mattered? Love for him was almost like a living being, she had come to realize, again recounting his many scribblings and the poems copied neatly in his notebook. *Having met her, I cannot cease to think of her,* she remembered distractedly. *Something new in my heart is awakening,* he had written. With a deep blush, she wondered, daringly, if those lines could have possibly been about . . .

But *were* they about her? Or were they about this Anna? The Anna he had tried to tell her about before she stupidly ran away from him. Why hadn't she been strong enough to stay and hear the answer? Well, she had told him she was weak—didn't this prove it?

She couldn't believe it of him that he was not honorable, that he could love two women at once. But how else could she explain this Anna? she thought, trying to find a more comfortable position on her pillow. Almost against her will, her mind strayed back now, for the hundredth time, despite her self-imposed confinement with Melody all day and evening, to how he had kissed her finger and then her hand, so . . . so tenderly. It had been intoxicating. She was weak there too, she knew. She swallowed hard and wondered what it might feel like to have his lips on hers . . .

Agitated, she kicked off the covers and walked to the little window. Melody had long since come up to bed, and Elsie listened now to her light snoring as she stood, absently fingering the small lace curtain and looking out at the dark, murky lake. The moon was small and on the horizon; it was almost dawn.

Who was this woman, Anna? she asked herself again. Keenly, she tried to remember what he had written about her in his journal. *Anna cries night and day* he had written, hadn't he? What did that mean? Was she some refugee from the war? *Mother wants me to the authorities go . . .* But maybe she was remembering it wrong or confusing it. *Someone I am trying to help*, he had told her. Surely there must be some rational explanation . . .

She found it hard to believe he had willfully deceived her, though she supposed that he *had* lied in a way, by omission, regarding his mother, if nothing else. It explained much, though—the unchanged bandages, his dirty clothes. Vexingly, it made her heart go out to him even more. But why should he have told her about his mother or Anna? she reasoned when she felt herself growing angry. What had Elsie been to him, at least initially? Just another student. He didn't owe her anything, so what reason would he have had to tell her about this woman before now? *I am not asking you to marry me,* he had said, and her face burned, again, at the memory. Was that because he wasn't free? as she had first supposed, or was it really because of the "confusion" he saw in her?

The truth was that she *was* confused, as much as she hated to admit it. A certain part of her thrilled, however, that someone seemed to know her so well, almost more than she knew herself, really. All afternoon, sitting with Melody, and all through the droll play that Charlie and Douglas had performed, she realized, shamefully . . . no, not shamefully, but wonderfully, terrifyingly . . . that she cared for Gunther more than she ever had another. In short, she was in love. Not in the flighty, girlish way she had thought herself in love with Harrison or Stanley, but in a deeper, more mature way. And though it was just the beginning, the initial, tender unfolding of these feelings, she could already see that it was something else altogether than anything that had come before. An image of Marianne Dashwood and Colonel Brandon from *Sense and Sensibility* came into her mind then, and she smiled, thinking of how they were similar in some ways to Gunther's Masha and Sergei Mikhailych. But she wanted more than that for them, if there was even to be a *them*.

Who was this man? Who was he really? she wondered, and she ached to know. And that was another problem, she sighed. What would she say to Grandfather and Aunt Agatha? She suspected—no, knew—they would say he was after her money, but something deep inside of Elsie did not believe this of him. *I am not asking you to marry me.* Elsie bit her lip. What *would* she say to them? Hiding behind the veil of the church had been her plan of escape from them, but now she would have to face them with nothing but her own courage, which was meager enough, and it terrified her.

And what about her desire to become a nun? she thought miserably, letting the lace of the curtain slip through her fingers. Is *that* what Gunther had meant by confused? Again, he had been able to see what she had not, and she blushed to think that Sr. Bernard had probably seen it too. That her desire to become a nun was fueled by fear, as most things in her life had always been. But her desire to study and become a teacher had not been; this she knew for a certainty. In fact, it had *caused* much fear in her, but she had desired it even still. And what . . . what if she did choose to make a life with Gunther—not that he was offering, she reminded herself—what would become of this desire? *Why can you not be teacher* and *wife?* he had asked. But did he really mean it? she wondered. Could she trust him?

Calling trust into question yet again brought Anna back to her mind, and she knew, as she watched the sky begin to fill with light before the sun even appeared on the scene, that the only way to resolve any of this was to go and talk to him. To let him talk, to let him explain and not to interrupt or judge him, no matter what his words would reveal, just as he had listened and not judged her. And she felt ashamed, again, of how she had acted, but she would try to make it right.

She dressed hurriedly, careful not to wake Melody, and tiptoed down the back stairs. She wrapped herself in her wool coat and slipped out the back door, knowing it would make less noise than going out the front, which would still be locked for the night.

She didn't know how she would find him, but she thought starting at Piper Hall would be the best bet. It was Sunday, so he wouldn't be expected to be working, and it was still very early morning. As she tramped across the crisp snow, her boots breaking the thin layer of ice to sink down into the powder beneath, she was filled with the determined excitement that accompanies any quest. It felt good to be doing something, to be acting and not merely reacting. The sun had crested the horizon, and she was blinded by its reflection off the pure, white snow in front of her. She shielded her eyes with her hand as she peered up at Piper Hall, looming before her.

She recalled, then, that he had told her he lived *behind* Piper. Blinking rapidly against the glare, she shifted her eyes to search the vicinity between the back of Piper and the actual lake, but all she saw was a small structure not far removed from the mansion that looked little bigger than a potting shed. Perhaps it *had* been a sort of shed, or caretaker's dwelling, back when some wealthy family had occupied the mansion, and Elsie could not believe that this was actually where Gunther might live. She saw smoke coming from a small pipe that crudely thrust through the roof and indeed a pair of boots sitting outside the door, both of which suggested, however, that this was somehow the case. Could this really be his home? she wondered, as she looked from it to Piper and back again. It must be, she finally reasoned. It seemed rather cruel of Sr. Bernard to house him here, but she supposed it would be unacceptable for him to be living inside a women's dormitory. Still, it seemed rather meager, and she wondered how he managed.

She diverted her path from the mansion, then, and strode toward the shed. As she approached, however, she disturbingly remembered that he had said that Anna sometimes lived with him. She wasn't sure what that meant, and she wondered if Anna was in there with him now. She hadn't thought of that when she set off on this morning mission, and she paused just outside the door, wondering now if this was a good idea after all.

Well, perhaps it would be good for her to meet this Anna and speak with her, Elsie rationalized, and was momentarily proud of her sudden bravery. She rapped lightly on the door before she could talk herself out of it. She waited, stamping her feet slightly and blowing on her hands—she had dashed out without her gloves. No one answered, and she wondered if she should come back a little later.

She was just about to rap one more time when the door suddenly opened, then, and Elsie was shocked to see a little girl standing in the doorway, looking dirty and disheveled, with ratty blonde hair. She couldn't have been more than four years old.

Elsie stared at her, a thousand thoughts exploding in her mind.

The little girl looked up at her warily, her finger in her mouth, her large, blue eyes fearful.

"Anna?" Elsie whispered.

The girl gave her a tiny smile and slowly nodded her head.

Acknowledgments:

This book was extremely fun to write because it took me back to my alma mater, Mundelein College in Chicago, Illinois. Through the story I got to imagine the college as it might have been back when it was a brand new school in 1929. Even when I was a student there in the late 1980s, Mundelein was still an all-women's school run and taught by the Sisters of the Blessed Virgin Mary and was still wonderfully old fashioned—with a chaperoned sign-in book for male guests and wooden phone boxes in our dormitory; a "secret" greenhouse on the seventh floor of the art-deco Skyscraper, as well as original elevators, complete with sliding grates and elevator girls to operate them; and a converted stone mansion with Tiffany stained glass and stunning views of Lake Michigan beyond. Sigh.

Mundelein, as such, is unfortunately no more, though it remains a separate entity within Loyola University, into which it was folded shortly after I graduated. And while I was saddened by its closing, as I am with all things that come to an end, I could not wish for a better steward of our little campus than Loyola. I was amazed when I recently returned for a visit to see what careful attention they have given to their former sister school. I very much enjoyed pouring through Loyola's extensive online archives and reading more about Mundelein's history than I ever knew when I was a student. I spent many fascinating afternoons reading through old school newspapers from the 1930s and perusing a wonderful collection of photographs of the students and teachers from that era. It was extremely enlightening, not to mention entertaining, and I hope I did a good job of weaving some of those rich details into *A Veil Removed*.

So besides being indebted to the Loyola University archives, there are a number of actual people I'd like to thank for helping me to bring this next adventure of Henrietta and Clive into the world.

First and foremost, I like to thank my publisher, Brooke Warner, of She Writes Press for championing women everywhere and giving a voice to those of us who would otherwise not be heard. Thank you for guiding and mentoring me. You continue to inspire with all that you put your hand and heart to; you are truly changing the world with your hard work and vision.

Secondly, I'd like to thank my brilliant project manager, Lauren Wise, who also took on the role of editor for me this time around, and it is through her astute guidance that the book comes to you in as fine a shape as it does—any mistakes found therein are entirely my own. Thank you, Lauren, for your superior editing skills, for being so organized, and for your sense of humor. You never cease to amaze me!

I'd also like to thank Crystal Patriarche and her team at Booksparks, many of whom work behind the scenes, tirelessly, to help so many authors succeed. In particular I'd like to thank my publicist, Liane Worthington, for so generously sharing your vast knowledge of the industry with me and for your insightful, intelligent advice and wise direction. Thank you, Liane, for all of your help in getting my series out to the bigger world. It means more than you know to have you in my corner.

Thanks, too, to my web master and newsletter guru, Yolanda Facio, who continues to help me, despite moving on to bigger and better things. Thanks for still keeping me on; I'd be lost without you, and that's a fact. Your speed and efficiency, not to mention your friendship, is much appreciated.

And what would an acknowledgments section be without a big thank you (again!) to my poor beta readers who slog through the mud for me and read sub-standard versions of what eventually ends up on a shelf somewhere, all sparkly and shiny. Thank you for your careful reading of the sludge—for your suggestions, your advice, and for patiently answering the million questions I pose to you about the plot, the characters and any number of little details. You help to shape these books, and that is no small thing. So, without further ado, I'd like to thank Margaret, Liz, Otto, Rebecca, Marcy, Susan, Phil, Kari, Wally, Paul, and Carmi for picking through the rubbish to find the gems.

And, again, thanks to my neglected family and in particular, my husband, Phil, who has taken on more household tasks than ever before and has sadly learned to live with others not getting done at all, or if nothing else then in a very untimely manner. But more importantly, you've been my constant support, my biggest fan, and my closet friend, and for this I truly thank you, my love.

About the Author

© Cliento Photography

Michelle Cox holds a BA in English literature from Mundelein College, Chicago, and is the author of the award-winning Henrietta and Inspector Howard series, as well as the weekly *Novel Notes of Local Lore*, a blog dedicated to Chicago's forgotten residents. Cox lives in the Chicago suburbs with her husband and three children and is currently hard at work on the fifth book of this series. In her vast free time, she sits on the board of the prestigious Society of Midland Authors and is a reviewer for the *New York Journal of Books*.

SELECTED TITLES FROM SHE WRITES PRESS

She Writes Press is an independent publishing company founded to serve women writers everywhere. Visit us at www.shewritespress.com.

A Girl Like You: A Henrietta and Inspector Howard Novel by Michelle Cox. $16.95, 978-1-63152-016-7

When the floor matron at the dance hall where Henrietta works as a taxi dancer turns up dead, aloof Inspector Clive Howard appears on the scene—and convinces Henrietta to go undercover for him, plunging her into Chicago's gritty underworld.

A Ring of Truth: A Henrietta and Inspector Howard Novel by Michelle Cox. $16.95, 978-1-63152-196-6

The next exciting installment of the Henrietta and Inspector Clive series, in which Clive reveals that he is actually the heir of the Howard estate and fortune, Henrietta discovers she may not be who she thought she was—and both must decide if they are really meant for each other.

A Promise Given: A Henrietta and Inspector Howard Novel by Michelle Cox. $16.95, 978-1-63152-373-1

Just after Clive and Henrietta begin their honeymoon at Castle Linley, the Howards' ancestral estate in England, a man is murdered in the nearby village on the night of a house party at the Castle. When Clive's mysterious cousin Wallace comes under suspicion, Clive and Henrietta are reluctantly drawn into the case.

The Great Bravura by Jill Dearman. $16.95, 978-1-63152-989-4

Who killed Susie—or did she actually disappear? The Great Bravura, a dashing lesbian magician living in a fantastical and noirish 1947 New York City, must solve this mystery—before she goes to the electric chair.

After Midnight by Diane Shute-Sepahpour. $16.95, 978-1-63152-913-9

When horse breeder Alix is forced to temporarily swap places with her estranged twin sister—the wife of an English lord—her forgotten past begins to resurface.

Cut: An Organ Transplant Murder Mystery by Amy S. Peele $16.95, 978-1631521843

When Sarah Golden, a well-respected transplant nurse, and her best friend, Jackie, get tangled up in the corrupt world of organ transplants, they find themselves on a sometimes fun, sometimes dangerous roller coaster ride through lifestyles of the rich and famous . . . one from which they may not escape with their lives.

7c 9/19 10/19